LIVVY

VALERIE S ARMSTRONG

Order this book online at www.trafford.com
or email orders@trafford.com

Most Trafford titles are also available at major online book retailers.

Printed in the United States of America.

ISBN: 978-1-4907-2891-9 (sc)
ISBN: 978-1-4907-2892-6 (e)

Because of the dynamic nature of the Internet, any web addresses or links contained in
this book may have changed since publication and may no longer be valid. The views
expressed in this work are solely those of the author and do not necessarily reflect the
views of the publisher, and the publisher hereby disclaims any responsibility for them.

Any people depicted in stock imagery provided by Thinkstock are models,
and such images are being used for illustrative purposes only.
Certain stock imagery © Thinkstock.

Trafford rev. 03/07/2014

Trafford
PUBLISHING®   www.trafford.com
North America & international
toll-free: 1 888 232 4444 (USA & Canada)
fax: 812 355 4082

This book is dedicated to my daughter, Loretta, whose love and friendship brings great joy to my life.

In acknowledgement of Anxiety Recovery Toronto, formed in 2001 as the Social Phobia Support Group. That same year, Paul Rennie became peer facilitator and the group became a nonprofit charitable organization. By 2008, the group had grown to over eighty members, one of the largest of its kind in North America and the original founder, Earla Dunbar, was awarded the Courage to Come Back Award. This award, created by the Centre for Addiction and Mental Health, recognizes six individuals across Ontario each year for overcoming the struggle associated with living with addictions and/or mental health issues. In 2013, the name of the organization was changed.

Chapter One

At number nineteen Cavendish Road in North London, Rachel Marshall stood anxiously by the kitchen stove waiting for the kettle to boil. She was weary from a day spent cleaning house and tending to her children and just wanted to sit for a while and enjoy her cup of tea and a couple of Peak Frean biscuits from the green and white cookie jar, she refilled every week. She could hear Olivia crying but it happened almost every night and this time she wasn't going to giving to her, she had more serious things to worry about now that the war in Europe had begun and she needed to think about sending the children out of London to escape the bombing. She carried her tea into the tiny living room and sank down on the only really comfortable chair with a sigh. She knew it wouldn't be long before Harry came home and asked for his usual snack of cheese sandwiches and cocoa before bedtime.

Harry Marshall was a man of many talents, he painted in oils and watercolours, frequently read educational books and was a professional musician playing the violin, saxophone and clarinet. As a young boy he sang in the choir at church but had since renounced all religions and was a confirmed atheist. As a very young man he played lead violin with the London Philharmonic Orchestra and later, formed his own dance band touring throughout England. His father deserted the family when he was four years old and Harry was left with his mother and younger sister Maude. Later in life he was disappointed to learn he might have had twin brothers except for the fact that they were stillborn, nevertheless he remained close to his sister until she died in a mental institution at the age of thirty two. She had always been a fragile girl and had married a man who not only abused her physically, but also mentally. Her emotional state deteriorated to such a degree that she could no longer function and although she was beginning to respond to treatment, her immune system was compromised and she succumbed to pneumonia after an outbreak in the institution.

Harry was devastated by his sister's death and while still grieving, met and married a very attractive girl he met while touring. Within a year they had a daughter, they named Sylvia, but the marriage was short lived and he soon lost all contact with his wife and child. When he met Rachel at a dance, he was twenty-six-years old and she was seventeen. Rachel had gone to the dance at the Streatham Ballroom with her sister Marie. It was a Saturday night and the highlight of their week. They both loved dancing and were hoping to meet some nice young man who would take them out now and again to a movie or even to dinner. Rachel had waved her dark brown hair and wore her favourite cherry red dress, which draped over her body and showed off her excellent figure. The sisters had just entered the ballroom when Rachel immediately noticed the conductor of the band. She was mesmerized by this man with the blond hair and blue eyes, and a marked resemblance to Kirk Douglas, and wanted to get to know him. It wasn't long before Harry became aware of the young girl with the dark hair in the red dress who was staring at him intently every time he looked in her direction and, when the band took a break, he took the opportunity to seek her out and introduce himself.

This was the beginning of a love affair that rocked Rachel's family. Over the course of the next three years Rachel had tried to keep the romance secret but her parents finally learned the truth. The Weinbergs were Jewish, both sets of grandparents having emigrated to England from Russia, and they could not accept the fact that their daughter was dating a gentile who was not only nine years older, but still legally married. There were six other daughters in the family and two brothers but Rachel was now the proverbial black sheep and things got so difficult at home that Rachel moved out and into a small flat in Palmers Green with Harry. She was very much in love but missed her family and was devastated when her father died without having made peace with him. After the death of her father, she discovered her mother had really been sympathetic with her situation and only went along with her father to keep peace in the household. Now, they were able to resume a loving relationship and Rachel was reunited with all of her siblings.

Soon after her father's death Rachel discovered she was pregnant and their son Matthew was born in September of 1934. Two months later, after Harry had managed to obtain his final divorce papers, Harry and Rachel were married and they moved into the house on Cavendish Road. The house was the mirror image of most of the row houses in the neighbourhood, three stories high with a small front yard and a fair size garden in the back which boasted a rhubarb patch but few flowers except for some giant hollyhocks. Their next-door neighbours on one side were the Brugnolis, a friendly family of Italian descent and on the other, the Pomfrets, a rather stuffy couple who paid little attention to anyone else on the street. Rachel's family rented the lower floor of the house while a rather odd and reclusive fellow, Mr. Wilson, lived in two rooms on the second floor and a very elderly lady occupied the remaining two rooms at the top of the house. Mr. Wilson and Mrs. Fossey shared a communal bathroom, the only one with a tub, and it was usual on weekends for Rachel's family to use the same bathroom for their weekly bath. During the week they were obliged to wash up in the kitchen and use the water closet, with merely a toilet, which was attached to the back of the house and opened up onto the garden.

After the move, Harry got a job repairing radios and going out on the occasional booking to play saxophone in a dance band while Rachel stayed home to care for little

Matthew. Times were tough and got even tougher when they had another child, this time a daughter who they named Olivia. Although over 8 lbs and above average weight for a girl she was not a pretty baby and had hair so long that, while still in the hospital, the nurses would tie it up with ribbon. Later, strangers would comment that she looked so different from her brother who, at two years old, had developed into a handsome child with an abundance of dark curly hair and large brown eyes.

Three and a half years after Olivia's birth, World War II began and Harry was drafted into the National Fire Service. He was considered too old to be conscripted into regular service but the job he was forced to do at home proved to be invaluable to all of those who suffered in the fires, which flared up throughout London during the bombings. Night after night he would be called upon to help put the fires out and rescue people trapped, both dead and alive, in the rubble.

On this particular night Harry had been out playing saxophone at a private anniversary party. It had been a long evening but the few extra pounds he brought home made it all worthwhile. As he entered the house and passed the children's room before heading down the short flight of stairs to the living room, he could hear Olivia crying. Rachel was still resting comfortably sipping her tea when he came through the door.

"What's the matter with Livvy?" he asked rather abruptly.

Rachel looked up a little annoyed that Harry's first concern was Olivia "She says she wants to go to the bathroom again. I've already taken her out of her crib twice this evening."

Harry turned to leave the room "I'll see to her this time."

Rachel jumped up and placed her hand on his arm. "No, she does this all the time. I think she just wants attention".

Shaking her hand off Harry turned away. "Maybe you're wrong and maybe she really needs to go."

When he opened the door to the bedroom Livvy was sobbing uncontrollably and shaking the bars on her crib while her brother slept on the other side of the room oblivious to what was happening.

"I want to go potty" she cried, "Please let me go potty."

Her father lifted her gently out of the crib and placed her on the chamber pot all the while soothing her with loving and reassuring words that everything was going to be all right. When she had finished, she placed her arms around her father's neck and hugged him with all her might. He was her hero, this tall handsome man who was there to protect her and she thought he was the best daddy in the world.

That night turned out to be Livvy's first living memory and one that would have a profound effect on her throughout most of her lifetime.

Chapter Two

Even before September 1939, civil defense preparations had begun in anticipation of attacks on British cities. To discourage low level attacks from enemy planes, thousands of huge barrage balloons were put up over heavily populated areas of Britain. These could be flown up to 10,000 feet and were moored to wagons by heavy cables. The cables were strong enough to destroy any aircraft that might collide with them. All over the country Anderson shelters made of corrugated steel and covered with earth were built in gardens and large civic shelters of brick and concrete were erected. Some homes had Morrison shelters, which resembled large crates made of steel plating with one side made of heavy wire mesh. These were often used as tables during the day because of the space they took up and at night two or three people would sleep in them. Gas masks were issued and the children were given specially designed masks that looked like Mickey Mouse and they carried them everywhere. A blackout was enforced and the tube stations, which were far below ground, became a haven for many people. It was a common sight to see men, women, and children sleeping on the platforms and everybody became united in spirit and friendship.

As the air raids continued, plans were made to evacuate the children from large or industrial cities into the countryside. In June, a few months before the blitz of November 1940, on a clear Saturday morning, Matthew and Olivia were on a train heading north with over sixty-three other children. One week earlier, Rachel sat five-year-old Matthew in Harry's favourite armchair and holding Olivia on her lap tried to explain what was going to happen. She was particularly concerned about Matthew because he had developed asthma and took medication as well as requiring exercise on a regular basis. All the documentation accompanying the children listed any medical or psychological conditions but Rachel had failed to recognize Olivia's need to run to the lavatory so often was anything of any consequence. "Now children, you know your daddy and I love you very much and we don't want you to get hurt so we have to send you away. We hate doing this and we'll really miss you but we have to for your own safety."

"No, Mummy!" Matthew cried shaking his head violently, "Where will we go? Who will take care of us?"

"That's all been arranged, Matt," Rachel explained. "You're going on a train with lots of other children to a lovely place in the country. Your teacher, Mrs. Graham, will be going with you on the train. When you get there some very nice people will be coming to meet you and they'll take you home with them. Whatever happens, Matt, you must be sure your sister stays with you. You can't be separated from her. Do you understand me?"

Matthew got up from the armchair and hugged his mother and sister. "Yes Mummy, but we don't want to go. We can't leave you and Daddy here. What will happen if a bomb drops on you and we never see you again?"

Olivia knew something was wrong and began to cry and Rachel had tears in her eyes but she had to be strong. "Don't worry about us Matt, we'll go to the shelters and be safe and when the bombing stops you'll come back home and we'll all be together again forever."

The next week was particularly difficult for Rachel. She couldn't imagine being left without the children but a series of heavy air raids convinced her they had no choice. Seven days later, on the station platform surrounded by other families being torn apart by the conflict, Harry and Rachel said their goodbyes but there was so much noise it was difficult to communicate. All around them people were crying and Rachel thought her heart would break. Olivia looked adorable in a fluffy pink cardigan and her new white dress embroidered with rosebuds and Matthew looked so grown up in gray flannel trousers and a navy blazer.

"Remember, Matt, what I've been telling you all week," said Rachel, "look after your little sister and, Livvy, you be a good girl and listen to your brother. You must stay together on the train and the bus and when you get to the village make sure nobody separates you. If you need anything you must ask Mrs.Graham to help you. We love you both so much and we'll come and visit as soon as we can."

Harry picked Olivia up in his arms and patted Matthew on the head "Yes son, you be a big boy and take care of Livvy."

"I will Daddy, I promise," Matthew replied trying to be brave but he was frightened and his little legs began to tremble as he reached up to kiss his mother. Five minutes later chaos erupted when the train's whistle started to blow, the stationmaster yelled 'all aboard' and Olivia began to scream. Harry tried to pry her arms from around his neck and eventually with the help of one of the civic workers he managed to get the two children and their luggage onto the train. They were well inside the carriage when the train pulled out of the station and never got to see their mother running desperately along the platform and collapsing in the arms of one of the porters.

While the train headed north Olivia slept with her head in Matthews's lap and Rachel and Harry made their way back to Cavendish Road. It was on the trip home that Rachel decided she needed a job to occupy her days and keep her from fretting about the children. She wondered how long it would be before they got word on where they were staying and how they were adjusting to their new life.

Leverington was a village in Cambridgeshire near the Norfolk border and a mile northwest of the town of Wisbech, capital of the Fen district. Most of the Fenland people earned their living on the land, which was fertile with dark rich soil, and produced many crops including potatoes, fruit, cereals and flowers. The church of St Leonard's, which was built of stone in the sixteenth century, was the center of the community and every Sunday all the villagers gathered for services while, during the week, there was always some activity in the church hall. It was here in this small village that Matthew and Olivia were to spend the next fifteen months of their lives.

At the train station in Wisbech, the children were fed with soggy egg sandwiches and warm lemonade from the station cafeteria before being split up into separate groups, while buses waited to take them to villages in the area. Matthew and Olivia were put on the Leverington bus with eleven other children and during the short trip all they could see were endless green fields and orchards full of apple trees. It was a clear spring day and the weather was unseasonably warm so, by the time they arrived in the village, they were hot and thirsty. Stepping off the bus, they were hustled inside a long one storey building, adjacent to a church. It turned out to be the schoolhouse with one large room where all the children were lined up in a row and asked to stand very still and not talk unless they were spoken to. Matthew was intrigued by the pictures on the walls, which ranged from indefinable blobs of paint to skillful renderings of birds and flowers. Olivia was so nervous, she clutched Matthew's hand when several people entered the room and began slowly walking up and down staring at them and muttering among themselves. They had no idea what was going on and what they were supposed to do.

Matthew looked up and cringed when an elderly lady stopped and put her hand on his shoulder. "What's your name son?" she asked in a croaky voice.

The woman had wispy white hair, drawn back in a bun, a face so wrinkled and brown she resembled a walnut and was so thin, her arms looked like twigs. "My name's Matthew," he said looking her in the eyes and willing her to go away. "This is my sister, Livvy, and we're together and so she has to stay with me all the time."

The woman, offended by his tone, quickly straightened up and stalked off mumbling, "Well I never, what a cheeky one; these city folks!"

Gradually the room began to empty as some of the children were taken away and soon there were only four children left. Matthew was hoping nobody would want them and they would have to go back to London. Meanwhile, Olivia was getting very tired and had to go to the lavatory again. "Matt, I have to go, please take me," she whined.

One of the women, inspecting the other two children, overheard her. "What's wrong dear, do you need to go to the lavatory?"

"Yes please," said Olivia jiggling from one foot to the other.

"I'll take you dear; it's just down the hall."

"No, Matt has to take me," she said as she tried to hide behind his back.

Matthew let go of Olivia's hand, "It's okay, you can go with the lady, and I'll wait for you here."

While they were gone, a man approached Matthew. He was not very tall and wore a wrinkled brown suit with a blue tie and a cap on his head but he had a pleasant honest face. He bent his knees so that he was eye to eye with the boy. "Hello son, my name's Mr. Richardson and what's your name?"

"It's Matt sir," he replied in a terse manner still hoping nobody would want them and wondering why this man didn't talk like the people back at home.

"I guess that would be short for Matthew?"

"Yes, sir."

"You're a fine looking boy, how old are you?"

"I'm almost six, sir."

"My, you're tall for your age. Tell me is the little girl your sister?"

"Yes sir, her name's Livvy and she's only four and she has to stay with me."

The man removed his cap and stood beside Matthew in silence, neither man nor boy knowing what to do, except to look down at his own feet.

When the woman returned with Olivia, she was holding her hand and, without letting go, she walked up to Matthew and putting her arm around his shoulder turned to her husband, "George, we have to take them both."

Now George Richardson was a kind and giving man and he had already agreed to look after a child and give them a safe place to stay while the bombing in the major cities continued. He had not, however, considered two children and was shocked when his wife suggested it. "But Mary, we don't have room for both of them. Where will they sleep?"

"They can both sleep in the big bed, there's plenty of room and we can't separate them. Look how adorable they are, George, how can you refuse?"

George loved his wife dearly and knew she had a loving heart so it took only seconds for him to agree. He smiled and nodded, taking the suitcase in one hand and Matthew's hand in the other, and said," Come along young man; you and your sister are coming home with us."

Chapter Three

George and Mary Richardson were in their early fifties and had been married for just over thirty years. They had both been born and raised in Leverington and George had worked on the land all his life. He had always been a devoted husband to his wife and a good father to their two daughters Emily and Millicent.

Mary Richardson was only five foot two inches tall, twenty pounds overweight, fair complexioned, with short graying hair, and hazel eyes that always seemed to be smiling. Most days she wore flowered shift dresses and stout Mary Jane style shoes except on Sundays when, in summer, she attended church in a pink cotton suit with its gored skirt or, in winter, a navy pant suit and a red and white polka dot blouse. Mary had been content staying at home taking care of her family and, now the girls were grown, she spent more time cooking George's favourite meals and had become more and more involved in community activities.

The youngest daughter, Emily, lived in the nearby town of March with her husband, John, and their two children while Millicent still lived at home with her parents. Millicent was almost thirty and had never had a lasting relationship with any of the available men in the area. She was the same height as her father, big boned with dark almost black hair, and dark skin. She was not a pretty woman and had a masculine air about her, always dressing in black trousers and heavy sweaters, even in summer. She rarely spoke, smoked like a chimney, and every morning had the strange habit of sitting at the table with her left hand in a basin of hot water. Every few minutes she would raise her hand and let the water drip from her fingertips back into the basin. George and Mary had accepted their daughter's odd behaviour years before and although they were disappointed she had not married and blessed them with more grandchildren they were grateful she caused them no trouble. The fact that she was still at home and got free board and lodging was offset by the fact that she helped out on the land, tended the large garden at the front of the house, and assisted her mother with the household chores.

There was one other member of the family, Pete, the four-year-old brown and white fox terrier George had brought home two years earlier, after finding him hurt and bleeding by the side of the road. They assumed a car had hit him but his injuries were not serious and after nursing him back to health and two failed attempts to find his owner, they decided to keep him. He was a loving, playful pet and spent most days following George around in the fields, chasing rabbits and any other small animal that crossed his path.

After all the paperwork was completed, George, Mary, and the children made the short walk home along a road bordered with trees, hedges and wild flowers where the only noise was the gentle wind and the birds singing. It was in this environment that Matthew and Olivia were welcomed.

Number 29 Gorefield Road was a long two-story structure made of stone with green shutters and a shingled roof. The position of the house was unusual because the left side abutted the roadway while the large front garden ran along the length of the roadway. As Matthew and Olivia stepped through the wrought iron gate they stared in wonder at the size of the garden and the riot of colours. Two archways covered with wisteria vines stood like sentinels at each end of a pathway that snaked around the perimeter and there were flowers everywhere, petunias, zinnias, marigolds, pansies and dozens of rose bushes in every shade of red, pink and yellow. There were also blackberry bushes and vegetable patches with tomatoes, cucumbers and lettuce but the time to explore this wonderful new world would have to wait because they were being ushered into the house. When Mary opened the front door, Pete came bounding along the hallway barking and wagging his tail in excitement but he skidded to a stop when he saw two strange little people on the doorstep. "Now, Pete, settle down," said George stroking the dog's silky head, "we've brought you some new friends. This is Matt and this is Livvy and they'll be staying with us for a while."

Pete sat down on his haunches with his head on one side appearing to inspect the intruders but when Olivia stepped cautiously forward and extended her hand, he got up and after sniffing her fingers he began to gently lick them. Matthew took a step towards Olivia and took her other hand. "Be careful Livvy he might bite you."

"That's okay, son," George assured him, "Pete would never bite anyone. We found him when he was small and sick and we've had him ever since, he'd never bite anyone."

Olivia put both arms around the dog's neck and he began to lick her face. "I like him, he's sweet," she said, "We never had a dog, and my mummy didn't want one. We had a cat, she was a girl and her name was Topsy but we had to give her away because she ate my daddy's dinner one night and he was really mad."

Mary knelt and patted Olivia's shoulder, "That's too bad, dear; well now you'll have a nice pet to play with. You are going to have a wonderful time here."

For a short time they had almost forgotten the trauma of being in a strange place with complete strangers and now the thoughts of home came flooding back and they both started to cry.

"Come along, you must be hungry after that long journey," Mary said gently, leading them into the large kitchen with its huge wooden table and eight sturdy ladder-back chairs.

Mary pulled out two of the chairs for the children. "Sit down, both of you, and I'll get you each a piece of rhubarb pie and a glass of milk. It won't be long before tea time and then you'll have a proper meal."

George, meanwhile, quietly left the kitchen carrying the suitcase up to the children's bedroom where he placed it unopened on the floor and then took the stairs back out to the garden where he could puff on his favourite pipe.

Mary placed the pie and milk before each child and, as they nibbled at their food with Pete quietly sitting beside Olivia's chair, they silently looked around the room. It was so different from their kitchen at home. This room had wallpaper with yellow chickens, brown rabbits and green leaves and all around the top of the room was a wide border with more green leaves. A huge black cast iron stove stood in one corner and there was a brick fireplace with a small pile of logs heaped in front of it. On one wall stood a long sideboard made of maple with a hutch full of dishes patterned with farmyard animals and the table, where they were sitting, was covered in a white lace tablecloth that draped so far over the sides of the table, that it fell in folds onto Olivia's knees.

Mary sat down next to Matthew. "I hope you like the pie. I made it with rhubarb from the garden."

"We have rhubarb in our garden at home," said Livvy proudly.

"That's wonderful, dear. I didn't know you had a garden. Now tell me would you like us to call you Matthew and Olivia or Matt and Livvy?"

"Matt and Livvy please," they both chorused at once.

Mary smiled, "I think it would be nice if you called Mr. Richardson, Uncle George and you can call me Aunt Mary. We don't like to be too formal around here."

After they finished their snack, Mary took them on a tour of the house and the garden. The living room, like all the other rooms in the house, was very large. Its bay windows with flowery drapes looked out onto the garden and it had fat chintz-covered sofas and chairs with a floor to ceiling bookcase housing hundreds of leather-bound books. George liked to read the classics in his spare time and had become something of a collector.

A door to the living room opened up to an enclosed staircase that wound up to the second floor. To the children it was like going into a closet and finding a secret set of stairs going to some magical place and when they saw their bedroom it did seem magical. The bed was a huge four-poster set on a slight platform so it appeared to be very high, in fact Livvy would find she literally had to climb into bed each night and it was covered in a plump cotton comforter in bronze and gold with two large matching pillows. Opposite the bed was a dresser made of a rich dark wood topped by a mirror and, on the dresser, a set of silver backed brushes and combs and the statuette of an angel in a long white dress and diaphanous wings. A wing chair graced one corner of the room and in the other, a washstand with a large china bowl and jug and a commode. The floor was hardwood which was stained a light brown and, on each side of the bed, were small woollen rugs that Mary had meticulously hooked in all of nature's shades of brown and green. The bay windows were draped in heavy gold velvet but were rarely drawn and there was a small window seat covered in the same velvet where one could sit and read or merely look out onto the garden. "This is your room now," Mary said gently, "you can spend as much time in here as you like. I have some toys my daughter Emily gave me for you to play with because her children are a little bit older and they don't need them anymore and also some books you can read."

Matt looked puzzled, "You mean this is really going to be our room and we're going to sleep in that bed? Where's Livvy's crib?"

With great effort Livvy climbed onto the bed and exclaimed, "I'm too big for a crib now," and she proceeded to bounce up and down in delight.

Mary laughed at this little girl who was suddenly feeling very grown up. "That's right, Livvy, you're a big girl now and you don't need to sleep in a crib anymore. You can sleep with your brother and if you need me I'll be right next-door. Now, we need to unpack your suitcase and put your clothes in the cupboard," and she proceeded to open the suitcase and laid the clothes on the bed. "I see you only have lightweight things here and I expect your parents will be sending your warmer clothes a little later."

"But where will they send them to?" Matt asked.

"Well," Mary replied, "the people who brought you here will let your parents know where you are and tomorrow I'll write them a letter to let them know you arrived safely and are settling in. Now let's put these clothes away and then I'll show you the garden."

When Mary brought the children outside, with Pete following on their heels, they were again enchanted by the garden. Matt walked along holding Mary's hand while Livvy ran on ahead under one of the vine covered arches and down the path bordered by beds of brilliantly coloured flowers and rose bushes. Suddenly she noticed what looked like a small shack on one side of the path and ran to the door but the latch was too hard for her to open and she called out to Mary, "What's in here, is it a playhouse?"

Mary released Matt's hand and approached the shack. "No dear it's the outhouse, if we need to go to the lavatory then we have to come here but I don't think you can open the door yet so you can use the commode in your room."

"Our lavatory is outside at home but it's not like this one, I want to see inside," said Livvy impatiently.

Mary opened the door and Livvy rushed in and was assaulted by the stench. She stared in amazement at what looked like a wooden box with a hole in it and then she looked up and noticed there wasn't a tank or a chain to pull. At that moment, to her horror, a large spider crawled up the wall beside her and she ran back out onto the path colliding with Mary. "It's scary in there, I don't want to go in there, please don't make me," and she clutched at Mary's dress with both hands.

"I already told you dear you don't have to go in there but, Matt, you're a big boy and I'm afraid you will have to get used to it, this is the country and things aren't the same here." She looked down at Livvy and stroked her head trying to comfort her, "Let's go and see the chickens and then I'll show you the washhouse which is where we do the laundry and take our baths."

The chicken coop was at the end of the garden and every morning Mary would go and feed the chickens and pick up the freshly laid eggs. Livvy was so fascinated that Mary promised she would take her to pick up the eggs the next morning.

After they returned to the house, Mary took the children into the living room where George was reading a book about the history of the fen district. He put the book down as they entered the room and smiled as he patted the sofa beside him. "Livvy, why don't you come and sit next to me and Matt can sit in the big armchair; you can tell me all about your family and your trip from London."

Livvy was a little leery of this man who was a stranger to her but she climbed up onto the sofa and scooted into the corner folding her legs under her.

When the children were settled George turned to his wife, "I guess you want to go and get things ready for tea Mary?"

"Yes George I do, so if you could look after the children for a while I'd appreciate it. By the way Millicent will be home soon. She's been at the library most of the day and I think she took a walk on the embankment."

After Mary left, and before George could speak, Livvy piped up, "Who's Millicent, is that your other doggie?"

"Don't be silly," chastised Matt, "how can a dog go to the library?"

Livvy giggled and George explained that Millicent was their daughter and she still lived at home with them. "Does she sleep with you and the lady?" Livvy asked.

Matt snorted in disgust while George tried to keep the grin off his face, "No, Livvy, she has her own room just down the hall from yours and remember now we want you to call us Uncle George and Aunt Mary."

"But you're not my uncle, I already have two uncles, one is Leslie and one is Lou and I have lots of aunts but I can't remember all their names."

"Their names are Cissy, Marie, Lily, Jennie, Sadie and there's one more," Matt paused chewing on his bottom lip, "Oh I remember its Doris," said Matt.

George was impressed. "Goodness, son, you have a good memory. That's a lot of relatives."

"Well, they're all my mummy's family, my daddy doesn't have any family except for my grandma and she's very old."

"How old is old Matt?" George asked knowing he was going to find the answer amusing.

"Well I'm not really sure but I think she's about fifty."

"That's very, very old indeed," George commented turning away so Matt wouldn't see the laughter in his eyes.

Just then the door opened and in walked a tall masculine looking lady with dark hair pulled back in a bun and clothed in black from head to foot. Her nose was rather like a bird's beak and she wore small round glasses with black frames, which made her look like a schoolteacher. She ignored George and stared first at Livvy, lowering her glasses as she did so, and then at Matt. Livvy sank back even further into the corner of the sofa and Matt folded his arms across his chest in defensive mode.

George waved Millicent further into the room. "This is Matt and this is Livvy," then turning to the children, he nodded towards his daughter, "and this is our daughter, Millicent."

The dark lady didn't move. "Mother told me all about them just now, I thought we were only getting one child," she remarked with irritation in her voice.

George sighed, "Yes I know, Millicent, but they are brother and sister and we couldn't separate them and you know how soft hearted your mother is. They won't be any trouble and they won't get in your way."

"Well I guess I will just have to put up with it," she said with a sigh, "as long as they don't bother me and don't make too much noise," and she left the room as quickly as she came in.

An hour later, George, Millicent, and the children were sitting around the huge kitchen table. Meanwhile, Mary fussed about setting out the tea. Back in London there had always been egg and chips, sausage and mash, corned beef or finnan haddie and sometimes canned fruit for dessert. Here, Mary put out an enormous platter of ham, a dish of potatoes whipped with butter, a second dish of whole baby carrots mixed with peas and, for dessert, there was another of Mary's pies but instead of just rhubarb, there were also raspberries and a pot of clotted cream to go on top. Matt and Livvy were used to having their plates put in front of them with the food already on it and they had no idea what they were supposed to do. Mary was already picking out small pieces of ham for Livvy then George, sensing Matt's discomfort, said, "It's all right son, you go ahead and take whatever you want. We're lucky here, we have plenty of food and we'll fatten you up in no time,"

Matt scrambled up onto his knees, spooned a mound of potatoes onto his plate and sat back down while Millicent shook her head in disgust. "Here take some ham and some carrots," said George spooning more food onto Matt's plate.

Everyone ate in relative silence until Mary put a pot of tea on the table and gave the children a glass of milk. "I think you should both go to bed early tonight," she said, "you must be tired and we'll all be going to church in the morning,"

"We've never been to church," Matt remarked.

Mary frowned at George, "We go every Sunday and in a few weeks you'll be able to go to Sunday school."

"But what happens in church, do we get to play games?"

Mary's frown deepened, "No, Matt, you learn all about the bible and about God and how to be a good person."

"My daddy doesn't believe in God."

Mary was now at a loss for words but Millicent saved the day and immediately rose from the table. "Mother, I think we should clear away the dishes," and she began piling up the dirty plates while Mary helped and George sat staring into his teacup.

After Matt was given his medicine and the children were alone in their room tucked up in the huge bed, Livvy cuddled up to her brother. "This bed is so big; I like it here, Matt."

Matt pushed Livvy away, "Well, I don't, Uncle George is nice and Aunt Mary is okay but I don't like Millicent, she's mean. Anyway I don't want to talk so go to sleep, Livvy."

Livvy rolled over and within minutes, she could hear Matt wheezing. In her crib back home, she wasn't so close to him and the noise hadn't bothered but now, she buried her head under the pillow. It didn't help much and then she had the urge to go to the lavatory even though she had just been. She crawled out of bed and pulled the chamber pot out from the washstand and sat there listening to Matt. She was beginning to feel a sense of despair. Two hours later, after using the chamber pot twice more, she crept down the stairs and opened the living room door. George was sitting listening to the radio with Pete curled up at his feet and Mary was knitting while Millicent was nowhere to be seen. Hearing the door open George looked up, "Livvy, what is it?"

Livvy slumped to the floor in a heap and began to howl, "I want my mummy, I want my mummy. Please, I want my mummy."

Mary dropped her knitting and jumped up running towards Livvy. She threw her arms around her rocking her back and forth. "It's all right dear, your mummy will come and see you soon and your daddy too," but Livvy continued to howl.

George crossed the room and put his hand on Mary's shoulder, "Let me take her, she can sit on my lap for a while and maybe she'll fall asleep." He then picked Livvy up and sat down in the armchair cradling her in his arms. Gradually her howling changed to sobbing and eventually a whimper and then silence. She stared into space, her face wet with tears and her thumb in her mouth, and stayed like that for a long time finding some comfort from the feeling of George's arms around her and eventually she fell asleep.

On Sunday morning, after a light breakfast of cornflakes and blueberry muffins Mary dressed the children for church. Livvy wore the only other good dress Rachel had packed for her, the powder blue cotton trimmed with lace around the Peter Pan collar and puffed sleeves, while Matt had to wear his gray flannel trousers and navy blazer. George looked very smart in a dark gray suit, white shirt and blue tie and the new cap he had just purchased in town and Mary put on a small pink veiled hat that matched her pink summer suit. Meanwhile Millicent appeared in her usual black trousers and black jacket but added some relief to the sober effect with a pale green and white silk scarf draped around her neck.

On the walk along Gorefield Road to St. Leonard's they met other villagers dressed in their Sunday best and although they exchanged greetings their mission was to get to the church on time, socializing would have to come later. It was a beautiful day with a slight wind making the trees sway gently to and fro and the clouds to drift slowly across the sky.

As they approached a bend in the road, Livvy broke away from Mary and ran to the edge of a large pond where the water looked a deep dark green and she could hear frogs croaking. George immediately ran after her. "Come here, Livvy, you mustn't go near the water, you might fall in," and he scooped her up and took her back to the road where they continued to walk past the cemetery to the church.

That Sunday morning was one of many the children endured throughout their stay with the Richardsons'. They remained in awe of the church itself and its magnificent stained glass windows but they were bored and restless as the minister, the reverend James Sinclair, droned on with his endless sermons preaching about the bible and the merits of good versus evil. Livvy would squirm in her seat always feeling the need to go to the lavatory and all Matt could ever think about was getting back to the house and the feast that awaited them. Every Sunday, at noon, there would be roast beef with crackling brown fat on the outside and thick brown gravy, crisp baked potatoes, bright green brussel sprouts and his favourite; Yorkshire pudding baked in a large dish and puffed up high with crispy brown edges. Dessert was always another of Mary's wonderful pies, strawberry, apple, rhubarb, blueberry or peach topped with clotted cream. Matt would eat and eat until he felt he would burst and Mary would just smile and try to feed him some more and, as time went on, even with his asthma which had caused him to be rail thin, he started to put on weight. Those Sundays were always special to Matt and he was fairly content.

Chapter Four

During the summer months, Matt and Livvy adapted to their new life except for the occasional night when Livvy would come downstairs and seek comfort in George's arms. She still crawled out of bed several times to use the chamber pot and Matt would often get angry with her for disturbing him and tease her about what a baby she was. During the day she found her own ways of coping with her problem and made up excuses for leaving the room or running into the house whenever she needed to. They had made friends with some of the villagers' children and spent most of their days playing in the orchard or in the fields, which stretched for miles behind the houses and occasionally, they would visit a farm and take Pete with them. They loved to play in the haystacks, which were piled with bales in a crisscross design leaving spaces they could crawl through. Little did they realize they would suffer the consequences when they came home with lice in their hair and were subjected to days of washing with carbolic soap and nightly ordeals, where Mary would pick the nits from their heads with a special comb.

Six weeks after their arrival from London, Livvy came home from playing with one of the neighbour's children to find Mary waiting for her at the front door. "I have a surprise for you, Livvy," she said. "Come inside".

Livvy was a little wary and stepped back, "What is it, Aunt Mary, is it something to eat; will I like it?"

"No it's not anything to eat but you'll love it, just come inside and you'll see."

Livvy stepped through the door and, as the door closed, she was aware of a shadowy figure hiding behind it. As her eyes adjusted to the light, she recognized the tall man with the fair hair and moustache, "Daddy, Daddy!" she screamed with delight.

Harry held out his arms and Livvy rushed into them then, swinging her up onto his shoulder, he murmured in her ear, "How's my sweet little fairy?"

Livvy was so happy she could scarcely breathe and grabbed Harry around his neck. "I'm okay, Daddy. Where's Mummy, is she hiding too?" she giggled.

"I'm sorry, Livvy, but she couldn't come this time. I rode down on the bicycle and she wasn't well enough to make the trip but she'll come next time, I promise. Now where is your brother?"

"I don't know Daddy he was playing with Ronny just down the road; let's go and find him?"

"Yes, let's do that. You don't mind do you Mrs. Richardson?" he asked addressing Mary. "We'll come right back as soon as we find him."

"I think that would be wonderful," Mary replied, "and please call me Mary."

Harry and Livvy took off hand in hand in search of Matt while Mary watched them go thinking what a nice looking man Harry was. They soon found Matt in a neighbour's garden but, although he was happy to see his father, he wasn't as excited as Livvy. Harry had never been too affectionate with the boy and could sometimes seem rather aloof and judgemental. Livvy, however, was too young to recognize these flaws in her father's character and looked up to him with complete adoration.

Harry had booked a room in Wisbech for the night and was leaving to go back to London early the next morning. As the daylight hours stretched late into evening, Mary persuaded him to stay for tea and spend more time with the children. Livvy wanted to show her father everything especially their room and the chicken coop where they collected the fresh eggs every morning. She chattered on and on, dragging Harry around the garden with Matt hurrying to keep up with them and Pete bounding along at their heels. Teatime was a lively occasion and even Millicent appeared to be gracious, joining in the conversation and talking to Harry about the effect of the war on the people of London. Mary outdid herself serving up a succulent leg of lamb with tiny new potatoes and green beans and toppimg it all off with a rich chocolate mousse. Harry was impressed with the Richardson family and felt secure in the knowledge that Matt and Livvy were safe and in good and loving hands.

When it came time to say goodbye, Matt was quiet and a little distant but Livvy was inconsolable and even after Harry lowered her to the ground, after holding her close for several minutes, she clutched at his trouser leg and wouldn't let go. That night she appeared at the living room door exhausted from crying and George gently picked her up and comforted her until she fell asleep.

As the summer drew to a close, Livvy became especially close with Janie, another evacuee who had arrived just two weeks before from Bristol. Janie lived a few houses away and most days they could be found playing together in the field bordering the garden or in the garden itself. Matt spent little time with Livvy preferring to play with the village boys and it wasn't long before he was befriended by one of the local lads. Vernon was seven and had been born and raised in Leverington where his family, the Kisbys', lived in one of the more modern houses on Gorefield Road, not too far from the Richardsons'. The Kisbys' were only in their thirties and had one other son, a little older than Vernon, and the whole family was outgoing and fun loving and treated Matt as one of their own when he came to visit. Little did Matt know they were to play an important role in his life in the future.

During the third week of August, Mary announced she had received a letter from Rachel and she and Harry would be coming to visit on the following Saturday. Livvy was giddy with excitement and spent the next few days wanting to know if it was Saturday yet. Matt, on the other hand, who had been pining for his mother but keeping those feelings to himself looked forward to the visit in anxious anticipation.

At eleven o'clock on the Friday night before Harry and Rachel were due to arrive and just as Livvy clambered back into bed, after one of her many visits to use the chamber pot, she heard the eerie wail of an air raid siren. Memories of the war and the noise of planes flying low over their house in London sent her hiding under the covers and curling up against Matt who was sound asleep. "Matt, Matt, get up the planes are coming!" she yelled in his ear. Matt mumbled and tried to turn over but Livvy started pounding on his back "Come on, wake up the planes are coming!"

He finally sat up, rubbing his eyes, but grabbed Livvy around her shoulders when he heard the undulating sound of the siren. For a while they just sat there clinging to each other and then the door opened and Mary came bustling into the room in her flowery cotton robe and fluffy pink slippers. She had curlers in her hair and looked a little flustered but she tried to remain calm as she approached the children. "It's all right dears, there must be some mistake. Let's go downstairs and have some tea while Uncle George tries to find out what's going on."

They all trooped down to the kitchen where they found Millicent fully dressed taking teacups from the cupboard, and they could hear the sound of the radio coming from the living room as George listened to the news. Five minutes later, he appeared at the kitchen door after hearing enemy planes had been spotted over the town of March, only a few miles away, where their daughter Emily lived. Mary immediately jumped up shaking her head in distress and wondering what they should do next but, just as she did so, the monotone of the all-clear siren filled the air and she sat down again heavily with a sigh, "Oh, thank the Lord I guess everything must be all right."

"Yes, this is the first time we've heard the sirens except for the training exercises and I hope we never hear them again," said George sitting down next to Mary and taking her hand, "I think it will be safe if we all go back to bed as soon as everyone's finished their tea."

"I'm staying up for a while," announced Millicent, "it's a beautiful night and I'm just going to take a walk around the garden."

"I'll come with you," said Mary rising from the table, "if you'll just wait until I tuck the children back in bed."

The following morning, Matt and Livvy were wandering in and out of the house aimlessly, waiting for their parents to arrive. Livvy started to get impatient and began to whine until eventually Millicent stepped in and told her to stop. At that Livvy trudged upstairs to her room and slumped down on the window seat staring vacantly outside. As the front of the house faced the garden she couldn't see anyone coming from the main road, which led through the town of Wisbech to the village, but she didn't want to face Millicent again. Just before noon, as she was starting to fall asleep, she heard Matt yelling,"Livvy, they're here, come outside, Livvy, Livvy!" and he waved up at the bedroom window where he had seen her with her face pressed up against the glass. Livvy jumped up and raced down the stairs out of the house through the garden gate, where Matt was hopping from one foot to the other. Just as she got there, Harry and Rachel were getting off the two-seater tandem bicycle they had ridden all the way from London. Livvy ran towards her father while he attempted to park the bike along the fence and Matt raced towards Rachel. It was a joyous reunion with hugs, kisses, tears and laughter until Harry finally broke away and suggested they all go in the house so that Rachel could meet the Richardsons'.

Rachel was a little embarrassed to be visiting George and Mary in the state she was in. On the trip down she had fallen off the bike into some nettles which left her a little bruised and her arms were covered with an itchy rash, but she was more concerned with the fact that her hair was windblown and her new ivory slacks were soiled from her fall. She counted her blessings that she had not been badly hurt, particularly in view of the fact she couldn't ride at all and merely sat behind Harry pedaling with her feet and hanging on to him all the way in absolute terror.

Mary stood just inside the door watching the happy reunion. She wanted to let the family have this special moment to themselves and it wasn't until Matt opened the garden gate that she ventured outside onto the pathway. "Hello, Harry, it's so nice to see you again," she said moving forward with her hand outstretched in greeting.

"It's nice to see you too, Mary," Harry replied shaking her hand. "I'd like you to meet Rachel; she's been looking forward to seeing you for such a long time."

Mary took a step towards Rachel and then spontaneously put her arms around her, "Rachel, my dear, I feel as though I know you already after the letters we've exchanged but it's so lovely to meet you in person."

Rachel was a little overwhelmed with the greeting but returned the embrace, "Thank you, Mary, I feel the same way. I can't believe I'm here and the children look wonderful."

"Well, they've been outside most of the summer so they've got some sun and I think it agrees with Matt, he isn't wheezing quite as badly as when he first arrived. We have so much to talk about so let's not stand out here; you must both be very tired. Why don't you come in and rest and I'll make you a cup of tea or some lemonade if you prefer," and with that she led the way into the house with the Marshall family following in her footsteps.

Once settled in the living room Mary explained that both George and Millicent had been called out to help a neighbour with her livestock but would be back before teatime. Then, satisfied her visitors were comfortable, she headed for the kitchen. Harry and Rachel relaxed with the children until Matt got impatient and decided he wanted to be Rachel's tour guide. While Harry remained in the living room with Livvy he took Rachel through the house and the garden and gave her a running commentary as they proceeded up and down the stairs and around the garden path.

When they finally got back inside the house, Mary approached Rachel with a jar of chamomile lotion. "I hope you don't mind," she said as she held out the jar, 'but I couldn't help noticing you have a nettle rash on your arms. If you put this lotion on it will help the itch go away."

Rachel took the jar, "That's so kind of you, Mary. As a matter of fact I fell off the bike just as we were coming into Wisbech and landed in some nettles. I have a few bruises and I got a little dirty but otherwise I'm fine."

"Thank goodness you weren't badly hurt. Surely you aren't going all the way back to London tonight?"

"No, we booked a room at an inn just a few miles from here and we'll head back in the morning. I hope you don't mind if we stay a little longer and spend more time with the children."

Mary looked aghast, "Heavens no, of course not, I was counting on you staying for tea and I want you to meet my husband and my daughter, they should be here very soon."

Rachel looked at Mary and could not believe how fortunate she was that her children had found this kind thoughtful woman to take care of them and she wondered if the rest of the family were just as pleasant. Just before five o'clock George and Millicent arrived home with Pete running along behind them. Pete seemed to remember Harry and approached him immediately licking his hand and wagging his tail. Harry petted the dog, rose to shake hands with George and Millicent and then introduced Rachel. It didn't take long for Rachel to decide that George was just as kind and thoughtful as his wife but she wasn't quite so sure about Millicent, who had abruptly shaken her hand and then left the room. She appeared again at teatime and helped Mary set the table but during the meal she said very little and nobody else paid attention to her, except for Pete who sat quietly under the table with his head resting on her feet.

The roast chicken Mary had prepared with whipped potatoes and cauliflower followed by a fresh fruit flan was a real treat for Harry and Rachel and they savoured every mouthful. They had already experienced the rationing of bacon, butter and sugar and knew many more foods would be rationed within the months to come including meat, fish, tea and cereals. While Harry and George discussed the war, Mary and Rachel were deep in conversation about more practical matters. The children were to be enrolled in school in September and they would need warmer clothes for the fall and winter. Mary suggested Rachel only send a few things as her daughter Emily had already offered to give Matt and Livvy clothes which her own children had outgrown, including boots and heavy coats. Livvy, who was listening to this conversation, frowned, "I want my own clothes Mummy, I want my red sweater with the teddy bears and my blue one with the big yellow buttons."

"Yes, darling I'll send the sweaters and some of your other things but it's very kind of Aunt Mary's daughter to give you her childrens' clothes."

"But I don't want their clothes," Livvy whined banging her fork on the table.

Everyone was very surprised when Millicent immediately leaned over to Livvy and, in a loud whisper, admonished her behaviour, "Don't be such an ungrateful child. I suggest you just sit there and eat and don't talk until we get up from the table."

Livvy, shocked into silence, bowed her head and picked at her food throughout the rest of the meal. Meanwhile conversation continued and even Matt, who was secretly delighted his sister had been scolded, joined in by telling George what he remembered about the air raids and a detailed account of their journey from London. George was intrigued to see how Matt had opened up while his parents were there and he vowed to try and get closer to the boy once they left.

Rachel offered to help clear away the dishes but Millicent took over and everyone else retired to the living room until it was time for Harry and Rachel to leave. By eight o'clock it was already getting dark and, not knowing the area very well, Harry thought it would be better if they made their way to the inn for the night.

Saying goodbye to the children was especially difficult for Rachel. She had promised they would come back in November but that was almost three months away and it seemed like an eternity. Matt tried to keep a brave face and hugged his mother fiercely before giving his father a brief kiss on the cheek. Livvy, on the other hand, was still sulking after the incident at the table and seemed strangely aloof. After her parents departed she went up to her room but did not appear back at the living room door to be comforted by George as expected. Unknown to all however, except for Matt who complained about the disturbance, she continued with her nightly ritual of getting in and out of bed several times to use the chamber pot.

Chapter Five

At the beginning of September, Matt was enrolled in the second grade and Livvy was in kindergarten. Eight different classes were held in the same one-room schoolhouse and the children were clustered in small groups with three teachers alternating between them. Matt was not particularly interested in learning and couldn't wait until the three o'clock bell so he could play with his friends. Both he and Vernon got into trouble on several occasions for talking when they should have been paying attention. Meanwhile Livvy loved learning about the alphabet and numbers but she was not happy when asked to draw or paint. She struggled with the confinement of the classes constantly feeling the need to visit the lavatory but fortunately the classes were short and she managed to suffer through them in silence.

On the thirtieth of September, Matt celebrated his seventh birthday. Harry and Rachel had sent him a package containing a bright yellow yoyo, an etchasketch and a royal blue sweater, made with wool left over from a cardigan Rachel had made for Harry the previous winter. The Richardsons' took both children on the bus into Wisbech for lunch as a special treat and, after filling themselves with wonderful salmon and cucumber sandwiches and huge ice-cream sundaes covered in chocolate sauce and whipped cream, they took a walk along the main street of the town and window-shopped.

After they got back to the house, the Richardsons' gave Matt a small wooden horse, George had carved, and a jigsaw puzzle picturing a cat with two kittens sitting in a basket. Livvy waited anxiously for Matt to finish opening the presents and then, rushing out of the room and up the stairs, yelled, "Wait here Matt, I'm coming back."

A few minutes later, they could hear her coming back down the stairs very slowly and it seemed to take forever for her to open the door. Finally she appeared holding something in her arms covered with one of Mary's tea cloths and she set it down on the table and grabbed at Matt's hand, "Close your eyes, Matt, and don't peek."

As George watched in amusement she whipped the cloth off, "Okay, you can open your eyes now," and she giggled at the expression on Matt's face when he saw the fish bowl complete with a goldfish inside.

"A goldfish, that's great, Livvy," and he kissed her on the cheek, "can I keep it in my room, Aunt Mary?"

"Yes, of course, Matt," Mary replied, " but you will have to take care of it. We have some food in the kitchen you can take with you when you go upstairs and George will tell you how much you should feed it."

Matt picked up the bowl and stared at the fish, "I'm going to call him Herbie."

Livvy groaned, "How do you know it's a boy, it could be a girl? Why don't you call it Sally?"

"No way, it's my present and I'm calling him Herbie," and he stalked off with his new prized possession in his arms and took off up the stairs.

George put his hand on Mary's shoulder "Don't worry, dear, I'll take the food up to him," then he looked down at Livvy. "I think he really liked your present, Livvy"

"Yes, I think so too, Uncle George, but Herbie is a silly name." and she took off up the stairs after her brother.

On the first weekend in October, Emily brought her children, David and Helen, from March to visit their grandmother and to meet Matt and Livvy. Emily was so different from Millicent and favoured her mother being rather short and a little plump with fair hair and distinctive pale blue eyes. She was also very outgoing and jolly and, within an hour of arriving at her parent's house, she had all four children caught up in a game of hide and seek. David and Helen were eighteen months apart in age just like Matt and Livvy but David was older than Matt by three years. Nevertheless, despite the age difference, they all seemed to bond together and had so much fun that, by tea time, they had worn themselves out and flopped down exhausted on the living room floor.

As promised, Emily brought a suitcase full of warm clothes for the children and even Livvy, who had turned up her nose at hand-me-downs, was impressed with the bright hand knitted sweaters, the pleated tartan skirt and the red wool coat with its two rows of black buttons. "Can I try everything on please, please, Aunt Mary?" she pleaded with her palms together as though she was praying.

"Yes, but you will have to wait until after tea dear. I'm sure you're going to look really pretty in all these lovely clothes."

Livvy could hardly wait and immediately after the dishes were cleared from the tea table she put on every single piece of clothing and paraded up and down the living room pirouetting every now and again, oblivious of the amused looks between Emily and her mother. Meanwhile Helen was not quite so amused, after all these were her clothes and she wasn't so sure she wanted Livvy to have them even though they no longer fit. She quickly changed her mind when Livvy, wearing the red coat, ran over and threw her arms around her neck," Thank you, thank you, Helen," she said, " I love all my new clothes. Tomorrow I'm going to show my friend Janie, she lives just down the road."

Helen hugged Livvy back, "You're welcome, Livvy. You'll have to come to our house one day with Matt, we have a new girl puppy called Lady and she is so sweet and we have a cat too named Delilah."

Livvy turned to Mary, "When can we go, Aunt Mary, I want to go to Helen's house and I want to see the new puppy. How far away is it? Can we bring Pete too?"

"Hold on, hold on," Mary replied laughing, "we have to wait until we are invited and then we can all go, including Pete."

Livvy was so happy she had made a new friend and anxiously waited for the day when she would see Helen again but it was almost Christmas before she finally got to meet Lady, who was now much larger than she expected, and Delilah who she fell in love with immediately.

As November approached and the days grew shorter and colder, the children began to get excited about seeing their parents again and continually asked Mary if she knew when they were coming. Livvy rushed in the door every day after school to see if a letter had come from her mother and finally she got the news she had been waiting for. Both Harry and Rachel would be arriving by train in two weeks and would be staying over the weekend. They were even going to be taking the children into Wisbech to stay with them overnight and would bring them back the next day at lunchtime before they returned home to London.

Livvy ran back and forth to the garden gate looking for Matt even though she knew he was probably off playing with Vernon somewhere. When at last she saw the two boys rounding the bend in the road she ran as fast as her legs could carry her to tell him the good news and for the rest of that day they couldn't stop talking about it.

Two days before Harry and Rachel were due to arrive, Mary received a telegram saying they had to cancel their plans and a letter was on its way. George took it upon himself to tell the children and that night Livvy was once again in his lap being comforted while she sobbed herself to sleep. There had been more intense bombing in London and residents were running for shelter day and night. George and Mary knew all about the attacks from the news and Rachel had already written and told them how difficult things were. They were not surprised when, after the telegram arrived, they got another letter explaining it was too dangerous to travel by train because the Germans were targeting rail lines as well as other means of transportation. Although they understood the situation and were afraid for the Marshalls' safety it was a different matter having to sit down with the children and assure them their parents would be all right and they would be coming back as soon as the bombing let up.

Chapter Six

Christmas at the Richardsons came and went without Matt and Livvy seeing their parents. Mary went out of her way to make it really special for them and baked for days making shortbread cookies, mincemeat pies, plum pudding and dark rich fruitcake. She decorated the kitchen and the living room with gaily-coloured garlands and holly and George brought home a huge pine tree and set it up in a corner of the room. Even Millicent seemed to get in the spirit as she decorated the tree with miniature candles, red and green balls, and tiny clay figurines of pigs, dogs, cats and birds and, to top it off, an angel with bright yellow hair and huge transparent wings.

On Christmas Eve, Matt and Livvy went to bed early while Mary and Millicent wrapped all the presents and set them under the tree. Livvy was up and down in the night even more than usual and Matt woke up early in the morning when it was still dark outside and couldn't go back to sleep. He counted the minutes hoping for daylight but his impatience got the better of him and, unable to wait any longer, he crept out of bed and down the stairs to the living room. Suddenly a loud clatter pierced the silence of the house and awoke everybody with a shock. Mary sat up with her hand on her heart, "My goodness, what's that?" she whispered as she started to get out of bed.

George hesitated for a moment and then started to chuckle "It's Matt, he found the Tommy gun!"

Mary slipped into her fuzzy pink slippers and blue flannelette robe. "Heavens above, it's the middle of the night. He's going to wake the neighbours up."

George continued to chuckle as Mary left the room and proceeded down the stairs and through the living room door where she was surprised to find Millicent already there. "It's okay, mother, you can go back to bed. Apparently this young man couldn't wait to open his presents and we didn't disguise the Tommy gun very well. If I had known it made this much noise I wouldn't have bought it for him."

At that, Matt looked up from where he was sitting in front of the tree in confusion "You bought it for me?"

Millicent appeared to be uncomfortable as she replied, "Yes, but you can't play with it in the middle of the night. Get up from the floor and get on back to bed. No more presents are to be opened until after breakfast," and with that she took the gun and put it behind the tree.

Matt walked over to Mary who put her arm around his shoulders and turned to go back upstairs. There they saw Livvy standing in the doorway and, having surveyed the exchange between her brother and Millicent, she was just as confused as Matt. Millicent was usually so aloof and could sometimes be mean and here she was buying presents. Livvy couldn't help wondering what Millicent had bought her and now she would have to wait until after breakfast to find out.

Christmas morning was cold and cloudy and there was a special service at the church at eleven o'clock. This gave the children plenty of time to open their presents after the special breakfast Mary had prepared of blueberry pancakes, poached eggs, bacon, fried tomatoes and freshly squeezed orange juice. They were excited as they tore the wrapping paper from boxes and Pete tugged at the ribbons, dragging them all over the living room floor. Inside were books, games, and toys from Harry and the Richardsons' and heavy argyle sweaters Rachel had knitted for both children. Matt had already recovered his Tommy gun from behind the tree and Livvy was still wondering what Millicent had given her when she opened the last of her presents and let out a cry of joy "Oh look Matt isn't she beautiful!" and she held up a magnificent doll, about a foot tall, with an exquisite porcelain face, long golden ringlets, dressed in a powder blue muslin frock trimmed with lace and embroidered with miniature white daisies. Matt was too interested in his own things to care about a doll and scarcely looked up as Livvy turned to Mary who had been wandering back and forth from the kitchen to make sure the children were all right and to comment on the presents, "Aunt Mary, look at my doll, isn't she beautiful? Did you buy her for me?"

"No, dear, Millicent got her for you. I'm so glad you like her," and she picked up the doll to examine it more closely, "she really is a lovely doll".

"Where's Millicent?" asked Livvy. "Can I go and thank her?"

"She's in the kitchen," Mary replied, "helping me with the turkey but you can go and see her if you like."

Livvy ran into the kitchen and astounded Millicent when she put her arms around her legs and hugged her. "Thank you for my doll, I love her. Can I take her to church with me today?"

Millicent looked down and put her hand on Livvy's head, " You're very welcome, Livvy, and yes, you may take the doll to church."

From that day forward the relationship between Millicent and Livvy changed and later, when springtime came, Millicent would take Livvy on her favourite walk along the embankment where buttercups surrounded them and they would stroll along hand in hand content in each other's company.

On St. Patrick's Day of 1941, Livvy turned five-years-old and Harry and Rachel came to visit even though enemy aircraft were still continually bombarding London. It had been six months since they had seen the children and there were so many stories to tell that the time flew by far too quickly and suddenly the visit was over. Life returned to a regular routine and in June, when school broke up for the summer, Matt and Livvy spent most of their time outdoors playing with the village children in the surrounding fields or in the orchard, where they would sometimes climb the ladders in an attempt to help with the apple picking. At other times they would pretend they were farmers' helpers and work in the field behind the house, harvesting the crops. Because of the richness of the soil, crops were abundant and were rotated often. That spring the field had been a blanket of tulips of all different shades and later there had been a strawberry crop where the fruit would often end up in little mouths rather than in the baskets.

As summer came to a close, and it was almost time to go back to school, Mary got a long letter from Rachel. It had been fifteen months since the children had left London and Rachel wanted them to come home. Harry was not happy about the situation and would have preferred things to stay as they were. Even though the blitz had eased off in May and there was a lull in the bombing, he still didn't think it was safe to be in the city but he knew how unhappy Rachel was and he finally agreed to bring the children back. When Matt and Livvy heard their father was coming to bring them home, they were both happy and sad. They missed their parents so much and talked about them often, but they had adjusted to their new life and now had to leave the friends they had made and the Richardsons' who they had grown to love.

George, Mary and even Millicent were visibly upset on the day Harry walked out of the garden gate carrying the children's suitcase. He had decided to give them a few moments alone to say goodbye and it was a very emotional time for everyone. Matt and Livvy promised to write and when it was finally time to leave, after all the hugs and kisses were over, the next-door neighbours, who had come outside to watch the children go, could hear Livvy's pitiful sobbing. Leaving Pete had been the most difficult for he had been their constant companion, playing in the fields. He gently licked her face when she knelt down to cuddle him and kiss him goodbye. She thought she would never see him again.

Chapter Seven

The journey back to London was one of excitement for the children. They were looking forward to seeing their mother and being home again and, it wasn't until they reached the outskirts of the city that they were reminded of the war that was still raging. As they neared King's Cross Station, they could see the ruins of bombed out buildings and began to feel nervous but their anxiety faded when they saw Rachel running towards them as they stepped off the train. It was a gray cloudy day but nothing could dampen her spirits. She looked lovely, in a bright sapphire blue coat and matching hat, as she swept both children up in her arms and kissed each one on the cheek, "Hello, darlings, Mummy is so happy to see you both. I want to get a good look at you," and she set them down on the platform. "Matt, you've grown so tall and you've filled out a bit and, Livvy, your hair is much lighter now. You look wonderful; I can't believe you're really here." She took their hands and turned to Harry smiling, "Let's go, Harry, it's getting late and they must be tired. I can't wait to get them home."

The family climbed to the top of the double-decker bus, that was to take them back to North London, and the children were amazed to see how many ruined buildings, and how much rubble, lined the streets. When they finally reached their neighbourhood and walked up Cavendish Road, they could hardly believe their eyes; every single house remained standing and their own house looked exactly as it had when they left fifteen months earlier.

Rachel had decided to keep the children home for a week before she enrolled them in school, only one street away on Romsford Road. She had been working full time in the stifling back room of a tailor's shop in the West End of London, basting linings into the lapels of men's jackets and hand sewing buttonholes, but it was a backbreaking and tedious job. She decided to take a week's vacation to be with the children and arranged to cut back her hours so that she would be home when they left school each day.

The first week was difficult for Matt and Livvy after being used to the freedom of being outdoors and the open space of the fields. They were bored despite the fact that Rachel took them out to the park most afternoons or to visit with cousins who lived nearby. The first time the air raid siren sounded, Livvy was frightened and her anxiety heightened in the Anderson shelter waiting for the all-clear. The siren sounded frequently after that and when school term began and everyone was hustled into the brick shelters, whenever there was a raid, it was impossible for the teachers to keep order. The children, having no real sense of fear, were happy to be out of the classroom and spent their time playing games.

As time went on Livvy was finding it more and more difficult to attend classes and, within a month of arriving home, she was given a note to take to Rachel requesting her to meet with Livvy's teacher, Mrs. Potter. Rachel was curious to know what the problem was. She had always considered Livvy to be a polite and obedient child and she was apprehensive when she entered the school office, where Mrs. Potter was waiting for her. "Good Morning Mrs.Marshall, do sit down," she said, pulling out a chair.

Rachel sat down meekly, laying her handbag in her lap and crossing her ankles. "Good morning, Mrs. Potter, is there something wrong with Livvy? She's always been such a good girl, I can't imagine her misbehaving."

"Not at all, you don't have to worry about that," Mrs. Potter replied, leaning her elbows on the desk, "but I am concerned about her. She is constantly interrupting class to go to the lavatory and I've tried to question her about it but she gets very upset and won't talk to me. Are you and your husband aware of the problem?"

Rachel began to nervously twist her wedding ring around her finger."Well yes, we've been aware of it but I've always thought she just wanted attention and we haven't taken it too seriously."

Mrs. Potter frowned, "I see, well far be it from me to tell you what to do, Mrs. Marshall, but don't you think you should take her to a doctor, she could have a medical condition?"

Rachel looked shamefaced and bowed her head, "You're right, I'll make an appointment this week. I should have done it a long time ago."

They continued to chat for a while and Rachel discovered her daughter was very bright and eager to learn, particularly when it came to arithmetic, and she couldn't help thinking she was going to be just like her father. Finally Mrs. Potter stood up, as an indication the meeting was over, "I'm so glad to have met you Mrs. Marshall, and incidentally you may want to get Livvy's eyes checked too, I notice she squints a lot when she's reading."

Rachel quickly rose. "Thank you, Mrs. Potter for taking the time, you've been very kind," and, after shaking hands, she hurried from the room feeling embarrassed and a little guilty but determined to do what she could to make things better for Livvy.

Two weeks later Livvy was in the office of Dr. Harold Lamb, a urologist recommended by the Marshall's family doctor, undergoing an examination, which she found both frightening and humiliating. Dr. Lamb concluded there was nothing physically wrong and Livvy would simply grow out of her problem and that would be the end of it. Now, Rachel felt justified in her belief that it was all in Livvy's head. She had no way of knowing just how much this condition would affect her daughter's life in the future.

Three weeks after the visit to the urologist, Livvy was fitted with, what were commonly known as, National Health spectacles. These were ugly round glasses with silver frames, free through the National Health Service. Livvy had a stigmatism in her left eye and was far-sighted and, as much as she hated her new glasses, she was forced to wear them and grimaced every time she looked in the mirror. She had changed a lot in the last year; she was very fine boned with a narrow face, true blue eyes and flaxen blonde hair, that seemed to have a mind of its own, and she had developed into a rather serious child. She was always very polite, never forgetting to say please and thank you. In years to come, Livvy's Uncle Ray, who was married to Rachel's sister, Lily, and was rather eccentric and very strict, would often comment on her exceptional manners and the fact that she was the only child in the whole family whoever bothered to ask him how he was.

Life at the house on Cavendish Road had settled back into a routine. Even visits to the civic shelters, or nights spent in the Anderson shelter, were part of everyday events. Matt and Livvy, when not at school, made friends with other children in the neighbourhood who had remained in London throughout the war or who, like themselves, had been brought back because of the lull in the bombing. None of them had any idea things were about to change and their lives would be turned upside down all over again.

Chapter Eight

Less than five months after the Marshall family had been reunited, air raids escalated over the major cities and Harry convinced Rachel they needed to send the children away again. Rachel reluctantly wrote to the Richardsons' hoping they would take Matt and Livvy back but the answer she received was bitter sweet. Mary felt that Matt and Livvy were getting a little too old to share a bed and they had no extra bedrooms. She suggested that, while they would welcome Livvy's return, Matt could stay with the Kisbys' who had agreed to take him in for as long as the war continued. Rachel knew little about the Kisbys' except that Matt used to play with the younger son, Vernon, but she was certain Mary Richardson would never have arranged for Matt to stay with anyone else unless they were a decent loving family.

When all the details had been taken care of, Rachel decided it was time to tell the children. She dreaded this moment but was surprised to see that Matt was not in the least bit upset at the news; in fact the idea of living with Vernon and his family seemed to please him. Livvy, on the other hand, had a temper tantrum, which was out of character and, when her anger finally died down, she proceeded to sulk and remained silent for hours not even talking to Matt.

Two weeks later, John Kisby drove his truck to the station in Wisbech to pick up Harry and the children and bring them back to Leverington. John had not dressed up for the occasion; he was wearing his usual red-checkered shirt and denim overalls and his old cloth cap and, the moment he saw Matt, he ran forward and embraced him. Harry shook hands with John thanking him for picking them up and for taking Matt in and, on the drive back to the Richardsons', sensing the kind of man John was, he put his mind at ease about the Kisbys'.

George, Mary, and Millicent were waiting with Pete at the garden gate when the truck pulled up. Livvy wriggled impatiently for Harry to lift her down then ran forward, as fast as her legs would carry her, while Pete bounded out of the gate nearly knocking her over in his excitement. Livvy threw her arms around the little dog's neck and hugged him tightly until he yelped out in pain but she hung on until Mary finally stepped forward and gently released her hands. The Richardsons welcomed Harry and the children back and invited John into the house for a cup of tea before leaving to take Matt home. It was a noisy afternoon with everybody chattering at once except for Millicent who, as always, just sat quietly with her hands in her lap. Millicent was not, in fact, as emotionless as it appeared. She had not realized until this day that she had missed Livvy so much and she looked forward to their silent walks on the embankment again. She had never felt very comfortable with another human being but somehow she had an affinity with this child and she regretted that she had never married and had a child of her own.

When it was time for Matt to leave, Livvy was visibly upset; she had never been separated from her brother before. Even though she knew he would be living just along the road, she was frightened to be on her own at night in the bedroom, where she would often see imaginary creatures in the shadowy corners. She didn't know then that in two weeks she would be sharing her bed with somebody else.

Tilly Parks was an eleven-year-old from Putney in southwest London and she was a cockney through and through. She arrived at the Richardsons' house with her mother who had, at long last, decided Tilly was better off in the country. Both mother and daughter were dressed in shabby clothes and looked like they were in need of a bath and a good meal. Mrs. Parks was bone thin with stringy mousy-coloured hair while Tilly was a replica of her mother except for her height. Through an agency, the Richardsons' had volunteered to take in another female evacuee but they had no idea someone like Tilly would land on their doorstep. Immediately after Mrs. Parks left, without so much as a tear being shed on either side, Tilly began to show her true colours. "Watcha got for tea?" she asked slumping down on one of the kitchen chairs and putting her feet up on another.

"We have baked chicken with boiled potatoes and peas," replied Mary as she pulled pots and pans from the cupboard.

"Don't like peas," Tilly said leaning her elbows on the table and glowering. "What's for sweets?"

Mary smiled to herself, "Peas are good for you and I haven't decided what we're having for dessert. I have some carrot cake; maybe you'd like a piece of that."

Tilly's diet had been very limited and she frowned, "A cake made of carrots, ain't never 'eard of it."

Livvy had been watching this exchange and decided it was time to speak up, "We had carrot cake at home lots of times, it has icing on the top. Why do you talk so funny?"

Tilly got up from the table and turned on Livvy, towering over her, "I don't talk funny, you do. 'Ow old are you anyway and where d'ya come from?"

"I'm six," Livvy replied," and I come from London. My mummy and daddy live in a big house there and my brother lives down the road at the Kisbys'. He used to live here but they didn't want a boy here anymore so they sent you instead."

Mary considered explaining to Livvy that they would love to have had Matt back but it just wasn't practical but then decided it would probably fall on deaf ears, as Livvy was too young to really understand. When Tilly realized Livvy was an evacuee and they would be sharing the same bed, any hostility she had been feeling began to fade away. The two girls went to bed at the same time that first night because Tilly was tired from the trip and she slept so soundly she didn't hear Livvy constantly getting in and out of bed. It turned out that Tilly had always been a heavy sleeper and it was a running joke in her family that even a bomb dropping next door wouldn't wake her. As she settled into her new life, she spent most of her leisure time out of doors, relishing the feeling of freedom away from the gray and run-down area in London she called home. Her brash manner softened, but only slightly, and Millicent couldn't tolerate her and avoided her, except at meal times when Tilly was at her worst. She fussed over every meal, even though in her whole life she had never seen so much food. She refused to eat brussel sprouts, cabbage or peas, in fact anything remotely green in colour and she turned up her nose at anything she didn't recognize. At home she had been exposed to a very different environment. She had never known her father and when her mother insisted he had died before she was born, she suspected her mother was lying to her. She had no real evidence her father was alive, just a gut feeling, and she vowed when she grew up, she would try to find him. Doreen Parks had not been a good mother to Tilly, always bringing strange men into the house and spending most of the spare money she earned, from her job at the local Woolworths, on herself. As a result of her mother's behavior, Tilly knew a lot more about sex than most children her age and she decided to pass on her knowledge to Livvy.

Livvy didn't believe a word Tilly told her about what went on in her mother's house but she was happy to participate in the 'Having a Baby' game Tilly liked to play, where she would stuff a big pillow under Livvy's dress and pretend she was the doctor. Mary caught them both in the washhouse one afternoon and was shocked, but a little amused, at the sight of Tilly with her ear pressed to Livvy's enormous stomach but she laughed it off and shooed them outside to play. From that time on, Mary was a little concerned about the effect Tilly was having on Livvy but there was little she could do as the girls spent so much time together. She had no need to worry about the relationship between the two girls for, as time went by, Tilly became almost like a mother figure. In an attempt to distance herself from her own mother, she evolved slowly into a gentler, kinder, and more passive youngster and developed a strong bond with Pete, who followed the girls around all day and slept in their room at night. Even Millicent, who had begrudged Tilly's monopoly of Livvy's time, noticed the change and remarked on it to George and Mary.

In the six months since Tilly had arrived, Matt had rarely been seen at the Richardsons' although he had been invited on several occasions to visit with his sister. During school days they would always be in the same room and would often spend a little time together at recess but, during his leisure time, Matt preferred to play with Vernon and his friends. He was happy staying with the Kisbys' and wished he had been raised in the country rather than in a big city with its narrow streets of row houses, dirty air, rancid smells and the constant noise of cars and buses. He even thought about coming back to this tiny village to live when he was old enough to leave home, but that seemed like years and years away and he had no idea then that his life would follow a very different path.

Commencing in September 1942, there was another lull in the bombing and Rachel pleaded with Harry to let the children come back to London for a while. Harry was angry that she would put Matt and Livvy's lives at risk, because of a selfish need to have them close to her, but he finally agreed and, two weeks after Matt's eighth birthday, he arrived in Leverington to take them home. Matt kept his emotions hidden as he said goodbye to the Kisbys' but he was desperately sad and, at the same time, angry that his father was taking him away from this family he had grown to love. John and Vernon walked him over to the Richardsons' house, where Livvy was lying on the living room sofa with her face buried in a pillow. She had been clinging to Tilly and Pete and crying for almost an hour when Harry took her on his knee and tried to comfort her. She was exhausted and just wanted everyone to go away and leave her alone because, in her simple childlike mind, she believed nobody wanted her around for very long.

Chapter Nine

Adjusting to their lives back home proved to be even more difficult than before for Matt and Livvy. They were a little older now and the friendships they had made in the village had become more meaningful to them. Matt missed his friend Vernon and was having problems making new friends at school, while Livvy seemed withdrawn and her anxiety attacks accelerated. On many occasions, she would interrupt class to be excused and would even skip the last class of the day altogether when her anxiety became too overwhelming. On those days, she would plead a sudden bout of sickness and, because she was such a bright child with such exceptional manners and obeyed all the other school rules, the teachers overlooked this erratic behaviour.

The children were forced to take care of themselves every day after school, now that Rachel had returned to working full time and they came home to an empty house, except for Mrs. Fossey, who lived like a hermit on the top floor. Harry was very strict and had made up a list of rules that had to be obeyed or they would be punished. Taking shelter the minute the siren sounded was one of the rules and they weren't allowed to invite anyone into the house, under any circumstances. One day just before Christmas, both Matt and Livvy were invited to the birthday party of a schoolmate who lived close by. Jimmy, one of the boys in Matt's class, had also been invited and Matt decided to sneak him into the house to play for a while but, against all odds, on one of her rare ventures out of the confines of her flat, Mrs. Fossey saw him and happened quite innocently to mention it to Harry. By the time Harry found out, the children were already at the party and they were shocked and embarrassed when he knocked on the door and demanded they come home immediately. Rachel tried to close her ears to the screams from Livvy as her father turned her over his knee and slapped her hard on the bottom while Matt, who had to endure the same fate, gritted his teeth and refused to cry. This was the first time they had ever seen their father this angry and it was an ominous sign of things to come. As the months passed, he became more reclusive spending nearly all of his spare time with his nose buried in a book and he never ceased to criticize Matt for his lack of interest in school. Rachel's defense of Matt aggravated him even more and voices would be raised, causing Livvy to cringe and retreat to the garden whenever she could. Harry appeared to have lost his patience with the children and he was tired of worrying about their safety, so it was no surprise when he insisted they be sent away from home for the third time. Rachel was devastated by Harry's decision, but the atmosphere in the house was getting steadily worse and she didn't want Matt and Livvy exposed to it any longer. She had been corresponding with Mary Richardson and was aware they were still caring for Tilly and had already made arrangements to take in another evacuee from Bristol, so there was no chance the children could go back to Leverington. Rachel did a lot of research trying to find an alternative place for them and Harry became more and more impatient. Finally he accused her of dragging her feet and, in order to keep the peace, she made a hasty decision and settled on a boarding school in Cornwall she had been considering, not realizing she would be sending the children almost three hundred miles away.

Matt soon became aware, after hearing his parents constant arguments, that they were being sent to the country again and on the Saturday morning, when Rachel had decided to break the news to the children, he approached his mother while she was in the kitchen cooking breakfast. Coming silently up behind her he tugged at her apron, "Mum, are we going back to Leverington?" he asked quietly.

Rachel dropped the spoon she had been using to stir the oatmeal and turned off the gas under the pot. Placing her hands on Matt's shoulders she replied, "No Matt, but you are going away again. Your father feels it just isn't safe for you here and it would be better if you were in the country but the Richardson's can't take Livvy and I can't let you go back to the Kisbys' without her."

"But, Mum, maybe the Kisbys' can take both of us. I don't want to go anywhere else; I liked it there. Why can't Aunt Mary take Livvy back?"

"Well, Tilly is still staying with them and they have another girl coming soon so there isn't room. I know you liked it at the Kisbys', Matt, but we had to find somewhere else."

Matt pushed Rachel's hands away, "No, we aren't going, you can't make us go. You're always sending us away. Livvy thinks you don't love her and I don't think you love me either," and he stamped his foot in frustration.

Rachel's eyes filled with tears and she pulled Matt into her arms. "You know that isn't true. Your father and I love you both very much and that's why we have to do this. I absolutely promise this will be the last time; when you come back home again it will be for always."

"You promise, you really promise even if Dad tries to send us away again?"

"I promise, Matt, no matter what your father says, so I want you to be a big boy and help me tell your sister."

"I will, Mum, but you still haven't told me where we're going."

"It's a long way away but it only takes a few hours by train. I found a boarding school in a place called St. Austell in Cornwall. It's supposed to be a very pretty place and there will be other children there."

Matt frowned, "What's a boarding school, Mum, and when are we going?"

"It's a school where you stay all the time. You'll have your meals there and even sleep there at night. The children sleep in dormitories, which are big rooms with lots of beds. You should have a lot of fun there and I'll be taking you there myself next Saturday so I'll see the school for myself."

"When are you going to tell Livvy?"

"This afternoon when we go to the park; she always likes it there and we'll take some bread to feed the ducks. I think it will be better if we tell her then."

Rachel underestimated Livvy's reaction. On hearing they were leaving London for the third time, she stiffened up and clenched her hands to her sides but when she discovered she wasn't going back to Uncle George and Aunt Mary, and she wouldn't be seeing Pete again, she let out a deafening howl and began racing through the willow trees bordering the duck pond. Rachel screamed at Matt to run after her and he finally caught her, wrestling her to the ground. He held her there, rocking her back and forth until Rachel reached them, then she lifted Livvy up and carried her all the way home sobbing on her shoulder. It was a dreadful afternoon and, as day turned to night, it only got worse when Rachel angrily recounted the whole episode to Harry and he reacted with little interest or concern.

The following Saturday, Rachel and the children started out early in the morning for their long journey. They took a train to Plymouth, near the border in Devon, a coach to the bus station in St. Austell, and then a taxi to Mount Thomas Boarding School. They were tired and hungry when they reached their destination and it wasn't until Rachel stepped out of the taxi that she really began to notice her surroundings. The building looked like something out of a Charles Dickens novel and her heart sank. There was something eerie about the large house looming just behind a line of towering oak trees. It had a pitched roof, pointed-arch windows and elaborate trimming along the roof edges. It was dark and foreboding and in a state of disrepair and Rachel approached the massive front door with trepidation, while Matt and Livvy hid behind their mother's skirts. After pounding on the door several times, with the large lion-shaped knocker, it suddenly opened to reveal a tiny woman wearing an apron and carrying a tray of dirty dishes. She looked up blankly at Rachel and asked abruptly, "Yes, what do you want?"

Rachel was a little taken aback at this greeting but smiled and replied, "I've brought my two children from London and I have an appointment with Miss Hargrove. Is she here?"

The little woman swung around and started to walk away, "Well," she said "you'd better come in. Wait right here in the hall and close the door behind you," and with that she vanished.

Rachel and the children crept quietly into the main hall and Rachel was appalled by what she saw. The floor, which was tiled in huge black and white tiles, was badly chipped and the windows, with their floor length black velvet drapes, looked as though they had never been washed. All around the perimeter were scratched wooden tables, displaying busts of children with staring eyes and gaping mouths, and there were dozens of chairs painted an ugly drab shade of green with torn seat covers. Rachel could feel Livvy trembling as she pressed up against her mother for comfort but Matt, who was scared too, wasn't afraid to speak up," We aren't staying here are we? This place is horrible, it's creepy and dirty and that lady was weird, she looked like a munchkin."

Rachel was on the verge of retreating back through the front door, even though she had no idea what to would do next, when she heard footsteps approaching on the tiled floor. When a figure appeared out of the darkness of an adjacent hallway, Rachel could see it was a woman with a ghostly cadaver like appearance dressed in a long black robe and heavy oxford style shoes. As she came closer, Livvy scrunched down behind her mother while Matt clutched Rachel's hand and whispered, "Let's go, Mum!"

Rachel looked down at Matt then at the woman, who she assumed was Miss Hargrove. "Good afternoon, I'm Rachel Marshall and you must be Miss Hargrove," and she extended her hand.

Miss Hargrove ignored the outstretched hand, inspected Rachel from head to toe and then, in an unpleasant tone, said, "Follow me please; we can talk in my office."

The little group followed her along a dark hallway, passing several doors until she turned into an office marked Principal and then she stood aside while they filed past her into the room. Once inside, she shut the door and sat down behind a huge wooden desk, covered in mounds of books and papers, and pointed to the one chair facing her. "Sit down please, Mrs. Marshall," she ordered, "the children will have to stand."

Rachel sat down and looked around the room while Miss Hargrove shuffled through some papers. The office looked more modern than the entryway, with the tiled floor and arched windows, but the furniture was old and worn and the beige linoleum floor was covered in scuff-marks and dirt. Rachel was still wondering what to do when Miss Hargrove finally looked up. "Well, I have all your papers here so I don't see any need to do anything more than have the children taken up to the dormitory and you can go on back to London. I'll go and get one of the monitors to come down right away and meanwhile you can stay in here and say goodbye."

Rachel couldn't believe her ears and stood up abruptly."Excuse me, Miss Hargrove, but I'm not leaving my children here without seeing where they will be eating and sleeping and attending classes. I want to make sure they'll be happy here and well taken care of."

While Rachel was talking, Miss Hargrove had risen from her desk and was visibly annoyed that anybody would dare to question her authority. She rounded the desk and confronted Rachel with a sickly smile. "Surely, Mrs. Marshall, you can't be serious, that will take time and I haven't got the time; I'm very busy. You've read all about Mount Thomas and you've signed all the papers so let's not make things more difficult for everyone."

Rachel stood her ground, "I'm sorry but if you won't allow me to look around and see where the children will be staying then we are leaving."

Miss Hargrove stretched to her full height in indignation, "Very well, if you insist, but this is highly irregular. Follow me please and no dawdling I have things to do," and she swept out of the room.

Rachel's tour of the building confirmed her worst fears. Even though Miss Hargrove set the pace and they were hustled along without time for any real inspection, it was enough for Rachel to realize this was no place for Matt and Livvy. The dormitory was co-ed with boys and girls together, sleeping on cots covered in thin wrinkled gray sheets and drab cotton quilts, and the dining hall consisted of long wooden tables and benches sitting on more dirty beige linoleum. The classroom at the back of the building, and overlooking the grounds, was cluttered with battered wooden desks stained with inkblots and defaced with crude carvings. No other human being, adult or child, was seen during the tour but Rachel could hear childrens' voices and assumed they were in some other area of the school that was probably even more dilapidated. Once they arrived back at the main entry hall, Miss Hargrove took Rachel's elbow and started to walk her towards the front door. "Well, you've had the tour, now you can go back to London so please quickly say goodbye to the children and leave. I will be in touch with you by letter in a week or so."

Rachel was outraged and pulled away then, taking the children by the hand, she turned and faced the principal, "How dare you, do you really think I would let my children stay in this place. It's ugly and dirty and I don't like your attitude so thank you for the tour but we are leaving!"

Miss Hargrove snorted and then laughed in Rachel's face, "And where do you think you will go? You won't find anywhere else around here; now you'll have to go all the way back to London."

Rachel wasn't to be intimidated, "It doesn't matter, I'd rather take my chances in London with bombs dropping than leave my children in a place like this," and she pushed Matt and Livvy out the door without looking back.

Once out on the road in front of the school, she had no idea where they were and was thinking they really needed to get something to eat when suddenly she caught sight of a taxi coming towards them. After hailing the taxi and asking the driver to take them to the main road, he recommended a popular tearoom and dropped them off less than five minutes later. Rachel found a table near the window and settled Matt and Livvy in their seats. The waitress took their order of fish and chips, with fresh bread and butter and a pot of tea but, even though she was famished, Rachel was too worried to enjoy her meal. She knew now that the only alternative was to take the children back to London and she knew Harry would be furious. At least they didn't have to make the trip back until the next day as she had already decided to stay over in Plymouth and Harry was not expecting her until the following evening. As she sat drinking her tea, the children were doodling on their napkins and talking about their adventure. They had been so nervous on the journey down, not knowing where they were going, and they had been terrified of Miss Hargrove but the thought that they were going home had changed all that. Little did they know that the tide was about to turn again.

Chapter Ten

The clock on the wall of the tearoom showed five o'clock when Betty and Jean Martin walked through the door, sat at a table in the corner, and ordered apple pie and coffee. Betty and Jean were sisters serving in the WACS but they were on a thirty-day leave, which had just begun, and had decided to leave their little cottage to come into town for dessert and then go to a movie. Betty was the older sister, tall, fair, and on the plump side, while Jean was just as tall and fair, but much slimmer. They both had boyfriends in the RAF, stationed in Biggin Hill, and they hadn't seen them in a while but, when the four of them did manage to get together, they thoroughly enjoyed each other's company. Betty couldn't help noticing the mother with her two children at one of the other tables and nudged her sister. "That lady over there doesn't look like she's from here and she looks a little lost."

Jean glanced over at Rachel and turned back to Betty, "Yes, you're right. Maybe we should ask her if she needs any help."

Rachel noticed the two young ladies looking her way and gave them a meek smile. She was surprised when they both got up, coffee cups in hand, and sat down at the table next to her. "I hope you don't think we're intruding," Jean said, "but you look a little lost and we were wondering if there was anything we could do?".

Rachel was so touched that complete strangers would take pity on them, her eyes filled with tears and she was soon telling the sisters everything that had happened that day never expecting, for one moment, they could help. Betty put her arm around Rachel. "There, there, it's okay. Why don't you come home with us for tonight we have lots of room and maybe we can figure out something. It doesn't make sense for you to take the children all the way back to London. They seem like really sweet kids and they must be exhausted."

Matt who had been listening to every word touched his mother's cheek, "Mum, can we go with them, please; Livvy and I are really tired. Look at her, she's almost falling asleep."

Rachel thought she had nothing left to lose and she gratefully, but reluctantly, accepted the Martin sister's offer. After bundling Rachel and the children into their old broken down Ford, Betty and Jean set off for home. They lived in a cottage with a thatched roof and a white picket fence, just like the ones Rachel had seen in picture books and movies and she was enchanted. Inside, all of the furnishings were covered in chintz and there were plants and cut flowers everywhere. The sisters decided to bunk together in Betty's room and put the family in the other. There was only a double bed but, because it had a footboard, they put Livvy along the foot of the bed and it left plenty of room for Rachel and Matt. It was only after the children were asleep that Betty came up with an idea. "My boyfriend, Jim, has an aunt who lives in Plymouth and she's been taking in evacuees since the war began. We just visited a couple of months ago and there weren't any children there then, so maybe she can help. There's one little snag, I know a lot of people are willing to help without wanting anything in return and some only want a little money for food, but Flo likes to get a little bit extra for herself. I don't think it's very much but I thought you should know that Rachel."

Rachel saw a glimmer of hope and clasped her hands together, "Oh money isn't a problem but how can we find out if she can take them and how will I know if they'll be all right there?"

Betty came over and sat down beside Rachel on the sofa, "Look, she has a telephone and I have the number so we'll go to the call box and ring her tonight and, if she says yes, we can drive you there tomorrow. Hey, this is exciting I hope she can take them; she has a really cozy house and she seems really nice, although I've only met her once."

"Can we really go out and ring her now?" Rachel asked, getting up and picking up her handbag.

"Yes, of course. Jean can stay and watch the children and we'll take a walk down to the call box," and taking Rachel's arm, they were off down to the corner chattering excitedly.

Rachel couldn't believe her good fortune when Flo agreed to take Matt and Livvy, and was prepared to do so the very next day. Rachel wasn't sure how she would catch the mid-afternoon train back from Plymouth to London in time but she decided to worry about that when the time came.

The next morning, the sisters were up at a quarter to seven and roused Rachel and the children for breakfast so that they could get an early start. After a meal of blueberry pancakes with syrup, sausages, and orange juice, they bundled into the car and set off on the road. It was a cold day but the sun was shining and Rachel was optimistic about what lay ahead. It was less than forty miles to Plymouth, but Betty wanted to show the children some of the coastal route so she headed off the main road towards the ocean. At Polperro, it was like a picture book with cottages perched on slopes overlooking the harbour and at Looe, with its historic bridge, they saw the wonderful old churches built in the thirteenth century and dozens of fishing boats being readied to venture out to sea, for the daily catch of mackerel, trout and even blue shark. Although the air was cool, Matt and Livvy were hanging out of the windows enchanted by the scenery and Rachel couldn't help but compare this beautiful serene place with home. It seemed like a different world here, without the threat of planes droning overhead and the constant noise of explosions from enemy bombs, and she wished they could stay here forever.

They arrived at Flo's house well before lunch and parked beside the picket fence. The house itself was a one-story brick dwelling with lovely bay windows and a front garden with a flagstone pathway, small areas of lush green lawn, and flowerbeds filled with chrysanthemums of all colours. As soon as Betty got out of the car, Flo came running out of the front door and through the garden gate to greet them. She was older than Rachel had expected with a stocky build and short curly brown hair and wearing a loose fitting white smock covered in bright red poppies. "Hello, Flo," Betty said, taking a step towards her and giving her a hug. "I didn't expect to see you again so soon."

"No my dear, I didn't expect to see you this soon, either. This must be your sister, Jean; she looks a lot like you," and she reached out to shake Jean's hand. "And you must be Mrs. Marshall," she said turning to Rachel, who had just finished helping the children out of the back seat. "I'm Florence Dawson but please just call me Flo; now let me see the little ones."

Rachel pushed the children in front of her, "I'm pleased to meet you, Flo, please call me Rachel. This is Matt and this is Livvy and I can't begin to tell you how grateful I am that you have agreed to take care of them."

"Well my dear, you're fortunate I don't have any other evacuees right now. They'll have to share a bedroom but they will each have their own bed. Why don't we discuss this in the house? I'll make us all a cup of tea and perhaps you will stay for lunch."

Matt and Livvy warily followed the grownups into the house, not quite sure what to make of Flo. While tea was being made in the kitchen, they were left in the living room and seated on a plump cozy sofa covered in rose coloured velvet. The walls were papered in a delicate floral design and beautiful wood framed paintings of seascapes filled most of the space, above a long wooden cabinet, displaying photos of Flo's family. It was a comfortable room and they began to feel a little more at ease but they knew Rachel would be leaving soon and wondered what would happen to them after she had gone.

Betty and Jean kept the children company while Rachel remained in the kitchen with Flo working out arrangements for the children's stay. She told Flo all about her experience at Mount Thomas and why she needed her help so desperately, then she talked about the children themselves and explained about Matt and his asthma and his need for special care and exercise every day. Flo listened, nodding her head every now and again and appeared to be sympathetic to all of Rachel's needs. She agreed to do what she could to make sure the children were happy and well looked after and promised she would enroll them both at the local school, the following week. Then she mentioned to Rachel, in a whisper, that she was a widow and had very little money and needed a little cash for herself, if it could be spared. Rachel assured Flo she would send her some extra money when she got back home and then send her something on a regular basis after that. Flo seemed content with this and suggested they join the others in the living room and Rachel felt at ease now that she had the opportunity to get to know Flo a little better. She appeared to be a kind and thoughtful woman and a little lonely after losing her husband after thirty years of marriage. She didn't have any children of her own but she had several nieces and nephews and a few friends from the neighbourhood and the church in Plymouth, where she had lived all her life.

After a lunch of fish paste and cucumber sandwiches, scones with plum jam and more tea, it was time for Rachel to leave to catch the train back to London. Betty and Jean were driving her to the railway station and then returning to St. Austell, leaving the children alone with Flo. Matt was his usual stoic self but Livvy couldn't let go of Rachel and cried bitterly as her mother was driven away, waving frantically out of the car window. It was only the appearance of Sheba, Flo's four-year-old white Persian cat that finally consoled her. Sheba had been tucked away under one of the wicker chairs in a corner of the living room surveying the newcomers. When she had grown bored and a little more curious, she eventually stretched out lazily on her back and then crept silently up to Livvy, brushing against her bare legs. Livvy thought she was the most beautiful creature she had ever seen and was mesmerized by her deep blue eyes and silky white fur. For Livvy, the love of an animal was unconditional and she doted on Sheba, while the cat returned her affection and gave her the love she had lost with the absence of her family. It took less than a week for Matt to discover Flo was not what she seemed.

Chapter Eleven

Within four days of Rachel's departure, there was a distinct difference in Flo's demeanor. Until that time, and only a few days before enrolment at school, she had treated the children well, even if she appeared somewhat aloof. She had helped Livvy select her clothes in the mornings, brushed her hair, and prepared wholesome meals for breakfast, lunch and tea. It was with the incident of the broken figurine, Matt had accidentally knocked off the living room cabinet, that her whole demeanour changed. She had instantly berated Matt in a loud voice gripping him by the arm, "You stupid boy, look what you've done. That was my mother's and now it's ruined. Why can't you be more careful, always running instead of walking? You are a stupid, stupid boy," and she twisted his ear violently. "Pick up all those pieces and make sure you don't leave any behind. I'll punish you if Sheba gets hurt because of your clumsiness. Your mother will have to pay for this, mark my words you little brat."

Matt didn't cry, even though his ear was smarting and he was starting to cough, but Livvy began yelling, "No, Aunt Flo, leave him alone, he didn't mean it. Stop it, you're hurting him," and she ran forward and pulled at the hem of Flo's dress trying to drag her away.

"Get off me, you little madam, how dare you put your hands on me. Go to your room and stay there until I say you can come out," and she let go of Matt and pointed down the hallway to the bedroom Livvy shared with him. When she had finished admonishing Matt, he was obliged to stand in the corner of the living room facing the wall for almost an hour, but he still refused to let Flo see he was upset and determined not to say he was sorry. This was the time when Matt and Livvy needed each other the most and they relied on each other for comfort. There was nothing they could do about their situation, even when Flo's impatience seemed to grow with each day, and she derived new ways of punishing them. Livvy was denied any access to Sheba, Matt wasn't allowed to play outside, dessert was denied them on many occasions, and so it went on. School gave them a welcome respite from Flo's constant tirades, over the smallest thing, but Livvy's anxiety, while confined to the classroom, escalated again and two weeks later another incident sent Flo into another fit of anger.

Whenever the weather got colder, Matt's asthma seemed to get better, especially if the air was crisp, and he was happier whenever winter approached but, one Wednesday afternoon, he would feel colder than he had ever felt before. He woke up that morning with a mild stomachache and, after a breakfast of cornflakes and milk and a small slice of dry toast, he felt even worse. Flo was in no mood to listen to any excuse for not going to school that day and sent him off with Livvy as usual. He suffered through his lessons until lunch time but, standing in line in the school cafeteria, he knew there was no way he could take a bite of the macaroni and cheese being dished out and he needed some fresh air. He had only been in the schoolyard a few minutes when Livvy came looking for him and found him sitting on a bench, doubled over and moaning. She became alarmed when he suddenly jumped up and started running towards the lavatories, which were at the far end of the building, but it was too late; his bowels seemed to erupt and, to his horror, he had an accident right there in the schoolyard, just as some of his schoolmates were coming out for recess. He froze in his tracks not knowing what to do but

Livvy, sensing what had happened, yelled to him, "It's okay, I'll get Mrs. Bell!"

Matt called after her in protest, "No, Livvy, don't do that, please don't do that," but his plea fell on deaf ears as Livvy ran to get Matt's teacher and returned almost immediately, clutching Mrs. Bell's hand and dragging her towards Matt. The teacher was used to tending to such emergencies and took Matt into the boy's lavatory while Livvy stood guard at the door. She removed his soiled clothes, putting them in a paper bag, cleaned him up, and then leaving him for a few moments returned with a pair of old oversize trousers she had found in an abandoned locker. Matt was no longer in pain and grateful for his teacher's help but humiliated when he had to pass all of his classmates near the front gate. Mrs. Bell suggested Livvy go with him just to be sure he got home all right and Livvy was more than happy to go. "Let's go to the park," she suggested tugging at Matt's coat sleeve.

"No, Livvy, we have to go home or else we'll get in trouble."

"Oh, okay," said Livvy grudgingly, "but she's gonna be mad anyway. I bet she starts yelling again."

"Don't worry, it wasn't your fault and I couldn't help it."

"I know but she'll still be mad, she's always mad," Livvy whined.

After they turned the corner and approached the house, they saw Flo coming up the pathway with her shopping bag but, when she saw the children, she put her bag down and yelled, "What are you doing? Why aren't you in school?"

Matt waited until he got a little closer and then called back, "I had an accident, Aunt Flo, so they sent me home."

Flo waited until both Matt and Livvy were through the garden gate and then looked Matt up and down, "You don't look hurt to me, sonny, and what on earth are you wearing?"

Matt tried to explain and as he did so Flo looked more and more disgusted. "Didn't the teacher give you a note?"

"She must have forgotten; don't you believe me?"

"Well, I'll soon find out if you're telling the truth. Get in the house, both of you," and with that she pushed them through the front door.

Livvy was instructed to sit in the living room and not to move while Matt had to wait in the bedroom. They could hear Flo clattering about dragging something along the floor and out onto the strip of lawn at the side of the house. Then they heard her running water in the kitchen sink and going back and forth, in and out of the door. Eventually she came in and confronted Matt, "All right young man, you get all those clothes off now and come with me."

Matt stepped backwards and folded his arms over his chest. "What, all of my clothes?"

"Are you deaf? Take those clothes off right now," and she stood with her hands on her hips waiting, just inside the door.

Matt slowly started to take off his coat, then his sweater when suddenly Flo began to shake her head. "I'm waiting and I haven't got all day so do as I say right now or you'll be in more trouble than you already are."

Matt finally managed to take everything off until he stood naked and embarrassed trying to cover himself, then Flo picked up the bag of soiled clothes he had brought home, turned on her heel, and proceeded out the side door, "Come along, sonny, move yourself."

Matt spent the next fifteen minutes sitting in a galvanized tub half filled with cold water and the soiled clothes, which Flo had ceremoniously dumped in with him. Livvy had left her place on the living room sofa and had been watching from the window but she knew there was nothing she could do for her brother. Matt shivered uncontrollably; he had never felt so cold in his life but he wouldn't let Flo see him cry and he didn't want Livvy to know how wretched he felt. That night both Matt and Livvy were at the lowest point in their young lives and they felt trapped and alone. They were unaware their lives were soon to take another turn.

Chapter Twelve

When Rachel didn't hear back from Flo after writing two letters she became very anxious. She had corresponded with Betty Martin thanking her for being so kind to them and decided to write to her again, in the hope that she would have some news. She let Betty know she had sent a letter to Flo, directly after returning to London, and told her she would be sending some money in her next letter then, two weeks later, she had written again enclosing money for food and a new winter coat for Matt, plus some extra for Flo. Betty thought it was strange that Jim's aunt hadn't replied to Rachel and, as she was going into Plymouth anyway to shop for a new pair of shoes, she decided to drop in unannounced. Flo was very surprised and a little annoyed to see Betty show up at her door but she greeted her as though she was pleased to see her and invited her in for a cup of tea. The children were overjoyed to see a friendly face and greeted her with a hug but, when Flo took off to the kitchen to put the kettle on, Livvy climbed on to Betty's knee and whispered, "I hate her, she's so mean. Please take us home with you, I promise we'll be really good."

Betty was shocked, "Why what did Aunt Flo do to you dear?" she asked drawing Livvy to her side.

Matt spoke up, "She's always yelling at us for nothing and we're always being punished. She made me sit in a bath of ice-cold water in the garden because of an accident I had at school. I wanted to write to my mum but she won't let me."

Betty was horrified but knew she had to be careful, particularly when Flo came back into the room and asked what they were talking about. "Oh, the children were just telling me about school but tell me, Flo, how have things been going? You look a little frazzled have you been feeling well?"

Flo was a little suspicious about this sudden interest in her health, "Of course I've been well," she replied a little too sharply. "I've just been busy with two little ones in the house. There's a lot to do, making meals, shopping, cleaning, and all the laundry but I'll manage somehow."

Betty immediately detected that Flo was being defensive and she needed to find out more about what was going on, without Flo taking it out on the children after she left. "I had a letter from Rachel, she told me you were going to get Matt a new winter coat. The clothes are so much nicer here in Plymouth, I'd love to see it."

Before Flo could respond Matt was on his feet crossing his arms over his chest, "I don't have a new winter coat and we didn't see any letter from my mum."

Betty looked expectantly at Flo who scowled at Matt before replying, "I haven't had time to get the coat yet and your mother's letter was addressed to me, young man."

Betty had heard enough to know all was not well and was already planning her next course of action. She knew she wouldn't get the chance to talk to the children again without Flo hovering over them so, when she left rather hurriedly, she embraced Matt and Livvy and told them she would be writing to their mother and she was absolutely certain they would be having a wonderful Christmas. She prayed they understood what she was trying to tell them and winked at Matt as she climbed into her car for the trip home.

As soon as Betty got back to St. Austell she contacted Jim at Biggin Hill and told him about the visit. She was astonished to hear Jim's mother, who was Flo's younger sister, had often told him that Flo was moody, and at times a little strange. She also placed a lot of emphasis on material things but Jim didn't think she was capable of being cruel. Betty thought the best thing to do was get the children out of Plymouth and back to London, in spite of the fact there was no evidence of the war winding down.

"I have an idea," Jim yelled down the phone line over the drone of engines revving up on the tarmac behind him, "I have a few days leave two weeks from now. I'd love for you to come up and visit and we can stay in that nice little inn we stayed at before. You could bring the children on the train with you and their parents could meet them at the station."

Betty could hardly believe it, not only would she be able to spend time with Jim but she could bring the children back home to Rachel, "Oh, Jim, that's a wonderful idea. I can't wait to see you. The children will be so excited about going home but I'm going to have to write to Rachel right away. She'll need to send a letter to Flo explaining that I'll be picking Matt and Livvy up."

"Okay, honey, phone me when you've made all the arrangements and I'll be at the station. That way, I'll finally get to meet these kids you seem to care so much about."

"You'll meet Rachel too, she's a lovely lady and she'll be so happy to get Matt and Livvy back. I'll call you, Jim. Take care of yourself, I love you," and in her excitement about the trip she hung up the phone before Jim could say goodbye.

Betty decided it would be better if she actually spoke to Rachel so she sent her a telegram asking her to telephone her the next evening, at her friend Jenny's house. Jenny was a hairdresser and worked at home, so she needed a telephone for her business, and was always obliging if any of her neighbours needed to get in touch with a friend or relative in a hurry. After Betty explained to Rachel what she thought might be going on at Flo's, Rachel was very upset and wanted to come and get the children immediately but, when Betty suggested she bring them back to London with her when she visited Jim, she decided to wait and she still had to tell Harry. She had promised them they would never be sent away again and was determined to keep her word, no matter what Harry said. That night, he was out fighting fires and Rachel was asleep when he got home. She was relieved that she would be leaving for work early the next day and didn't have to face him right away. She was certain what his reaction would be. Harry didn't disappoint her and he became so angry that she had made the decision to bring the children back without consulting him that, at one point, he raised his hand to strike her but she faced up to him and refused to show she was in the least bit afraid. During the next few days, they didn't speak to each other and this was a pattern that was to be repeated over and over again.

Chapter Thirteen

Life back at home for Matt and Livvy was much like before and Matt appeared to adjust without too much problem but Livvy found it much more difficult, even though her mother assured her they would be staying in London. She was very insecure and continued to have trouble at school skipping classes and constantly asking to be excused. Harry got less and less work playing the saxophone, something he enjoyed and which gave him a pleasant change from his everyday life, and he became moodier and more aloof. He and Rachel argued constantly about the children and Rachel always had to defend Matt, who still had problems applying himself at school. Rachel would have been proud if her son had been an intellectual like his father but understood, only too well, why some children found learning difficult. Livvy, on the other hand, excelled at arithmetic and English and Harry tended to favour her, leaving Matt feeling inferior and unwanted. In truth, although he had fallen back into the routine of school and home life, Matt secretly wished he was back with the Kisbys' where he could play freely in the open fields or in the orchard with his friends.

There were occasions when the family spent some good times together. They would sometimes go to Southend for the weekend and spend time playing on the beach or in the ocean. The tide seemed to go out for miles and once, after Matt and Livvy had walked out a fair distance, the tide came in so quickly that Rachel, who couldn't swim, became hysterical and was screaming at them to hurry back. Harry had gone for a walk and had no idea what was going on but was relieved to see both children safely playing on the beach when he returned. Matt and Livvy thought it was a great adventure and weren't in the least bit scared, even when Livvy had difficulty wading through the water after it reached waist level. They both loved the ocean and were already learning to swim at school. Rachel was nervous just standing in the surf but Harry was an excellent swimmer and had even won medals for diving off the high board. He encouraged both children and, as they grew older, he would take them further out into the ocean and teach them the rules of safety and respect for the water. At these times they would forget there was a war on and it was only when they returned to London that they were forced to face the terrible conditions there.

Mrs. Fossey, who was still living on the top floor, was now almost eighty and very frail. It was not surprising that after catching the flu, it developed into pneumonia and she was taken to the hospital where she remained for two weeks without any visitors, other than Rachel, and then quietly passed away. After Mrs. Fossey's death, Rachel decided to take over the two vacant rooms and turn them into bedrooms for Matt and Livvy. Livvy got the larger room overlooking the garden and Rachel decorated it in a deep rose colour. There was rose patterned linoleum on the floor with two small-fringed rugs, a rose quilted comforter and matching silk drapes and Livvy loved it. She scoffed at Matt's room, which was much smaller and finished in shades of brown, but he was perfectly content.

Rachel wasn't particularly pleased that the children had to pass Mr. Wilson's flat to get to the top floor. He was a very quiet man in his early fifties but he had a strange untrustworthy air about him and he had recently started keeping a number of birds in his living room. There was always an odor permeating the hallway on the second floor and it seemed to creep down the stairs to the main level. Harry and Matt ignored him while

Rachel tried to be civil whenever she ran into him and Livvy avoided him completely.

Now that the children had vacated the back room Rachel decided to make it into a bedroom for herself and Harry and turn the front room into a place where she could entertain family. Rachel put her heart and soul into decorating with deep red wall-to-wall broadloom, beautiful ivory regency striped wallpaper and large comfortable furniture and, on the coffee table, she placed her prized Venetian glass vase. She would often just go into the room and look around and feel a sense of pride but she felt cheated too because they hardly ever entertained and few people ever saw the room or enjoyed its comfort.

Harry had no family left; his mother had died the year before after suffering from dementia and being cared for in a nursing home for six months. Harry was not a materialistic man and for years he had given his mother money on a regular basis to make her life a little easier. He was shocked to find, after her death, that she had not spent a penny of the money he had given her and had deposited all of it into an account, which was now his.

Rachel's mother was in the last stages of a terminal illness and not expected to live more than a few months and her eight siblings and their families were scattered throughout the London area. All but two of her siblings had maintained their religious upbringing and married partners of Jewish heritage but Harry couldn't deal with the rituals they followed, especially when it involved their strict dietary laws, and he discouraged Rachel from inviting them to the house. It was a happy coincidence that the two sisters, Cissy and Marie, who had married gentiles lived only two streets away and Rachel and the children visited them often. Harry tried to be sociable whenever they came to the house but he had difficulty making conversation and it made Rachel feel uncomfortable. Since she met him he had never had any friends and she often wondered why but Rachel had lost touch with old friends too. Except for an old schoolmate, who lived in Essex and who she corresponded with now and again, but never got to see, she only spoke to her neighbours when seeing them in the back garden or meeting them on the street.

Life became a routine for the whole family despite the bombings, which had continued for so long. People went about their business from day to day and took shelter when the sirens sounded, as though it was a normal occurrence, and when there was loss of life, injury, or damage to property, they rallied together to comfort and help those affected. Rationing was difficult to deal with and Rachel would buy eggs and tea on the black market just to give the family a little extra and the children would bring home packets of cheese and powdered hot chocolate, which the Americans donated regularly to the schools.

On June 13, 1944, the nature of the war changed when the first buzz bomb hit London and, by the end of the month, they averaged about fifty a day and came to be known as doodlebugs. These weapons were like bombs with wings and were launched from the coast of Belgium and France. When overhead, they made an odd sound that could clearly be heard by those on the ground. It was when the sound stopped, only fifteen seconds remained to take shelter before the bomb hit the ground and caused devastating damage. A few weeks later, on a July evening, Harry and Rachel were sitting listening to the radio and the children were playing draughts on the dining room table when they heard the noise of a doodlebug overhead. Harry stood up immediately and, sensing danger, grabbed Rachel and the children and pushed them into a corner of the room. At that moment, the noise stopped and, hugging his family, Harry said very softly, "This is it!" Everybody held their breath, for what seemed like an eternity, then suddenly there was a loud explosion and the house shook. The bomb had dropped on the next street taking out five houses and all of the people in them and the Marshalls' counted their blessings. This was the closest they ever came to any real danger but they experienced many anxious moments until the end of the doodlebugs in March 1945. Two months later on May 7th, Germany surrendered and, the next day, V-E Day was declared and it seemed like the whole world went crazy. People were dancing in the streets, kissing and hugging complete strangers, and the pubs were overflowing with everyone celebrating the end of the war in Europe. A week later, on Cavendish Road, they built a huge bonfire and burnt an effigy of Hitler and there were dozens of trestle tables set with trays of sandwiches, cake and lemonade. The blackout was finally over and all across London the bonfires burned, lighting up the night sky. This was the end of an era and for some it was a new beginning, while for others it was a difficult adjustment.

Livvy had just turned nine-years-old when the war ended and incredibly her anxiety attacks suddenly stopped. In later years, she came to believe it was because she no longer had a fear of being sent away from home and she never expected to suffer these attacks again. It was a blessing she had no idea what the future would bring.

Harry was a victim of the new found peace. He was no longer needed in the National Fire Service and had a lot of time on his hands. He was suffering with a mysterious pain in his stomach, which he claimed was an ulcer, but the doctor wouldn't confirm his diagnosis. He was very particular about what he ate, claiming many foods upset him and he drank gallons of milk. His condition wouldn't allow him to play his favourite instrument, the saxophone, and slowly he began to sink into a depression becoming moodier and more difficult to live with and occasionally becoming physically violent with Rachel, when they got into arguments. Eventually, he had a nervous breakdown and took to his bed for four weeks but, even without treatment, he finally had the inner strength to overcome his depression and began to take an interest in the inner workings of the latest introduction to the world of entertainment, television.

Chapter Fourteen

At the age of fourteen, Livvy was attending an all-girl high school and had made some new friends. She was of average height for her age, very slim and often wore her now honey blonde hair braided crisscross fashion on top of her head. Her slightly aquiline nose, which she inherited from Harry, gave her a refined look and two years earlier she had discarded her hated glasses and could see perfectly well without them. In junior school, she had always been first or second in her class but now she was competing against students like herself from other schools and she was finding it difficult to place above fourth of fifth. Harry was still proud of her achievements and praised her often while continuing to belittle Matt, who had failed to attain his GCE and was in secondary school and due to leave that year.

Livvy had three special friends, Maureen Jensen, Stella Garwood and Luisa Silva. Luisa was her closest friend and the one she spent the most time with. They lived only two streets apart and would meet every weekday morning for the mile walk to school and always walked home together. They had both reached puberty at the young age of eleven but Luisa was much more developed with a very curvaceous figure. She constantly expressed her embarrassment about her large attention-getting breasts but when she wasn't wearing her school uniform, which consisted of a white tailored shirt, navy skirt, and blazer, she never took the trouble to hide them. By the time the girls reached the age of fifteen they began to experiment with make-up and were soon wearing heavy kohl eyeshadow and the palest lipstick. Livvy rarely took any of her friends home because Harry was so critical, it would make her feel uncomfortable so, during the week, she would often go to Luisa's house to study. On the weekends, when they were allowed to stay out until ten o'clock, they would either go to a movie at the local cinema, commonly known as the Flea Pit because of its run-down state, or they would congregate at the popular ice-cream parlour on the main street.

One Saturday night in summer, when the weather was exceptionally warm, they decided to go for a walk to the park and took the route over a bridge spanning the railway lines. Livvy had on a simple lilac dirndl skirt with a white cotton top while Luisa was wearing her favourite dress with an all-over pattern resembling a newspaper. The pattern itself looked authentic at first but, on closer inspection, it was an illusion and none of the words made any sense. Anyone seeing the dress for the first time was intrigued and attempted to read it and the area stretched across Luisa's ample chest would always attract the most attention. They were halfway across the bridge when Livvy spotted four teenage boys coming in the opposite direction and she failed to recognize any of them. Noticing no one else in sight and feeling a little nervous she grabbed hold of Luisa's elbow and forced her to stop. "I think we should go back, I don't like the look of those boys coming towards us."

Luisa tossed her long auburn hair over her left shoulder, "Well I'm not scared of them, what do you think they're going to do?"

"I don't know," Livvy replied, "but I don't like the look of them especially the tall one, he looks mean and he's staring at us."

"Let him stare, see if I care," said Luisa stubbornly as the group got closer.

The tallest boy, who looked about eighteen, strode away from the others and came face to face with Luisa who had stepped protectively in front of Livvy. "Where d'ya think you're going?" he demanded staring straight into Luisa's eyes.

"None of your business," countered Luisa tossing her hair again.

"Yea, well I could make it my business if I wanted to. Little girlies like you shouldn't be wandering around on your own, you need some company. Oh, and by the way, sweetheart, nice dress you've got on there," and he lowered his gaze to stare at Luisa's breasts. Luisa didn't move but looked directly over his shoulder at the other three boys who were hovering in the background. The tall boy finally looked up again into Luisa's eyes, "I said, where d'ya think you're going?"

"And I said, none of your business," said Luisa staring back.

"Think you're pretty smart don't ya? I'll show you how smart you are," and with that he pulled back his fist and aimed for Luisa's nose while Livvy gasped. His fist didn't connect but missed by an inch or two and Luisa didn't even flinch. This so unnerved the thug, he stood motionless for a few seconds while continuing to stare then shrugging, he turned to his mates and signalled them to start moving. "Let's get out of here, these two ain't no good," and with that, they sauntered past the two girls and off the bridge.

The encounter with the four boys was long forgotten but, just before Livvy's sixteenth birthday, a chance meeting in the ice-cream parlour brought the whole episode back. Luisa was sick with the mumps so Livvy had arranged to spend Saturday night with Maureen. They went to the Flea Pit to see the movie, Come Back Little Sheba, and then decided to walk along the main street, finally ending up at the ice cream parlour. They were sitting at the counter sipping on malted milk shakes when Livvy noticed a boy sitting alone at one of the corner tables. She knew she had seen him before but couldn't figure out where and it bothered her so much, she couldn't take her eyes off him. Maureen was chattering on about her younger brother Bobby, whom she constantly had to babysit, when she suddenly realized Livvy's attention was elsewhere. "You're not listening, Livvy. Who are you looking at?"

"It's that boy over there in the corner. I've seen him somewhere before and I can't think where. It's really bothering me."

Maureen swivelled around on her stool scanning the room and then she saw the object of Livvy's curiosity. He looked to be about medium height with fair hair drooping over one eye and wearing a heavy, dark gray duffel coat, black pants, and army style boots. He was too far away to get a really good look at but, from a distance, he seemed rather average looking and didn't appeal to Maureen. She turned back to her milkshake. "Why don't you go over and speak to him if you're so curious then maybe you'll figure out who he is."

"No way," said Livvy, "let's just forget about it, maybe he just looks like someone else, a movie star or someone."

As Livvy was talking the boy had left the table and was approaching the counter but the girls didn't see him until he came right up behind Livvy and tapped her on the shoulder. "Hello," he said as she turned to face him. "Haven't I seen you somewhere before?"

"That's funny," Livvy replied, "I was thinking the same about you. When we came in and I saw you sitting there you looked really familiar."

"Well I guess we'll remember sooner or later. My name's Brian, what's your name?"

"Livvy, and this is my friend, Maureen."

"Hello Maureen, do you both live around here?"

Livvy was looking at Brian still puzzling where she had seen him when Maureen replied, "Yes, Livvy lives on Cavendish Road and I live on Whiteman Road, how about you?"

"Oh, I live up over the railway bridge on Chelmsford."

As soon as he mentioned the railway bridge, Livvy recognized him as one of the four boys who had stopped her and Luisa the summer before and she decided the conversation had gone far enough, "Maureen and I have to go, maybe we'll see you again sometime," she said abruptly and pushed Maureen off her stool.

Maureen was astute enough to know something was wrong and started to walk towards the door but Brian was a little surprised at this sudden change in Livvy's attitude and decided to get to the root of it, "Did I say something wrong?"

"No," replied Livvy moving past him, "we just have to get home that's all."

"But it's only nine o'clock," Brian protested, "are you sure I didn't say something to upset you?"

"No, no," Livvy repeated walking away, "we have to leave and please don't follow us."

Brian frowned, puzzled by her remark, "Why on earth would I do that?" and then suddenly the light went on and he remembered the girl with the honey blonde hair, hiding behind her friend that day on the bridge. "Wait a minute, now I know where I've seen you before. It was last summer on the bridge when my cousin Tony tried to frighten you. That friend of yours was really something; she wasn't the least bit scared. Anyway you needn't have worried, Tony's all bluff; he's always going around doing stuff like that."

Livvy looked Brian up and down with distaste, "I suppose you think it's amusing?"

Brian was contrite. "No, I don't. Tony's a jerk and I hardly ever see him. He lives on the other side of London and only comes to visit a couple of times a year. The other two boys were my other cousins, Tony's brothers. Look I'm sorry let me buy you and Maureen a coffee or something."

"Why should I believe you? Sorry, but we're going."

"Please," Brian pleaded, "I'm telling you the truth. Look I'm here all alone, just have coffee with me."

Maureen looked across at Livvy and nodded her head then started to walk back to the counter. Livvy hesitated for a minute and then smiled, "Okay, you can buy us coffee but we can't stay for long, we still have to walk home."

Later that night, unable to get to sleep, Livvy couldn't stop thinking about Brian. She had only had two encounters with boys in the last few months but there wasn't anyone she had thought about too seriously. When she was fourteen, she had developed a crush on John Pengelly who was at least three years older and lived almost directly across the road. She would sneak into the front room and watch for him from behind the lace curtains when he came home from work but, whenever he ran into her, he would just nod and keep on going. About three months earlier, he had suddenly seemed to notice her and would stop and chat and then, out of the blue, he asked her to go to a movie with him. Livvy was so excited she was in a turmoil trying to figure out what to wear and finally opted for her cherry red Burberry coat and her new gray suede shoes. John came to pick her up and asked to speak to Rachel, wanting to assure her they would be home by eleven o'clock and that Livvy would be in safe hands. Rachel was very impressed, and so she waved them on their way and hoped they enjoyed themselves. They travelled on the bus to Finsbury Park and took the tube to Piccadilly Circus and, when they arrived it seemed like a magical place to Livvy. She had been on field trips with the school to the West End and to the historic areas of London and she'd been shopping with Rachel on Regent Street, on a number of occasions, but this was different. After the movie, they went for a hamburger and coffee and Livvy just stared out of the window, enchanted at the sight of all the neon lights and the crowds of people parading up and down Leicester Square. It was then she realized she didn't have much to say to John and, on the journey back home, they were both uncomfortable. Livvy was glad when she reached the house and John walked her to the front door. She thanked him for a lovely evening and, just as she was wondering what he was going to do next he leaned forward, kissed her lightly on the lips, said he would call her, and left. Rather than being devastated, Livvy was relieved that, not only was the date over but, she was over her crush on him. Thankfully he didn't ask her out again.

Livvy's only other encounter was with another boy she had met at the ice-cream parlour. Luisa had been with her that day and they got talking to two brothers, Kenny and Stan, and had gone to the Flea Pit with them the following Saturday. Stan had taken Luisa home and Kenny had walked Livvy up Cavendish Road. He was exceptionally good looking with jet-black hair swept back from his forehead, deep brown eyes and at least six feet tall. Luisa had been disappointed when he had taken a shine to Livvy but she had graciously gone with Stan, without any fuss. When they finally reached the house, Kenny suggested they slip into the small alleyway, just a few feet away so they could talk undisturbed, and Livvy agreed although she was a little nervous about being with a boy she hardly knew. It only took a few minutes before Kenny became very amorous and Livvy didn't mind the kissing, in fact she found it rather exciting but, when he started groping at her clothes, she pushed him away. "Don't do that, I don't like it."

Kenny put his arms around her holding her tightly against his chest, "Aw, come on, Livvy, you don't mean it. You didn't seem to mind me kissing you."

Livvy struggled to get out of Kenny's grip, "Let me go, kissing is okay but that's as far as you go."

Kenny continued to hold onto her, "Don't be such a baby; don't tell me you haven't done this before. I don't believe it, all you girls say that."

Livvy pushed as hard as she could and freed herself from his grasp. "Well believe it creep," and she ran out of the alley and back to the house, praying he wouldn't run after her. Once inside the door she breathed a sigh of relief and crept downstairs to the living room where Harry and Rachel were watching the news.

Rachel was surprised to see Livvy come home earlier than expected. "Hello, Livvy, you're early. Is everything alright?"

"Yes, Mum, the movie wasn't very good and then Luisa had a headache so she wanted to go straight home."

Harry looked up, "It's about time you got home early for once, always gallivanting about."

"I wasn't gallivanting, Dad, I was out with my friend," she protested.

"Your friend, Luisa, has no manners," he mumbled and turned back to the television.

Livvy was tired of Harry's criticism, "I'm going to bed so I'll say goodnight and I'll see you in the morning," and she gave both Rachel and Harry a quick kiss on the cheek and went on upstairs.

Now in the quiet of her room, she wondered what her father would think of Brian. She wanted to believe his story about his cousin Tony and she liked his quiet manner so she had agreed to go out with him. She made a date to meet him the next day to go to the park and she had a feeling she would be seeing a lot more of him in the future.

Chapter Fifteen

The next day it was cold and windy and the skies were heavy with dark clouds but Livvy was excited about seeing Brian. Both Matt and Livvy always got up late on Sundays because they had nothing much to do and the heavy roast beef dinner Rachel prepared every week, was usually their first meal of the day. Livvy was wearing her navy pleated skirt with a royal blue turtleneck sweater and she was hoping Brian would take her to the teahouse, so that she could take off her coat and show off her outfit. Harry sat down at the dining room table and eyed Livvy suspiciously, "What are you all dressed up for?"

Rachel glanced at Livvy and then intervened, "She's just going out with one of her friends. You're going to a movie aren't you, Livvy?"

Livvy was grateful Rachel was covering for her, "Yes, Mum, I'm going with Luisa and Stella may come with us too."

Harry looked out of the window at the darkening clouds, "Well, you'd better put your heavy coat on and take an umbrella and don't you be late back for tea."

Livvy was relieved Harry had accepted Rachel's story and, after dinner, she rushed through her Sunday chore of cleaning up the dishes so that she would be on time to meet Brian on the railway bridge.

Over a pot of tea with warm scones, creamy butter, raspberry jam and Dundee cake, Livvy wanted to know all about Brian. "There isn't much to tell," he said as he settled in his chair overlooking the pond and the willow trees, swaying in the high wind, "I live with my mother, stepfather and older sister on Chelmsford Road. My mother is great, she's always let us do whatever we wanted and it's a wonder we turned out the way we did. She's very independent and goes out a lot with her friends, I don't know why she married Bob because she's hardly ever home."

"What happened to your real father?" Livvy asked spreading more jam on her scone.

"He took off when I was about four years old so I don't really remember him but my sister Judy does. She really missed him for a long time but she's pretty happy now; she's going steady with some Yankee airman stationed in Oxfordshire."

"It sounds as though you don't like him."

Brian hesitated for a moment "Who Marty? No he's okay; actually he's a nice chap. He's always buying Judy little gifts and she's hoping one day they'll get married and then she can move to California."

Livvy looked pensive, "It sounds so romantic. I'd love to go to America one day, wouldn't you?"

"I'm not sure; I suppose I'm a bit put off by all these servicemen dating all the girls here. They have so much money and they've got those darn uniforms. Women always like men in uniforms."

"You told me the other day you were training to be a car mechanic, do you like it?" asked Livvy.

"Yes, I'm learning a lot and I'll earn a good wage when I get my license but it's a dirty job. Anyway, enough about me; what about you? What are you going to do when you get out of school?"

Livvy was thinking about the coming June when she would be finished with her education and didn't know whether to be happy or sad, "I'm not sure what I'm going to be doing yet. I would have liked to go to college but my parents couldn't afford it. I'm looking forward to going to work and earning some money. I'm really good at math so I may try something in accounting or work in a bank."

Brian remembered Livvy had an older brother, "What about your brother, does he work?"

"Yes, he works for a silk screen printer and he likes it because he's quite artistic. My dad isn't happy about it though; he's been really hard on my brother because he didn't pay much attention in school. I love my dad but sometimes he's really difficult to get along with. The other day he got in an argument with my mum and tipped the table over, dishes and all. Oh, I guess I shouldn't have told you, now you'll be scared to meet him."

Brian smiled and covered Livvy's hand with his own, "Does that mean you're going to invite me to your house?"

Livvy smiled back, "Yes, but not just yet, it's my birthday next month and I'll be sixteen. I don't think my dad would like me going out with anyone before that."

"I don't mind waiting to meet your parents as long as I can see you before then."

Livvy squeezed Brian's hand, "I would like that very much; maybe we can make a date to go to the movie next week."

By the time Livvy invited Brian to her house. she had already had her sixteenth birthday and was working as a clerk at Barclay's Bank in Wood Green. She spent most of the day adding up piles of cheques on a huge Burroughs calculator, while the other employees either ignored her or talked down to her, as though she was a second-class citizen. After three months she couldn't tolerate it anymore and broke down in tears one evening after she got home. Harry was immediately sympathetic advising her to quit and the next day she handed in her notice. Working out the last week on the job was torture and she had no idea what she was going to do next. School now seemed like a vacation and she couldn't imagine spending the next forty years or more going to work every day. Harry suggested she take a little break and the timing was perfect. Rachel's oldest sister, Sadie, was considering a trip to the continent and had already talked to Rachel about taking Livvy with her. It was a seven-day trip and Livvy was excited about going to a foreign country, but she didn't want to leave

Brian. She had formed a bond with his mother and was always welcome in his home and he had become a permanent fixture in her life. Even Harry tolerated his presence while insulting him behind his back by calling him Popeye.

The journey across the English Channel from Dover was one Livvy would never forget. Even seven years after the war had ended, some items were still rationed, including sweets, but once they were beyond the three-mile limit, passengers were free to buy as much candy as they liked. Livvy made the mistake of buying a huge slab of milk chocolate and greedily eating the whole thing, while sitting on a stool that swivelled round and round, as the ferry rocked back and forth in the rough waters. Livvy wasn't the only one who was sick that day and she ended up along with scores of other passengers hanging over the side and praying for the journey to end.

On landing in Calais, buses were waiting to take them up the coast to Holland where they stayed in a tiny village overnight and got some sense of the country. The next day, they were awakened at six o'clock by the noise of the village people washing their shop windows and singing merrily in the morning sunshine and they understood why the Dutch had the reputation of being so scrupulously clean.

After spending the day sightseeing they travelled south, back across the border, to the Belgian town of Ostend and, on the journey, made friends with two young men from Nottingham who were sitting across the aisle. Johnny and Jeff had a great sense of humour and both Sadie and Livvy were enjoying their company. Livvy didn't realize Jeff was attracted to her but, after they settled in the small hotel and the whole tour group had enjoyed a meal of veal stew with dumplings and deep-dish custard pie, he asked Sadie for permission to take a walk with Livvy. Sadie had a daughter of her own, Livvy's cousin, Jeanne, who was twenty-one, and she had never tried to monitor her friends or control her, other than to insist she come home at a reasonable hour. She decided to take the same approach with Livvy and sent them on their way with the promise that they would be back by eleven o'clock. Jeff, who was twenty-three, turned out to be the perfect gentleman particularly when he discovered Livvy was only sixteen. They took a leisurely walk along the beach, waded in the surf, and bought Belgian waffles covered with heaps of strawberries and whipped cream. It was a perfect summer night and Livvy couldn't help wishing Brian was with her. They had been sitting on the beach for a while both feeling quite comfortable with each other when Jeff checked his watch and suggested they had better be getting back to the hotel. They were shocked to discover, although it was only ten-thirty, the front doors were securely locked. Fortunately Sadie and Livvy occupied a room on the second floor, facing the main street, and after Jeff pitched several small pebbles at the window Sadie stuck her head out and saw the two of them waving frantically below. Rather than being annoyed at being dragged out of bed and downstairs to let them in, she found it rather amusing and recounted the tale to a dozen people on the bus the next day.

The last three days of the trip were spent on the French Riviera at Juan-le-Pins between Cannes and Nice and they lazed about in the hot sun, dined on some wonderful French food and swam in the glorious Mediterranean. Most of the time, they kept company with Johnny and Jeff and were having so much fun that Livvy wanted to stay even longer but, every now and then, Brian would pop into her mind and she realized how much she missed him. The ferry crossing back to Dover was calm and Livvy loved every moment staring out across the channel and watching the seagulls swooping overhead and, when they finally arrived in London, she was sad having to say goodbye to the two young men who had made their holiday such a pleasant one.

While Livvy was away, Brian was worried she might meet somebody else. He talked to his mother and sister about her constantly and mooned around the house just waiting for her return. Marion Warner was sympathetic towards her son and always seemed to know the right thing to say. One morning after Livvy had been gone for four days she quietly woke him up for work and asked him to come down early for breakfast. He finally appeared at the kitchen table dressed in his overalls and heavy boots looking downcast. "Morning, Mum, what's for breakfast?"

"Hello, son," Marion replied, placing a glass of orange juice next to his empty plate, "how would you like some eggs and bacon today?"

Brian couldn't help chuckling "You mean I don't get to choose between corn flakes, shredded wheat or weetabix?"

"No, and don't be such a smart guy," his mother replied nudging him gently on the shoulder, "I just thought you needed something nice to buck you up. I know you aren't very happy this week with Livvy away but, before you know it, she'll be home and you'll forget how miserable you were."

"I know, Mum, but what if she meets some other chap while she's over there? Some of those French men are real charmers."

Marion smiled as she slid two eggs out of the frying pan and onto his plate, "Well, even if she did meet some charming man, he's there and you're here so she'll soon forget about him. Anyway nobody's more charming than you so you don't have to worry."

Brian looked up as his sister strode into the kitchen dressed ready for work in a sapphire blue suit, Marty had bought her, and high heeled patent leather pumps. He couldn't help thinking how attractive she was with her deep auburn hair curling softly over her shoulders and an expression on her face that was one of utter contentment. She glanced at her mother and then at Brian, "Good morning you two, hey what's going on? I see you cooked eggs, Mum."

Brian puffed out his chest, "Yes, she cooked them especially for me, didn't you, Mum?"

Marion turned from the stove to face her two children. "Morning, Judy, those eggs were for Brian but I can make some for you too if you want. There's also bacon and toast and you can have some of that Camp coffee."

Judy's mouth dropped open in astonishment, "But it's a weekday, what's the occasion?"

"Mum was just being nice because I was feeling a little miserable."

"Oh, I get it, pining for Livvy. Won't she be home on Sunday?"

Brian sighed, "Yes, but it seems so far off and I really miss her. Don't you miss Marty when he's at the base?"

"Yes, but it's a bit different, I know he's working. This is the first girl you've really cared about Brian and she probably won't be the last."

Marion decided it wasn't what her son wanted to hear, "Judy, did you want any eggs or not because I need to get to work too?"

Judy realized her mother had interrupted her on purpose, "Oh, sorry, Mum, no I'm just going to have some toast and tea and then I'm off. You sit down and eat and I'll get my own breakfast," and she rested her hand on Brian's shoulder, "Everything's going to be okay, believe me," she said reassuringly.

Everything was okay when Livvy returned. After returning home, she began her search for another job and, within a week, she was working at the St. James Club, an exclusive hotel in the heart of the city, just minutes away from Buckingham Palace and Piccadilly Circus. Working in the accounting department kept her confined to an office most of the day but, occasionally, she would be required to go to the front desk and talk to some of the guests. She soon discovered most of the people who stayed at the St. James Club were very rich and came from all over the world and she was amazed to learn they were exceptionally polite and friendly. One day she even had a chatty conversation with a very elegant woman from South Africa who was dripping in diamonds and was astounded to hear the porter, who was transporting her seven pieces of luggage, address her as Lady Harrington.

The other three girls in the office lived in South London, so socializing with them after work was difficult but every lunch hour, during the warm weather, one of the them would accompany her to Green Park and they would lounge on the grass eating their lunch and watch the tourists, who were easy to identify with their cameras slung over their shoulders. The experience was so unlike her time at Barclays Bank that Livvy couldn't wait to go to work in the morning despite the long trip by bus and tube. The highlight of her week was always when she saw Brian, which was usually on a Wednesday, when he left the garage early and on the weekends. On a Saturday night, they often went to movies, either at the Flea Pit or occasionally to the West End and they loved to sit at the back of the cinema and cuddle up, while munching on Maltesers. If there was a hockey game on at the local arena they would go just to be able to skate around the rink afterwards, along with dozens of others.

Brian rarely came to Cavendish Road to visit, as Harry still made him feel uncomfortable, so they spent a great deal of time at Brian's house and Livvy was always welcomed there. She enjoyed talking to Judy and when Marty was in town he would tell her all about his home in Long Beach and she would daydream about going there one day. She tried to keep in touch with her friend, Luisa, and got together with her occasionally at the ice cream parlour, or at Luisa's house, but she felt guilty about not spending more time with her. Her heart now belonged to Brian and their relationship seemed to take precedence over everything else. Matt was also becoming more removed from her life. He preferred to spend time with his friends and when he was at home he was often in the cellar attending to his tropical fish. He had two aquariums filled with vibrantly coloured specimens, and all kinds of rocks and greenery, and he took pride in making sure the fish were well looked after. Harry was fascinated with Matt's hobby and it was pleasant to see father and son finding some common ground. That September, when he turned eighteen, he was conscripted into the army and sent to a base in Scotland for two years. Rachel was upset that he was being sent so far away; knowing the eleven hour train ride would mean he would rarely come back to London on leave. Matt, on the other hand, was looking forward to the change and was pleased when Harry agreed to look after his precious fish. In the end, it would turn out to be a positive experience for Matt. The two years he spent in the clear air of Scotland cured him of the asthma that had plagued him most of his young life.

Chapter Sixteen

In December of 1952, smog descended on London, lasting for four days and killing thousands of people. London was known for its pea soup fog but this was the worst the population had ever encountered. Those with existing respiratory conditions had great difficulty breathing and many ended up in hospital, or dead. As smoke from chimneys mixed with natural fog, the air began to turn yellow and, as it got colder and more coal was burned, it got blacker. It was as though the city was in complete darkness and it was hard to see one's hand in front of one's face. There were hundreds of traffic accidents and any buses, left on the road, had to be guided by off-duty drivers, walking ahead with lanterns. The soot from the swirling smog permeated everything; white undergarments looked gray and hands and faces, exposed to the air, were covered in a film of grime. There was a blanket of silence which was eerie and made it even more difficult to get any sense of direction and the city virtually shut down, as people were forced to stay home.

Brian was desperate to see Livvy during this time but it was impossible to navigate from his home to the Marshall's house. He was grateful telephones had now become a common way of communication and they talked every night, but it was difficult.

There was no privacy with Harry lurking about listening to the conversation and Livvy could never say what was in her heart. They agreed that, as soon as the smog lifted, they would be together again and they went to bed praying they would wake up to a clear bright morning. When the smog finally cleared, nearly everyone who had been housebound couldn't wait to get out of their homes and when Rachel suggested going to a movie on Saturday night, Harry was easily persuaded. They hadn't been to see a movie in a long time and decided to make a real evening of it by traveling to the West End and having a bite to eat at one of the upscale restaurants in Leicester Square. Knowing her parents wouldn't be at home, Livvy thought it would be the perfect opportunity to invite Brian for tea and spend some time alone with him. She decided to confide in her mother, not only because it made her feel less guilty but because she also wanted her advice on what to cook and how to prepare it. Rachel suggested a simple meal of pork chops, peas, chips, and canned peaches for dessert and, as she left for the movie with Harry, she gave Livvy a hug and hoped she had a wonderful evening.

Livvy was extremely anxious; she hadn't cooked very often and Rachel hadn't spent too much time teaching her. She helped with other chores around the house, vacuuming the living room rug every evening after work and scrubbing the kitchen and hall floors every Thursday night, as well as keeping her own room immaculately clean. The only exception was when she was eleven years old and Rachel had a hysterectomy, putting her in a hospital and rehabilitation center for four weeks. Livvy was left to run the household and neither Harry nor Matt lifted a finger to help her. She thought she had done a really good job and was proud of herself but devastated later, when she overheard Harry tell Rachel she did pretty well, except for the cooking when she gave them meager portions and everything tasted bland. Tonight, everything had to be perfect and she was in a dither peeling and slicing the potatoes and pounding the pork chops, hoping it would make them tender. She was thankful both the peas and the peaches were in cans and no preparation was needed, this would allow her time to change her clothes, brush her hair, and put on a little makeup before Brian arrived. She had been trying to decide what to wear all day and finally picked a rose wool dress with a scoop neck out of her closet. As she sat down in front of the mirror brushing out her hair, which now fell to her shoulders, she contemplated what might happen later after they had eaten. They had been dating now for nearly nine months and innocent kissing had progressed to heavy petting but they were still very young and Livvy didn't know if she was ready for complete intimacy. Sex education at school had been sketchy at best and the subject had never been discussed in the Marshall home. Nearly everything Livvy had learned had been through other young people and she wasn't even sure what they told her was true. As she put down the brush and applied a little rouge and a touch of lipstick, she wondered if this was the night when she would find out what really went on in the bedroom.

At just after six o'clock, the front door bell rang and Livvy raced up the short flight of stairs to open the door. Brian was leaning heavily against the sidewall dressed in his heavy gray topcoat and carrying a bunch of pink chrysanthemums. Livvy was excited to see him and beckoned him inside, "Hello, Brian, I've been dying to see you. Come in and get warm, you must be freezing."

Brian pushed himself away from the wall and grimaced for a second before smiling, "Hello Livvy, these flowers are for you, I hope you like them."

"Oh, they're beautiful; thank you so much," and she took them from him, burying her nose in them and opening the door even wider so he could pass through. He slowly climbed up the two stairs to the hallway and she couldn't help noticing the pained look on his face. "What's wrong? Is it your knees? You have to get near the fire and you'll feel better. Dad brought a lot of logs in earlier so it should be blazing all evening. Here let me help you," and she linked her arm through his and helped him along the hall and down the stairs into the living room.

Brian was in a great deal of pain that day but he didn't want to disappoint Livvy. As a youngster he had rheumatic fever, which had left him with a weak heart and, when the weather was cold and damp, his joints swelled and ached. His knees were the most painful and he often had difficulty walking and even aspirin didn't help. Because of his weak heart, he sometimes joked that he wasn't long for this world and this would upset Livvy because she couldn't imagine her world without him. After taking off his coat, Livvy noticed he had taken particular care with his appearance and was wearing a shirt and tie, light gray flannel slacks and a new burgundy corduroy jacket. The colour really suited his fair complexion and his hair, which usually flopped into his eyes, was slicked back from his forehead. She gave him a kiss on the cheek, "My goodness you look nice tonight; I love your jacket."

Brian lowered himself into Harry's favourite chair. "Do you really? I was hoping you'd like it. Mum bought it for me; she knew I was coming here tonight for a special evening so she thought I needed something new."

Livvy frowned, "Why did your Mum think it was going to be so special?"

Brian looked a little embarrassed and hesitated before replying, "Well, she knew you were cooking for me and you've never done that before. By the way, Livvy, you look really pretty tonight, I like that dress."

"You're changing the subject but thanks anyway. Now, I have everything ready to start cooking in the kitchen and it should only take about ten minutes so why don't you just sit here and I'll get you a shandy."

Brian shook his head, "You need beer for shandy."

"Yes I know that, there's a whole lot of beer in the refrigerator and my Dad won't notice if I take one".

Brian shook his head again, "Are you sure? I don't want you getting in trouble."

Livvy looked coy, "If that's the only reason I get in trouble tonight I'll be okay won't I?"

"What do you mean by that?"

"Nothing at all; I'll get that shandy now," and Livvy rushed out to the kitchen afraid she had just made a fool of herself.

The pork chops were perfectly cooked and the chips were crisp on the outside and soft on the inside, just the way Brian liked them. After smothering everything in ketchup, he declared Livvy had done a great job but he was too full to eat dessert. In spite of Livvy's attempts to get him to eat the peaches, by opening a can of Devon cream to go with them, he insisted he had had enough and just wanted to relax. Livvy could never relax until all the chores were completed so she left Brian by the fire, cleared the table and washed and dried all the pots, pans, and dishes. She didn't want any evidence left behind to show Harry she'd been entertaining anyone, especially Brian. When she came back into the living room, Brian had slid down from the chair and was sitting on the rug with his legs stretched out in front of him. "Are you all right?" she asked, concerned he was still in pain.

"Yes I'm fine now, Livvy. Why don't you just leave that little lamp on and sit down here with me," and he patted the spot beside him.

Livvy turned off the glaring overhead light and sat down and, when Brian put his arm around her, she rested her head on his shoulder and they both sat in silence gazing into the fire watching the flames, flickering in the semi-darkness. After a few minutes, which seemed like an eternity to Livvy, Brian turned and kissed her tenderly, "You know I love you, Livvy, and we've been going out for a long time."

Livvy cut him off before he could say anymore, "Yes I know, Brian, and I love you too. I want us to be together, you know what I mean, but I'm scared."

"There's no need to be scared, Livvy, I promise I won't hurt you. I knew this was going to be a special night, everything's going to be okay." Slowly he turned her around and started to undo the tiny buttons on the back of her dress and finally, after he had removed all of her clothes, she suddenly felt quite beautiful with the firelight dancing over her body and she just lay there and watched, while Brian stood and removed his own clothes. Livvy had often seen her brother, when he was small, running around in his birthday suit and she had seen lots of pictures of naked men but she had never seen one in the flesh before. She started to panic when she saw the aroused state Brian was in and then she knew all the stories she had heard were true. She was trembling when he got down on the rug beside her and stretched out full length taking her into his arms. "Its okay, Livvy, I told you I'm not going to hurt you. I promise I'll be very gentle."

Livvy buried her head against his chest. "I know and I trust you but I don't want to get pregnant."

"You don't have to worry about that, I'll stop in time," and he stroked her hair and kissed her lightly on the top of her head.

He was true to his word and Livvy went to bed that night believing she had experienced the most intimate act between a man and a woman. She enjoyed the closeness but had felt neither pain nor euphoria and she wondered what all the fuss was about. She had no idea, it would be many years before she would discover how truly wonderful it could be.

Chapter Seventeen

The following spring of 1953, Brian and Livvy talked about going on holiday together and although they knew Brian's family wouldn't object, they were surprised when Harry and Rachel agreed it would be a good idea for them to get out of the city. The largest annual racing regatta in the world was being held in August, at Cowes on the Isle of Wight, and they were fortunate enough to book two rooms at a small bed and breakfast in Ryde. Although they would have to take the bus to Cowes to see the regatta they had plenty of time, as this was the first year the race had been expanded from three to eight days. Brian tried to talk Livvy into booking one room but she was far too nervous in case her parents tried to contact them and she didn't mind the extra cost. She had been saving every spare penny for this holiday and had only bought a few new clothes. She could hardly wait to go on holiday but in June, like the rest of the country, she was distracted with the coronation of Queen Elizabeth. It was estimated that twenty seven million people watched the event on television and three million people lined the streets of London to watch the procession. Brian and Livvy were among the crowds on the Mall that day and, even though they could only see the tops of the heads of the horse guards as they trooped by, they were excited just to be there. It had been over a year since the young princess had been proclaimed Queen and the British people were filled with a sense of pride. After the coronation, July seemed to last forever but August finally arrived and, the day before their departure, Rachel was helping a very excited Livvy pack. She was examining some of the new clothes she'd bought and was particularly taken with a pair of bright yellow shorts with cuffs and a red butterfly motif on the pocket. "My goodness," she remarked smoothing them out on the bed, "these are really cute. What are you going to wear with them?"

"Thanks, Mum, I like them a lot. I think I'll wear my white cotton top with them."

"I have a better idea, I have a yellow top that is just about the same shade and I've never worn it. You can have it, Livvy, and anyway it will probably look better on you than on me."

Livvy gave Rachel a hug, "I remember that top, Mum, and it would be perfect with my shorts. Are you sure you don't mind me borrowing it?"

"No, of course not, in fact you can have it. I just want you to have a nice holiday but please be careful, Livvy, you are still very young and I don't want you to get into any trouble."

Livvy couldn't look her mother in the eye so she busied herself with folding her clothes, "Don't worry, Mum, I'll be fine and I won't do anything to make you ashamed of me."

Rachel appeared to be reassured by Livvy's reply but deep down she worried whether they were doing the right thing in allowing her to spend a week alone with Brian.

The following day, Brian and Livvy took the train to Portsmouth and the ferry across to Ryde. It was a short trip and the Solent was calm so Livvy didn't have to face another experience like the crossing to France the year before. They arrived at the Burchfield Guest House in late afternoon and were shown to their rooms by a sweet-faced lady named Mrs. Grimes. She explained that breakfast was served each morning, between eight o'clock and nine-thirty, and gave them a list of tearooms and other places in the area where they could eat. After unpacking in their separate rooms, they went for a walk along the esplanade and, unable to resist the sight of the waves gently rolling onto the beach, they took off their shoes and socks and waded in the surf. They could see the mainland but felt isolated from all the routine of everyday life back home and couldn't believe they had a whole week to spend alone together. Further along the beach they found a seafood shack and bought two bags of plump salty shrimps and a bag of cockles, which they ate at the end of the pier gazing out across the water. Later as the sun started to go down and the sky turned a wonderful shade of pink, they walked back along the esplanade and stopped off to buy double scoop vanilla ice-cream cones at a stall, who's owner they came to know well during their week's stay. That night, after retiring to their own rooms, Brian waited until he thought all the guests were asleep and then crept into Livvy's room. Working in the garage, he was used to getting up early but the next morning, when returning to his own room, he could already hear signs of life in the rooms below. This was a routine he went through every night during their holiday but, despite the element of risk, both he and Livvy thought it was worth it and they treasured every moment they spent together.

The week flew by so quickly, neither Brian nor Livvy wanted to go home. They had been all over the island by bus or by hiking and would never forget the sights they had seen. The view of the Needles, towering stacks of chalk and flint rising out of the sea at the western extremity, was breathtaking and they could see the old lighthouse at the outermost point. Then there were the cliffs at Blackgang Chine and Alum Bay where they collected coloured sand in glass tubes provided to the tourists. They even got to spend two full days in Cowes watching the regatta and imagined what it would be like just to sail away forever on one of the yachts. One day they had a real adventure when they took a motorboat out and suddenly the engine died. The sea was rough that day and waves were coming into the boat and Livvy was scared to death until a fishing boat came close enough to hear Brian yelling frantically for help and they were towed back to shore. They laughed about it afterwards but Livvy had visions of them drifting out to sea or drowning and she had never forgotten the lessons Harry had taught her about respecting the ocean. For Livvy, the end of the holiday brought back her ever-present feelings of insecurity. While with Brian, almost twenty-four hours a day, she felt comfortable and safe in the relationship but on the last day, as they were leaving to catch the ferry, she was overcome with fear not knowing exactly when she would see him again.

Chapter Eighteen

Over the next six months, life reverted to its normal pattern. Livvy went back to her job at the Overseas Club and continued to see Brian two or three times a week. In March, just before Livvy's eighteenth birthday, Brian suggested they have a special night out and he booked a table at an upscale restaurant in the West End. Birthdays had not been celebrated with too much enthusiasm in the Marshall household, except for the time when Livvy was eleven. Rachel had redeemed dozens of ration coupons to provide two huge cans of peaches, whipped cream, and all kinds of candy for Livvy's party. Several children who hardly knew each other had been invited but the whole thing fell flat and not even the food could salvage the day. It was not surprising then when Harry and Rachel had no objection to Brian taking Livvy out on her birthday as they had nothing planned, other than giving her a lovely gold-plated watch with a narrow wristband that looked perfect on her slim wrist.

Livvy dressed in a two-piece, fine wool, periwinkle skirt and matching top with a cowl neck which was very form fitting and showed off her slim figure and Rachel loaned her a long rope of pearls and small pearl drop earrings to finish off her outfit. She wore her hair loose around her shoulders and put on a little more make-up than usual. She had long discarded the heavy kohl eyeliner and pale lips and now preferred a touch of mascara, rouge, and deep rose lipstick and, as she surveyed herself in the mirror, she was happy with what she saw and looking forward to the evening with growing excitement. At the restaurant Brian did his best to act like a man about town and ordered for both himself and Livvy. When the waiter brought Livvy her vichyssoise she was shocked when she took a mouthful and it was cold. She put her spoon down immediately, leaned towards Brian and whispered, "Its cold Brian!"

Brian grinned, "Yes I know Livvy, it's supposed to be cold, taste some more you'll like it."

Livvy picked up her spoon again and frowned at the bowl in front of her. But what is it?"

"It's a leek and potato soup. My mum made it once when she was feeling creative in the kitchen."

Livvy took another sip and tried not to make a face, "It's different; I'm not sure if I like it. I'm really sorry, Brian, I know you wanted everything to be perfect."

Brian took Livvy's hand, "Everything is perfect, Livvy. You don't have to eat the soup, I've ordered sole amandine and a special dessert I know you'll like."

The sole with fresh green beans and tiny new potatoes was delicious and Livvy was already feeling full, "I don't think I can eat anymore, Brian. That was wonderful."

"Nonsense, I know you love chocolate, wait till you see what's coming," and, as he spoke, four waiters descended on the table singing Happy Birthday, in perfect harmony, and carrying a chocolate layer cake covered in flickering candles. Livvy was mortified and could hardly look up when she realized what was happening and, when all of the other diners started to applaud, she blushed a deep shade of red.

Brian interrupted her thoughts, "Come on, Livvy, blow out the candles before the wax melts onto the cake." It took her two attempts to blow out the eighteen candles and she was only too happy to allow their waiter to slice the cake and serve it.

Livvy had always liked coffee but had rarely had the real thing. At home, they always had tea or made Camp coffee, which was a thick condensed liquid mixed with water. At the restaurant, they had the most wonderful coffee she had ever tasted and she was on her second cup when Brian asked, "Are you sure you've had enough Livvy?"

"Oh, Brian, it was wonderful. Thank you so much everything was perfect."

Brian laughed, "Except for the vichyssoise!"

Livvy giggled and looked a little embarrassed, "Yes, except for the vichyssoise."

Brian took Livvy's hand, "The evening isn't over yet there's more to come."

"Where are we supposed to go, my mum and dad are home and so is your family?"

Brian laughed again, "You've got a one-track mind. That's not what I was talking about."

"Oh! Well, what were you talking about?"

"This, Livvy," and he took a small velvet box from his inside jacket pocket and handed it to her. Livvy nervously took the box and looked up at Brian questioningly. "Go on, open it. It's not going to bite you."

Inside the box was a ring that looked like the one Livvy had been admiring in the jeweller's shop on Bond Street. The round stone looked about half the size of her mother's genuine one-carat diamond ring and was set in a silver band and it was very pretty, but Livvy knew it couldn't possibly be real. She took it out of the box but hesitated before putting it on. "Is this what I think it is Brian?"

"Yes, Livvy, it's time we got engaged. We've been going out together for a long time and one day we'll get married."

Livvy suddenly no longer cared that she was in a public place and leaned over to kiss Brian on the lips. She was ecstatic that Brian loved her enough to want to marry her and she couldn't wait to show off her ring to everybody she knew.

In the fall, after being engaged for only six months, Livvy sensed a change in Brian. On some nights, when she expected to see him, he began making excuses that he had to work late and she suspected he wasn't always telling the truth. They had made some new friends at the ice-cream parlour but one of them, Brenda Buckley, made her uncomfortable. Brenda lived with her mother and father at the other end of Cavendish Road, close to the main street. She was a year older than Livvy and about an inch taller with dark red hair, which fell in waves to her shoulders. Because of her stick thin figure with small breasts, wide shoulders and a rather pronounced nose, she was not considered attractive but she had a way of flirting with the opposite sex that got their attention. At the end of November, Brenda invited several friends to a party at her house, including Brian and Livvy. Her parents were away visiting relatives in Essex and she had the house to herself for the weekend. She was planning a wild get-together with lots of beer, sandwiches, salad, potato chips and music including some of the early rock and roll of the Crew Cuts and Bill Haley. Livvy was not a party person, she much preferred to spend her time in one-on-one situations rather than with a crowd of people, especially when they were drinking and things started getting out of control. When they arrived at Brenda's house they could hear the music blaring and they had to knock several times before anyone responded. Finally Brenda's cousin, Will, answered the door and ushered them into the living room which was filled with about twenty people, some lounging about drinking beer and some gyrating to the sound of Elvis Presley. Brenda didn't even acknowledge their arrival; she was too engrossed in her partner, a rather tall lanky boy with jet-black hair, dressed in blue jeans and an argyle sweater. Brenda was wearing a pair of tight black slacks and a white man-style shirt, which only accentuated her rather masculine appearance but her actions left no doubt, she was all female. Livvy felt overdressed in her red poodle skirt, black off-the-shoulder top, and black high heels and wished she'd worn something more casual. Brian, however, was wearing his navy cuffed pants and teal blue shirt with button down collar and seemed to fit right in. After greeting a couple of friends and some people they had met once or twice before, Brian escorted Livvy to a straight-back chair in the corner of the room and said he'd see what he could find to drink. While he was gone, Livvy studied the crowd and took a good look at her surroundings. She was surprised when she noticed the room

was a little shabby, paintwork was peeling in places, wallpaper
had been stripped off in spots, the carpet was threadbare
and faded, furniture needed re-upholstering, and everything
seemed to be beige with not a hint of colour anywhere. She
had met Brenda's parents once or twice and they were such
outgoing and likeable people, she expected their house to be
bright and cheerful. Perhaps, she thought, they didn't need
material things to create a happy home.

When Livvy was sixteen, with the blessing of her father who
chain smoked foul looking cigarettes, which he rolled himself,
she got into the habit too. Her mother had always thought it
was unhealthy and it was impossible for Matt to smoke because
of his asthma. Livvy always felt much more sophisticated with
a cigarette in her hand and she lit one up while waiting for
Brian. A young man she had seen in the ice-cream parlour
approached her and asked for a dance but she could see Brian
weaving his way back through the crowd, with a beer bottle in
one hand and a glass in the other, so she gracefully declined.
As the evening progressed, they mingled with the other guests
and danced several times with each other but, when Livvy saw
Brian dancing with some of the other girls, she didn't hesitate
to accept the invitation of several of the young men. This
was the first grown-up party Livvy had been to and she was
beginning to enjoy herself.

It was almost eleven o'clock when she noticed Brian and
Brenda were not in the room and wondered where they were.
She had noticed earlier, they had danced together a number
of times and Benda had been openly flirting, batting her
eyelashes, and staring into Brian's eyes. She was starting to
get suspicious and decided to go to the kitchen to see if they
were there. She tiptoed down the hallway but, at the door to
the kitchen, stopped dead in her tracks, Brian had his arms
around Brenda and was kissing her passionately. She could
see his face but he had his eyes closed and didn't see Livvy
standing there. She felt her heart drop into her stomach and
backed slowly away from the door then ran frantically back
to the living room. Flopping down on the sofa, she began
nervously tapping her foot and tried desperately not to cry;
she couldn't believe Brian would cheat on her. She felt utterly

betrayed and knew she had to get out of the house. As she was about to get up Brian came back into the room and sat down next to her but she couldn't even look at him and stared down at her feet, "I want to go home now," she said abruptly.

"It's early yet, Livvy", he said reaching for her hand, "let's stay for a while. I thought you were enjoying yourself."

Livvy pulled her hand away, "Well I'm not anymore. I want to go home now and if you won't take me then I'll go by myself."

Brian was puzzled unable to understand why Livvy's mood had changed so drastically, "What's the problem, are you feeling sick?"

Livvy was angry now, "I just want to leave, I've had enough."

Brian got up and put his arms around her, "Okay, suit yourself, go home and I'll stay for a while and talk to you tomorrow."

Livvy couldn't believe her ears and pushed him away, racing for the front door and running as fast as she could back to her own house, where thankfully Harry and Rachel were in bed. Later, she wished she hadn't run out but her response to bad situations had always been impulsive and she often regretted her actions. That night she tossed and turned for hours sobbing into her pillow until finally she fell asleep from sheer exhaustion.

Chapter Nineteen

For a week, Livvy waited for Brian's call but it never came and finally she couldn't bear it any longer and called his house. Marion Warner answered the telephone and was surprised to hear Livvy's voice, "Hello, Livvy, it's lovely to hear from you but is something wrong? Brian told me he was meeting you to go to a movie."

Livvy choked back tears, "That's not true, Mrs.Warner, I haven't seen Brian for a week, in fact I haven't even spoken to him."

Marion was flabbergasted, "Oh no, I can't believe this, what happened, Livvy? Did you two have a fight?"

"Not exactly, we went to a party last Saturday and something happened but I think Brian should tell you all about it. I was upset and went home by myself and I haven't spoken to him since that night. I know I shouldn't have walked out but I didn't expect this. We're supposed to get married one day, why is he ignoring me?"

"I'm so sorry, Livvy, he hasn't said a word to me and I don't know where he is. I'm annoyed he lied to me tonight but when he gets home I'm going to have a talk with him and I'll make sure he calls you, even if I have to stand over him. Try not to worry dear. I'm sure everything will be alright."

Livvy's hopes started to rise, "Thank you so much, I'd be really grateful if you got him to phone. I don't understand why he hasn't got in touch with me and why he would make up a story about meeting me."

Marion was starting to think back over the past week and realized Brian had not been behaving like his usual self, "I don't understand it either but I'm sure there must be an explanation. You have some rest now and I'll talk to you soon."

"Thank you, Mrs. Warner, and goodnight."

"Goodnight, Livvy, dear and try not to worry," but Marion was worried because she had never known Brian to lie to her before and she intended to find out the truth.

It was almost midnight when Brian arrived home but he wasn't surprised to see his mother still sitting in the living room watching television while his stepfather was already asleep in bed. Marion was a night owl and had trouble sleeping and she often stayed up until the small hours of the morning, reading a novel or watching a late movie. He hung his coat in the hall closet and poked his head around the door, "Hi Mum, watcha watching?"

Marion turned off the television. "Oh, it's just some boring film. Come in and sit down, Brian, I want to talk to you."

Brian was instantly wary and had a feeling this was not going to be a pleasant conversation, "What's up, Mum?" he asked as he slumped down in his stepfather's favourite armchair.

"I'm not going to give you the chance to lie to me again by asking what movie you saw with Livvy tonight, son. She phoned here and you haven't talked to her for a week. What's going on?"

Brian lowered his head not wanting to look his mother in the eye, "I can't face her, Mum, I don't want to get married now and I don't even want to be engaged but I don't know how to tell her."

Marion was not a naive woman; she had been married twice and had many affairs so nothing really shocked her, "Why Brian, what happened last week to make you change your mind?"

"I'm sure Livvy saw me kissing some girl at a party but that isn't the reason. I've just been feeling tied down lately and I want to be free to do whatever I please, I'm only nineteen, Mum."

Marion got up and perched on the arm of the chair putting her arm around Brian's shoulders, "I understand, I really do but you just can't ignore Livvy. You have to go and see her and tell her how you feel."

"I know, Mum, but she's going to be so hurt and I feel rotten about it but I can't help it. What else can I do?"

"Nothing, son, you have to make the break. It will be hard at first but she'll get over it and one day she'll meet someone else. Now first thing in the morning, you promise me you'll phone her and go and see her?"

"Okay, I promise, but what am I going to say to her?"

"Tell her you want to see her to talk and that's all, you owe it to her to tell her to her face. Livvy is a lovely girl and she deserves to be treated properly." She ruffled Brian's hair affectionately, "Now I suggest you go to bed and get a good night's rest."

The next morning true to his word Brian called Livvy and arranged to meet her at a small coffee shop on the main street. He arrived early, sitting at a table near the window, where he'd be able to see her walking past, and he was nervous. Ten minutes later when she suddenly appeared, he knew he should jump up and meet her at the door but he couldn't seem to move and, as she looked around, he raised his hand so that she could see where he was seated. Livvy had dressed carefully for the occasion. She was wearing her dove gray pleated skirt and lilac cable knit sweater and had brushed her hair until it gleamed under the subdued lighting. Brian had always told her how lovely she looked in lilac and this was his favourite outfit. As she shrugged out of her navy gabardine coat and hung it on the coat rack near the door, she tried to stay calm and in control. "Hello, Brian," she said quietly, as she pulled out a chair on the opposite side of the table, noticing how nervous he was folding and refolding his serviette.

Brian tried to look Livvy directly in the eyes but he kept looking down into his coffee cup, which was now almost empty, "Hello, Livvy, would you like some coffee, I'm going to have another cup?"

"Yes, please," Livvy replied rather abruptly and watched while he got up and went over to the counter. It seemed like an eternity before he came back with two cups of coffee and two glazed doughnuts, "I bought you something to eat as well."

Livvy took the coffee but pushed the plate away, "I'm not hungry, Brian, so you'll have to eat them both yourself."

Brian tried to take Livvy's hand but she put both hands in her lap, "I know you're angry, Livvy, and I'm sorry about what happened at the party, I shouldn't have let you go home alone. It's just that we don't seem to be having too much fun lately and I think we need to take a break."

Livvy clenched her fists under the table, "What do you mean, take a break; are you telling me you don't want to go out with me? Are you sure you're not seeing Brenda now, you seemed pretty cozy when I saw you together or did you think I didn't know anything about that?"

"No, I figured you'd seen us in the kitchen but it was nothing, Livvy. I'm sorry; I guess I just don't want to be engaged anymore. I thought I wanted to get married but I'm too young to get tied down and so are you."

Tears began to form in Livvy's eyes and she clutched at the sleeve of her sweater. She'd gone over every scenario in her mind including the fact Brian may not want to see her ever again but she wasn't prepared to face it. It was obvious he was trying to end their relationship but she couldn't let him go. Her breathing started to accelerate and she felt a little dizzy, "Please Brian, you told me you loved me. If I can't see you for a while how do I know you won't meet someone else?"

"You don't know, Livvy, nobody knows what might happen in the future, and you may meet someone else too."

Livvy shook her head violently, "No, no I won't. I love you. I'll wait for you."

Brian knew from Livvy's reaction he had to be honest with her. She was a good person and he had loved her for her kindness and generosity of spirit but he was no longer in love with her. "Livvy, this isn't going to work. It's better if we make a clean break and then we can both get on with our lives. I can't let you go on thinking I'll come back to you because it might never happen."

Livvy sat stunned for a moment and then stood up, with eyes blazing, and Brian had never seen her so angry before, "You just want to be free to fool around with other girls. I thought you were different but you're just like all the other guys around here."

Brian was astounded and, jumping up, he reached across the table and grabbed her by the arm, " How can you say such a thing, you know that isn't true? We've been together for a long time and I've never looked at another girl except for that one time at the party."

Livvy shook off his hand and backed away, " Yes, and she wasn't even pretty, so what happens when you meet someone who is? I hate you and I don't want to see you anymore so don't call me and don't come to my house," she yelled as she grabbed for her coat and ran out the door.

Brian didn't know whether to go after her or not, he was so shocked at the way she had reacted. After a few seconds, he dropped back down onto the chair and put both hands over his face trying to block out his last image of Livvy. A tap on his shoulder by the waitress made him look up, "Are you okay?" she asked.

Brian looked around the coffee shop and suddenly became aware of a dozen faces looking his way and he was embarrassed, "Yes, thanks, I'm all right and I'm sorry about that little scene."

"Don't give it a second thought," the waitress said kindly, "it happens to all of us sometime or other."

While Brian remained behind drinking another cup of coffee, Livvy was stumbling along the main street choking back tears. She knew she had been impulsive again and now she had probably lost Brian forever. So many thoughts were going through her head and she just wanted to go home and shut herself in her room. When she arrived at the house she quietly let herself in and tried to creep up the stairs to the third floor but her mother intercepted her. Rachel had known all week something was going on because Livvy had been so quiet, and she had been at home every night. Once when she had asked why she wasn't with Brian, Livvy had muttered something she couldn't understand and fled from the room. Livvy stopped midway up the steps to the second floor when she heard Rachel calling. She was going to pretend she hadn't heard her but something in her mother's voice told her she was already aware something was wrong. Slowly she turned and started back down to the hallway where Rachel was standing waiting for her and, when she got to the bottom step, she just threw herself into her mother's arms and howled in despair. Rachel walked backwards into the front room dragging Livvy with her and sat her down on the sofa. Then, sitting beside her, she put her arm around her shoulders and hugged her tightly. "Okay, what's this all about, Livvy? You haven't been yourself all week and you haven't seen Brian so you must have had a fight." Livvy was crying so much, it was hard to make out what she was saying but Rachel finally got the gist of it. She hated to see her daughter so unhappy but she didn't really know how to comfort her except to just hold her close. Rachel had always been a good mother, looking after both of her children by providing them with the best food and clothing the family could possibly afford, but she had trouble expressing her feelings and providing emotional support. She could now only offer the usual cliches, "You're better off without him, Livvy. You'll see, after a while, you'll forget all about him."

"No, I'll never forget him, Mum, what am I going to do?"

"You'll meet somebody else; you're still very young and when you do, you'll wonder what you ever saw in him."

"No, you're wrong," Livvy protested, "I'll never meet anybody else."

"Now that's silly sweetheart, of course you will. There's plenty more fish in the sea."

Livvy could not be pacified, and she was so emotionally drained, that eventually Rachel led her up to her bedroom and covered her with the comforter so she could get some rest. When Harry came home and Rachel told him what had happened he was less than sympathetic, "Well I'm not sorry, I never liked that boy and he wasn't good enough for our Livvy, she'll get over it".

It took Livvy three full months to even begin to get over Brian.

Chapter Twenty

Just after Livvy's nineteenth birthday, since she had been isolated in the house for so long, Matt suggested she tag along with him and his friends when they went dancing one Saturday night. He had just finished his two years of service and was chumming around with four other young men from the neighbourhood. Terry, Colin, Gerry and Laurie were all rather conservative with short hair, wearing pleated slacks, button down shirts, and jackets while Matt was the odd one in the group with his Teddy boy look. His hair was thick, curling over the back of his collar, and on most days he wore an Edwardian style draped suit, with drainpipe trousers and a narrow black tie. He looked oddly out of place among his friends but he was popular because of his sense of humour. He had only recently begun to date, and had been seeing one girl in particular, but he had no thoughts of having a serious relationship and still enjoyed being with his friends on a Saturday night. Livvy was grateful her brother was concerned about her but she couldn't face going alone with them and she had abandoned all her friends during the last year while she was with Brian.

"Why don't you call Luisa," Matt urged, "you haven't seen her for ages. She's a great girl and I'm sure she'd like to come too."

Livvy shook her head, "How can I just phone her up now after so long? She's probably annoyed I haven't kept in touch with her and I can't really blame her."

"Well, it's too bad you gave up all your friends for that good-for-nothing but what have you got to lose? Come on, Livvy, you can't sit around the house for ever, you have to get out and start enjoying yourself again."

"Okay, I'll do it but I hope she doesn't start yelling at me, I feel bad enough as it is."

Contrary to what Livvy expected, Luisa was pleasantly surprised to hear from her after so long. She had no idea Livvy's relationship with Brian was over and like a good friend, listened sympathetically while Livvy told her what had happened and then excitedly accepted the invitation to go dancing with Matt and his friends. They all went dancing frequently after that and it soon became obvious, Jerry and Luisa were becoming more than friends, while Livvy kept her distance emotionally, even though she was very attracted to Laurie who, though rather short in stature, was good looking and had an amazing singing voice. One Saturday night while dancing a slow waltz with Colin, she came face to face with one of the two people she was desperate to avoid. Brenda Buckley was dancing with the same lanky young man she had seen her with at the party and she was grinning and waving at her, as though nothing had ever happened. Colin was surprised when Livvy suddenly took the lead and whirled him off of the dance floor, "What's going on Livvy, did I step on your toe or something?"

In spite of the fact she had been momentarily stunned by Brenda's appearance she couldn't help but smile, "Sorry, Colin, I just saw someone I don't particularly like and I don't really want to speak to them."

Colin was just about to ask Livvy if she was talking about Brian when he noticed the stricken look on her face and turned around to see Brenda coming towards them. She slipped her arm through Colin's grinning up at him, "Hello, Colin, I didn't know you liked to dance," and, without missing a beat, she looked over his shoulder at Livvy, "and, Livvy,

I didn't know you came here either. Where's Brian, isn't he here too?"

Before Livvy could reply Colin intervened, "Livvy's here with Matt and me and a couple of other friends."

Brenda looked puzzled and faced Livvy directly, "But where's Brian?"

Livvy couldn't believe Brenda didn't know about the breakup, "I thought if anyone knew where he was, you would know," she said haughtily.

Brenda was genuinely confused, "Why on earth would I know where your boyfriend is? I haven't seen him since the party, last November."

"Yes, the party where you were kissing him in the kitchen, I saw you both. How could you do such a thing, you knew we were engaged?"

Brenda looked down at Livvy's left hand and noticed she was no longer wearing her engagement ring, "Wait a minute, are you telling me you two broke up because of what happened at the party? We had a couple of drinks and it was all harmless. I swear to you, Livvy, I haven't seen Brian once since that night."

Livvy's shoulders slumped and Colin put his arm around her, "Brenda, why don't you leave Livvy alone right now? We came here to have a good time and help her get over Brian. You aren't helping matters so it would be better if you just took off."

Brenda took a step towards Livvy and put her hand on her arm, "I'm sorry, Livvy, I really am and I hope we can be friends. I'll probably see you around. Bye, Colin," and she turned and walked slowly away melting into the crowd.

"Are you okay, Livvy?" Colin asked tipping her chin up to make sure she wasn't crying.

"Yes, I'm fine," she replied. "I guess it just hurts even more, in a way, to know he didn't leave me for someone else but just because I wasn't good enough for him."

"He wasn't good enough for you, Livvy, and you're well rid of him. I know Matt didn't really like him, although he never told you that, and he thinks you're better off without him. You're an attractive girl and I've seen a lot of the guys looking at you. If you weren't Matt's sister I'd probably ask you out myself."

Livvy couldn't help laughing, "You're just saying that to make me feel good. I know you like that skinny little blonde, Margie, who lives on Whiteman Road."

Colin blushed and hung his head, "Okay you got me, but I still say you can have your pick of guys. Now let's shake this place up and do some serious dancing before the place closes down."

Livvy's spirits were always lifted after a night out with Matt and his friends and she felt strangely unaffected by her encounter with Brenda. She knew now that she had made a big mistake in blaming her for the breakup and she wondered what she would say to her if she saw her again.

The following weekend, Livvy decided she needed a change and made an appointment at the beauty salon. She had been wearing her shoulder length hair framing her face for the last few years and, although it was a pretty golden blond, she was tired of the colour. When she emerged later that Saturday afternoon, she looked like a different person. The popular poodle cut of the day suited her delicate features and the platinum blonde, a la Marilyn Monroe, was a dramatic change. She felt like she was walking on air and when she arrived home and both Harry and Rachel told her she looked beautiful, she felt like she was ready for anything. That night, she put on the sleeveless white sweater with mandarin collar and tiny pearl buttons all the way down the front; she had knitted herself, and her short navy skating skirt. She was meeting Luisa to go skating at the local rink and, after slipping on her gabardine coat; she slung her new white ice skates over her shoulder and headed off down the road. Luisa was shocked to see the change in Livvy, when she met up with her at the rink, but she thought she looked wonderful and, with her confidence boosted, Livvy set out to have a fun time. Several young men escorted her around the ice during the evening but she preferred to speed around on her own, feeling the wind rushing past her ears. About an hour before the rink closed, she was getting a glass of water and a bar of candy from the concession counter when she sensed someone standing behind her. Her body tensed as she heard Brian's voice say, "Hello, Livvy," and she slowly turned around. He looked the same and he sounded the same but she wasn't the same anymore.

The tension left her as she smiled and leaned casually against the counter, "Well, hello, Brian, how are you?"

"I'm doing okay; I didn't know you'd be here. You look great, I love your hair it really suits you," and he meant it sincerely. He had been watching her for almost half-an-hour skating around the rink and he was astonished at how attractive she looked.

Livvy had received so many compliments all day that Brian's no longer seemed important and she ignored it, "I come here a lot, it's fun and I meet a lot of nice people."

Brian caught the innuendo and frowned, "Have you met anyone else yet, Livvy?"

"No, and I'm not looking for your information," she replied haughtily, "how about you?"

Brian looked embarrassed, "No, I haven't met anybody, at least nobody like you."

Now Livvy was angry and she started to walk away, "Well I guess you're in luck then because I wasn't good enough."

Brian stared after her wondering if he had done the right thing in letting her go but he knew it was too late, he could see she had changed not only in looks but in her whole demeanour.

Chapter Twenty-One

A week after seeing Brian, Livvy ran into Brenda as she was coming home from work. Brenda was coming towards her and there was no way she could avoid her. She considered walking right past or crossing the road but, in her heart, she knew Brenda had nothing to do with her broken engagement. Brenda was the first to speak, "Hello, Livvy, I wasn't sure if it was you, you look so different. I really like your hair, the colour looks great on you."

Livvy didn't have a clue what to reply so she fell back to being her usual polite self, "Thank you, Brenda. How have you been?"

"Oh, I'm good thanks. Look I'm sorry if I upset you that night at the dance. I hope you believe me about Brian and I wish we could be friends. Why don't we go out one night, we could go to the West End and see a movie and hang out at the Wimpy Bar?"

Livvy was surprised at Brenda's offer of friendship but it was like a lifeline. Lately Luisa had become more and more involved with Gerry and she was seeing a lot less of her. Before she had time to really think about it, she found herself smiling back at Brenda, "That's sounds like a great idea, I'll give you my telephone number and you can ring me up sometime."

Brenda seemed genuinely pleased, "Okay, scribble it down for me and I'll ring you later on this week. Maybe we can go out on Saturday."

Livvy hunted for some paper in her handbag and finally retrieved a book of matches and wrote her number down, "Okay, that would be lovely; don't lose my number."

Brenda took the matchbook and slipped it into the pocket of her jacket "Don't worry I won't, I'll ring you and we'll go out for sure. I'd better get going now; I'm meeting my dad to help him pick out a present for my mum's birthday."

"Oh, okay, I hope you find something nice for her, bye for now, Brenda."

"Bye, bye, Livvy."

Livvy watched Brenda skip off down the road and felt elated. It made her feel that the tide was turning and someone she thought was her enemy might actually turn out to be a friend.

The following Saturday night at six o'clock Livvy met Brenda outside her house, near the main street, and they took the number twenty-nine bus and Piccadilly tube into town. Brenda had called as promised and, after making arrangements to meet, they had spent nearly forty minutes on the telephone just chatting casually as though they had been friends for years. They decided they would go to a movie and then go to the popular Wimpy Bar and, just in case they happened to meet any young men, they agreed to dress up a little. Brenda looked more feminine than usual in a deep aqua-coloured jacket with a gray pleated skirt and Livvy wore her favourite classic ivory suit which showed off her slim figure and made her feel very sophisticated. Both girls had wanted to see Picnic with William Holden and Kim Novak and neither of them was disappointed. It was a dreamy, romantic, movie and every now and again thoughts of Brian would drift into Livvy's head but she no longer deluded herself about a future with him and was ready to move on.

It was almost ten o'clock by the time they got to the Wimpy Bar, ordered coffee, and were sitting at a table near the window watching the crowds and they couldn't help noticing the number of good-looking American servicemen passing by. Within ten minutes, three young men came into the restaurant and sat at a nearby table. All three were wearing American Air force uniforms and were tall, slim, and extremely attractive. Brenda stopped talking in mid-sentence and nudged Livvy who was busy looking in the other direction and, as Livvy turned to see what was going on, one of the airmen looked over and smiled at her. Brenda kicked her under the table encouraging her to respond but Livvy ignored her and concentrated on drinking her coffee. "What's wrong with you?" Brenda whispered, "Say hello to him, he's cute and so are the other two."

"I know, but he took me by surprise." Livvy whispered back and she glanced over at the other table, only to catch the young man smiling at her again. Brenda kicked her under the table again, only harder, and Livvy reacted. "Ouch, stop kicking me, that hurt."

Just then the young man got up and sauntered over, "Hi there ladies, how would you like to join me and my buddies for a coffee?"

The three airmen were stationed in Oxfordshire, which gave Livvy something to talk about because she had had many conversations with Marty about the base, when she was going out with Brian. Chuck and Irwin had known each other before being sent overseas and had lived in the same neighbourhood in Philadelphia. They were boisterous and a lot of fun but Jimmy was really quiet and shy and, at eleven o'clock, he left the quartet to go off on his own.

Brenda and Livvy went out with Chuck and Irwin often but they dated other American servicemen too. They enjoyed being taken out to dinner and the movies and sometimes went on trips to Oxford or Brighton and it wasn't long before they got a bit of a reputation as being party girls. One American sailor particularly impressed Livvy. He was six foot four and muscular with fair hair and a boyish face and he looked spectacular in his uniform. Livvy loved to show him off and repeated his name, which was Romeo Eugene LaPlante, to everyone they met. One day she even took him to the tailor shop where her mother worked and Rachel graciously gave him a hug, even though the top of her head barely reached his chin. The other American, Livvy always remembered with great fondness was Frank, who asked her to marry him on the fourth date. He had movie star looks, tall and dark with a rugged face and deep brown eyes. In fact, when he came to pick Livvy up one day from her house and Rachel answered the door, she came running down the stairs in a fluster. Frank was very gentle and kind but he had an annoying habit of picking at his food like a little bird and Livvy could hardly bear to watch him when he ate. When she found out he came from a small town called Franklin in New York State, not New York City as he suggested, she lost interest. Even though Livvy was intimate with a few of the young men she dated, she cut herself off emotionally and decided just to have fun. It was the kind of fun, staying out at night and going on trips that caused a rift between her and her father and he started to be verbally abusive, calling her hurtful names on many occasions. This was when she decided it was time to get out of Cavendish Road.

Chapter Twenty-Two

Brenda and Livvy had often talked about leaving England and going to America to live but soon discovered that the only way to get anywhere near achieving their goal would be to immigrate to Canada first. The British government was subsidizing immigrants to both Canada and Australia, based on a partial payback scheme. Both girls naturally chose Canada as their destination as they believed the Canadian people closely resembled Americans. They poured over maps and watched documentaries and eventually came up with a grand scheme. They were going to go to Toronto to work, save some money, and then travel all through the States, finally ending up in Caracas, Venezuela, which on film looked awesome. When Livvy approached her parents about immigrating, Rachel was very upset but Harry encouraged her to follow her dream. Despite the abuse directed at her in the last year, Livvy knew her father really loved her and she genuinely believed he wanted her to be happy.

In order to qualify for their immigration papers, it was necessary to have a Canadian sponsor who would vouch for the girls once they arrived and support them if it became necessary. Fortunately, Brenda's father had a cousin who lived in Toronto and he was more than happy to sponsor them and to find them a place to live. Waiting for their immigration papers to come through seemed to take an eternity but, when they were finally approved, there was so much to do that the time just flew by. They needed passports, shots, and travel reservations, and they also had to notify their employers they were leaving. Livvy had very mixed emotions about saying goodbye to the people she had worked with at the St. James Club. She had never made any really close friends there but she had an easy camaraderie with everyone and she was particularly fond of her boss, Philip Stone, who was an imposing man in his fifties and who she had just learned was dying of bone cancer. She knew, even if she came back for a visit, she would never see him again.

Matt was particularly interested in everything Livvy could tell him about Canada and she had a strong suspicion he might join her there, but not alone. About a year before, he had met a waitress in an underground espresso bar in Leicester Square and he was crazy about her. Gina was a vivacious Italian, slim with short dark hair and dark eyes. She spoke with a fairly heavy accent and always wore bright scarlet nail polish that drew attention to her hands, which always seemed to be in motion. The most notable thing about Gina was that she was fifteen years older than Matt and much more sophisticated. Livvy liked her immensely and was fascinated that she had fallen in love with her brother.

On December 6th, 1956, the Marshalls' and the Buckleys' gathered on the platform at Euston Station to say goodbye to Livvy and Brenda. There were many immigrants travelling from London to Liverpool that day and the air was full of excitement, but also sadness. Harry and the Buckleys' were in a happy mood, encouraging the two girls to make the most of their new life in Canada while Rachel held her handkerchief to her face and sobbed continuously. Livvy tried desperately not to add to her mother's despair and hugged her over and over again trying to reassure her they would be all right and they would write as soon as they got settled. She was glad she had already said goodbye to Matt the night before because, she was certain now, he might follow her and she could only imagine the scene on this same platform if he followed through with his plans. When the train whistle blew signaling everybody to board, something echoed in Livvy's mind and she vaguely remembered a similar time when, as a small child, she was taken away from her parents. This time she had made the choice to leave and although she knew it was a huge step, it was an adventure she was anxious to take.

On arrival at the Liverpool docks, the girls were in awe when they saw the ship that would carry them across the Atlantic. The Empress of France was part of the Canadian Pacific fleet. Weighing 20,000 tons, she was built in the 1920's and was originally named the Duchess of Bedford. During the war she was used as a troop ship, then retrofitted for commercial use, and in 1948 her name was changed. Neither Livvy nor Brenda had ever seen an ocean liner before and it looked enormous. All around them, their fellow passengers were chattering excitedly, anxious to get on board to explore the ship and begin their journey to a new life. It seemed to take forever to check all the documents needed before they were allowed to finally climb the gangplank and be escorted to their cabin, which appeared to be in the bowels of the ship. Once inside, they looked around in dismay. The cabin was so small they immediately felt claustrophobic, in spite of the tiny porthole window which appeared to be almost on a level with the water, but was actually several feet above it. The furniture was sparse with two sets of bunks, a small three-drawer dresser, a narrow closet, one chair, and a washbasin with a mirror. Livvy immediately hauled herself up to the top level of one set of bunks, "I'm sleeping up here," she announced.

Brenda sank dejectedly onto the lower bunk "That's okay, I'd rather sleep down here; I'm not too fond of heights."

Livvy laughed, trying to overcome her disappointment with their accommodation and lighten the mood, "This isn't high, wait till you go on the top deck and look over the side."

Brenda was just about to respond when the cabin door opened and a woman entered dragging a small suitcase behind her. She was very tall and thin with gray hair, caught into a bun at the back of her head, and she wore a pair of silver framed glasses that made her look like a schoolteacher.

When she saw the girls she nodded and, in a very thick accent, introduced herself, "Hello, my name is Helga Bauer and I am very pleased to meet you."

Livvy jumped down from the bunk and held out her hand, "How do you do, I'm Livvy Marshall and this is my friend Brenda Buckley. Will you be staying in our cabin with us?"

"Well, they gave me this cabin number so here I am. I see there are four beds so maybe we will have another passenger as well."

Livvy smiled, "I think three of us are quite enough, you couldn't even swing a cat in here. Anyway, just in case someone else does come, Helga, you had better choose whether you want to sleep on the upper or lower bunk."

Helga set her suitcase down next to the others in one corner of the cabin, "I am too old to be climbing so I'll stay on the bottom."

Brenda had been surveying Helga, wondering just how old she was and why she was going to Canada but, before she had a chance to satisfy her curiosity, Helga sat down on the lone chair and looked up at the two girls, "I am fifty years old and I came from Germany. I have been living in England for one year working as a housekeeper for a doctor and his family. They are moving to Montreal and I am going with them but they are up in first class while I am stuck down here with the immigrants."

Brenda took offense at this remark, "Excuse me, but do you have something against immigrants because as far as I can see you're one yourself?"

Helga shook her head, "I am so sorry, I didn't mean to offend. Sometimes my language is not so good."

Livvy intervened, "It's okay Helga, you'll be fine here with us and I'm sure we'll all get along like a house on fire," and she shot Brenda a warning look.

Helga got up and laid her hand on Livvy's arm, "Thank you, my dear, you are very kind."

Later, they learned that Helga had been a victim of the war and her sister had died in a concentration camp. She kept to herself throughout most of the journey and either stayed in the cabin or sat on deck wrapped in a blanket reading and she never attended any of the after dinner entertainment.

When the ship eventually left Liverpool, the girls were up on deck with hundreds of others watching the English coastline slipping away. It was a bright sunny day, but bitterly cold, and they couldn't bring themselves to go below and continued to hang over the railing, with their arms around each other and tears streaming down their faces. In the dining room, that first evening, they soon forgot how sad they had felt when they were suddenly confronted with more food than they had ever imagined. They were seated at long tables and served by dozens of waiters, who flitted back and forth chattering with the passengers in accents, which were hardly understandable. Nearly all of the young lads serving on the ship were from Liverpool and they had a dialect all their own; one that would become familiar to most of the world with the popularity of the Beatles. The meal, consisting of four courses, was a feast and it was to be that way every night. The first course was melon or salad, then cream of asparagus or tomato soup, then an entree of lake trout or roast beef and finally chocolate layer cake or apple charlotte. Tea and coffee cups were constantly being refilled and there was even wine to celebrate the beginning of the journey. Livvy could hardly imagine what the passengers in first class were being served. She soon realized there were a lot of passengers at their table who didn't speak English. Most of them were very young and seemed overly excited about the trip and, she eventually learned, they were Hungarian refugees. After the Hungarian revolution was crushed in November, the Canadian government had eliminated all the red tape and given priority treatment to the refugees. The government also elected to pay for all travel costs without requiring any repayment at a later date. It was estimated that approximately 37,000 Hungarians eventually settled in Canada following the revolution. Every evening in the main salon, the Hungarians would gather together, play the accordion and sing and dance. This would go on until the early morning hours and many of the other younger passengers, who only spoke English and didn't understand a word of the songs, would try to join in.

For the first two nights, Livvy and Brenda stayed behind in the salon to enjoy the fun but on the third day when they started to encounter heavy swells, Brenda got seasick. For two days, she attempted to fight the never-ending nausea but fainted twice in the dining room and had to be carried out. On one occasion, after having her hair set in the ship's beauty salon she slumped down from beneath the drier and rolled head over heels onto the floor. Livvy, who had been sitting right beside her, went into a fit of laughter at the sight of Brenda out cold in her pink rollers but finally collected herself and got her back to the cabin and into her bunk. Brenda stayed in bed the next day while Livvy went off with a group of young cockney lads she had met on the second night. They were from the East End of London, full of mischief, and flirted with Livvy outrageously, but she just ignored it all as good clean fun. She had already made a connection with their waiter and was enjoying a shipboard romance, indulging in clandestine meetings late at night on deck, behind one of the huge funnels. Eddie was from Liverpool, just like most of the other waiters and Livvy suspected he had a romance every time they crossed the Atlantic but she was having fun basking in the attention. She had grown her blonde hair long again and loved to wear calf length slinky wool dresses that clung to her slim figure. Every time Eddie saw her he would tell her how attractive she was and, even when he was serving her in the dining room, he would cheekily whisper flattering remarks in her ear and make her blush. On the last night on board there was a dance held in the main salon but, as they approached Cape Race, Newfoundland, the storm that had been threatening for hours suddenly set the ship rocking violently. Everyone on the dance floor was warned they should sit down but Livvy and Brenda totally ignored the warning and, five minutes later, Brenda toppled over onto her face while her dance partner fell on top of her and his knee connected with the back of her neck. Livvy, who was right beside them, actually heard the crunching noise as Brenda's nose broke from the impact and she threw herself down next to her and screamed for someone to get the ship's doctor. It was fortunate for Brenda that there was a doctor so close at hand and he immediately put splints up her nose and stuffed it with cotton batten but she was terrified, because she couldn't breathe and thought she was going to die. Livvy sat with her in the cabin for hours encouraging her to breathe through her mouth and assuring her she would be all right and, when Brenda finally fell asleep, she took a walk on deck just to get some air while Helga kept watch.

Five days after they had left Liverpool, they landed at St. John, New Brunswick. Long before they got to port, all of the passengers were out on deck straining to see the coastline of Canada and they weren't disappointed. It was just as they had imagined it, all fir trees and snow and it looked beautiful. Brenda was not happy about arriving with splints up her nose and got a little indignant when a couple of the immigration officers, checking her papers as she disembarked, decided to call her Punch. Livvy didn't notice Brenda's discomfort; she was too busy trying to see if Eddie was watching from one of the decks but she finally gave up, disappointed that he hadn't come to say goodbye. Within hours they were shuttled onto a train by the young volunteer redcaps, who came to help out when they had nothing else to do, and they were finally on their way to Toronto.

Chapter Twenty-Three

After a twenty-two hour train ride, Livvy and Brenda arrived in Toronto. Livvy had stayed awake throughout the whole trip staring out of the window and only stopping to make a trip to the concession car or to go to the ladies room. The journey was tedious with nothing but acres of countryside and the occasional dwelling but Livvy didn't want to miss a thing and she had never been able to sleep while traveling except, of course, on the ship. She was intrigued to see the size of the cars parked alongside the houses they passed; they seemed enormous compared to the cars driven back in England. As the train pulled into Union Station, it was already dark but the snow was falling in huge fluffy flakes and, to all of the newcomers, it looked like a fairyland. Brenda's relatives, her second cousins Bill and Amy Sellers, were waiting for them on the platform and holding up a huge placard that read Welcome to Canada, Brenda and Livvy. Brenda spotted them immediately and ran towards them dragging her suitcase awkwardly behind her while Livvy tried to keep up.

The cousins were a warm and friendly couple and embraced both girls. As it was already getting late, they invited them to stay with them for the night and then they would get them settled in their own flat in the morning, so they all bundled into the Seller's dark green Chevrolet and drove west to Ossington Avenue. The Sellers' lived in a semi-detached house with a porch, which resembled most of the rest of the houses on the street, but it was too dark for the girls to really get a good look at their surroundings and, they were so exhausted from the train ride, they just wanted to get some sleep. It was almost two hours later before they finally got to bed, in the spare room at the back of the house. Amy had insisted on feeding them a light snack of grilled cheese sandwiches and hot chocolate and Bill wanted to know every detail of their trip, especially how Brenda had broken her nose. She had already removed the splints, as the ship's doctor had instructed her, but was still wearing a heavy plaster dressing, which was to stay in place for another two days.

The next morning, Bill drove them a few blocks to their new home on Queen Street. After climbing three flights of stairs they encountered five doors and soon discovered that only two of the doors opened up to their rooms. These were located kitty corner from each other across a poorly lit landing, covered in dark green linoleum. Bill opened the door to the first room, which appeared to be a large kitchen with an unfinished wooden table surrounded by five matching chairs and a window looking out onto a treeless snow covered back yard. "I know it isn't much," he said, gesturing with his hand, "but you don't have jobs yet so I had to get something you could afford. There's a stove and an icebox and I think the iceman comes every Friday. You'll have to make arrangements to get the ice replaced every week or else any food will go bad. You'll probably spend most of your time here because the other room is just a bedroom and the bed is pretty big and takes up a lot of space. Follow me and I'll show you."

Bill wasn't exaggerating about the bed, it had a brass headboard and a lime green chenille cover and it dominated the room. The only other furniture was a long low maple dresser with six drawers and a three-way mirror, and a straight back chair in one corner. The floor here, and in the kitchen, was covered in the same dark green linoleum as the landing but the bedroom also had a small-fringed lime green rug. "That's it girls, so I'll leave you to get settled. Oh, by the way, there's another couple that live in the two other rooms and there's a communal bathroom, I'm sure you won't mind sharing."

Before Bill left to return home, Brenda and Livvy stoically thanked him for going to so much trouble to find them a place and promised to see him at Christmas. At the front door, he gave them the keys then jumped into his car and waved out of the window calling, "Good luck, take care," as he drove off.

Slowly the girls climbed silently back to the third floor, sank down onto the bed with their arms around each other and cried like babies. "It's horrible!" sobbed Brenda, "I hate it. My parent's house wasn't much but this is disgusting. We should never have come here."

Livvy wiped away her tears and blew her nose, "I know, it's horrible but we have to make the best of it. We'll get some flowers and things and make it look better and after we both get jobs and save some money we can move somewhere else."

Brenda kept right on crying, "That could take forever. I don't know if I can take this place for long."

Livvy tried to console her friend, "Look, why don't we unpack our things. You take three drawers and I'll take three and there's a closet for our other stuff. After that we can go for a walk or go for a ride on the streetcar. Bill said there's one that goes right along Queen Street to the middle of town."

An hour later, the two girls were outside shivering on the street. The snow had stopped falling but it was bitterly cold and they realized they needed to get boots and heavier coats in order to survive the winter. Looking around them, they noticed a car dealership directly across from them decorated with dozens of colourful flags flapping in the wind and next door was a bar, The Drake Hotel, which was closed. The whole neighbourhood had a seedy quality to it and it made them even more determined to move as quickly as possible. After waiting for ten minutes, they finally saw a bright red streetcar approaching and, when it stopped, they clambered aboard thankful to get out of the frigid cold. The driver was very patient as they counted out the exact change from the nickels and dimes they had in their purses. The currency was a complete mystery to them and they had no idea of the value of any of the paper money or the coins. Both Livvy and Brenda were staring hopefully out of the window, expecting the gray looking street to change, and were surprised when the driver announced they should get off at Yonge Street. They stepped down from the streetcar and looked around but everything looked the same as before so they nervously approached a young woman, walking with her dog, and asked where the center of town was. Surprise turned to shock when she informed them they were standing right at the center but everything was closed on Sunday. Two large department stores took up two corners of the intersection and their windows were filled with Christmas scenes, some based on religion and some on fairy tales, but very few people were window shopping and the area seemed deserted. Livvy was so cold she suggested they try and find somewhere to get a hot drink and, after a short walk, they finally saw a small restaurant with an open sign on the door. It was here, over mugs of steaming cocoa, they decided they would try and get a job at one of the department stores the next day. Christmas was just over two weeks away and they knew nobody would be interested in hiring them for office work until the New Year but a temporary position in a store would tide them over.

They were in luck; the next morning both girls were hired in the packaging department of Simpson's where they wrapped all the mailorder purchases in sturdy brown paper and applied all the labels. It was a tedious job but all of the other temporary workers were friendly and they were allowed to chatter away to their hearts content. The supervisor of the department was twenty year old, Douglas Ingram. He had progressed from clerk to supervisor in a very short time, due to his maturity and ability to handle people, and Brenda set her sights on him immediately. At the end of the very first day she cornered him on her way out of the mailroom. She explained that they had just arrived from England and didn't know their way around town and maybe he could tell her where to go to have fun. Douglas Ingram was not only smart, he was very aware when anyone had an ulterior motive and he decided to take advantage of the situation. "Sure, I know where to have some fun. Why don't you let me show you around?"

Brenda smiled provocatively, "Well that would be lovely but I have this friend, Livvy. Look she's over there getting her coat, and I'd like her to come along too if that's okay with you." Douglas glanced over to where Livvy was pulling on her wool cap, "That's no problem; in fact I have a friend who would probably like to join us. I'll speak to him and see if he wants to come along and then I'll phone you."

"Oh dear, we don't have a phone. I think there may be one on the second floor landing where we live but I don't know the number."

"Not to worry," Douglas reassured her. "I'll talk to my friend tonight and I'll see you here tomorrow. By the way what's your name?"

"Brenda, Brenda Buckley and my friend is Livvy Marshall."

"Well, I'm Douglas Ingram, so I guess I'll say goodnight. See you in the morning, Brenda."

Brenda was beaming, "Goodnight, Douglas," and she turned and ran over to Livvy.

"What were you talking to the supervisor about?" Livvy asked.

"You'll never guess. I told him we didn't know our way around town and he suggested he show us. Not only that, he's got a friend and he's going to see if he wants to come too."

Livvy was horrified, "Brenda, we've only been here five minutes and you're already picking up men. What's the matter with you?"

Brenda grinned, "Don't be such a prude, Livvy. The only way we're going to have any fun in this godforsaken place is to get ourselves a couple of fellows. Douglas seems like a really nice chap and he's not bad looking either. Maybe his friend is even better looking and then you'll be happy."

Livvy was not happy at all with Brenda's brazen approach but decided she would go on the double date just to keep the peace.

It was six o'clock before they got back to their rooms that night and, when they reached the third floor landing, they almost ran into an elderly woman who was exiting the bathroom. "Excuse me," said Livvy politely, "we weren't looking where we were going." Brenda glanced at Livvy incredulously thinking it was the old lady's fault, not theirs.

"That's all right dear, it get's a bit crowded on this landing sometimes. You must be the two girls from England and now we'll be neighbours. I'm Dolly and my husband is Fred. He's in bed right now; we were just having a little siesta, if you know what I mean?" and she giggled lasciviously.

Livvy got the implication immediately. She was shocked that this woman, who she guessed to be in her late seventies, was not only still having relations with her husband but boasting about it too. Somehow she managed to introduce herself and Brenda and then hurried into the kitchen, with Brenda following right behind her. They each collapsed onto a chair and buried their heads in their arms laughing hysterically. "Can you believe it?" Brenda roared, "she's still making out at her age and look at her, she's not only fat she's ugly too."

Livvy looked up and shook her head, "I know, I'm shocked too but you don't have to be unkind. She can't help the way she looks."

"Well she could at least wear some clean clothes. Did you see the robe she was wearing? It was covered in stains and her hair looked like it needed a good wash."

"Okay, you made your point, let's just drop it. These are our neighbours now and we have to get along with them; they are probably nice people."

"I suppose you're right," Brenda said grudgingly, "but I don't have to like it."

Following their first day at work the girls were tired and there was nothing to do except read or listen to the radio so, at nine o'clock, they climbed into bed, huddling under the blankets and promptly fell asleep. It seemed like only moments, but was actually over an hour, when they were awakened by a commotion outside. Both girls crawled out of bed and, despite the cold, opened the window and looked out. The window overlooked Queen Street and they were already aware they would have to put up with the noise of streetcars rattling by but, they didn't anticipate the havoc created by drunks from The Drake Hotel on the sidewalk below. For ten minutes they watched the scene as a fight broke out and police arrived, hauling two men and one woman away, then Brenda pulled Livvy away from the window and slammed it shut, "Well, that's just one more reason why we're getting out of here just as fast as we can."

In the mailroom at Simpson's the next day, Douglas approached Brenda just as she was returning from her lunch break, "Hi Brenda. I've been trying to get down here to speak to you all morning but I've been tied up in a meeting. With Christmas just around the corner, things are pretty busy around here."

"That's okay, Douglas, I figured I'd see you sooner or later," Brenda replied confidently.

"Good, because I spoke to my friend, Russ, and he'd love to go on a double date so how about if we get together on Friday night? We can go to a movie and then go for a drink somewhere and listen to some music."

For Brenda the next few days seem to crawl by, while Livvy was quite content to forget about Friday altogether. This would be her first date with a Canadian and she wasn't sure what to expect. She already knew from her encounters in the few days since she arrived, Canadian men were not in the least like American men and she was disappointed. On Friday afternoon, Brenda was getting excited and kept teasing Livvy by imagining what Russ would look like. "He's probably six feet tall and gorgeous," she kept repeating over and over again until Livvy finally forgot her manners and told her to shut up.

Douglas came to get the girls at just after five o'clock and took them across the road to a coffee shop for a bite to eat and to wait for Russ. Livvy and Brenda both ordered hamburgers and French fries and as they ate Brenda talked a lot about their life in England and why they had come to Canada. They were just finishing their coffee when Douglas stood up and waved to the young man who had just come through the door, "Here's Russ now," he said. Livvy looked up expectantly and immediately felt let down, Russ was no Rock Hudson but he did resemble the movie star Russ Tamblyn, who she had seen in Seven Brides for Seven Brothers. She glanced over at Brenda to see her reaction and, after Brenda finally tore her eyes away from the two young men who were now standing a few feet away talking, she turned to Livvy and shrugged.

As Russ approached the table, Livvy noticed he had a severe case of acne and this did nothing to add to any attraction she may have felt but she was courteous as always and smiled, extending her hand at the same time, "Hello Russ, pleased to meet you, I'm Livvy."

Russ took her hand and held it for a moment without shaking it, "Hi, I've been looking forward to this evening," In actual fact he had been dreading the evening, even though Douglas had told him Livvy was a very attractive girl. Now, after meeting her, he felt enormous relief because, not only did he think she was attractive but he was already impressed with her manners.

One of the most popular movies playing that night was Love Me Tender with Elvis Presley and the theatre was packed. Throughout most of the movie, Livvy was totally enthralled with the audience reaction. Girls were catcalling every time Elvis appeared and running down the aisles towards the screen as though they were worshipping some god. She had never seen anything like it in England and wondered if Canadians reacted to all movies like this. After the movie, Douglas suggested they walk up Yonge Street and drop in to Le Coq D'Or, "I think you'll enjoy the music, Ronnie Hawkins is playing and he's really popular."

"Sounds like a good idea to me," Brenda responded enthusiastically as she grabbed onto Douglas's arm and raced off ahead of Russ and Livvy.

Russ took Livvy's hand, "Looks like your friend's in a big hurry, hang on to me and we'll catch up."

Livvy laughed, "Take no notice of Brenda she's just in the mood to have some fun, that's all."

"Well, I hope you are too," Russ countered. Livvy felt herself blushing and hoped he wouldn't notice in the dark.

It was almost impossible to talk inside the club, with the live band playing, and Livvy spent most of the time sipping on rye whiskey and ginger ale. Douglas had recommended it but, back home at the local pub, she only ever drank gin and tonic and wished she had one now. Douglas and Brenda were soon snuggling up together and making Livvy feel rather uncomfortable. She was hoping Russ wouldn't try to put his arm around her; she really wasn't attracted to him even though he seemed to be considerate and had a quiet way about him that she found appealing. She was relieved when, at eleven o'clock, Brenda decided it was time to leave but her relief turned to concern when she realized that Brenda was going off with Douglas and she would be left alone with Russ. Russ seemed to sense that Livvy wasn't happy and asked if he could escort her home. She declined his offer graciously but didn't have the heart to refuse his invitation to meet him on Monday night and have dinner with him. Behaving like a gentleman, he walked her to the streetcar stop and made sure she was safely on her way before he made his own way home with the strong feeling that his life was about to change.

Russ was working in the downtown area at a small print shop and arranged to meet Livvy at the corner of Queen and Yonge Streets just outside Simpson's. That same day at noon, Livvy had rushed up to the women's department to find a new winter coat and then rushed back down to the shoe department for boots. At a little after five o'clock, she was standing on the corner in her new outfit and feeling rather sophisticated except for her woolly hat. She had managed to get a black coat with a white fur collar and cuffs and a pair of high-heeled, black suede boots, which she knew were impractical but couldn't resist. She was hoping she wouldn't have to wear her red woolly hat but the snow was falling heavily and she didn't want to get her hair wet. As she stood there waiting for Russ, she was wondering why she had gone to so much trouble about her appearance when she had no real interest in having any relationship with him and had already decided, this was probably the last time she would see him.

Russ was a few minutes late and apologized twice then commented on her new coat, telling her she looked like a Russian princess and making her feel very special. They walked for a few blocks, through the snowy streets; finally arriving at a Hungarian restaurant which, Russ assured her, had wonderful food and a fireplace giving it a cozy atmosphere. Livvy looked around and noticed the waitresses were all dressed in Hungarian costume and only three tables were occupied. She assumed, because it was early and also a Monday night, this was probably normal and when the hostess showed them to a table by the fire she was grateful the place was as empty as it was. The menu was so extensive, Livvy had trouble making a choice but, with Russ's help, she finally settled on an appetizer of roasted goose liver and then cabbage rolls with sour cream. They were so busy enjoying the food, there was little conversation and then Russ insisted she have the dessert of grape and apple strudel with hazelnuts and she gave in, despite the fact she felt completely stuffed. It was only after the last dish was cleared away and they were completely relaxed, each with a glass of wine that Livvy realized she was really having a nice time and she wanted to get to know more about Russ. "That was a lovely meal thank you, Russ. The dessert was absolutely scrumptious. How did you find this place?"

"Douglas told me about it last year. I've only been here once before but I really like the food, it reminds me of my grandmother's cooking."

Livvy settled back in her chair, "Tell me about your family, where were you born?"

"I was born right here in the city. I don't have any brothers or sisters but I have lots of aunts and uncles. My family is Ukrainian and my grandmother, we call her Baba, has a house in northwest Toronto. My grandfather died a long time ago but then Baba got remarried, to Walter. All of Baba's children are from her first marriage; there are three sons and four daughters. The youngest son, my uncle Alex and his wife, Evie, live with her; they just got married a year ago. My mother and Baba's other two sons live in Toronto and my three aunts live in California."

"Your family sounds like mine, "Livvy remarked, "My mother has six sisters and two brothers."

Russ was impressed, "Wow, that's even more than in my family"

Livvy giggled, "Yes, there are a lot of names to remember especially when they are all married and have kids. I have so many cousins and they are nearly all girls."

"Are you an only child too?"

"No, I have a brother, he's eighteen months older than me and I wouldn't be surprised if he comes to Canada too." She hesitated and then asked, "Wasn't it lonely growing up by yourself?"

Russ looked sad as he remembered his childhood, "Yes, it was. My mother was always flitting off somewhere, mostly between California and Toronto. She's been married three times and none of them worked out. She was always palming me off on an aunt or Baba; I never really knew where I would be from one year to the next."

Livvy was listening and thinking how much they had in common but she decided to let Russ tell her about himself and maybe later she would tell him about her own childhood, "What happened to your father, don't you ever see him?"

"Occasionally this guy shows up called George Walker, who my mother claims is my father. I have his name so I suppose it's true but I wish it wasn't. He's a drunk and I don't like him and, as far as I know, he's never given my mother a penny but then I never know whether my mother is lying or not, she's really generous but hard to get along with."

Livvy was more and more intrigued, "Do you live with your grandmother too?"

Russ shook his head, "No, I live in a basement apartment on Runnymede Road. It's not bad and the rent's cheap; you'll have to come over and see it some time."

Livvy considered the invitation for a moment, "Anywhere would be better than where Brenda and I are living, we can't wait to get out of there."

"Well, all the more reason to come to my place one evening. I could make us something to eat. You may not believe it but I can cook a little even if it's only soup."

Livvy liked Russ's sense of humour, "Soup eh?? As long as it's not vichyssoise."

Russ frowned, "What's that?"

"Never mind," Livvy replied laughing. "It's just a joke. I'd love to come over one night."

Within a week, Livvy was spending nearly every evening at Russ's apartment. It was small but comfortable and she felt at home there. On the first night, he had fed her cream of mushroom soup and she had become addicted to it. After that she would taunt him into making it for her and, because he was falling in love with her, he couldn't refuse her anything.

Livvy felt no guilt about leaving Brenda to her own devices. Brenda was constantly out on the town with Douglas or some other young man she had batted her eyes at. The two girls still saw each other all day in the mailroom or late at night when they would tumble into bed, barely able to stay awake, except to relay the very latest gossip and to say goodnight.

When Christmas came, Livvy had still not met any of Russ's family and she knew that for two days she would probably not be seeing him. According to Russ, his family celebrated Christmas by opening their gifts on Christmas Eve and then going to midnight mass and, the next day, Baba would cook a feast and everyone would gather around the huge dining room table and eat until they could hardly move.

Livvy and Brenda spent Christmas Eve having a quiet dinner alone at a small restaurant downtown and discussing what they were going to do after the holidays. They both realized they had to start looking for jobs or they would have trouble making ends meet so they made a pact that, on the second day of January, they would spend the day together checking the newspapers and calling the employment agencies. Christmas Day was spent with Brenda's second cousins on Ossington Avenue. Amy cooked a large turkey with all the trimmings and a traditional English plum pudding, especially for the girls. The Seller's daughter Jane, with her husband and two children, made the day a lot more festive and Livvy was particularly happy when they arrived with their new Airedale puppy that she could fuss over. Her grandmother had owned an Airedale named Barnaby who had died two weeks after her grandmother and the breed had always been Livvy's favourite. Livvy and Brenda bought a huge poinsettia plant between them to give to Bill and Amy and, in return, they each received a small bottle of Chanel No.5 perfume and a lace trimmed, linen, handkerchief. Even though the food was wonderful and the company enjoyable, both of the girls missed their families desperately and they were glad when the day was over.

In the week before New Year, Livvy and Russ resumed their pattern of getting together nearly every night and they were becoming more and more comfortable with each other. Douglas had made arrangements for the two couples to spend New Year's Eve at the Palais Royal on the lakefront. The celebration included a lavish buffet, champagne, and dancing, and the girls were excited. They had both bought new dresses for the occasion; Livvy's was a bright emerald green silk with a tight bodice and thigh-length bouffant skirt and Brenda's was a midnight blue, crepe sheath with a high neckline that camouflaged just how thin she was. On the actual night, they spent an hour fiddling with their hair, first putting it up and then down, then finally deciding they wanted to look sophisticated so they both swept it up again and prayed it wouldn't fall apart.

It was a wonderful evening and, although Russ wasn't a very good dancer, he had a unique style and enjoyed himself. There was a live orchestra and a buffet table laden with platters full of salads, sliced turkey, ham, roast beef, shellfish and all kinds of desserts and the champagne seemed to be limitless. Livvy was beginning to wonder how much the evening was costing Russ. She knew he didn't have much money and she was concerned but at midnight, for the moment, all her worries melted away when Russ took her in his arms, kissed her passionately, and whispered in her ear, "I love you, Livvy." In the wee small hours of New Year's Day, at Russ's apartment on Runnymede Road, they became intimate for the first time.

Chapter Twenty-Four

Livvy and Brenda stuck to their plans and, by the second week of January, they started working for a small insurance company in the downtown financial district. Livvy's duties in the accounting department were not exactly what she was accustomed to. At the St. James's Club in London, she had been able to use her mathematical skills but now she was being assigned menial tasks and she wasn't happy but she knew, if she worked hard, she had the potential to be promoted. Brenda was more content, although she was one of three members of a typing pool and was used to a secretarial position, she was grateful she no longer had to worry about paying the rent or wondering where their next meal was coming from.

Just before the end of January, on a frosty Sunday afternoon, Russ's grandmother greeted Livvy at the front door of her house on Caledonia Road. She had been anxious to meet Livvy after Russ had confided in her that he had met the most wonderful girl. Livvy had been nervous but was immediately put at ease when Baba opened the door, muttered something in a foreign language and gave her a hug. When she finally released her, Livvy found herself looking down at a small round woman with a wrinkled, weather beaten face and the sweetest smile, wearing a flowered apron over her long navy dress. While Baba excused herself to fuss in the kitchen, Russ introduced Livvy to Baba's husband Walter, his Uncle Alex and his wife Evie. Evie wanted to stay and hear all about England but had to excuse herself to help with dinner and Livvy was left with the three men in the living room feeling a little less nervous, but not entirely comfortable. Ten minutes later she heard the front door open and a woman's voice calling for Russ. She knew it had to be Russ's mother and she braced herself to meet her. The woman who entered the room was not what Livvy expected. Of average height, with short blonde hair; she looked very much like her son except her face was more peasant like and her nose much rounder. She didn't appear to be wearing any makeup which was a mistake, considering her face was pitted with acne scars, but she was fashionably dressed in an apple green sheath with a double row of pearls and matching pearl studs in her ears. Vivien embraced her son, nodded at her stepfather and brother, and then strode across the room to where Livvy was standing rather awkwardly but, before Vivien had a chance to speak, Livvy managed to smile and say, "Hello, Mrs. Walker, I'm very pleased to meet you."

Vivien glanced over at Russ then looked Livvy up and down before replying, "It's Mrs. Chandler."

Livvy may have been young but she was astute enough to recognize Vivien Chandler was going to be a force to be reckoned with, nevertheless she maintained her composure and, without missing a beat, said, "My apologies, I'll try to remember in future."

Vivien realized she had failed to intimidate the young woman her son had just introduced to her family and turned to Alex, "I think I'll go and help Baba and Evie in the kitchen."

Alex was only too pleased to see his sister leave the room," Why don't you do that, Vivien, I think they were just about to serve dinner."

After his mother had gone Russ took Livvy's hand, "I warned you didn't I?"

Livvy just shook her head, "I don't think she likes me very much."

Alex laughed, "Take no notice Livvy, Vivien's always been a bit of an odd duck."

Walter, who had been brought up to believe one had to honour one's father and mother, regardless of their shortcomings, wagged his finger at Russ and, in a heavy accent, admonished him, "You must be respectful to your mother my boy and you do not help, Alex," he continued, turning to his stepson.

"Yes, Walter," Alex said condescendingly, "now why don't we all go into the dining room, I think I hear Baba calling us."

"I don't hear anything," Walter said, as he shuffled out of the door with the others following behind him.

The dining room table was covered in platters and dishes heaped full of food and Baba was already seated at the head of the table. She nodded and smiled at Livvy then patted the seat beside her and Livvy was relieved that she didn't have to sit next to Vivien. Conversation during dinner was a mixture of Ukrainian, Polish, and English and half the time Livvy had no idea what was being said but she was too involved with what was on her plate to really be concerned. There was borscht, a wonderful soup made of beetroot and sour cream, chopped herring, chicken Kiev, and perogies, little parcels of dough filled with cheese and mashed potatoes, boiled, then fried with onions. The food was delicious and she didn't think she could eat another bite until Baba set a strudel made with apples and poppy seeds in front of her and insisted, "Eat, eat!"

After dinner Livvy offered to help with the dishes but Vivien made it very clear she wasn't needed in the kitchen and that she and Evie would take care of everything. Reluctantly, she returned to the living room with a cup of coffee and sat quietly smoking a cigarette, half listening to the men discussing the previous night's hockey game and wondering where Baba was. She couldn't help thinking about her own grandmother and, although her memory was vague, she remembered the times she would visit her and her dog Barnaby and feast on potato pancakes, chopped liver, knishes and wonderful fresh challah bread. Russ interrupted her daydreaming when he got up from beside Walter and parked himself on the arm of her chair, "Is everything okay, Livvy, you seem very quiet?"

Livvy smiled up at him, "Yes, Russ, everything's fine."

By the time Livvy's twenty-first birthday arrived in March, she had visited Baba's house three times. She got to meet Russ's other two uncles and their families but didn't see Vivien again. Baba had invited Livvy to celebrate her birthday at the house but she excused herself, claiming that she was going out to dinner with Russ and her friend Brenda. Russ was disappointed she had declined his grandmother's invitation until Livvy told him she really needed to spend some time alone with him to talk. He pressed her to tell him what was on her mind but she insisted he wait and he could only imagine the worst; that she wanted to end their relationship.

Livvy felt she had to forewarn Russ that she had something important to tell him but first she needed to talk to Brenda about her predicament so, the night before her birthday, she sat with Brenda at the kitchen table and, choking back tears, told her she was almost sure she was pregnant. Brenda wasn't totally surprised but felt sorry for Livvy, who was obviously upset, "Have you thought about having an abortion if you really are pregnant?"

"No, I'm too scared to do that and I wouldn't know how to go about it," Livvy replied, "I just don't know what to say to Russ."

Brenda thought the direct approach was best, "Just tell him, you think you're having a baby."

Livvy wasn't convinced, "Can't I lead up to it somehow? I can't just come out and say it."

Brenda was adamant, "Of course you can, what's he going to do? He'll probably ask you to marry him."

"But I don't want to get married, at least not to Russ."

"Well, you should have been more careful. Look, I know you aren't madly in love with him but if you really are pregnant and he does want to marry you I think you should go ahead with it. He worships you, Livvy, and I'm sure he'll make a good husband and father."

Livvy shook her head, "I think a lot of him, I really do, but I'm not sure."

Brenda took both of Livvy's hands in hers, "You know, Livvy, you've always been a bit of a martyr but you can't go through this by yourself. Russ is a good person and you should give him a chance."

Livvy was thinking about Brenda's advice when she rang Russ's doorbell the next afternoon. Russ had been waiting for her anxiously, not knowing what to expect, but he greeted her with a kiss on the cheek and a huge bouquet of red roses, "Happy birthday, Livvy, come in and get warm."

Livvy was silent as he took her coat, "I'll put the roses in water for now and you can take them home later."

Livvy took the bouquet, "I'll do it Russ, they really are beautiful, thank you," and she vanished into the kitchen.

Russ followed her and watched as she filled a vase at the kitchen sink, "Would you like to go out to dinner later, Livvy?" he asked.

"No, I think I'd like to stay in, I'm not very hungry and we need to talk."

Russ noticed Livvy's hand start to tremble, "Okay, let's go and sit down," and he took the vase from her and set it on the counter top.

Once they were settled on the living room sofa, Russ faced Livvy and braced himself for what he thought was about to come, "Well, Livvy, what do you want to talk about?"

Livvy decided Brenda was right, "Russ, there's no easy way to tell you this so I might as well come right out with it; I think I may be pregnant."

Russ looked stunned for a second and then breathed a sigh of relief, "Oh, Livvy, I thought you were going to tell me you didn't want to see me anymore."

"You didn't hear me, Russ. I said I think I may be pregnant."

"But I did hear you, Livvy, and I think it's wonderful."

Livvy got up from the sofa and started pacing the floor, "It's not wonderful, Russ, and I'm not sure what I'm going to do."

Russ looked puzzled, "What do you mean? We'll get married of course or don't you want to marry me, Livvy?"

Livvy walked to the window and gazed out at the maple trees blowing in the wind, "I don't know Russ; maybe I can bring the baby up on my own."

Russ walked over and put his hands on Livvy's shoulders, "Livvy, turn around and look at me. I love you and I think you love me a little. I've never really had a family growing up. I've always been pushed around from one place to the other and now I have the chance to have a family of my own. I've never met anyone like you before so marry me and I promise I'll look after you."

Livvy turned and saw the tears in Russ's eyes. At that moment, she felt something for him she hadn't felt before and, whether it was pity or love, she heard herself saying, "All right, Russ, I'll marry you."

Chapter Twenty-Five

A doctor's appointment, less than a week later, confirmed Livvy's baby was due at the end of October and, four days after that, she was able to tell her brother all about it in person. As expected, Matt and Gina had made plans to follow Livvy to Toronto right after she left England and their papers had come through in record time. Livvy was apprehensive about Matt's reaction to her news and he didn't disappoint her. He was not pleased but he was too preoccupied with his own problems to lecture Livvy and finally found it in his heart to congratulate her.

Vivien had left to spend the rest of the winter in California, with her sister Joan, and Russ decided not to tell any of his family about his marriage plans or about Livvy's pregnancy until after the wedding. He had no doubt there would be serious objections and he couldn't deal with it, even though Livvy tried to convince him Baba would be upset she wasn't there to see him get married, and his mother would probably throw a fit. They decided to get married as quickly as possible, and applied for a license at City Hall, but all their plans almost fell through when Livvy discovered Russ had been harboring a deep secret. She had always believed Russ had been born on March 5, 1936 and was mortified when she noticed the year recorded on the license was 1939. She quickly realized Russ was only eighteen years old and had been seventeen when she first met him. Russ knew, sooner or later, Livvy would discover his true age and had been terrified whenever they were around members of his family, afraid someone would let the cat out of the bag. He had hoped they would be married before she found out and now he had to convince her, he lied because he truly loved her and didn't want to lose her. Livvy confronted him angrily, "You've been lying to me all along, Russ. How could you do that? I can't marry you, you're only eighteen and I'm three years older."

Russ was devastated and trying hard to hold back tears, "I always meant to tell you the truth, Livvy, but I just couldn't do it. When we first met, I knew if I told you how old I was you wouldn't have gone out with me again."

Livvy was furious and turned her back on him, "So when did you ever intend to tell me?"

Russ hung his head, "I don't know; I'm sorry, Livvy. It doesn't make any difference, does it? I'm still the same person; I haven't changed just because of a date on a license."

Livvy raised her voice in anger, "That isn't the point, you deceived me. What else haven't you told me; how can I ever trust you?"

The words uttered by Livvy that day would come back to haunt her but, on this particular day, Russ persuaded her they were doing the right thing by getting married and providing a mother and father to raise their baby.

The wedding party was very small. On May 4, 1957 in the chapel on Glebe Road, Livvy and Russ were joined by her brother Matt and Gina, and their friends Brenda and Douglas. Livvy wore her new pale green outfit and a white lacy hat and Russ wore his best brown suit. In his formal attire, he presented quite an attractive figure. He was a tall young man, very slim, with curly dark blonde hair and his acne had almost cleared up, after taking Livvy's advice to get medical treatment and give up chocolate. Inside the chapel, waiting for the minister, Livvy was very nervous and hung on to Russ's hand while Brenda stood beside her and Douglas took up his place beside Russ. When the short ceremony began, Livvy thought she was going to faint and had the extreme urge to run to the bathroom. She was so distraught she could hardly repeat the wedding vows and Brenda, sensing her discomfort, leaned in towards her and pressed her whole body against Livvy's. It was extraordinary, because it worked like magic and Livvy's anxiety faded away almost instantly, and she was able to get through the rest of the ceremony without a hitch. They celebrated by going out to an early dinner and ordering champagne but Livvy had given up drinking while she was pregnant and had even stopped smoking. The wedding night was spent at the Park Plaza hotel in a regular suite, because they couldn't afford the honeymoon suite, and because Livvy was sure it was where her baby was conceived. One weekend they had booked into the hotel on a whim just because they wanted to be pampered for a change and they had thrown all caution to the wind.

The following day, they moved into a two-room flat on the second floor of a house on McPherson Avenue, in the Rosedale area. It was a lovely neighbourhood and they were happy living there but Russ's mother had other plans for them. As predicted, Baba and the rest of the family were disappointed they were not told about the wedding, or the baby, but once Russ sat down with them and explained, they accepted it and welcomed Livvy into their hearts. Vivien was another story; she was furious and blamed Livvy for all the secrecy but, at the same time, she wanted to do what was best for her son and the only way she knew how to do that was with her generosity. After only six weeks in their new flat, Vivien insisted they move into her furnished apartment at the corner of Church and Wellesley Streets, which she was giving up permanently while she stayed in California. Livvy was not happy about having Vivien manipulate their lives but she liked the apartment, which was on the main floor, with lots of windows, and had a nicely furnished living room and bedroom, and a small kitchenette.

Livvy now had to wear maternity clothes, because of her bulging belly, and she decided it was time to stop working. She was also experiencing a great deal of back pain and consulted with her doctor to try and determine what the problem was. It turned out she had pyelonephritis, a condition which affected the kidneys, and for two months she was forced to sleep sitting up to relieve the pressure on her back. This was a trying time for Livvy and, most of the time after she stopped working, she was bored and restless but one day in the middle of August, when it was extremely hot and humid, she was involved in more drama than she bargained for. On a Monday, just after noon, she got a call from Brenda asking Livvy to come right away because she needed her desperately. Livvy knew Brenda had not been feeling well lately and she didn't hesitate to find her way back to Queen Street and climb the three flights of stairs to the bedroom they had once shared. When she got there, she was exhausted but any thoughts of herself were replaced with concern for her friend who was lying in bed moaning and as pale as a ghost. She put her hand on Brenda's forehead, "Oh, goodness, Brenda, you're burning up. You must have the flu."

Brenda shook her head and tears came into her eyes, "It isn't the flu, Livvy."

"Well what is it then, have you seen a doctor?"

Brenda shook her head again, "Livvy, I had an abortion this morning and now I'm bleeding so much and I feel so rotten, I'm scared."

Livvy was shocked, "Oh my god, why didn't you tell me you were pregnant? Why didn't you tell me you were going to have an abortion? Who's the father, is it Douglas? Did you go to the doctor all by yourself?"

Brenda had to smile despite the pain she was in, "Slow down, Livvy, and I'll tell you everything. I've been seeing this man, his name's John, but he's married. He said he loved me and he'd leave his wife for me but when I got pregnant he didn't seem so keen on the idea, so I decided to have an abortion. I've been so stupid, Livvy."

"But what happened this morning, how did you find a doctor who would do it?"

"John found him for me. It was horrible, I don't know exactly what they did but they sent me home and told me the baby should come out in a few hours and not to tell anybody where I'd been?"

Now a look of horror came on Livvy's face, "Are you telling me you had the baby here in this room?"

"Yes, I thought I was going to die, it hurt so much and now I'm bleeding a lot and I don't know what to do."

"Where is it?" asked Livvy

"What are you talking about?"

"Where's the baby?"

"Under the bed in a bowl. You can see it if you want to."

Livvy knelt down and slowly pulled the bowl from under the bed. She couldn't believe her eyes when she saw an almost perfectly formed tiny little body lying in a mass of bloody matter, "Oh Brenda it's amazing, I've never seen anything like it before."

"I know, but we have to get rid of it somehow."

Livvy knew the first order of business was to make sure her friend was okay and she demanded that Brenda give her John's phone number so that she could call him to help. She wanted Brenda to go to the hospital but Brenda was adamant about staying where she was and Livvy thought the least she could do was get some ice to help stop the bleeding and she needed a car for that. John was surprisingly cooperative and arrived within a half hour of Livvy's angry call. She immediately instructed him to go back out and get bags and bags of ice and, within another half hour, he was lumbering up the stairs weighed down by three heavy bags. They sat with Brenda for hours, constantly changing the ice on her stomach, and she seemed to improve. Eventually, after phoning Russ to explain where she was, Livvy decided to stay for the night and John was given the task of disposing of the fetus by taking it as far away as possible and burying it.

By the next day, Brenda was still bleeding enough that Livvy insisted she go to the hospital. She forced her to get dressed and take a cab to the emergency room where she was questioned extensively about where the abortion had been performed, but she refused to give them any information and had deliberately not told Livvy any details so that she would not be forced to lie, if drawn into the investigation. She spent the next three days in the hospital, after undergoing dilation and curettage, and then went back to the flat to rest for the weekend. She never heard from John again and, less than a year later, she met the man who was to become her husband.

Chapter Twenty-Six

As Livvy's pregnancy progressed, she became more restless. She was not accustomed to being idle and always needed something constructive to do. Her kidney infection began to clear up and she attributed her constant trips to the bathroom to her condition. Then one day when Russ borrowed a car and, along with Brenda and Douglas, they took a trip up to Lake Wilcox, just north of Toronto, she was thoroughly humiliated when she had the urge to stop at nearly every gas station in sight, and they were forced to make the journey in six stages. They stayed at the lake for most of the afternoon but Livvy was dreading the ride home. It came as a complete surprise to her when she made the trip back without stopping and she began to wonder what was going on.

Vivien made an unexpected appearance at the apartment one morning while Russ was at work. Livvy had no idea she had returned from California and had no choice but to invite her in and attempt to be cordial. Livvy made tea, which Vivien appeared to drink by the gallon, and she was surprised when they had a pleasant conversation chatting about all manner of subjects. Less than three weeks later, after Vivien had traveled back to her sister's in San Diego, a letter arrived addressed to Russ. Livvy couldn't contain her curiosity and decided to steam it open to see what Vivien had to say. She was infuriated to learn that Vivien questioned whether Russ was really the father of her baby. Now she knew what a snake in the grass his mother was and she vowed to be on her guard from then on.

Near the end of October, when Livvy was in her eighth month, they discovered the owners of the building had a strict rule that children were not allowed and they were forced to move. At the time, it was difficult to find a place to live that they could afford, and especially on such short notice. It was Russ who finally found somewhere where he thought they could stay, at least until after the baby was born.

When Livvy walked into the flat on Charles Street, she was horrified when she saw where they would be living. It consisted of only one room with a shabby sofa and a double bed, shoved up against some double doors, and a kitchenette painted a ghastly shade of yellow. The floors were covered in brown linoleum and the windowpanes were so dirty that the brick wall opposite was barely visible. She cringed in disgust and turned to Russ in despair, "I can't stay here; it's an awful place."

Russ put his arm around her, "I know it isn't very nice but it's the only place I could find at such short notice."

Livvy started to cry, "I don't care; I'm not bringing my baby up here. Oh, Russ, what are we going to do?"

Russ tried to comfort her as best he could, "Look we'll stay here just for tonight. It's getting late and we have nowhere else to go and, I promise, tomorrow I'll find somewhere else, if it's the last thing I do."

Livvy wiped away her tears and sank down on the shabby sofa, "But what if you can't find anywhere else?"

"I will, don't worry and if the worst comes to the worst we'll go and stay at Baba's for a few days."

Livvy brightened up at the thought of being in Baba's house, "Okay, but as soon as you go to work in the morning, I'm leaving with you. I don't want to stay here a minute longer than I have to."

The night seemed to be endless, particularly when they could hear all sorts of ominous noises in the next room and could actually look through a crack in the double doors and observe what was going on. Livvy was sure they were living in a brothel and prayed for the sun to come up. The next morning, true to her word, Livvy left the flat with Russ and arranged to meet him at five o'clock on the corner of Bloor and Yonge Streets. Most of the morning, she bided her time riding on the streetcar or sitting in the park reading a magazine, even though the weather was cold and windy. She stopped for lunch at Fran's, ordering a club sandwich and dawdling over her coffee, and then decided to go to a movie. By the time the movie was over, it was still only three o'clock so she window-shopped and rode the streetcar again until it was time to meet Russ.

During his lunch hour Russ had checked the newspapers and telephoned the one place that appeared to be suitable. He suggested they have supper before going to look at the place but Livvy couldn't wait. They soon found themselves walking through the gate of a large house, set back from the road, at the far end of Wellesley Street bordering on Riverdale Park. When they knocked on the door, a small, very thin woman, with a pinched face and gray hair, answered and invited them to follow her upstairs. The whole layout of the room was almost identical to where they had just come from, except it was much larger and brighter and there was a television. Livvy wasn't impressed but she really didn't want to look like a poor relation by going to Baba's and the landlady seemed to be very pleasant so they decided to stay. The neighbourhood was extremely quiet but the household was not. The very next day, Livvy discovered the landlady had a daughter who was an absolute shrew. She had her own room on the same floor as Russ and Livvy and forbade her mother to enter it without her permission. She screamed at her mother constantly with such profanity. Livvy could hardly bear it but she kept silent for fear of retaliation.

Two weeks after Livvy's due date, she was dancing the polka at the wedding of one of Russ's cousins. She had already gained over thirty pounds but she felt good and was full of energy and hoping all the activity might encourage her baby to make an appearance. Close to midnight, six days later, Russ and Livvy were walking slowly along Wellesley Street trying to find a cab to take them to the hospital. Every few minutes,

Livvy bent over groaning in pain and they were forced to walk almost four blocks before they finally saw a taxi and flagged it down. After they arrived at the Western Hospital and Livvy was admitted into the labour ward and examined, Russ was told he might as well go home because it would be a while before the baby would be ready to be delivered. Livvy was left completely alone for hours, suffering through each contraction, never crying out, but quietly crying while gripping the bars on her hospital bed. Every so often, a nurse would come in to check on her progress but she had no one to talk to or comfort her as she watched the clock opposite her bed and saw the sky go from dark to light, outside the window.

At exactly ten minutes after two o'clock, on the afternoon of November 19, 1957, her baby was born and Livvy was delighted to learn she had a little girl but she didn't feel the instant bond she had heard other mothers talk about. She had no idea then, this child would become the most important person in her life and, as long as she lived, she would love no other person as much. When Russ came to see her, later that day, he was beaming, "Oh, Livvy, I went to see the baby and she's so beautiful. She's got blonde hair and blue eyes just like you and she's so tiny."

Livvy smiled and took Russ's hand, "She is pretty but I think she looks more like you and she's not that small. She weighed seven pounds two ounces and the nurse told me it's a good average weight for a girl."

"We still haven't decided on a name, what are we going to call her?" Russ asked.

Livvy sank back against the pillows exhausted, "You know I wanted to call her Gabrielle."

"No way, Livvy," Russ objected, "then everyone will call her Gabby and I don't think she'll be very happy with that. I'd like to name her after one of my two favourite movie stars."

Livvy looked at him apprehensively, "Oh, and who are they or dare I ask?"

"Well, one is Natalie Wood and the other is Mitzi Gaynor."

Livvy giggled, "Mitzi? You have to be joking. I'd never give a baby a name like that. I don't mind Natalie so much, although I still prefer Gabrielle."

Russ was elated when he eventually got his way. Natalie Anne Walker was welcomed into the world and that Christmas, when she was only five weeks old, it was a magical time for the family. They spent the holidays at Baba's house with all of the aunts and uncles and the other new baby in the family. Evie had become pregnant at almost the same time as Livvy and had recently given birth to Michelle, a dark eyed, dark haired, chubby little girl.

Vivien arrived on Christmas Eve bearing mountains of gifts and immediately fell in love with Natalie, insisting on holding her for most of the afternoon, and only giving her up to be fed by Livvy or to be changed. That evening they all sat around the tree, opened their gifts, drank eggnog, and sang carols then later everyone, but Livvy and Evie, went off to celebrate midnight mass. On Christmas Day, everybody slept late except for the two new mothers, who had to get up to attend to the babies, and Baba who was already in the kitchen before dawn preparing all of the traditional holiday foods and her favourite Ukrainian dishes. Matt and Gina were invited to spend the holiday at Baba's house and Livvy was happy to have a member of her very own family around her. She missed her mother and father and wished they could be there to enjoy all of the festivities. Visitors streamed in and out of the house all day and neither Matt nor Livvy had ever experienced a Christmas like it before and the snow, which had been falling all night, made it even more magical.

At the beginning of the new year, just as Livvy was settling back into the routine of taking care of Natalie and being home alone all day, Russ lost his job and Livvy had to remind him constantly that it wasn't his fault. The printing company he worked for was closing down and she urged him not to be discouraged although, when he failed to find work, she was worried about how they would manage. When Harry and Rachel received a letter from Livvy telling them about their misfortune, they immediately offered to pay for their passage to England if she would come back and bring her family with her. To Livvy, it was a chance to be with her parents again while for Russ it was an adventure he couldn't pass up, even though there was no guarantee he would find work in London.

Despite the pleas from Baba and Vivien, and even Brenda, that they stay in Toronto, in mid February, when Natalie was just three months old, they were on a train heading for New York and their journey across the Atlantic. The train ride was almost unbearable, even though they had a sleeper car. There was hardly room to move and with Natalie's carrycot taking up one bunk, Livvy and Russ had to sleep in the other. It took just over twelve hours to reach Grand Central Station and they were exhausted but had no time to waste if they were going to be in time to board the Cunard Line's ship, Ivernia. When they finally reached the pier suddenly, without any warning, Livvy had a panic attack. Her heart began to race and she felt the desperate urge to go to the bathroom. In an effort to cover up what she was really feeling, she feigned a dizzy spell and begged Russ to find her a chair where she could sit for a few minutes trying to fight off her anxiety. Once on board, she soon settled down and discovered the crossing would not be anything like her first experience on the Empress of France. Most of the passengers were going back to England for a vacation and the mood, although upbeat, couldn't compare to that of immigrants sailing towards a new land.

After five days at sea, they arrived in Southampton and, as they came through the customs shed, Livvy could see her parents waving frantically. They welcomed Russ with open arms and showered Livvy with hugs and kisses but Rachel couldn't wait to pick Natalie up and cradle her in her arms. If Livvy expected life in London would be any different than before she was sadly disappointed. Living with her parents was not an ideal situation and she became bored and restless. When Russ managed to find a job at a gas station, she thought they might be able to find a place of their own but soon discovered his salary wouldn't support the idea and she seriously considered getting a job herself. Looking after a baby was difficult for Livvy; she loved Natalie but taking her for a walk in her pram every day and getting up at six o'clock every morning to wash diapers was not very rewarding. She longed to do something that would give her something to think about but both Russ and Rachel both discouraged her from working. For the time being, her guilty conscience kept her at home but she slowly began to formulate a plan to get herself out of the situation she was in and help her to regain her independence.

Rachel was very generous and would not dream of charging Livvy and Russ more than a pittance for their room and board and, after almost a year, they had saved a sizeable amount from Russ's earnings. It was at this time, in answer to a letter from Vivien, that Livvy subtly suggested she would like to go back to Toronto and Vivien immediately took the bait and offered to supplement any shortage in their fare. It took very little to persuade Russ to return home; he was not happy in London and was constantly being hassled and told yankee go home, by those still opposed to the American servicemen based in England. Harry and Rachel were not pleased about Livvy leaving home for the second time and Rachel was particularly upset that her grandchild would be thousands of miles away but, fifteen months after they arrived, Russ, Livvy and Natalie were sailing back across the Atlantic to Canada.

After sailing up the St. Lawrence River and arriving in Quebec City, they took the train to Toronto and were met by Vivien at Union Station. She seemed genuinely pleased to see Livvy and overjoyed to see Russ and Natalie and she had a surprise for them. She had rented them an apartment over a store on Eglinton Avenue and couldn't wait to show it to them. Livvy was overwhelmed with Vivien's generosity when they walked through the door. The living room and bedroom were both completely furnished and the kitchen was stocked with dishes, pots, pans, and silverware and the refrigerator held enough food for a week. Vivien was a little surprised when Livvy, who was genuinely grateful, put her arms around her, "Thank you so much, this is wonderful. How can we ever repay you?"

"It's a gift, Livvy, I want you to stay here in Toronto and not go traipsing off to England again. I missed my little granddaughter," and she reached out to take Natalie from Russ's arms.

"I don't think there's any chance of us going back again, Mom," Russ said, "unless we go over for a vacation one day. That will be a long way off though because we have to get back on our feet and I haven't even got a job."

Vivien rocked Natalie gently, "Well, I have something else to tell you. I know someone who's looking for a sales rep to sell beauty products to salons and I've set up an interview for you for tomorrow."

"Wow, that sounds great but I don't know anything about selling and I don't have a car so how can I get around?"

"You can borrow my car for a few weeks," Vivien suggested "then, as soon as you have enough money, you can buy a second hand car. You can finance it and I'll cosign the loan for you."

Livvy intervened, "That's really generous of you, Vivien, but we can't let you do that, you've already done enough."

"You're my family and I want to help," Vivien insisted, "especially my little sweetie here," and she covered Natalie's face in kisses.

Livvy knew there was nothing she could do to dissuade Vivien and she really appreciated all of her help but at the same time she wondered if Vivien had an ulterior motive. She still hadn't learned to trust her mother-in-law after she had inferred Natalie was not Russ's child.

While Livvy and Russ were in England, Brenda had married a man she had met while still working at the insurance company. Livvy thought it was ironic when she learned that Victor was from Manchester and had only been in Canada for two years. She liked him immediately when she was first introduced to him and found him to be rather attractive, not so much because of his looks but because of his sharp mind and spontaneous sense of humour. Brenda had already suffered a miscarriage, which she felt was God's punishment for having had an abortion, and Livvy tried to assure her she was being too hard on herself and not to give up hope. Matt had also married within the last six months and he and Gina were living happily in a rented house in the north end of the city but planning to build their own house, even further north, as soon as they could afford it.

Russ got the job at the beauty supply company and was enjoying traveling around visiting all of the salons but he longed to get his own car and, after he received his sixth weekly pay cheque plus a sizeable sum for commissions, he arrived home with exciting news for Livvy. He burst into the apartment as Livvy was preparing supper waving some papers at her, "Hi honey, you won't believe what I have here."

Livvy laid down the fork she had been using to mash the potatoes, " What is it, Russ, you look so excited?"

"Come outside with me and I'll show you."

"I can't do that, I have supper on the stove and I can't leave Natalie here."

Russ stepped over to the stove, and switched off all the burners, then walked over to the playpen, where Natalie was chewing on a piece of bread, and scooped her up in his arms, "Now you can, it will only be for a few minutes and you won't even need your coat."

Livvy couldn't help but laugh at Russ's enthusiasm, "Okay, you win, lead the way my lord and I will follow."

Instead of going out of the front door of the building Russ headed for the back door, which led onto the parking lot, and then he just stood there waiting for Livvy to react to his surprise. It only took a few seconds for Livvy to rush past him and run a complete circle around the black Pontiac parked where his mother's car used to be "Is this ours?" she yelled, "Is it really ours, Russ?"

Russ was amused at how excited Livvy was and even Natalie was pointing at her and mumbling Mama over and over again. "Yes, it really is ours; it's four years old but it's in really good shape and I got a great deal on it. I didn't feel comfortable driving Mom's car; she only let me use it to do my job but now we can go anywhere we like. I have a great idea, how about we go to a drive-in tonight?"

Livvy ran over to Russ and kissed him on the cheek, "That would be fabulous. I've never been to a drive-in."

Having their own car gave them a real sense of independence but Livvy was still not content. She desperately needed to work and finally decided to look for a job and a babysitter. She was fortunate that her neighbour, who lived one floor above them, was willing to look after Natalie. She was a young mother herself and an immigrant from Poland and was grateful for the extra money. Once that was settled,

Livvy started looking for work and, because she had already had some experience in the insurance field, it only took a week before she was hired by one of the largest insurance companies in Canada. The claims department was a busy and interesting place and Livvy would have been content if it had not been for her supervisor. Freddy was a fifty-year-old single woman with a chip on her shoulder and she ruled the department with an iron hand. If a mistake was made, she could be particularly vindictive and she had a habit of intimidating her staff any chance she got. It took Livvy about two weeks to realize, the only way to handle Freddy was to ignore her. Freddy wasn't used to being ignored and tried to intimidate Livvy even more but it didn't work and eventually she completely changed her attitude, almost to the point where she was kowtowing, and Livvy was secretly amused. As the weeks progressed, Livvy became Freddy's favourite employee and even toned down her behaviour with the rest of the staff.

For the next year, life for Livvy and her family settled into a comfortable routine. Natalie was a pretty child with pale blonde hair and a sweet face and she was so good-natured, Livvy hardly ever had cause to admonish her. She tended to be a solitary soul, playing for hours with her dolls and stuffed animals and appeared to be content. On weekends when they weren't working, the family would often go to Baba's house where there were always aunts, uncles or cousins visiting. Sometimes Vivien would show up and would insist on fawning over Natalie proclaiming her to be the most beautiful little girl in the world. One day Livvy finally met Russ's father, George Walker. He showed up at the apartment with Vivien and Livvy disliked him on sight. She knew he was an alcoholic and he had all the trademarks of someone who drank heavily. He was short and stocky with straight fair hair, a round face, and pockmarked red nose, and he had a way of looking at Livvy that made her feel uncomfortable. Russ treated his father like some stranger and was anxious to get rid of him and Livvy was relieved when they finally left, after two hours of small talk and more of Vivien's gushing over Natalie. It would be a few years before Livvy saw George Walker again.

Chapter Twenty-Seven

Everything changed for Livvy when Russ failed to come home for supper two or three nights a week and always had the excuse he was working. Livvy insisted he should at least call to let her know when he would be late but Russ claimed he was so busy he didn't always have time to stop and phone. As time progressed, the hours Russ stayed away became longer and longer and Livvy knew in her heart he was probably cheating on her but she had no way of proving it. It went against her nature to snoop but she found herself going through Russ's pockets trying to find evidence of an affair and, when she found a phone number scrawled in an unfamiliar hand on a matchbook in his jacket, she made the call that would confirm her suspicions. On hearing a young female voice say hello, she hesitated and then said, "Is, Jane there please?"

The voice replied, "No, there isn't any Jane here, are you sure you have the right number?"

Livvy repeated the number and added, "I'm sure this was the number my friend gave me. Who's speaking please?"

Unwittingly the girl on the other end answered, "This is Carla, and I really don't know anyone named Jane."

Livvy felt a degree of triumph as she said goodbye and apologized for being a nuisance but, it only took a minute for her to realize, confronting Russ would be unpleasant and she might get to learn the ugly truth.

At nine o'clock that night, after Natalie was tucked up in bed and fast asleep, Livvy sat quietly contemplating what she was going to say to Russ when he arrived home. She felt sure he would deny any affair and prayed Carla was just a business acquaintance, but she was nervous, and finally started pacing the living room anxious to get the confrontation over with.

At ten o'clock, Russ bounced in the door looking like the cat who swallowed the canary and, before Livvy could speak, announced, "Hi honey, sorry I'm late but I made a huge sale today and I went out with Douglas to celebrate with a few beers. Wait until you see my commission cheque."

Livvy looked at Russ with contempt, "Do you really expect me to believe you were out with Douglas, what kind of a fool do you think I am?"

Russ was startled but decided not to take the bait and so he drew Livvy towards him and looked her straight in the eyes, "I don't know what you're talking about. I told you I was out with Douglas. Why don't you call him if you don't believe me?"

Livvy was sure he was bluffing, "You know I'm not going to do that. It's too humiliating checking up on my own husband but I know you're lying to me." Her voice started to rise in anger, "You're getting just like your mother, that's where you learned how to lie."

Russ was getting angry now, "Wait just a minute, my mother's no saint but don't start insulting her."

"Why not, like mother like son. If you're not lying then tell me, who's Carla?" Russ's mouth dropped open and he turned to walk into the kitchen. "Oh no, don't you run away, "Livvy demanded, "I asked you a question. Who's Carla?"

"I don't know anyone named Carla."

"You're lying again, because I found her phone number in your pocket."

Russ whirled around with eyes blazing, "You really want to know who Carla is? She's some girl I met in one of the salons and I've been seeing her for months."

Livvy suddenly felt sick to her stomach, "Why Russ, aren't you happy? How can you do this to me and to Natalie?"

Russ shook his head, "I can't help it Livvy. We should never have got married, I was much too young and I wasn't ready to settle down. I can't take all this responsibility; I want to have some fun."

Suddenly Livvy felt such rage she couldn't contain herself and screamed, "Well go and have your fun then. Get out and don't come back, I never want to see you again." Russ was shocked at her reaction and attempted to put his arms around her. "Don't touch me!" she yelled pushing him away, "Just go. Get out."

Russ staggered backwards, hesitated, and then left the apartment slamming the door behind him and Livvy sank to the floor sobbing. She couldn't believe what had just happened. She had thrown her husband out of the house and now she chastised herself for being so impulsive. She wished she could take back every word and prayed it wasn't too late. She was awake most of the night trying to figure out what she had done to make Russ behave this way. She thought she had been a good wife and knew he loved little Natalie. It was true he was very young and had never been brought up in an environment with a responsible parent; maybe he was just following the same pattern. Thoughts tumbled through Livvy's head over and over but eventually as daylight started to creep through the window she fell asleep.

Later that morning, she called Freddy to tell her she wasn't feeling well and wouldn't be in to work but she took Natalie to her neighbour as usual because she couldn't deal with looking after her. She waited anxiously for Russ to call and considered phoning Baba's house in case he was there but didn't want to alarm her. At noon, he walked through the front door and was surprised to find Livvy at home, "What are you doing at home today?" he asked.

"I was waiting for you to come back," Livvy replied meekly.

Russ looked angry, "Why? You threw me out yesterday and you expect me to come back just like that?"

"Can't we talk about this, Russ? I was upset and I didn't mean what I said. I don't want you to leave; I want us to stay together as a family. You can't abandon Natalie, she loves you and I love you."

"I'm sorry, Livvy, but I can't stay. I've just come to get some of my clothes and then I'm leaving again."

Livvy felt utterly defeated, "Please Russ, you can't do this. Don't you even want to say goodbye to your daughter? How will I get in touch with you?"

"I'll see Natalie real soon and if you need me you can leave a message with Alex, or Evie, at Baba's."

"But we'll need money Russ, I can't afford to keep this apartment and pay for babysitting by myself."

Russ was getting impatient, "Don't worry, I'll get you some money when I get paid. Now if you don't mind I have to get going so I'm just going to grab some things." Livvy watched him go into the bedroom and emerge with a pile of clothes over one arm. She couldn't believe he was really going through with it and she felt numb. When he reached the front door he turned briefly, "You'll be all right, Livvy, I'll see you soon." And then he was gone.

Livvy rushed to the window overlooking the street to watch Russ getting into their car and, as he pulled away from the curb, she couldn't help noticing someone else was in the passenger seat, a dark haired young woman. An hour later, she was on the telephone telling her mother what had happened and crying uncontrollably. Rachel couldn't believe what she was hearing and was worried about how Livvy would manage on her own with Natalie. She begged her to come back home.

Everything happened so quickly after that, Livvy never went back to her job and didn't even tell Freddy she was leaving. Matt agreed with his mother that Livvy would be better off in England and he helped to arrange her flight home while Gina helped her to function during the day, by doing the laundry and some household chores and providing her with pills, so that she could get a good night's sleep. She walked around the apartment in a daze most of the time but finally got up the courage to call Evie and ask her to let Russ know she was leaving with Natalie and not coming back. Evie was stunned, she had no idea Russ had walked out and had no idea where he was staying. She begged Livvy to reconsider, but it was too late. The next call Livvy made was to Brenda who wished she could come with her because she was so homesick.

They cried a lot on the phone and promised to stay in touch and get together when Brenda went home to visit her folks.

Exactly two weeks after Russ left, Matt was driving Livvy and Natalie to the airport. Livvy had never flown before and, under normal circumstances, she would have been nervous but she was too upset to be afraid. She had not heard from Russ and he hadn't even bothered to come and see Natalie. As far as she was concerned, they would never see him again. Saying goodbye to Matt was difficult but she hoped he would come to England for a vacation and she promised she would write and send pictures, so that he could see what Natalie looked like as she grew up. Matt picked three-year-old Natalie up and kissed her on the cheek, she looked so adorable in the blue and white gingham dress Vivien had bought her.

The first leg of the journey, landing in Montreal, was on a small plane carrying about thirty people and it seemed as though they had just become airborne when, a short time later, they were coming in to land. Livvy was too busy watching Natalie, making sure she was comfortable and secure, to pay much attention to what was going on around her but, when they walked out onto the tarmac to catch their connection to London, she was shocked. On the tarmac sat the biggest plane she had ever seen, it was a Bristol Britannia, and she couldn't see how it could possibly get off the ground. Once on board, they settled in for the long trip, stopping in Gander and then Prestwick for refueling and then Manchester before their final destination. As the plane descended in Manchester, Livvy got airsick and felt exactly as she had on the ferry crossing to France when she was sixteen but, after an hour on the ground, she recovered and was anxious to see her parents again. Harry and Rachel were in the arrivals lounge when they eventually reached London but after the long and arduous trip, the very minute Livvy saw them, she knew she had made the biggest mistake of her life.

Chapter Twenty-Eight

When Livvy left Canada, she left behind her husband and her home and, most of all, her independence. Living back at home with her parents and without Russ was like becoming a child again and Rachel and Harry watched over her every move. Whenever, she left the house they asked her where she was going and when she was coming home and, although she knew they meant well, she hated the way it made her feel. The depression she had experienced before her arrival back in London deepened and this proved to be the darkest period of her entire life. Not even Natalie could lift her spirits and eventually, because of her neglect, the sweet child she had always known turned into a holy terror. Mealtimes were an exercise in futility, when Natalie would climb under the table and refuse to eat, and Harry would lose his patience and storm off in exasperation but Livvy couldn't deal with it and her mother was left to cope.

Two weeks after Livvy's arrival, she got a job with an advertising agency in Russell Square which meant she had to travel to the center of town each day and leave Natalie with a neighbour. Work had always been a distraction from any trouble she had experienced in the past but this time, she was unable to focus and would arrive home exhausted, just wanting to sleep so that she didn't have to think. Every night, after putting Natalie to bed at just after seven o'clock, she would go to bed herself and lie awake for hours before finally falling asleep. Sometimes she would stare at the window and contemplate jumping out but then she thought about what would happen to Natalie and she knew it wasn't an option. To make matters more difficult, no one in Rachel's family had ever been divorced and she insisted that the reason Livvy had returned home be kept a secret. Livvy argued with her mother asking her what she expected her to tell people and finally, in frustration, she confided in both of her aunts who lived close by. It was a relief for her to visit them and be able to talk about her situation and they were both understanding and very supportive.

Five weeks after she left Toronto, Livvy was surprised when she received a telegram from Russ saying he was arriving in London in three days. Contrary to being excited, she was anxious and guarded but her mother took it as positive sign that there would be no divorce. When Russ came through the arrival gate, the reunion with Livvy was tense and awkward but Rachel tried to make Russ feel at ease and threw her arms around him, welcoming him back into the family. On the way home, he tried to reassure Livvy that he had come to England to see if they could work things out and then he would arrange for them to return to Toronto but Livvy wasn't convinced she could ever trust him again. She still loved him and wanted nothing more than to go back to Canada but she was apprehensive about the future.

Natalie was playing in the garden when Russ arrived at the house. She hadn't seen her father for seven weeks and looked at him as though he was a stranger, even when he got down on his knees, held out his arms, and said "Hi Natalie, it's Daddy, aren't you going to say hi to me?"

It took Natalie a few days before she bonded with her father again but the relationship between Russ and Livvy remained strained even though he tried again to assure her, he wanted his family back. Livvy wanted the same thing but, more than anything else, she wanted to go back to the place where she had first asserted her independence. Her resolve became even greater when Russ told her he would only be staying for a month and during that time; he was constantly traveling to the centre of London to visit the Canadian Embassy. When she questioned him on his activities, he claimed he had to clear up some travel documents but she suspected he was having his mail addressed there and didn't want her intercepting any letters from his mother or possibly, Carla. It suddenly occurred to her that she had entered Britain without any papers for Natalie and there was no way she would get back into Canada without getting her a passport of her own. Any application had to be signed by Russ and he promised to take care of all the details but, by the time he left to return to Toronto, the passport had not arrived and Livvy was so anxious, she fell into another deep depression and found it even more difficult to concentrate on her job. When she was called onto the carpet for her lack of interest in her work and given a warning, it didn't faze her; all she cared about was finding a way to get back to Toronto.

Foolishly, she had given most of her savings to Russ so that he could return home and, when she didn't hear from him after another month went by, she knew in her heart she would have to start over. In desperation, she wrote to Freddy asking if she could borrow some money and promising to pay it back but, although Freddy was no longer angry Livvy had left her job without even giving notice, she felt she could not trust her enough to lend her a penny. A week after receiving Freddy's letter, Natalie's passport arrived and Livvy was filled with a profound sense of relief. It was obvious to Harry and Rachel that she was determined to leave as quickly as possible. That same evening, Rachel told Livvy she wanted to talk with her privately in the front room. Livvy was surprised because her mother had never actually sat down and had a serious conversation with her before. It came as a greater surprise when Rachel expressed her concern about Livvy's treatment of Natalie and warned her, if she didn't change her attitude towards her daughter, she would grow up to disrespect her and maybe even grow to hate her. Rachel then offered to pay for Livvy and Natalie's flight back to Toronto, provided Livvy could assure her she had enough money to tide them over while she looked for a job and got settled. Livvy had no alternative but to lie to her mother and assure her that she had plenty to see them through and she had no reason to worry. It was much later in her life that Livvy realized the sacrifice her mother had made for her that day.

Chapter Twenty-Nine

Two weeks later, Livvy and Natalie flew out of Heathrow on their way to Toronto and, when the plane touched down at Toronto International, Livvy was completely transformed. Despite the fact that she had only thirty-five dollars in her pocket, she felt like the luckiest person in the world and she was determined to survive and mend her relationship with her daughter.

Not wanting to call Matt because she knew he didn't approve of her leaving England, Livvy called the one person she knew would help them without question. Baba welcomed them with open arms and begged them to stay for as long as they liked but Livvy felt uncomfortable knowing Vivien could show up at any moment, and she wanted to get a place of her own. Leaving Natalie with Evie, she set out the very next day looking for a job, an apartment, and a babysitter and it took her exactly seven days to find all three. She had applied at four different companies for a position in accounting and was accepted at a large market research company as a payroll clerk. When Mrs. McGowan, who ran the accounting department, interviewed her, Livvy decided to be totally honest and explained why she had suddenly left her previous job without giving notice and her honesty paid off. Now that she knew there would be a pay cheque in a week, Livvy put down a deposit on a basement apartment in a house on Castlefield Avenue and managed to find a babysitter directly across the street. The apartment had a large living room with very little furniture, other than a pull out davenport, and a small television, and the bedroom was all but taken up with a large brass bed and one dresser. The kitchen was long and narrow with a long table against one wall where they could eat, and the cupboards were filled with pots, pans and utensils but the whole place was dark and drab and the floors all covered with linoleum. Like Baba, the owners of the house were Ukrainian and often cooked traditional food and even brought a dish down now and again for Livvy to sample.

Natalie was perfectly happy being taken care of by the babysitter, a young Italian woman, who had two children of her own and looked after four other children as well. Every night, when Livvy came home from work to pick her up, the children would be sitting around the huge kitchen table chewing on chunks of home made bread and it was difficult to get Natalie to eat any supper. At the best of times, she ate very little and was very slight but Livvy didn't believe in forcing her to eat and she was an exceptionally healthy child.

Russ finally showed up at the apartment almost a week after they moved in and claimed he was still trying to put their lives back together. Livvy wanted to believe him and asked him to stay and he agreed, but it took very little time for Livvy to realize he was still lying to her about where he spent his time and they fought constantly. She confided in Brenda but her friend could not understand why she put up with Russ and advised her over and over again to throw him out, while Matt was even less tolerant.

The following spring, Livvy did something that took a lot of courage and once again split the family apart but she needed to know the truth once and for all. One evening, after discovering Russ had deceived her about his whereabouts for the umpteenth time, she informed him she was going out for a while. Russ immediately became agitated demanding to know where she was going but she refused to answer him. When she returned about fifteen minutes later, he suspected she might have phoned Carla. This unnerved him so much, he quickly scampered out of the front door but he was too late to stop Carla because she was already on her way to see Livvy.

Carla turned out to be a very young, slim, Spanish looking girl with an attractive face, long dark hair, and wearing a black dress that showed she was obviously pregnant. When Livvy opened the door she maintained her composure, asked her to come inside and even offered her a cup of tea. Carla didn't seem in the least bit nervous and settled herself at the kitchen table while Livvy put the kettle on to boil, filled the teapot, and placed some cookies on a plate. When she knew she couldn't delay the inevitable much longer she finally sat down, looked Carla straight in the eyes, and asked, "How far along are you?"

"Four months," Carla replied without any sign of embarrassment or guilt.

"I guess I don't have to ask if it's Russ's baby."

"No, it's Russ's."

"What has he been telling you, Carla? Has he told you he's been living here or has he made up a story about living somewhere else?"

Carla looked downcast, "He told me he was staying at his grandmothers."

Livvy smiled, "So, of course he couldn't take you home. You probably think you love him but you can't trust him. He's been lying to you all along because, when he's not with you, he's here with me. Maybe you think having his baby will force him to stay with you but it won't work. I feel sorry for you, I really do, but you're very young and you have your whole life ahead of you. You'll find someone else eventually."

Carla looked agitated, "No, I want Russ and he wants me. He tells me he loves me all the time and he wants this baby. I'm sorry, Livvy, but he says he doesn't love you anymore."

"Then why is he still here with me? Why is he lying to you all the time? I asked you here hoping Russ would be here too because he can't keep deceiving both of us. If we both confront him together he has to tell the truth." The minute she stopped speaking, Russ walked through the door into the kitchen and froze in his tracks. He looked visibly shaken and

Livvy could see that he was actually trembling. She looked up at him with disgust, "Well you finally returned and, as you can see, your girlfriend is here."

Russ now became angry "What the hell is going on? What are you doing here, Carla?"

"Livvy asked me here and I just found out you've been staying here all along. Now you can't lie anymore, you have to tell the truth."

Livvy nodded in agreement, "Yes, you have to make up your mind once and for all who you want, Carla and her unborn baby or Natalie and me."

Russ hesitated then smirked, "I don't know what I want. Maybe I don't want either of you."

"Oh, no you don't," cried Livvy, "this is it, Russ. You're not getting out of this, make up your mind."

She held her breath as she watched him hesitate, then slowly walk over to Carla and put his hand on her shoulder. Looking Livvy straight in the eyes, he said, "Okay you want the truth, I want, Carla."

At that moment, Livvy felt as though someone had stuck a knife in her back. She really hadn't expected him to choose Carla and she was outraged. She got up from the table and, pointing to the door, screamed, "Get out, both of you; just get out." Minutes later, in the pouring rain, she was throwing Russ's clothes out onto the front lawn while he watched helplessly from just down the street, with Carla at his side.

The very next morning, she received a phone call from Russ telling her he didn't mean a word he had said and still loved her and Livvy wanted with all her heart to believe him. She just couldn't let go. Russ didn't move in with Carla, as Livvy had expected, but moved in with a friend she had never met. He claimed his new friend, Norman, worked as a hairdresser in one of the salons he serviced and Livvy had already established that Carla was a hairdresser and she assumed that they probably knew each other. When she finally met Norman, she was surprised. He was funny and really taken with Natalie but he was obviously a homosexual, with bleached blond hair, and very effeminate.

Chapter Thirty

When Rachel wrote she wanted to come for a visit in August of 1962, Livvy was overjoyed but anxious about the situation with Russ and the conditions they were living in. Rachel arrived and was relieved to see that Livvy and Natalie appeared to be happy but she was upset when she found out where they were living. Because she was concerned about leaving Harry alone, she had only arranged to stay for two weeks but Livvy took a vacation from work so she could spend time with her mother. Ironically, just after Rachel returned to England was when Livvy really needed her. In early October, she thought she had the flu and was forced to take some time off, even though it was very unusual for her to be sick and never ill enough to stay at home. She was completely drained of energy and, when she looked in the mirror, her skin looked almost translucent. When she had been living in Toronto, prior to her return to England, Vivien had referred her to the family doctor. Dr. Freeman was born in Jamaica and had spent a lot of time in England but, on rare occasions, one could hear the musical lilt of the islands in his voice. He was a friendly and caring man and had treated every member of Baba's family. When Livvy called to see if he could visit her, he was away on vacation and his young assistant made the house call. He examined her and asked a lot of questions, finally determining she had a kidney infection and prescribing medication.

A week later, she was feeling a little better and decided to go back to work but she was concerned because, for no known reason, she was spotting slightly. That evening, she made an appointment to see Dr. Freeman and arrived at his office the next day just before noon. After examining Livvy he asked her to get dressed and come into his office so that they could talk and Livvy had a feeling something wasn't quite right. She smiled as she walked in the door. "Well Dr. Freeman, what's wrong with me?"

The doctor smiled back, his perfectly even teeth pure white against his black skin, "Well Livvy I think you have an ectopic pregnancy."

Livvy was shocked, "What does that mean?"

"It means you have a fertilized egg growing outside of the uterus in the fallopian tube and we have to remove it."

Livvy was so shocked she began to cry, "Oh my god, Russ and I are separated and I've only been with him a couple of times in the past few months, how could this happen?"

Dr. Freeman got up, came around his desk, and placed his hand on her shoulder, "Livvy, it doesn't matter how it happened but the point is something has to be done right away. Now, I'm not one hundred percent certain about my diagnosis so I'm sending you over to see a specialist this afternoon and he'll decide what to do next."

Dr. Edward Stone was a gynecologist with offices at the Doctor's Hospital and he ruled the nurses and interns under him with an iron hand, while treating his patients with care and compassion. He questioned Livvy extensively about her symptoms and, after examining her and noting her shocked reaction when he placed pressure on her lower right abdomen, he ordered her into the hospital that evening in preparation for an exploratory operation the next morning.

Livvy immediately called Russ and told him he had to take care of Natalie and he readily agreed, provided he could take her to stay at Norman's house. Under the circumstances Livvy had no choice and reluctantly turned Natalie over to him early that evening. Later that night after being admitted, as she was lying alone in a small dark room, she worried about Natalie and prayed that whatever was wrong was nothing serious and she would be released within a day or two. Over the course of the next two hours, a young intern returned a number of times to take her temperature and blood pressure and he became more agitated as time went on. When Livvy's temperature finally rose to 103 degrees and her blood pressure began to drop dramatically, he panicked and called Dr. Stone at home and the doctor reacted immediately. By midnight he was escorting Livvy to the operating room and yelling at the top of his voice while the intern and two nurses pushed the gurney at reckless speed and Livvy could only stare at the lights racing by overhead. After arriving in the operating room, for some reason, Livvy was perfectly relaxed and even joked with the anesthesiologist and, although her vital signs were spiraling out of control, she didn't feel any discomfort or any pain.

When she woke up, she was in recovery and her stomach felt heavy and extremely painful. She asked the nurse, who was hovering over her, what had happened and was told very gently that the doctor would explain everything to her after they had settled her in her room. An hour later she was being wheeled back along the corridor, moved from the gurney onto a bed, where they fussed over her, inserting an IV and taking her vital signs, and then she promptly fell asleep. On opening her eyes, Livvy blinked twice trying to make sure she wasn't hallucinating. Just near the foot of her bed, in a very large chair, sat an impish looking man with a broad smile on his face. He nodded at Livvy and then said in a lilting Scottish accent, "Hello me bonnie wee girl and how are you feeling now?"

Livvy was so taken aback by this strange little creature, she replied rather abruptly, "Who are you?"

"Why, I'm Angus Campbell, and what's your name?"

Livvy was really not up to answering questions and she groaned as she tried to raise herself up on the pillow, "Livvy Marshall."

"You poor wee girl, I ken see you're in pain but I have to tell you, you looked so beautiful when I saw them wheeling you along the hall with your face all painted up like a movie star."

Livvy couldn't help but grin, "You mean, I still have all my makeup on?"

"Yes, and you look pretty as a picture, not like a lot of the old biddies around here although that Dora in the next room is a fine figure of a woman even if she's a bit old for my liking".

Livvy winced but she couldn't help but laugh and then, suddenly, a nurse bustled into the room and seeing Angus pointed her finger at him, "Now Angus, you know you're not supposed to be in here. You go back to your room," then turning to Livvy she shook her head. "He's a patient in case you hadn't figured it out and he loves the ladies but you need your rest right now."

Livvy gave a feeble wave to Angus as he crept silently out of the door and wondered when the doctor would come. It was a few hours later when he visited Livvy and sat down next to her bed with a grim look on his face. He explained that they had found an abscess the size of an orange in one of her fallopian tubes and it had already ruptured, spilling its toxic contents throughout all of her reproductive organs and leaving them no choice but to remove everything.

Livvy was shocked but not upset, "You mean; I had a hysterectomy?"

"Yes," Dr. Freeman replied, "but we had to remove your ovaries and cervix as well and we'll need to put you on hormone replacement therapy but we can talk about that later. Right now, you have to concentrate on getting better. You're young and healthy and we just don't understand why you weren't experiencing severe pain when you were admitted."

"I didn't feel anything, "Livvy remarked, "in fact I felt much better than I did a week ago."

Dr. Freeman shook his head, "It's a miracle you decided to come and see me otherwise I don't like to think what would have happened."

"How did I get this abscess doctor?" Livvy asked.

"We're not really sure, but we have to assume it came from some kind of infection."

Livvy digested this information and tucked it away somewhere in the back of her mind then she grinned, "I guess this means no more cramps every month."

"You've got that right, Livvy," replied Dr. Freeman, smiling from ear to ear, "and you can have a lot of fun now because you don't have to worry about getting pregnant."

Livvy thought about that for a moment, "You know, doctor, I'm so glad I have Natalie, she's five now and I didn't want anymore children. I just want to know how long I'm going to be here and how long before I can go back to work."

"You'll be here for two weeks in the hospital and then you need to stay home for at least five more weeks to recover completely. You've had major surgery and you have a very large incision that needs to heal before you go back to your normal routine. I'll be back in to see you while you're here and Dr. Stone will be in later today."

Before he left, Dr. Freeman gave Livvy a hug and she thanked him for sending her to the specialist and probably saving her life.

The next two weeks Livvy spent in the hospital were surprisingly pleasant, except for the fact that she was in discomfort most of the time and because of an incident that occurred on the third night. It was almost midnight when the phone rang beside her bed and, when she picked it up, she heard a woman's voice telling her that Natalie had been left alone in the house while Russ and Norman had gone out on the town. Livvy was sure the woman was Carla but when she questioned her, she abruptly rang off. Now she was left agonizing over what to do and imagining the worst. She knew Norman's father also lived in the house but he was as deaf as a doorpost. If Natalie got up and wandered out of the front door, he wouldn't even hear her and she might be run over or get completely lost. Livvy painfully crawled out of bed and approached the nursing station where she broke down in tears but, when the nurse suggested she contact the police, she declined and went back to her room and began calling Norman's house every ten minutes. At two o'clock in the morning, Russ answered the phone and Livvy screamed at him demanding to know why he would leave Natalie alone and insisting he check and make sure she was alright. Russ made all manner of excuses, even claiming they had been home all the time but had the radio up so loud they didn't hear the phone and he feigned outrage that someone would call Livvy and make up a story. Livvy didn't believe a word and prayed for the day she could go home and take Natalie back with her. During those first two days in the hospital, Brenda and Victor, Matt and Gina, and some of the girls from her office visited her but she wasn't very good company. On the third day she felt a lot stronger and was walking the corridors, bent over and holding her stomach, but still making an effort while most of the other women who had less serious operations remained in their beds. Angus was recovering from a heart operation and doing well. He became a wonderful friend to Livvy and kept her spirits up, telling her stories about his strange assortment of relatives and constantly cracking jokes that had her laughing and wincing at the same time. One day he even climbed into bed with the fine figured Dora who giggled uncontrollably until her nurse arrived and ordered him out. Livvy actually shed a couple of tears when she said goodbye to some of the patients. She had grown close to many of them during her two weeks there and she was particularly sad to leave Angus but overjoyed to find Natalie waiting with Norman in the car when Russ picked her up.

The first five weeks at home were difficult. Rachel wanted to come back to Toronto to look after Livvy but she had only just returned to England and Harry needed her there. He was so distraught when he heard about Livvy's operation that, according to Rachel, he turned stone deaf for two days. Brenda was a good friend and spent the first two days and nights cooking and cleaning and looking after Natalie and, after she left, Natalie's babysitter brought over supper every day for the next week. Meanwhile, Russ was of no help and kept his distance knowing Livvy was still angry with him for being so negligent while she was in the hospital. Eventually she returned to work and, within two months, she was promoted to supervisor of the accounting department and given a considerable raise in salary. This prompted her to consider moving out of the basement apartment and Brenda suggested she move into the building where she lived in the Don Mills area. This was particularly appealing to Livvy as her company was relocating to Don Mills and she thought it would be an ideal place to bring up Natalie. The move was simplified by the fact that she had no furniture of her own but now she needed to invest in the basic necessities, so they could at least have somewhere to sit and sleep. Brenda donated a few items for the kitchen and, after purchasing a royal blue chesterfield suite, a bedroom suite with a queen size bed, and some additional kitchenware, Livvy had enough money in her savings account to buy a small television. The move gave her a deep sense of pride and independence knowing she had provided a new home for herself and Natalie but, in her heart, she still missed Russ and wanted her family back together again.

A French Canadian woman lived in the next apartment with her daughter Monique. Monique was exactly the same age as Natalie and they became fast friends and were enrolled in the same school. Often, while the two girls were playing together, Livvy would visit with Brenda who was now finally pregnant but terribly homesick and looking forward to going back to England for a few weeks after her baby was born. Livvy was now fairly content but constantly battled with Matt every time she spoke to him on the telephone. The conversation always turned to Russ, who Matt despised, and he chastised her for having anything to do with him. Everything came to a head one day when Matt happened to be driving downtown and saw Russ in his car accompanied by a woman. A confrontation resulted in Matt punching Russ and then being reported to the police, which was unfortunate because Matt had just applied to join the police force and they wouldn't tolerate that kind of behaviour. When Livvy heard about the incident, she immediately intervened and persuaded the police that Matt had been provoked and it was out of character for him to be violent. Her intervention paid off because Matt was accepted into the force, but it did nothing to heal his relationship with Livvy.

Russ finally broke all contact with Carla after she gave birth to a daughter and he persuaded Livvy to take him back. He had given up his job selling beauty supplies and was now a waiter in the restaurant of one of Toronto's finest hotels. Having to interact with other people for the last few years had changed Russ. He had developed into something of an extrovert and, as he and Livvy got to know more of their neighbours, he loved to host parties in the apartment. It seemed like every other weekend, Livvy was left to entertain while waiting for Russ to get home from his shift and supply liquor and food, which he had managed to salvage from the restaurant. Often he would bring home a whole filet mignon and, at midnight, it would be served up with baked potatoes and sour cream and fresh bread. After a while, Livvy became rather bored with the parties; the guests were always the same and flirting appeared to be on the agenda no matter who one's partner was. One married couple, Sally and Rod, who were from South Africa, were the life and soul of every party. Sally, although not very attractive in person, did some modeling and she was a lot of fun and Rod took a shine to Livvy but she didn't return any of his outrageous advances. Sally and Rod introduced Livvy to several of their other friends, Cal another South African, who was very handsome, and Liz who turned out to be a lesbian. They were an interesting group. Brenda refused to attend because she wanted nothing to do with Russ and, shortly after the birth of her son Jason, she took off to England for six weeks on vacation and left Victor behind.

As Russ had a lot of spare time during the day he took on another job driving a catering truck and he would often drive up to the apartment building and give out free cookies to the children playing outside. Natalie got a big kick out of the fact that all of her little friends swarmed around her father when he arrived and he made them all laugh with his teasing.

When Livvy had first moved to Don Mills, she had acquired a black and white cat which she named Topsy, after the cat she had when she was a small child, but she couldn't bear to see her sitting all alone every night when she got home and finally gave her away. Soon after Russ moved in, he brought home a puppy as a surprise for Livvy. The puppy was a black miniature poodle and Livvy named him Nicky but he was alone all day too, impossible to housebreak, and he cried incessantly so that the neighbours complained. Eventually, Livvy had to give him away and it upset her so much, she vowed she would never have another dog unless she had a house with a yard. Two weeks later, she woke up to find Russ kneeling at the side of her bed with a six week old Doberman puppy in his arms and although she found him adorable she just couldn't keep him.

Livvy desperately wanted to learn how to drive so that she could be independent and have some control over her anxiety attacks. Russ now owned a two-year-old yellow Thunderbird and Livvy spent hours practicing in the parking lot of the apartment building and on the quiet two-lane roads outside of the city. Eventually she felt secure enough to take a driving test but failed when she attempted to parallel-park and scraped another car. On her second attempt, she made another mistake at a stop sign and the instructor was not about to overlook the error. She never attempted to learn to drive again.

On weekends, during the summer months, they would go camping. Their favourite place was Wasaga Beach where they could drive along on the sand and pitch their tent near the edge of the lake. Livvy wasn't comfortable in the car on these long trips but she managed to control her anxiety and never once conveyed how she felt to Russ. Once at the lake, she loved every moment, cooking on an open fire, sleeping under canvas, swimming and sunbathing, and Natalie was in her element, taking to the water like a fish. One weekend they traveled for hours to Timagami where Russ's father was now working as a forest ranger. They were supposed to stay at his cabin, along with two other rangers, but when Livvy walked in the door and saw dishes piled high in the sink and dust everywhere, she persuaded Russ to come up with an excuse so that they could leave. George Walker was not pleased to hear that, after just arriving, they were already going back home and, the more he protested, the more Livvy realized what an obnoxious person he was. The trip to Timagami had been an ordeal for Livvy and she decided, without Russ's knowledge, to consult with a psychiatrist but her first appointment turned out to be her last and she was deeply discouraged. The psychiatrist diagnosed her as having a deep-seated problem with sexuality and drew her pictures of body parts, including genitals. Livvy was both shocked and angry and vowed never to go back.

It was during this time that Livvy met Maggie. Maggie had just been hired as the switchboard operator where Livvy worked and their friendship developed very quickly. Neither one of them had any idea that their friendship would last a lifetime. Maggie was tall, slim, attractive with bright red hair, and ten years older than Livvy. She lived with her husband and four children and, on the surface, was a happy outgoing person but Livvy soon discovered she had a terrible secret. Her husband abused her and while she made every attempt to cover up the signs of abuse, she wasn't always successful. Eventually, she separated from her husband and Livvy welcomed her into their circle of friends with Russ assuming the role of matchmaker.

Brenda returned from her trip to England deeply depressed. Livvy thought she would be cured of her homesickness, but she was wrong. Brenda was determined to return to England for good and tried to persuade Victor to go too but he refused and slowly their marriage began to crumble. Even the fact that Brenda became pregnant with her second child didn't deter her from her ultimate goal and, just after her second son was born, she left Canada and Victor for good. Livvy missed her friend, they had shared a lot together, but she resented the fact that Brenda had made no effort to accept Russ and in some respects it was a relief that she had decided to return to London. Meanwhile, Victor kept the apartment and became a frequent visitor in Russ and Livvy's home.

In the summer of 1964, Livvy suspected Russ was cheating on her with Sally but she had no real proof and then somebody else appeared on the scene. A friend of Sally's arrived for a projected visit and that's when life changed again for Livvy. Velma was rather short, a little on the stocky side and quite a bit older than Russ but she had her own home in Florida. Russ's attempt at being a responsible husband and father had run its course and he couldn't resist the idea of being foot loose and fancy-free and Velma was his ticket to a new life. Livvy was aware trouble was brewing but she wasn't prepared for what was to come. Six weeks after Velma arrived, she returned home from work one afternoon to find the apartment eerily quiet. She didn't expect anyone to be home but she sensed something was wrong and, when she discovered all of Russ's belongings were missing, she knew he had gone for good. In a state of shock, she confronted Sally who confirmed her worst fears; he had taken off to Florida with Velma. Livvy picked up Natalie, returned to the apartment, and tried to explain to her that her father had to go away for a while. Later in the evening Rod, Sally and Cal came to comfort her and Cal suggested that because she was so distraught, he should stay over and sleep on the sofa. Livvy was confused as she lay in her bed that night and almost prayed Cal would come in and make love to her. She so desperately needed someone to hold her but, the following morning, when she woke up; she was completely devoid of emotion as far as Russ was concerned. It was like a weight had been lifted off her shoulders. He was finally out of her life.

Chapter Thirty-One

During the next year, Livvy was supported by the friends she had made. Sally and Rod were good neighbours and Victor was often there with a helping hand. She dated often and spent a lot of time with Natalie who showed no evidence of missing her father. On only one occasion did she appear to be disturbed, when Livvy was late picking her up one night, and she reacted with what almost looked liked a seizure but Livvy soon reassured her she wasn't going anywhere.

The following year both Rachel and Harry came for a visit and Livvy took them sightseeing all over Toronto, then to Niagara Falls, and across the border to Detroit, and they even spent one idyllic day swimming in Lake St. Clair. It was during this time that Rachel began to talk about moving to Canada permanently and Harry seemed to go along with the idea. Later that same year, Livvy took Natalie to Atlantic City. This was their first real holiday together and the bond between mother and daughter became even stronger.

When Livvy's friendship with Maggie grew and Natalie became more involved with Maggie's children, she decided to move into an apartment in the same building on Esterbrooke Avenue. The building had an outdoor pool and Natalie was in her element in the summer months when she, and Maggie's youngest son Buddy, would swim for hours on end. One day Maggie introduced Livvy to an old friend who was visiting with her husband and children. Susan seemed like the typical housewife, a little overweight, and conservatively dressed, and at the time she made very little impression on Livvy. She would have been surprised to learn this woman would become a lifelong friend and an important element in her life.

Through Baba and Russ's family, Livvy learned Russ and Velma had moved to San Diego and were now living near Vivien who had remarried an American and moved there permanently. Russ sent greeting cards on birthdays, and at Christmas, but had very little contact with either Livvy or Natalie then, in November, just after Natalie's tenth birthday he suggested she come to San Diego the following summer and stay with him for a month. Livvy had no objection, she wanted Natalie to have a relationship with her father, but she didn't like the idea of her being away for so long. It was finally arranged that, after Natalie had been there for a week, Livvy would come down and stay in a motel with Natalie for two weeks then she would return her to Russ for the final week.

In April, prior to the San Diego trip, Livvy was to meet the man who would become, first a lover, and then a friend for the rest of her life. One night while bar hopping with a casual friend from her office, Livvy jokingly remarked that she could make the next man who came through the door, come over and speak to her. Her friend, Clare, watched with amusement when the door opened and two men walked in, the first one being of average height, average looking, but with a boyish face. Livvy quickly determined he was a suitable candidate for her little scheme and stared at him intently, never taking her eyes off him and, whether he sensed it or not, she suddenly found he was staring right back. Five minutes later he was introducing himself and offering to buy Livvy and Clare a drink. "Good evening ladies," he said grinning from ear to ear, "I couldn't help noticing you when I came in. May I buy you something to drink?"

Livvy smiled at Clare knowingly, "That's very kind of you, I'll have a scotch on the rocks please and I think Clare would like a Tom Collins, isn't that right, Clare?"

Clare nodded looking a little dumbstruck, knowing Livvy had enticed this man to their table so easily.

"My name's Dan Charette, may I sit down?" and without waiting for an answer he promptly pulled over a chair from the next table, inched up beside Livvy, and signaled for the waiter. He then nodded at Clare and said, "Well, I know your name, it's Clare but what's your name?" and he turned to Livvy staring intently into her eyes.

"I'm Livvy, Livvy Walker, is there anything else you'd like to know," she said teasingly.

"As a matter of fact there is. You sound English, are you?"

"Yes, but I've been here for twelve years."

Just then the waiter interrupted them and after Dan placed their order he asked him to take a beer over to his friend who was still sitting alone at another table.

"What's wrong with your friend?" asked Livvy "Why don't you ask him to join us?"

Clare glanced over at the friend and then kicked Livvy under the table.

"Nothing's wrong with him," Dan replied, "he's just not in the mood for socializing. He had a bad day at work and just wants to sit there and drink his beer."

"Don't you think you should keep him company?" asked Livvy.

"No he'll be fine for a while, anyway I think he's leaving soon as it's getting late."

Livvy looked at her watch, "Yes, it is getting late and it's a work day tomorrow so we'll be leaving soon too."

"I can drive you home," Dan offered.

"No, I couldn't ask you to do that, I live in Don Mills and Clare lives out on the Danforth. It's a nice night and we don't mind taking the TTC."

Dan continued unsuccessfully to persuade Livvy to let him drive them home but she finally gave him her phone number and agreed to see him again. Twenty minutes later outside of the bar, he took her hand and said, "Well, I guess this is goodbye for now but somehow I have a feeling I'll still know you when you're fifty." Livvy was a little stunned at this remark because it was said so intently. She imagined he probably said it to all the girls he met, but then again what if it really happened?

Chapter Thirty-Two

On her first real date with Dan, he took Livvy to a wonderful restaurant and they had just been seated when he remarked, "I'm so glad you decided to come out with me this evening, I've been thinking about you a lot."

Livvy frowned and picked up her napkin, placing it in her lap, "But you only just met me the other night for a very short time."

"I know, but I find you very attractive, I've never been out with someone who looks like you before."

"What do you mean?" Livvy grinned and shook her head. "Have all the women you've taken out been ugly?"

Dan knew Livvy was teasing and he grinned right back, "No, but they all seem to have been rather skinny."

Livvy thought this was getting funnier by the moment, "Are you implying I'm fat?"

Now Dan wasn't sure whether she was serious or not. "No, no, of course not, it's just that you look like the kind of woman every man dreams of going out with. You're blonde and have curves in all the right places; that's all I was trying to say."

Livvy was enjoying the attention. She knew her figure had changed dramatically after the birth of Natalie and she was no longer the flat chested teen that boys would sometimes make fun of, "Well, thank you Dan I'm very flattered." The waiter interrupted them to take their order and returned almost immediately with a bottle of Merlot. Once the wine was poured and they waited for the food to be served, Livvy asked Dan about his life and discovered he was separated with two small children. "I've only been separated for six weeks," Dan said swirling the wine in his glass, "and it's been hard because I miss the children. Ellen and I haven't been getting along for some time and we should never have had a second child."

"How old are your children?"

"Ben is five and Kelly just turned two. I get to see them every other weekend but don't often see them during the week because they live in Hamilton."

"Isn't there any chance of you and your wife getting back together?"

"No, I don't think so, all we seem to do is fight and that's no good for the kids."

Livvy was remembering her own childhood, being brought up in a home where her parents fought and knew it was not a healthy environment to be raised in, "I'm sorry, it must be very difficult for you. Where are you living now?"

"I have an apartment on Jamieson Avenue, it's only small but it's big enough for me. Maybe after we've eaten I can take you there for a nightcap."

Livvy wasn't sure how to answer and finally replied, "Let's see how the evening goes before we make any plans for later."

Dan looked disappointed, "Okay but I'll keep my fingers crossed."

They dined on Caesar salad, filet mignon topped with asparagus and bearnaise sauce, creme broulaise, and espresso coffee, and finished the whole bottle of wine between them. Livvy could hardly move but she felt wonderfully mellow and she was enjoying the company. When Dan again suggested they go back to his place she was feeling so comfortable with him that she agreed, even though she was aware that he probably expected her to sleep with him. The way things turned out, Livvy's first sexual experience with Dan was a bit of a disaster. He was so attracted to her and so eager that it was over in minutes and Livvy just wanted to go home. Dan was upset and tried to reassure her he really was a good lover and the next time would be so much better. Livvy wasn't even sure there would be a next time but she didn't know then that Dan would make her feel like a real woman for the first time in her life and make her realize how naive she had really been.

Two weeks after meeting Dan, he persuaded her to go to Ottawa with him for the weekend. Livvy had never visited the nation's capital and when Maggie offered to look after Natalie she eagerly looked forward to the trip although she was somewhat anxious about the long car ride. Dan was so attentive and so easy to be with that she felt little anxiety as they traveled north and she began to relax and enjoy herself. After they arrived at the hotel and checked in, Dan immediately suggested he take her to see the Parliament Buildings and other tourist spots and, although he had been there dozens of times before, his enthusiasm was contagious. Later that night after a wonderful dinner at one of the most popular restaurants, Livvy learned what it was really like to be made love to. Dan was the most sensual man she had ever encountered and they spent most of the next morning in bed before driving back to Toronto. She continued to see him two or three times a week and he introduced her to his children. Ben was a little aloof but Kelly was too young to really be affected by her parent's separation and she took to Natalie right away. For the most part, when the children came to visit, they would spend most of the time together and Dan always had something planned, like a visit to Riverdale Park, a movie, or a short road trip.

In July, Livvy put ten-year-old Natalie on a plane headed for San Diego. She was nervous letting her travel alone but the stewardess had already taken her in hand and Russ had assured her he would be waiting for her at the airport when she arrived. It was only when she got a phone call later that day to tell her Natalie was safely at Russ's house that she was able to relax. Then, one week later, Livvy was making the same flight south and she was overjoyed to see Natalie at the arrival gate with her father. Natalie was bubbling over with excitement, "Oh, Mom you should see the ocean and the beach, it's beautiful and Dad's got two dogs. They're boxers, Caesar and Max, and I just love them," then turning to her father she added, "Can Mom see the dogs please?"

Russ looked awkward, "Well, I'm not sure about the dogs but your mom can sure see the ocean. First of all we have to get you to the motel and get you settled in." He then directed his attention to Livvy, who he had embraced rather nervously when she arrived, "You're looking really good, Livvy, I hope you had a good trip. I got you a motel on the beach and it's just a short distance from my cafe, all you have to do is walk along the boardwalk."

Natalie interrupted, "Yes Mom, you should see Dad's place. I've been there nearly every day and Dad has this friend named Ratso who's really funny."

"I heard you opened a cafe, I'm looking forward to seeing it," said Livvy.

"Oh, it's not much; we just serve up fried chicken, salad and sandwiches, that kind of thing. It's really casual, mostly kids coming in off the beach for a bite to eat."

"Sounds great, I'm looking forward to seeing it and meeting Ratso of course," and she grinned at Natalie.

The motel room consisted of a bedroom with a queen size bed and a very small sitting room with a sofa and television. The decor left a lot to be desired but it was, as Russ had said, right on the beach. Forever after, Livvy would claim that the best holiday she ever had was the two weeks she spent with Natalie in San Diego. Nearly every minute was spent experiencing something new and seeing all the places she had only ever seen at the movies. After two days exploring the Mission Beach area and the San Diego zoo, renowned for it's collection of animals, they took a bus to Los Angeles and went on a guided tour of the movie stars' homes. Livvy stared in wonder at the grand houses of Jimmy Stewart, Lucille Ball and many of the most famous actors and actresses of the day. Natalie finally understood how she got her name when she placed her own tiny hands in Natalie Wood's handprints in the forecourt of Grauman's Chinese theatre. Just two days later they were in Tijuana, a seedy town just south of the border in

Mexico. Livvy saw another side of life right after they passed
through customs and noticed hundreds of run down shacks on
a hill and people in rags begging for money. Tijuana itself was
colourful and a popular tourist spot for visitors to Southern
California. The town relied on the tourists for its survival and
there were stalls everywhere selling serapes, sombreros, and
crafts made from wood and clay. One of the main attractions
was the bullfight but Livvy had no desire to see any animal
taunted and injured or possibly killed.

The night after their trip to Mexico, Livvy visited Russ's
cafe with Natalie. She had been there briefly after they had
first arrived but had not yet met the elusive Ratso. Russ was
efficiently throwing chicken legs and wings into a deep fryer
and serving up beer to the many young people perched on
stools along the counter and Livvy could see he was in his
element. When Natalie got tired, Russ took her into the back
room and settled her down on a mattress on the floor, where
she promptly fell asleep. It was a few minutes later when Livvy
met a few of Russ's friends, including Ratso who had inherited
his name because of his uncanny resemblance to Dustin
Hoffman in the film Midnight Cowboy. At ten o'clock when
the cafe closed, they all trooped into the back room where
Russ promptly offered pot to everyone. Sitting on the floor
in a chocolate brown jump suit and with her long blond hair
naturally frizzy from the dampness, Livvy felt perfectly at
home but she had never smoked pot before. "I don't do drugs",
she said. "Anyway your daughter is right over there and I don't
think you would be setting a very good example if she woke up
and saw you."

Russ rolled his eyes, "Come on, Livvy, lighten up, Natalie's
dead to the world and it's no big deal."

Ratso and the others echoed Russ's words and finally
goaded Livvy into joining them. Soon she started to relax and
found herself giggling at the most inane things and beginning
to feel at home with these people, who dressed like hippies
and talked endlessly about the Vietnam War and free love. It
was almost dawn when she was forced to wake Natalie up to go
back to the motel but they walked along the beach just as the
sun was about to come up and it was a glorious sight.

That afternoon, Natalie persuaded Livvy she just had to see the dogs at Russ's house but Livvy had no idea how she could possibly see them without running into Velma. When Natalie explained that the dogs were usually in the backyard and they would be able to see them through the fence, she reluctantly agreed to go. The house was a two story yellow brick, surrounded by tall palm trees and with a large back yard where Caesar and Max were running around on the grass chasing each other. "Look Mom," said Natalie pulling at Livvy's hand, "look through the fence. The bigger one is Caesar, isn't he beautiful?" Just as Livvy was admiring them, the two dogs, sensing their presence, came bounding towards the fence wagging their tales in excitement. "Hi Caesar, hi Max," Natalie whispered, "how's my boys?"

Livvy was getting nervous, sure that Velma might come out into the garden at any moment, "Come Natalie, we have to go. I don't want Velma to catch us here and I don't want your father to know we were here either."

Natalie slowly backed away from the fence, "Okay, let's go but Velma isn't so bad. I don't think she'd be mad at me."

"It's not you I'm worried about," said Livvy, "I haven't been invited and I'm not likely to be, so let's keep it our little secret."

That evening Russ took Livvy and Natalie out to dinner. They drove for a few miles up the coast and Livvy started to feel anxious again. She had seemed so relaxed traveling all over the place with Natalie but then she had been the one in complete control and she wondered if control was what her problem was all about. The restaurant, perched on a jetty right over the ocean, served seafood and although Natalie was not really keen on eating shrimp, lobster, or anything else on the menu, she contented herself with a giant sundae covered in nuts, chocolate sauce and cherries. When they arrived back at the motel, Natalie was tired so Livvy put her to bed and then joined Russ in the tiny sitting room. She was surprised when he produced a bottle of wine and filled the two glasses he had retrieved from the bathroom. Livvy took the glass he handed to her and sat down on the sofa, "I don't think I need anything more to drink, Russ."

Russ shook his head, "There you go again Livvy; you have to loosen up." "That's the second time you've said something like that in the last couple of days. Am I really so uptight, Russ? You know, when I first met you, you were pretty uptight yourself. You've changed so much. You like having a lot of people around you, and you've become quite a social animal."

Russ sat down beside her and took her hand, "You know, Livvy, I've always thought you were a great person. You're a good mother and I'm sorry I haven't been around for Natalie. It wasn't your fault we split up, it was my fault. I never learned how to be responsible for anything and I just couldn't handle it. I did what my mother always did, I ran away."

"But are you happy now, Russ?"

"Yes and no, Velma's a good woman, but I don't really love her. She was my way out and I guess I used her and I'm not proud of that. My life's pretty good though, I like living here and I like running the cafe. I don't know if Velma and I will stay together but who knows what's in the future?"

As the night wore on and they continued to talk it seemed like the most natural thing in the world for Russ to lean over and kiss Livvy lightly on the lips but it didn't end there. Since their separation both Russ and Livvy had experienced sex unlike any they had shared when they had been together and, on this night, they realized they were no longer the naive young couple they once were. Livvy had no regrets about sleeping with Russ and no expectations for the future. She decided to go on with her vacation as though nothing had happened.

The next day, Livvy and Natalie were on a bus traveling through the Mohave Desert to Las Vegas. The trip took seven hours but Livvy loved every minute of it. They stopped in Barstow for refreshments and it was over one hundred degrees but that didn't faze Livvy, she just wanted to take in every sight, sound, and smell around her. Mostly, all she could see was sand but it was all so new and, as they got closer to Las Vegas, there were giant billboards all along the route advertising the Sands, the Dunes, the Flamingo, and all of the hotels and entertainment venues. When they got to the city, they stayed in a small downtown hotel and immediately took the local bus to the Strip and it was magical. Livvy had never seen so many lights and it looked like a fairyland. They walked up and down surrounded by tourists and finally ended up in Caesar's Palace, where Natalie wasn't allowed in the Casino and had to wait at the entrance while Livvy kept one eye on her and one eye on the slot machine.

Two days before Livvy was due to leave San Diego they went to a Jimmi Hendrix concert at the new sports arena. Livvy had been determined to get tickets because Hendrix was a superstar and even though she wasn't fond of his kind of music, she knew it would be a once in a lifetime experience. The air was blue and Livvy thought they would both get high from the smell of pot that pervaded the stadium. There wasn't a vacant seat and the crowd went frantic, dancing in the aisles, chanting Jimmi's name and trying to get on stage. It was an experience Livvy never forgot and would recount to any guitar playing Hendrix fan she met.

On her last day, Livvy wasn't happy leaving Natalie behind but she knew she would be coming back home to her in a week and she was anxious to see Dan again.

Chapter Thirty-Three

Livvy stepped off the plane in Toronto looking like an advertisement for the USA. She wore navy and white vertical striped slacks and a tank top that appeared to had been made from the American flag. Her skin was a light bronze and her hair was blonder than ever and she felt fabulous. Dan, who was watching for her, spied her blonde hair through the crowd as she came through the arrival gate and ran forward eagerly. Livvy was surprised and delighted when he picked her up and swung her around before setting her down again, "Welcome home, Livvy, I really missed you."

"I missed you too Dan," she replied kissing him on the lips, "but I had the greatest time. I have so much to tell you."

Dan took hold of her hands and held her at arm's length, "I just want to look at you; you look beautiful. I can't wait to get you home and see if you're tanned all over!"

Livvy laughed, "You're bad, you're just going to have to wait, I need to unpack my things and I'm starving."

Dan pretended to sulk and then grinned broadly, "Okay, I can wait. I'll take you home and after you've unpacked I'll take you out to dinner at Carmen's"

Seeing Dan again made Livvy particularly happy, he was obviously delighted to have her back home again and he always made her feel so special.

One day in August, on a particularly sunny day, when everything seemed right with the world, Livvy got a call from Matt and she knew immediately something was terribly wrong. When she picked up the phone in her office that afternoon all she heard was, "Livvy?" and then his voice broke and he was sobbing uncontrollably.

"Matt, what is it, please tell me," Livvy asked anxiously gripping the phone and holding her breath.

Through the sobs, she finally made out the words, "It's Gina; she's got cancer."

Livvy was shocked, she knew Gina had been having stomach pains and was getting some tests but they had assumed it was an ulcer. When the doctor's couldn't determine what the problem was they had suggested she have an exploratory operation and discovered she had pancreatic cancer and it was terminal. Livvy immediately dropped what she was doing and went to her brother to both comfort him and see if there was anything she could do to help, but he was inconsolable. Ultimately he was going to have to face this ordeal alone.

In October, Rachel and Harry immigrated to Canada and Dan drove Livvy to Montreal to meet the ship. Livvy was overjoyed to see her parents waving frantically from one of the upper decks but, because of all the red tape, they were unable to wait to drive them back to Toronto and they arrived by train at Union Station the next day. Livvy had arranged for them to stay with her until they could get on their own feet but it proved to be a bit crowded in the apartment. Soon she found her life style, which now included Dan, was being severely cramped but she tried to make the best of it. At Christmas, she surprised her mother by inviting Rachel's oldest sister, Sadie, who now lived in Connecticut, to stay for a few days. Dan and Livvy picked Sadie up from the airport and when she walked through the door of the apartment Rachel was ecstatic.

During the holiday they visited Gina, whos condition was deteriorating rapidly. At one point, she had been allowed to go home but Matt was no longer able to look after her and she was back in the hospital. Livvy couldn't believe the woman lying in the hospital bed was the same vivacious woman she had once known. Gina was now a shadow of her former self, she had lost so much weight and her skin had a yellow cast. Every four hours the nurses would administer morphine but it wasn't enough to ease her suffering and when she cried out in agony, Livvy couldn't bear it and had to leave the room. Gina died in January and was cremated after a brief funeral service. That night, a fire from a neighbouring building lit up the sky near Livvy's apartment and the whole family stood at the window each wrapped up in their own memories of Gina.

Natalie was now ten years old and a delightful child. Harry found it hard to accept that she was the same unruly toddler he had been forced to contend with back in London, seven years before, and he enjoyed spending time with her. When he finally managed to get a job as a janitor in an apartment building and a free rental unit for himself and Rachel, it turned out to be bitter sweet. He was thankful for the work and the security it would bring but he missed seeing Livvy and Natalie every day.

In May, Dan invited Livvy to go to Bermuda with him. He worked for a national business forms company and was one of their top salesmen, dealing mainly with the health care industry, and the trip was a reward for those who had contributed the most to the success of the company during the past year. Livvy was apprehensive when she learned all of the other salesmen were bringing their wives and she felt her relationship with Dan might be frowned upon. "I'm not sure it's a very good idea, my coming with you," she remarked after thinking it over.

"Why's that?" Dan asked, wrinkling up his brow.

Livvy bowed her head then took his hand, "Look, Dan, you told me all of the other men are taking their wives and I'm sure most of them know your wife. They probably won't approve of me and I'm sure they won't like us sharing the same room."

Dan had never been one to follow the crowd and was amused, "Livvy, I don't care what anybody says or thinks. I'm proud of you and I want you to be there, imagine how miserable it will be for me if I'm there alone. You've heard me talk about my boss, Alan, well he's also a friend and he'll be there too. He's a great guy, I want you to meet him and I know you'll get along with his wife, Jeanine."

Livvy hesitated for two reasons; she was nervous about meeting new people and being thrown into a situation with them for five whole days, and she was anxious about the actual journey where she would no longer be in control, "I'd like to think about it some more, Dan, please can you wait until tomorrow for an answer?"

Dan was not happy but figured he could wait that long. "Okay, but I don't see what the problem is, Livvy."

Livvy was stalling for time but the next day she knew she had no legitimate reason for refusing Dan's offer and she finally gave in.

After leaving Natalie in Rachel's care, Livvy boarded the plane for Bermuda. All of the men had traveled down two days earlier to attend a seminar before enjoying their leisure time and she was forced to travel with all of the wives. She sat alone throughout the journey and had no idea which of the women was Alan's wife, Jeanine, but she preferred it that way. It had always been easier for her to travel alone where she had only to answer to herself and not be at the mercy of others. When they arrived at the small island airport and stepped off the plane, she could see Dan waiting among a crowd of other men and he was beaming from ear to ear. Livvy had dressed more conservatively than usual, so that she wouldn't solicit any negative comments from the other women, but she looked very feminine in a blue and white-checkered pinafore style dress with a sheer white organdie blouse. Dan greeted her with his usual enthusiasm and proudly introduced her to several of his colleagues, including Alan and his wife. Livvy found Alan to be a very mature, kind, and intelligent man and Jeanine, who was from Belgium, was similar in nature but much quieter.

Dan had arranged for them to stay at Harmony House, just steps from Gibbs Beach. The hotel consisted of several small villas and they were completely private, preferring to spend most of the time alone but occasionally meeting up with Alan and Jeanine for a few hours of swimming and sunbathing, or for a meal in one of the large hotel restaurants. The long, lazy days together brought Dan and Livvy closer as they spent hours lazing in the sun, playing in the ocean, or riding a moped all over the island. They both wished they could stay longer but, at the same time, Livvy missed Natalie and she was anxious to see her.

In July, the whole world was in awe when a man walked on the moon and Dan and Livvy joined hundreds of people in Nathan Phillips Square and watched the event on a giant screen. Toronto had changed since Livvy had arrived and the square, with its new city hall, which was built four years earlier, was now a focal point where people gathered and it now represented part of the revitalization of the city. The next day, everyone was buzzing with news of the moonwalk but, for Livvy, the euphoria of that time soon vanished when the following weekend Dan came to her with unexpected news. Livvy was dressing to go out to dinner when he arrived at her door an hour early. When she heard the buzzer ring in her apartment and heard his voice over the intercom she thought she had made a mistake about the time but, when she saw the grim look on his face, she knew whatever he had to say would not be pleasant.

"Hi, Livvy," he said hardly able to look her in the eye, "I need to talk to you."

Livvy turned, walked away from the door, and sat down on the nearest chair, "Well obviously this isn't going to be good. What is it, Dan?"

Dan came over and pulled her up from the chair. "You know how much I love you, don't you?"

Livvy pushed him away, "Don't beat about the bush, if you've got something to say, please say it."

"Okay, Livvy, I'm so sorry but Ellen and I have decided to try and make a go of our marriage for the children's sake.

We've talked it over and we know it's the best thing for Ben and Kelly, they need me in their lives and I do miss them."

Livvy was shocked and not ready to give Dan up without a fight, "What do you mean, they need you in their lives? You are in their lives, you see them every other weekend and you spend quality time with them. Do you really think living under the same roof as two parents who don't love each other is the best thing for them? Look at Natalie, she's the most normal child you know and she only has me, she doesn't need her father. You can't do this, please don't do this, Dan," she pleaded and her eyes filled with tears.

Dan put his arms around her and she buried her face in his shoulder, "Oh, Livvy, I do love you, really I do but I have to give my marriage a chance. Even though I don't love Ellen anymore, we're two civilized people and I think we can make this work."

"Does this mean you're going to give up your apartment and drive back and forth to Hamilton every night?"

Dan nodded, "We haven't worked out all the details yet but I suppose that's what will happen. I still have a few months left on my lease so I'll probably keep the apartment for a while. Look, Livvy, I know this is really hard on you but I've never made any promises and I know you'll find someone else although I don't really want to think about that."

Livvy pulled away and looked into Dan's eyes, "I don't want anyone else; I want you. We've had so much fun together and I can't imagine not seeing you anymore. Natalie's going to miss you too, she really likes you."

Dan sighed, "I know and I am so sorry, but this is the way it has to be. I promised Ellen I would spend tonight and the rest of the weekend with her and the kids so I'm going to have to go. I hope you will forgive me for causing you so much pain."

Livvy tried to hold back but couldn't help herself, "Please don't go, Dan, please stay a little while longer."

Dan took Livvy's face in his hands and kissed her gently on the lips, "I can't Livvy, I'm sorry," and he walked towards the door opening it slowly and repeating, "I'm so sorry."

Livvy watched him walk out of her apartment and felt such an overwhelming loss, she sank down onto a chair and sobbed until she was unable to shed anymore tears. She was thankful Natalie was staying at Maggie's for the night and she didn't have to face her; she just wanted to be alone.

She spent the next three weeks in a depressed state; she hadn't realized how much effect Dan had made on her life. He was an interesting man and a lot of fun to be with and the days seemed so much emptier without him. She had always wondered in the back of her mind if he would go back to Ellen and the children and had worried about his attraction to other women. He had a certain charm about him that others seemed to find appealing so there always seemed to be someone else on the scene whether innocent or not. Livvy had always tried to convince herself that he had never had time for anyone else because they spent so much time together, but now that didn't matter anymore. After three weeks had passed, Livvy realized she had to get on with her life and spend more time with Natalie, who also missed Dan and the weekend visits with Ben and Kelly. So, it was a complete surprise, when early one evening, Livvy heard a gentle knock on her apartment door and opened it to see him standing there with Gary, one of his associates from work. She looked from one to the other but didn't speak. There was an awkward silence until Gary said, "I think I'll leave you two alone," and took off down the hallway.

Dan shifted nervously from one foot to the other and then asked, "Can I come in please, Livvy?" Livvy still didn't speak but opened the door and stood aside while he entered the apartment. "I know you're wondering why I'm here. I was going to phone you first but I thought I'd have a better chance coming to see you."

Livvy had followed Dan into the room and stood protectively with her arms crossed, "A better chance at what?"

Dan gestured towards the chesterfield, "Please sit down. I need to talk to you." Livvy slowly sat down and, after sitting down beside her, Dan attempted to take her hand but she pulled away from him. "Oh, Livvy," he said shaking his head, "I made a big mistake. I really thought Ellen and I could work things out. I told you I didn't love her anymore but I thought it would be best for the children but I was wrong. I've been so miserable and you were right, the environment is bad for Ben and Kelly, they're better off with an absent father who sees them every other weekend and can enjoy them. Being away from you, I realized how much you meant to me and I hope it's not too late for you to forgive me."

Livvy's eyes had filled with tears as he spoke but they were tears of happiness, "I'm sorry for the kid's sake it didn't work out but I'm not sorry to see you here. I missed you as much as you missed me and Natalie missed you too, she will be so happy when I tell her."

Dan edged closer to her and took her in his arms, "Where is Natalie?" he asked.

Livvy laughed, "She's just outside playing and should be home any minute so don't get any ideas."

"Who me?"

"Yes you, I know how your mind works."

This was the kind of banter that made Livvy's relationship with Dan such fun. He was a very sensual man and showed it at every opportunity. He had a great deal of respect for women and particularly admired any female he considered to be intelligent and hard working. In Livvy, he seemed to find all of the attributes he was most attracted to and he felt relieved that she had decided to take him back and overlook the pain he has caused her.

Chapter Thirty-Four

In April 1970, Russ flew to Toronto to see Livvy. They met in a restaurant without Natalie's knowledge because they didn't want to subject her to any unpleasantness. Russ was seeking a divorce and wanted Livvy to sign the papers so that he was free to remarry. He had split up with Velma and was involved in a serious relationship with a woman he had met while investigating the possibility of starting up his own catering business. Livvy had no issue with setting Russ free and wished him well. Although nervous when he first walked through the door of the restaurant, she soon realized that while she felt a bond with him because of Natalie, she no longer had any romantic notions about him. Ironically a month later, Livvy found herself in Dan's apartment, sitting on a rumpled bed, while Dan's wife and her current boyfriend stood silently in a corner of the room. Ellen wanted a divorce on the grounds of adultery and Livvy agreed to set up a scenario, which both Ellen and a witness could attest to having observed, as proof of an adulterous affair.

During the next few months Dan attempted to persuade his company to set up a division dedicated specifically to health care and, when they rejected his suggestion, he considered the idea of leaving and starting up on his own. He knew his clients relied on him for his knowledge in their specialized field and gambled on the fact that some of them would want to retain his services. In August 1970, he moved to an apartment on Wellesley Street, close to many of the hospitals he had been calling on, and two months later he quit his job and set up his own business, working from his home. While he was an excellent salesman and had good negotiating skills, he had no knowledge of finance or accounting and decided to hire a part-time clerk to help him out. Livvy wasn't surprised when she discovered his first employee was a young and very attractive Asian girl named Alice, with long black hair that fell like a curtain almost to her waist. It didn't take her much longer to realize Alice was not very bright and her duties also included making Dan lunch, doing his laundry, and possibly providing other fringe benefits. Livvy suspected this was not the first time Dan had cheated on her and she didn't really know why she accepted the situation except for the fact that they spent so much time together, she enjoyed his company, and didn't want to lose him. When she finally found a long black hair in Dan's bed, she confronted him angrily, "I knew something was going on, what's this?" and she held the hair directly in front of his nose.

"What are you talking about?" Dan replied defensively "What's that?"

"Well, your hair is fair and short and mine is blonde so I guess this could only belong to somebody else and the only person I know with hair like this is Alice," Livvy spat out sarcastically.

Dan walked away, "I don't know how it got there; maybe it fell out when she changed the sheets."

"Oh, so she changes sheets now and I suppose that means she does the laundry too? She's supposed to be keeping the books and from what I see she's not doing a very good job. You're not making enough money to even pay her so there must be some other reason why you have her here."

Dan knew he'd been cornered, "Well, what do you suggest I do? I need someone to do the books and I wish I could offer you the job but I can't afford to pay you what you earn now."

Livvy was surprised at this turn of events but wasn't about to let him off the hook so easily, "Well, isn't that convenient. Obviously you can't be serious, would you really like me to work for you?"

Dan nodded and took hold of both of Livvy's hands, "Yes, of course, it would be great working together. Ever since I've known you, I've admired the way you've always taken your job so seriously and never even thought twice about working overtime. Look at all the hours you spent moonlighting in the keypunch department just to make some extra money so life would be easier for you and Natalie."

Livvy moved away and sat down with a thoughtful look on her face. Although she was happy with her job, the idea of being with Dan and disposing of the likes of Alice held a great deal of appeal. After what seemed to Dan like an eternity, she looked up and smiled, "Maybe we can work something out, let's try and see what we can come up with."

A month later, Dan discovered a business acquaintance, Gary Kennedy, had also started up his own business and was looking for help, but couldn't afford to pay someone full time. Dan suggested they both use Livvy and split her salary and then she would be earning the same as in her current job. Livvy gave the idea a lot of thought. She had long-term security where she was and a lot of benefits but, after ten years, her work had become mundane and she was eager for a challenge. At the beginning of April, she handed in her resignation and while her colleagues were shocked she was leaving, they all wished her well. Maggie was particularly sorry to see her go but they had become such good friends they knew Livvy's departure would not affect their relationship and they would continue to see each other socially. On April 30th, she walked out of the building where she had worked for so long, feeling the weight of the world had been lifted from her shoulders. She had no idea then how difficult it would be going from a company with four hundred employees to working with two people who were rarely ever around.

She found Gary to be very easy going. He was happily married with two children, lived in the suburbs, and had a regular job as the advertising manager for a large pharmaceutical company. A friend had got him interested in a sideline selling playboy products through the mail. For Livvy, this was a dramatic departure from the kind of work she was used to but it proved to be a fairly simple process. Dan had rented a very modern one-room office in the upscale Bloor-Avenue Road area of the city and this was the perfect setting for Gary to showcase his products that included desktop games, paperweights, keys etc. and a rather large executive sandbox that served as a coffee table. Occasionally clients would drop in and, on one occasion, a rather eccentric and flamboyant movie crew arrived to determine whether they could use anything for the new film they were producing. Working for Dan was another matter and it opened up a whole other world to Livvy. Very quickly she was forced to learn how business forms were manufactured and how to deal with health care clients on the telephone. In the first week, when Dan would run in and ramble at her, she had no idea what he was talking about and ended up in tears one night because she felt so inadequate. The following week, when she realized Dan was inept at giving instructions and very gray in his approach to everything, she decided to take matters into her own hands and do what made the most sense to her. Her instincts soon proved to be right and it wasn't long before she began to enjoy what she was doing, although being alone most of the day was difficult to deal with.

After the first month Dan decided they needed a break and they took a long weekend away in Quebec, chasing Dan's family tree. It was an enlightening experience for Dan and, in their travels through the countryside searching through records and talking to the locals in the small town of Saint-Anicet, he discovered he was the descendant of a french cardinal named Bernard. Work was completely forgotten and the whole trip was a welcome change for Livvy, but she was not comfortable with all of the driving and vowed to seek help for her anxiety problem when she got back to Toronto.

Soon after the trip to Quebec, Livvy helped organize setting up a booth, to exhibit Gary's playboy products at an exhibition on the CNE grounds. This was a whole new experience for Livvy and, for two whole days, she was surrounded by people rather than being shut away in her tiny office on Bloor Street. During her absence, Dan took the opportunity to fly to Austin, Texas to negotiate a deal with a company that sold stock forms to nursing home facilities throughout the United States. He managed to persuade the company to give him exclusive rights to resell in Canada plus a thousand brochures, free of charge, and he committed to purchasing a small supply of each of the forms they produced. When the cases arrived at his apartment, he hardly had room to move and he and Livvy spent fourteen-hour days compiling mailing lists, making labels, and transporting brochures to the post office, to be sent to nursing home facilities across Canada. When orders started coming in, they were overwhelmed and, eventually, Dan realized he could afford to pay Livvy himself and no longer needed Gary's help. Within a week Livvy stopped selling playboy products and became totally involved with Dan's business.

Despite the demands on her time Livvy had already made up her mind to seek out a hypnotherapist who used methods to reinforce positive thinking. When she entered the office of Dr. Martin Silverman she had no idea what to expect. Dr. Silverman was a short, slightly overweight man of about fifty with dark hair, piercing dark eyes, and a rather unsmiling face. He listened while Livvy told him about her history and her reason for being there and he immediately decided that not one word she said from then on could be negative. When the word 'No' wasn't allowed in her vocabulary Livvy, being a realist, knew she had had enough and, after three more visits, decided not to go back. During this time, when she was so caught up with work and trying to solve her anxiety problem, she experienced her first conflict with Natalie. Now age fourteen, Natalie was becoming a young woman and starting to feel her need for independence. Livvy had always been very lenient except for the fact that she would not allow Natalie to answer her back or be disrespectful and so far she had been a model child. She had adopted the dress currently worn by most teenagers, ripped jeans that dragged on the floor, despite being worn over clunky shoes with platforms almost two inches high, but Livvy had no problem with that. In the last few months she had become close friends with a girl in her class who was the total opposite in so many ways. Kathy was tall with long unruly red hair, freckles, and extremely extroverted. Her parents, who had adopted her when she was two years old, were very British, and very strict. Their parenting skills left a lot to be desired and Kathy decided to rebel at a young age and was already quite heavily into drugs. While Livvy felt assured Natalie would not be influenced by Kathy to take the same path, she felt she had to place some restrictions on her and insisted she be home by ten o'clock every night, including weekends. One night, when Natalie casually strolled through the door, almost an hour late, Livvy decided she had to put her foot down. She didn't wait for Natalie to get very far before she cornered her, "Have you seen the time young lady?" she asked.

Natalie pouted then shrugged her shoulders, "It's not very late."

"I didn't ask you that," Livvy said, annoyed at Natalie's casual attitude, "you have a curfew and you're supposed to be in by ten. I don't care where you've been or what excuse you come up with I expect you to be in on time."

Natalie turned her back on her mother. "It's not fair and you're being mean, other kids don't have to go home so early."

Livvy grabbed Natalie by one shoulder and spun her around, "Don't answer me back, you'll do as you're told."

Natalie pulled away and staring her mother directly in the face replied, "Leave me alone, I don't have to do what you tell me."

Livvy was so shocked that, for the first time, she lost control and slapped Natalie across the face, "Yes, you do have to and if you can't, then you can just leave right now." Even as she said it Livvy knew she was taking a gamble but she couldn't seem to stop herself. She was even more shocked when Natalie walked towards the front door and said, "Okay, I'll leave," and suddenly she was gone.

Livvy wasn't sure what to do next, it was now after eleven o'clock at night and Natalie had gone off in the dark. She sat down at the kitchen table and tried to think through what had happened and then came to the conclusion that Natalie would have gone directly to Kathy's house, which was only a short distance away, and Kathy's parents would probably phone her. Even an hour later, when she didn't hear anything, she was convinced Natalie was safe and would come to her senses. In any event, she had to stick to her guns and make sure Natalie knew exactly who was in charge. She spent a rather sleepless night tossing and turning and was worried when she hadn't heard anything by early the next morning then, at ten o'clock, the phone rang and it was Natalie. Livvy decided to pursue her tough love approach, "What do you want?" she asked abruptly.

Natalie sounded rather meek, "I want to come home," she said.

Livvy decided to make her position as clear as possible, "In that case, you make sure you're here by three o'clock at the very latest, either to pick up your things and leave for good, or to stay and change your attitude. What's it going to be?"

There was only a slight hesitation and then in a very quiet voice Natalie answered, "I want to come home to stay."

"Okay," said Livvy abruptly, "I'll see you later."

When Natalie finally arrived early in the afternoon, Livvy gave her a hug and they never discussed what had happened. Natalie immediately reverted to being the obedient child she had always been and forever after, mother and daughter only ever had one or two cross words and they respected each other enormously.

In order to be nearer to her work, Livvy decided to move closer downtown and rented an apartment in the St. Clair/ Yonge area, close to the subway line. At the same time, Dan decided he could no longer continue to store inventory in his home and the office was much too small to use as a warehouse. He found an ideal spot, not too far from their current premises, in the basement of a furrier shop. There was a large main office which could be used as a reception area, a smaller office, and a huge backroom with a great deal of shelving where they could store all of their forms inventory and supplies. It didn't take Dan long to realize it would be much more lucrative if they produced their own forms in Canada and stopped importing them from Texas. Within weeks he had purchased a small printing press, hired a pressman, and installed them both in the back room. They were now able to manufacture most of the sheet fed forms they sold, including those being purchased by Dan's hospital clients, while the balance they continued to contract out to other printers. Both Dan and Livvy were still working long hours and found the effort of building a business stressful but they enjoyed the challenge and, when Dan acquired the order to design and manufacture all of the forms for a new hospital soon to open in the west end of the city, they were ecstatic.

Chapter Thirty-Five

In the early spring of 1972, after having worked so hard for so many months, Dan and Livvy attended a conference in Washington DC and then took some time to do some sightseeing. Livvy never imagined she would find herself inside the White House and be exposed to some of the most famous monuments in the world, like the Lincoln and Jefferson Memorials. They spent hours in the Smithsonian Institute, walked through Arlington Cemetery, and bowed their heads in respect at the grave of John F. Kennedy. Livvy couldn't have wished for a better travel companion. Wherever they went, Dan made what they saw more interesting because of his thirst for knowledge and his passion for history. Two months later, they took a trip to New York City and visited Livvy's cousin, Jeanne, who lived there with her husband, Sam, and their baby daughter, Sara. Once again, Livvy experienced the joy of being with someone like Dan who absorbed all the sights and sounds and who made the visit so memorable.

After the trip, Livvy was to experience one of the saddest days of her life when Harry suddenly had a stroke. When Rachel called Livvy at work she was already at the hospital where Harry had been taken by ambulance, "Livvy, its Mum" she whispered into the phone, "I'm at the hospital. Dad fell out of bed and can't move or speak, I think he's had a stroke."

"Oh, Mum" Livvy cried, "I'll come right away. Have you called Matt?"

"No, but I'm going to try and get hold of him now or leave a message for him."

"Okay, Mum, tell me exactly where you are and I'll get Dan to drive me over or take a cab."

Fortunately, Dan was in his office and, after Livvy knew exactly where to find Rachel, she rushed in to ask him to take her to see her father. Dan was always the kind of person to react immediately when there was any kind of crisis. He could be relied on to do anything to help but, once he knew things were under control, he tended to step back and bow out of any difficult situation. He grabbed his jacket with one hand, grabbed Livvy's arm with the other, and pushed her out the front door while yelling to the pressman to watch the phones. Once in the car, he patted her knee trying to reassure her, "I'm sure he's going to be okay, Livvy, he's only sixty-eight and they got him to the hospital right away. If it really is a stroke, it may take some time for him to recover but they have so much physiotherapy now and they can do wonders."

Livvy tried to hold back her tears, "It's my fault; my dad never really liked it here, they should have stayed in England but I encouraged them to immigrate."

"Now that's ridiculous, Livvy, they've been here for four years and I've never heard your dad say he didn't like it here. From what you told me about him he never had any friends or family in London anyway and here he's had you and Matt and Natalie, so don't ever blame yourself for anything."

Livvy hunted in her purse for a tissue to dry her eyes before she saw her mother and nodded, "I guess you're right but what are they going to do now? He can't work as a janitor anymore and they'll have to give up their apartment and move somewhere else. They don't have much money and I don't know how they'll manage."

"First of all, we have to see exactly what the situation is and if they are having financial difficulties maybe we can find a little job for your mom. We're getting busier and I know you could do with some help."

Livvy was so grateful for Dan's support, "Thank you, Dan, I really appreciate you wanting to help. I don't know what I'd do without you."

The prognosis for Harry's recovery was not good. When he was eventually released from the hospital, his right side was partially paralyzed. He had to wear a brace on one leg, his arm was virtually useless, and his speech was impaired. In addition he had lost a great deal of weight and looked like a shell of the man he used to be. Livvy would look at her father and remember, when she was a child, how she would look up at him and think he was the most handsome man in the world and now she felt tremendously sad. There was no question, Harry would never be able to work again and Rachel was forced, with Dan, Livvy's and Matt's help, to move into a new apartment in another building. When Dan suggested he might be able to find some work for her, Rachel insisted that they could manage and she couldn't possibly leave Harry alone to fend for himself.

These were difficult days for Livvy emotionally but she had support, not only from Dan but also from her friend Maggie who had the most empathetic nature of anyone Livvy had known. It was during this time that Maggie met the love of her life but she would confront a lot of heartache before she found real happiness. Byron Cummings was a teddy bear of a man with a shock of fair hair, a round boyish face and eyes that twinkled when he smiled, which was often. He was the kind of person who endeared himself to everyone who knew him and Maggie was swept off her feet the first time she met him. Unfortunately Byron was married, with two grown children, and a seven-year-old daughter who was severely overweight just like his wife, Gwen. It would take two years for Byron to resolve his relationship with his family, finally leave Gwen, and commit to Maggie for the rest of his life.

Matt was also discovering a new romance and, when he met Kathy, he fell head over heels in love. Kathy already had a son from whom she was estranged but Livvy never got to hear the details of Kathy's former life. She liked Kathy well enough but found her a little self-absorbed. She was always concerned about her appearance and always went to bed in full make-up, which probably accounted for the fact that her skin was not in the best condition for a woman of only thirty-seven. Despite her reservations, Livvy was happy for her brother who had only had one short serious relationship with anyone since Gina died.

In the spring, Dan and Livvy spent an idyllic weekend visiting his oldest friend, Alan, and his wife, Jeanine, in Montreal. They welcomed Livvy with open arms and accepted her as the new love in Dan's life, even though they had been close to his wife. Because Dan had to remain in Montreal on business, Livvy flew home alone and was surprised when the flight attendant passed her a note addressed to the occupant of seat 5B. Whether it was the black turtle neck, combined with her black mini skirt, and her long blonde hair, it appeared that the gentleman in seat 20F who had sent the note was under the impression she was the infamous Xavier Hollander, author of The Happy Hooker. He was anxious to meet her and wanted to arrange a speaking engagement for her at the University of Western Ontario. Livvy was both amused and mortified and didn't dare look behind her. As soon as they landed in Toronto she exited the plane as quickly as she could and melted into the crowds at the airport. When Dan heard about it, he found great pleasure in recounting the tale to nearly everyone he met. He was proud of Livvy and liked to show her off to his friends, acquaintances, and even business associates. When he found a picture in a current issue of Playboy magazine that closely resembled her, he showed it to a particularly lecherous individual, who happened to be a client, and claimed it really was her. She spent years attempting to deny it.

By the summer, Livvy decided she needed to get away and took Natalie on a trip to the Bahamas. They stayed in Nassau and spent their days swimming and sunbathing and just being together. Natalie was no longer a little girl and Livvy enjoyed being with her more and more as the years passed. She realized too, on this trip, being in control of almost everything that happened helped to alleviate any anxiety she had. She often wondered if she would be better off without a man in her life and able to make all of her own decisions, but her love and affection for Dan far outweighed any further thoughts in that direction. Soon after their return from Nassau, during the new school term, Natalie met Robert Quinn. Robert was two years older than Natalie and was the youngest of a large family. His mother had walked out of the marriage years earlier and he now lived with his father in a large house in the east end of Toronto. Livvy didn't expect this relationship to last and expected Robert to be the first in a long line of boyfriends. She would not have believed then how wrong she would turn out to be.

The following year was difficult. The business was growing and both Dan and Livvy were still spending long hours working. At the same time Livvy was aware that an ominous figure had appeared on the scene that was disrupting their personal lives. Whether Dan had encouraged the relationship or not, Livvy had no way of knowing, but it was obvious that one of his female clients, Judy Callaghan, had become completely enamoured of him and was out of control. She telephoned the office constantly, pretending to be someone else so that Livvy wouldn't recognize her. She waited outside the office for Dan, hiding behind cars parked on the street, and she even appeared at his apartment door one day when Livvy was there and she was obliged to chase her up the stairs to get rid of her. Livvy was infuriated with Dan because he treated Judy with kid gloves and Livvy, believing in tough love, thought he should be firm and tell her to stop harassing him. Eventually Judy moved away but, within a few months, Livvy became suspicious about the connection between Dan and another client, Diane Barrows, whom she had always found to be very soft spoken and particularly pleasant to deal with. Diane was, apparently, involved with one of the men she worked with but that didn't stop Livvy from picking up clues that there was more going on than business between her and Dan.

During this time, they hired another salesman, Jim Doyle. Jim was Irish through and through and he looked it, short and stocky with jet-black hair, and blue eyes. He was married, had very strong views about morality, and thought himself totally inept when he first started to learn about the forms business. It didn't take him long, however, before he became a competent addition to the team and despite his brash manner he created some close associations with many clients.

When Livvy wasn't at the office or checking in on her parents, she tried to spend time with Natalie but she found Natalie had her own agenda and was heavily involved with Robert and his family. She was surprised when Dan suggested, now that Jim was capable of running the store, they should consider taking a vacation over the Christmas holidays. She was even more surprised, and a little perplexed, when he suggested they go the London as she had given up any idea of seeing her hometown again. When she returned to Canada, with Natalie sixteen years earlier, she had experienced a recurring nightmare for months where she was trapped in London and couldn't get out and she always woke up with a sense of profound relief that it was only ever a dream. Because Dan had never been abroad before, and he was so excited about the prospect of seeing all the places he had only ever read about or seen in the movies, Livvy finally but reluctantly agreed to go. She felt guilty about being away from Harry, Rachel and Natalie at Christmas but they assured her they would all be fine and she deserved to take this time for herself.

She wrote to her Aunt Cissy, who she had been closest to when growing up, and told her they would be staying at the Regent Palace Hotel in Piccadilly Circus but would love to come and visit with her on Christmas Day. Cissy immediately wrote back to tell her that her Uncle Leslie would pick them up and drive them out to their house and the whole family was anxious to see her again. A few days before Christmas, Dan and Livvy were sitting on the marble floor of the Toronto International Airport along with dozens of other passengers waiting for news of their departure time. It was ironic that, after Livvy's experience with the infamous London fog, they were now being delayed by heavy fog in Toronto. Livvy was so stressed out by the delay, she couldn't relax any longer and spent the next few hours pacing and running to the bathroom every half hour. When they finally heard that they were being bussed to Montreal she was a nervous wreck and didn't know how she would ever cope with such a journey, which would take at least five hours. It took all of her courage to climb on board the Voyageur coach but she settled down when she realized there were washroom facilities on board. They eventually reached Dorval Airport, almost six hours later, and were immediately set up in a hotel to await their flight the next day.

Dan was particularly upset and exhausted. He had been having a problem with lower back pain and at this point could hardly walk so when they returned to the airport the following morning, Livvy arranged for him to be transported onto the plane in a wheelchair. Another delay, when a catering truck damaged the plane they were ready to board, sent them back to the hotel until early afternoon. They finally arrived in London at five o'clock in the morning, when it was still dark but surprisingly mild for December, and they took a taxi to their hotel and immediately fell into bed for a few hours.

When Dan woke up he was in an even worse state but bravely insisted they should take a quick tour of the West End and, when he finally hobbled out of the hotel entrance and found himself in the middle of Piccadilly Circus, he stood there in awe. "I can't believe I'm here, this is amazing," he said leaning against Livvy for support.

"I know, Dan, and there's a lot more to see but we're not going anywhere with you in this state. I'm going back to the desk and I'm going to see where we can rent a wheelchair and then I can wheel you all over London."

An hour later, after hailing a taxi, they found a shop on Regent Street that supplied all types of devices to assist the disabled and true to her word; Livvy was soon wheeling Dan through Westminster Abbey, St. Paul's Cathedral, Trafalgar Square and the Tower of London. The wheelchair proved to be a benefit on two occasions when they were allowed to precede a four hour line up at the British Museum to see King Tut's tomb and they were placed at the front of a crowd of onlookers at Buckingham Palace, by two jovial members of the British police force. At the museum, Dan was so overwhelmed by the sight of the original copy of Chaucer's 'Canterbury Tales' that tears came to his eyes and they had the good fortune to see all of the members of the royal family leaving the palace for Windsor Castle, to celebrate the holidays.

On Christmas morning, after Livvy's uncle met them at the hotel and drove them home, Livvy saw some of her relatives for the first time in years. Along with her Aunt Cissy, her cousin Angela, and her husband, her other uncle had also arrived with his wife, Betty. Dan was welcomed with open arms by everyone and he was touched by the hospitality he received but he was in a lot of pain and was eventually forced to seek refuge in a bedroom, where he could lie down and rest.

The following day Livvy took the train to Aldershot, about an hour outside of London, to make a surprise call on her old friend Brenda. She took the chance that Brenda still lived at the same address where she had last been in contact with her, but it had been several years since they had spoken. Dan was left behind to spend most of the day in bed to try and recover but Livvy assured him she wouldn't be too long. When she arrived at 140 Campbellford Road, it was Brenda's mother who came to answer her knock. When she saw Livvy, she hesitated for a moment and then recognition dawned and her mouth dropped open,"Oh my God, it's Livvy!" and she immediately turned her head and yelled, "Brenda, come quick, look who's come to see you."

In the dark hallway Livvy could just make out Brenda's shape as she crept tentatively forward to see who had arrived on their doorstep but when she saw Livvy she broke into a run and threw her arms around her. "Livvy!" she screamed, "I can't believe it's you. What are you doing here? How did you find me?"

Livvy hugged her friend and laughed while Brenda's mother stood watching the reunion with a huge grin on her face, "I'm here on holiday and just took the chance of coming to the last place I'd heard from you. Of course you could have been off in Timbuktu by now, why didn't you answer my letters?"

Brenda looked shamefaced, "I'm sorry Livvy, you know I was never any good at writing and so much has happened. Look, don't stand on the doorstep, come inside and we can talk 'til the cows come home." She then turned to her mother,

"Mum, don't just stand there, you'll catch your death, why don't we all go inside and have a cup of tea."

Once in the house, Brenda brought Livvy up to date on her life. She had remarried and now had three children, all boys, and she was very happy. Her new husband worked as a real estate agent and Brenda was anxious for Livvy to meet him, "Len will be home soon for his dinner, that's lunch to you," she said smiling, "he's been so good to me. I told him all about you and everything that happened in Toronto so he'll be so pleased to see you. Anyway enough about me; tell me all about what's been happening to you."

While Mrs. Buckley fussed with tea and cookies, Livvy told Brenda all about her relationship with Dan and how much Natalie had grown and changed into such an attractive young lady. They spent the next half hour pouring over photos and then taking pictures of themselves with the new camera Livvy had brought with her on her trip. She never got to meet Brenda's children, as they were all still in school, and she had to get back to London but she did meet Len and found him to be a very quiet and gentle man who appeared to be delighted to meet her. Before Livvy left the house, they arranged to meet in the West End the next night and have supper at one of the most popular restaurants. By the time she got back to the hotel it was almost five o'clock and she was surprised to see Dan sitting in the lobby dressed up in a suit and tie waiting for her. He was clearly upset that he had been left on his own for so long but he soon changed his attitude when she ran to the room and returned in less than five minutes, dressed and ready to see the town.

The next afternoon Livvy paid a visit to the hotel hairdresser and had her long blonde hair washed and set. To achieve the latest style of the day, they wrapped her hair around her head and blow-dried it so it fell straight and shining past her shoulders and when Dan saw her later, dressed in a new black miniskirt and white lacy top, he let out a low whistle. They had a wonderful evening, with Livvy and Brenda talking about old times, while Dan and Len had a rather intellectual discussion about the Canadian lifestyle compared to that of the British people. It was almost midnight when they said their goodbyes and Brenda and Len drove off in their battered little Mini-Minor. Livvy was especially sad because she didn't think she would ever see her friend again but her somber mood was gone by the next morning when Dan picked up a rental car, arranged by the hotel, and they set off on their trip to Paris. Dan was still unable to walk without a great deal of pain and was still using a wheelchair and, although he was apprehensive about driving any distance particularly on the other side of the road, he was too excited to notice any discomfort. When they arrived at Dover it was already mid-afternoon. They boarded the ferry, which would take them and their car across the English Channel to Calais, and they stared in wonder as they left the coastline and watched the towering white cliffs fade into the distance. It was dark when they approached Calais and the ferry was being prepared for the exodus of cars. All they could see were lights twinkling in the distance but Dan, sitting in his wheelchair, oblivious to the wind and the cold was so emotional that he blinked back tears. They stayed the night in Calais in an old inn. The sign on the door to their room said Louis X1V Suite and it contained a massive four-poster bed with a crimson comforter edged with gold. Dan attempted to look very regal when he climbed between the sheets and Livvy took a picture of him while she giggled uncontrollably.

The next morning, on the last day of the year, they drove to Paris, stopping on the way to buy a baguette and delicious dark roasted coffee in a small village. The quiet of the countryside was in significant contrast to the bustle of the city and they experienced a hair-raising drive through the streets to their hotel. They spent the whole day exploring Paris, the Left Bank, the Eiffel Tower and the Louvre and that night, on the Champs-Elysees, they celebrated the New Year with thousands of people including many other Canadians waving their flags with great pride. It was a wonderful holiday and Livvy hoped it would never end. It felt as though she and Dan had never been closer but she realized he had been dependant on her throughout the whole trip and once back home and feeling better, his attitude might change.

After returning to London they took a direct flight back to Toronto and when Dan dropped Livvy off at her apartment and continued on to his own place, she felt a profound sense of loss. It was only when Natalie greeted her at the door that she realized just how happy she was to be home again.

Chapter Thirty-Six

Within a few weeks of their return from vacation, Livvy's worst fears began to materialize. She noticed Dan was becoming distant and making excuses for spending less and less time with her. Diane Barrows was calling the office more often than usual and Livvy suspected it had nothing to do with business then, one morning, she knew with certainty that she had been right. She had not been idle in her curiosity about Diane and discovered she lived in a house very close to her apartment building and which she passed every day on the bus going to work. When she saw Dan's car sitting in Diane's driveway on a Tuesday morning in early March, she was devastated and didn't know how she could possibly face him that day. At about nine o'clock he bounced in and greeted Livvy in his usual manner as though he had nothing to hide, "Hi, Livvy, how are you doing kiddo?"

Livvy could hardly look at him as she replied, "How do you think I am? I thought you were up to something and now I know for sure. I saw your car in Diane Barrow's driveway this morning."

Dan looked stunned but didn't deny it, "Yes, I know, I was just dropping off some samples she needed to take to the hospital today."

Livvy was infuriated and got up from her desk so that she could confront him and look directly into his eyes, "What kind of a fool do you think I am? You're a liar; since when do you call on clients at their homes?"

Dan was getting defensive and found himself in an awkward position, "Look, this isn't the time or place to discuss this and I have work to do. We can have dinner tonight and talk about it."

"That's it, run away, Dan. I'd like to discuss it now."

"Well I can't. I have a meeting I have to get to, so it will have to wait. Will you have dinner later or not?"

Livvy knew she was beaten and went back to her desk, slumping down in her chair in defeat, "Okay we'll get together after work, but I don't want to hear anymore lies."

The rest of the day seemed to drag by indeterminably even though there was so much to do. Livvy had a hard time concentrating and she had no idea how she was going to handle the situation, although she knew she wasn't ready to give up without a fight. When Dan eventually returned to the office at six o'clock to pick her up, she was a bundle of nerves. They went out to dinner at one of their favourite restaurants and he finally admitted that he had spent the night with Diane but it had all happened in a weak moment and it wouldn't happen again. With his usual charm and affectionate nature he succeeded in winning Livvy over and convinced her she was the only woman he really cared for. Livvy wanted to believe everything he was telling her but even after they slept together that night and Dan was as loving as ever, deep in her heart, she knew she was losing him.

In the weeks that followed, Livvy discovered many occasions when Dan had deceived her and she was now absolutely certain the affair with Diane had become serious. In spite of this it was impossible for her to walk away. She tried to salvage the relationship but it became increasingly difficult and they argued constantly. In an attempt to take a break from the situation, she flew to Boston one weekend to attend a seminar given by the National Business Forms Association. On the first day there, she ran into Mort Cummings, an entrepreneur running a one-man operation in New York City.

She had come into contact with Mort once before when she and Dan attended the conference in Washington D.C. and she found him to be urbane, witty, and with a great sense of humour. After a meeting on Saturday, they had dinner together at one of the most popular seafood restaurants in Boston and, on their return to the hotel, Mort kissed Livvy goodnight at her door and suggested they have lunch the next day. She went to bed that night and slept surprisingly well. She was grateful for the relief from all the stress she had been under and was flattered by the attention she was receiving from Mort.

At lunch the next day and, after all the business sessions were over, Mort talked Livvy into staying over another day and moving into the Ritz Carlton with him that night. In a rash moment, and feeling that she was taking revenge on Dan, she agreed but when she called the office to say she would not be back until Tuesday she left a message with Jim and avoided speaking to Dan himself. The time she spent with Mort proved to be a lot of fun and she enjoyed his company. They went sightseeing all afternoon, ate dinner in the hotel's most luxurious restaurant, and ended up in the king size bed of a suite, which was large enough for a family of six. When Livvy got up in the morning she felt no sense of guilt and Mort kept things light between them by insisting they have a wonderful breakfast before they left for the airport, and he kept her laughing with his outrageous sense of humour.

Mort's flight back to New York left before Livvy's and it was only while she was waiting for her own flight that her anxiety began to kick in. At one point she thought she was going to have a panic attack and decided, for the first time in her life, to see if there was some type of medication she could buy that would ease her symptoms. The pharmacist in the airport could only recommend a mild non-prescription drug, but Livvy was desperate and took double the dose recommended before she could force herself to face the trip back. When she arrived in Toronto, she was surprised to see Dan waiting for her and, after driving her back to her apartment, he asked her to have dinner with him later that day. He seemed very loving and told her how much he had missed her so she assumed he had come to the realization she was really important to him. Wanting the evening to be special, she dressed rather provocatively in a long green halter gown and paid a lot of attention to her hair and makeup. During dinner Dan took her hand, "You look really lovely tonight. I really missed you and I'm sorry for all the times I've hurt you. We've been together so long, Livvy, and I should have married you long ago. I need you to give me the chance to clear things up between us so I am asking you to bear with me for one more week."

Livvy had not expected Dan to mention marriage and her hopes soared but she wondered what was coming next, "What do you mean, Dan, give you one more week? What do you intend to do?"

"Well, I've made arrangements to go away with Diane next weekend and this will give me the opportunity to tell her I can't see her anymore."

Livvy withdrew her hand in anger. "How dare you; once again you think I'm stupid. You don't have to go away with her to tell her that and you don't have to wait until next weekend. You can tell her tomorrow, right here in Toronto."

Dan shook his head, "No Livvy, I owe it to her to do it this way. Trust me, once the weekend is over, everything will be all right."

Livvy knew in her heart nothing Dan was saying made any sense but she didn't want to give him an ultimatum so she finally relented and told him, she didn't want to hear anymore about it until he got back on the following Monday.

The rest of the week dragged by and the weekend was even worse, even though Livvy had made a date with Maggie, and her friend Susan, to go to a movie on Saturday night. After the movie, Maggie expressed her feelings about the way Dan was treating her and suggested she move on, but Livvy couldn't just throw away six years as though they had never happened. She knew Maggie was right but she prayed that when Dan came back from his trip, he might even suggest that they move in together.

On Monday morning, from the moment Dan walked into the office, Livvy was aware it was not going to be a pleasant day. He could hardly look her in the face and, when he told her he had to have a serious talk with her after work, she was filled with a sense of dread. At five o'clock, he told her he'd had enough work for one day and asked her to get her jacket and meet him at his car. They drove in silence a short distance away to a coffee shop and he guided her to a table, where she sat nervously while he ordered two cups of coffee at the counter. When he returned to the table Livvy couldn't contain herself any longer, "Well Dan, I assume you brought me here to tell me something."

Dan stirred his coffee, then without looking up said, "Livvy, I don't know how to tell you this, but we have to end our relationship. I thought I could finish with Diane but going away with her this weekend made me realize my true feelings for her."

Livvy reached across the table and grabbed the spoon from Dan's hand, "Stop doing that and look at me. You said you were going away with her to tell her it was all over between you and now you tell me it's me you want to finish with?"

"I'm so sorry, Livvy, we've been great together but we've stopped having fun. The last thing I want to do is hurt you but I can't do this anymore. I don't think I've ever felt as miserable as I did last night when I got home. I spent nearly all night thinking about you. You've been the greatest person I've known but it's over, Livvy and we have to move on."

"So all that talk the other night was a lie. You said you should have married me a long time ago. What was that all about? We've been through so much together and we can start having fun again if we just stopped working so hard. If I'm the greatest person you've ever known then why are you throwing me away and going with Diane?"

"Oh, Livvy, I know I need to explain it to you; you deserve that. It's just hard to make you understand how things have changed between us. I just don't feel the same way about you anymore."

Tears flooded Livvy's eyes while she searched for a tissue in her purse, "I can't talk about this anymore tonight, Dan, please just take me home," and she started to rise from the table.

"Livvy, don't do this, we have to talk, I don't want it to end this way."

"I want to go home, Dan, please take me or I'll get home by myself."

"Okay, if you insist, of course I'll take you."

They drove to Livvy's apartment without a word being exchanged between them and when Dan pulled up outside the building; Livvy reached over and grasped Dan's hand for a second and then quickly opened the door and jumped out. Natalie was already home from school when Livvy arrived and sensed immediately that something was wrong. For Livvy, it was a relief to cry on her daughter's shoulder and receive the comfort she so desperately needed. Later, she spent hours lying awake trying to figure out what to do. She loved her job but she didn't see how she could possibly be exposed to Dan every day and she was bound to come into contact with Diane, which would make it even more difficult. The next morning, she walked into Dan's office and gave him two weeks notice and he was stunned. He begged her to reconsider and asked her to give him more time to think about. He had not expected her to resign and didn't know how he could possibly cope without her. Two days later, when she approached him again, insisting she was serious about leaving, he suggested she do some freelance part-time work for an associate in the meat import business and keep working, part- time, while training someone new to take her place. Livvy realized this situation might allow her to start her own business providing help to small companies needing accounting services and, after some thought, she agreed to Dan' suggestion.

The next few months were some of the most difficult Livvy had ever experienced. As well as producing the accounting records and financial statements for the meat importer, which was a challenging and complicated task, she also acquired another small account, but she wasn't happy. It took very little time for her to realize she wasn't cut out for freelance work and she preferred being in one place and dedicating herself to one company. Though her encounters with Dan were awkward, she felt most at home when she was back in her old office even though she was training someone new to replace her. At the end of the summer, it was Dan himself who asked Livvy to come back. He wasn't happy with his new employee and he felt, now that some time had passed, that they could work together without any problem. He was also thinking about purchasing his own printing plant and desperately needed someone he could trust and rely on. Late one afternoon he asked Livvy if she would come into his office, "Hi Livvy, have a seat," he said, gesturing to the chair beside his desk. Livvy sat down with some trepidation. She expected Dan to ask her just how much longer the training would take. "How are things going?" he asked.

"They're okay I guess," Livvy replied.

"You don't sound too happy. Don't you like what you're doing?"

Livvy hesitated, not sure whether she should be honest about how she felt, "Well, to tell you the truth this freelance work is not really what I'm cut out for. I guess I like my roots too much and going from place to place just doesn't suit me."

When she finished speaking Dan grinned, "I figured as much and that's why I think you should come back and work full time."

Livvy was shocked and not sure how to react at first. When she realized this was what she had wanted all along, she smiled too, "Are you serious? Do you really think we can work together so closely again?"

"Yes, of course I do. When I first met you I told you I'd know you when you were fifty and I still believe that. I'm planning on buying this printing plant and I couldn't do it without you. You're the only person I can trust around here and I need you, Livvy"

Livvy felt a sense of euphoria but also had some concerns about having to get rid of the new trainee, "What about Chris, are you going to let him go?"

"I don't think I have much choice, there isn't any other position for him. Face it, Livvy, he hasn't proved to be that efficient and he certainly isn't you. If you can get rid of all your other commitments in two weeks, I'll let him go and you can have your office back."

It took Livvy less than two weeks to dispose of her other responsibilities and she was more than ready to take back her old job. On her first day back, Dan suggested they have lunch so that he could tell her all about his plans for the printing plant and, although she was apprehensive about spending time with him outside of the office, it turned out to be a pleasant experience and one that was completely related to business.

The fall of 1974 gave Livvy a new lease on life, after she moved into a new apartment near Allan Gardens in downtown Toronto. She was back doing the job she loved and Natalie, who was now almost seventeen was a well-adjusted young lady and a joy in her life, and she had begun to go out socially again. Earlier in the summer, Maggie had persuaded her, on many occasions, to join her and Byron at the Scotch Room, which was a popular dancing spot at the Inn on the Park Hotel in Don Mills. Byron had finally left his family and he and Maggie were now a steady item and Byron loved to dance. Maggie's friend, Susan, loved to dance too and would often join the threesome and, before long, Livvy and Susan began to form a friendship of their own. Susan was now divorced and had sole custody of her two children, Dina who was a year younger than Natalie and fourteen-year-old, Tom. Susan had changed considerably since the first time Livvy had met her in Maggie's apartment. She had lost weight, changed her hair style, and her fashion sense, and her personality seemed to have changed too. She was no longer a rather conservative housewife, but a fun loving young mother looking for some excitement in her life. Livvy even began dating again but she still had feelings for Dan and couldn't imagine anyone taking his place.

In July, Livvy went on a weekend trip to Kitchener with Maggie, Susan, and Maggie's sister-in-law, Marion. They stayed in a caravan belonging to Byron that was parked in a camp ground near a river and were having a lot of fun skinny dipping, climbing trees and enjoying the sun. Then, on Saturday night Maggie practically accused Susan of being interested in Byron and from that point on their friendship began to erode. Livvy felt as though she was in an awkward spot but rather than openly take sides, even though she thought Maggie was mistaken, she continued her relationship with both women.

That same month, Livvy's brother, Matt, married Kathy, who was about to give birth to their son, Colin. Matt was excited about becoming a father for the first time at the age of forty and Livvy was excited for him but, in November, her upbeat mood came to a crashing halt when Harry was admitted to a nursing home after nearly setting a chair on fire. He had never stopped smoking his favourite hand rolled cigarettes and Rachel had always been nervous leaving him alone, while she ran out to do a few errands. When he dropped a lighted butt down the side of a cushion on the chair where he was sitting, the effects of the stroke restricted him from doing anything about it. It was divine intervention that Rachel came home in time to save him from being burned to death and he escaped any injury, but Rachel couldn't cope with the worry or the risk anymore. Seeing her father moved to the nursing home was a traumatic event for Livvy. When she walked in the door she was aware of the odour of urine permeating the air and the blank faces of the residents sitting in their wheelchairs completely oblivious of others around them. Then, when she sat down on Harry's bed, she cried because it felt as hard as the floor she had just walked across and she couldn't bear to think of her father, with his pitifully frail body, lying there day after day. Rachel, however, showed little emotion about leaving Harry in the home and Livvy again felt the lack of connection between herself and her mother and only wished they could have had the same close relationship she had with her own daughter.

Christmas that year was a rather sad affair, even though they were able to bring Harry home for the day. He looked like a very old man and when Livvy gave him a gift of some books, she knew he would love to read, he shed a few tears. Livvy was certain that he knew, he wouldn't share many more Christmas's with his family.

Chapter Thirty-Seven

One Friday night in April 1975, Susan was meeting a male friend at the Copper Lounge, a nightclub just upstairs from the Scotch Room at the Inn on the Park. As Livvy was at loose ends that weekend, Susan asked her to go along too, suggesting she might meet someone new. The Copper Lounge was a popular spot and many people traveled from all over the city to enjoy the music and to dance. It was Livvy's favourite place to go and it didn't take much to persuade her to join Susan on this particular night. When she arrived, Susan was already there with her friend Greg. Livvy didn't take the relationship very seriously as she knew Greg was married and just staying over in town until the morning. This wasn't the first time Susan had become involved with a married man and Livvy didn't particularly approve but she kept her opinion to herself. It was ironic that she was about to fall in love with a man who was living with his wife and three small children.

After an hour of drinking and dancing with a few men, who Livvy found rather dull and boring, Greg suddenly stood up and gestured to someone on the other side of the room. When Livvy looked over, because of the low lighting, she could barely make out the person who was now rising from his seat and starting to walk towards them. When he arrived at their table, Livvy found herself staring up at a very handsome man, just over six feet tall, broad shouldered, with thick dark hair, slightly graying at the sides, and a thick dark mustache. She was reminded of her father, when she used to look up at him as a young girl, and she was instantly attracted. Greg remained standing and shook the man's hand, "Hi John," he said "how are you? I thought it was you sitting over there all by yourself. Why don't you come and join us."

John looked from Susan to Livvy and in a deep masculine voice answered, "I really don't want to intrude on these lovely ladies."

"No intrusion," Greg continued, "I'd like you to meet Susan and this is her friend, Livvy. Ladies, this is John Freeman, he works with me."

After ordering more drinks and some small talk, John asked Livvy to dance and that's when she discovered what a wonderful dancer he was. She had never been very coordinated but he led her around the dance floor so easily, she felt like she had been dancing all her life. At the end of the evening, when John asked her if he could drive her home she threw caution to the winds. She had no idea whether he was married or single; she only knew she wanted to see him again. On the drive, which took about twenty minutes, John wanted to know more about her, "Livvy is an unusual name, is it short for something?"

Livvy smiled, "Yes, my name is really Olivia and sometimes I think I'd like to go back to being called Olivia but I don't think anyone else will go along with it."

John slowly nodded, "Olivia is a pretty name, but Livvy suits you."

After more questions John discovered she was divorced, lived with her daughter, and worked for a company involved in the health care industry but, when Livvy attempted to find out more about John, it was a little too late, they had already arrived at her apartment. She wondered if he would kiss her goodnight and was disappointed when he didn't, but he asked her for her phone number and said he would call.

The rest of the weekend seemed to drag by and Livvy thought about John often but she didn't expect to hear from him for a while, if at all. She was genuinely surprised on Monday evening when her phone rang and she heard his voice. It was then that she learned he had gone home to Sarnia for the weekend to visit his family and was back in town and wanting to see her. When he picked her up the next evening to go out to dinner, she still had no idea about his marital status and having always respected another individual's privacy she didn't like to pry.They drove a short distance to a restaurant in the neighbourhood she had recommended and, after ordering a scotch on the rocks for Livvy and a beer for himself, it was John who opened up about the situation with his family. "Do you mind if we talk for a while before we order", he asked "or are you really hungry?"

Livvy put down the menu she had been studying, "No, I'm fine for now," she replied, "was there something in particular you wanted to talk to me about?"

John hesitated, looking a little uncomfortable, "Well, I know our conversation was very brief last night and I guess you must have wondered what was going on when I told you I'd been to Sarnia over the weekend. You probably realize by now I'm married but things aren't quite as simple as they seem. My wife and I separated last year for about six months; she was the one who actually left home, then she came back and we have been trying to work things out for the sake of the children but neither of us are really happy."

Livvy had been listening carefully and had very mixed emotions, "How many children do you have, John?"

"I have three boys between the ages of thirteen and sixteen and when their mother left it was really difficult for them. I had my job, which keeps me traveling back and forth to Toronto almost every week, and they had to do a lot of fending for themselves. It's much better for them with their mother at home and I don't have to worry about them every day I'm away."

Livvy was curious and wanted to know more, even though it went against her nature to ask personal questions, "Why did your wife leave in the first place?"

John chewed on his lower lip, pondering how to answer without appearing to place the blame, "Well, I was gone so much during the week and we'd been married for twenty years so Marilyn was feeling neglected. She sings in the choir at the church and she got involved with one of the other choir members. They spent a lot of time rehearsing together for a songfest the church was putting on for the community, and just got closer and closer. Neither of them was happy, so I suppose they were drawn to each other and eventually they both left home and actually lived together for those few months. He was married too, so it caused a bit of a scandal and eventually the pressure of the community and the concern about all the children involved made them both decide to return home."

"So obviously you've forgiven her."

"I suppose I have, but there's nothing between us anymore."

Livvy was wrestling with her thoughts, " I have to be honest John, I've never been out with a man who was married and actually living with his wife."

John nodded slowly then reached across the table for Livvy's hand, "I don't expect anything, Livvy, but I'd like to see you again. The minute I met you I wanted to know more about you."

Livvy hesitated and then smiled, "I'm not sure it's a good idea John but why don't we just enjoy this evening together, I think I can handle that."

As the evening progressed Livvy found herself more and more attracted to this man, who insisted in knowing all about her life and paid attention to her every word. After a wonderful dinner of chateaubriand, which they shared, John persuaded Livvy to go back to the Copper Lounge where they first met, and they danced the night away until the band finally announced they were playing their last song. Once again John drove Livvy home but this time he gave her a quick peck on the cheek and asked if he could see her again before he went back to Sarnia. Despite her misgivings, Livvy agreed to see him again on Thursday and so their romance began.

During the next month they spent at least two evenings each week together and always seemed to end up at the Copper Lounge. Although John was very affectionate on the dance floor and his kisses grew more passionate each time he drove Livvy home, it never went beyond that. Livvy had not even invited him up to her apartment because she didn't want to expose Natalie to the fact that she was having an affair with a married man. Then almost a month to the day when they first met, despite Livvy's attempts to keep their relationship as platonic as possible, she could no longer deny her strong physical attraction to John and her desire for intimacy between them. After the last dance of the evening when she suggested they go up to his hotel room, John readily agreed but, when they got to the room, he was obviously very nervous. Their first physical encounter was a disappointment but Livvy made excuses for John, rationalizing that he was feeling guilty and assuring him it didn't matter as long as they were together. She had no idea that his reluctance to consummate their relationship was the sign of an even more deep-seated problem.

Every weekend, when John returned to Sarnia he would find some excuse to get to a telephone to call Livvy and tell her how much he missed her and their feelings for each other grew stronger. Then, in June, when Livvy went to Miami with Susan for a week's vacation, even though they were apart, she felt closer to him than ever. While in Miami they met up with Maggie and Byron, who were going on a cruise to the Bahamas, and Livvy spent a wonderful morning walking on the beach with them while Susan relaxed in their hotel room. Later, along with Susan, they were allowed to board the ship to say their farewells and Livvy got a taste of what cruising was all about.

After returning to Toronto, the affair with John continued and Livvy realized she was really in love for the first time in her life. Even though their physical relationship couldn't compare to the one she had experienced with Dan, Livvy felt John was someone who truly cared for her and he never failed to express his feelings over and over again. One day, when having lunch with him at the Stable Restaurant near her office, she noticed Dan at another table with a client. When he saw Livvy and noticed the way she was interacting with the handsome man across from her, he was disturbed and even somewhat jealous. Ironically she had not yet encountered the side of John that wouldn't allow him to accept Dan as someone in her past. In August, Livvy decided to take a two-week trip alone to San Francisco and Vancouver. She had always wanted to attempt a trip on her own and knew being in control of her own actions made her much less anxious. When she arrived in San Francisco she booked into the Hyatt, visited all the well-known tourist spots including Golden Gate Park, Alcatraz, Fisherman's Wharf, Ghiradelli Square and Lombard Street, and wrote a long letter to John telling him about her travels. After a week, she flew to Vancouver and spent four days there before she took the twenty-two hour train ride to Calgary, stopping briefly in Banff. Travelling through the Rockies was an awesome experience and she didn't sleep a wink during the journey. She finally flew back to Toronto, arriving on a Sunday, and was happy to see Natalie, who at seventeen was quite capable of looking after herself and still very much involved with Robert. Then the very next day she found John on her doorstep as loving as ever and anxious to resume their relationship.

It was at this time, Livvy decided to introduce John to her mother and so, on a Sunday afternoon, they visited Rachel's apartment where she offered them tea and cookies but had very little to add to the conversation. Livvy was so proud of John, he was wearing a light blue summer suit and he looked especially handsome that day. He was also a complete gentleman and Livvy knew Rachel was impressed. She wanted John to meet her father too, but the nursing home was depressing and she decided to wait a little longer to see if their relationship would develop further. Meeting Rachel encouraged John to introduce Livvy to his own mother and, the very next week, she came face to face with Jane Freeman. Jane lived in a tiny senior's apartment and Livvy and John had to sit on the bed because there was only one chair. She was very nervous because she had no idea what Jane really thought of the situation with her son. It didn't take long to find out that she was no fan of John's wife and was quite pleased he was dating someone else. She also discovered John didn't think too highly of his mother as she was an alcoholic and had been drinking since the early sixties, when her husband had died unexpectedly. Right after the encounter with Jane Freeman, Livvy noticed she had a rash that began to spread all over her arms, legs and chest, and irritated her so much, she was unable to sleep. The doctor told her it was just nerves and prescribed a skin cream to help relieve the itching but it didn't help and, after six weeks, Livvy decided to visit a dermatologist. Dr. Bertrand was a tiny little woman, with gray hair pulled tightly in a bun and small black-framed glasses perched on the end of her nose and she didn't pull any punches with Livvy. She immediately confirmed the doctor's diagnosis of nerves and suggested she be put on a treatment of Valium. When Livvy objected to any tranquilizers, Dr. Bertrand was adamant she needed help and couldn't always fix things on her own and so, she finally acquiesced and began taking the pills prescribed.

The next month proved to be one of the most difficult Livvy had experienced. Despite the support of Natalie and John, Livvy felt like a zombie and the rash continued to bother her. Finally Natalie suggested they go away for a weekend to Montreal so that Livvy could have a change of scenery and so, together with Susan and Natalie's friend Heather, they traveled by train to Montreal and stayed in the renowned Queen Elizabeth Hotel, in the heart of downtown. On Saturday, after a day of shopping, they had a wonderful supper at one of the city's finest restaurants and Susan and the girls were raring to go out on the town, but Livvy was unable to keep her eyes open. Leaving the others, she returned to the hotel room, fell into bed, and slept for fourteen hours. It was then she decided she had had enough and on her return home, later that day, she uncapped the bottle of Valium and flushed the pills down the toilet, strong in her belief in mind over matter. The next morning, when she got up for work, to her amazement, the rash had disappeared but she knew the real problem hadn't gone away and she had to resolve her relationship with John. Early in the afternoon, she received her usual phone call from him desperately wanting to see her that evening. She didn't want him to pick her up and made an excuse so that she could meet him at the Quo Vadis restaurant near her apartment.

When she arrived at just after seven o'clock, John was already there and rose to embrace her the minute she walked through the door. Livvy returned the embrace but John sensed a change in her mood that he had never seen before. He draped his arm lightly around her shoulders and guided her to her chair, "How's my sweetheart?" he said.

Livvy looked up into John's face, once again thinking how handsome he was, "I'm fine; a little tired but glad to be home."

"You look good Livvy, how was your weekend and how's the rash?"

"The weekend was great except I mixed Valium with alcohol and slept for hours on end and that's when I decided I wasn't going to take anymore drugs."

John looked concerned, "Do you think that's wise Livvy, after all you're not going to get better if you don't follow the doctor's orders."

"So much for the doctor; I was tired of feeling like a zombie so I threw my pills away last night and this morning my rash had vanished. I believe in mind over matter, John, I just wish I could use my mind to control some other aspects of my life."

John frowned, "What do you mean Livvy?"

Livvy thought about her problems with her anxiety but she had never confided in anyone who wasn't a professional and she wasn't ready to confide in John now, particularly as she was about to tell him she couldn't see him anymore. She twisted her napkin around her fingers, "Oh nothing, but I do need to talk to you about us."

"I don't like the sound of that, Livvy, what do you want to talk about?"

At that point the waiter arrived at the table to see if they were ready to order something to drink and Livvy was grateful for the interruption. "Let's just have a glass of wine and something to eat before we talk John."

It was over an hour later, when they finally finished supper and were sitting quietly having coffee and liqueurs, when Livvy reached across the table to touch John's hand, "John, there isn't an easy way to say this but I can't see you anymore. I've never felt this way about anyone before but it just isn't right. You need to resolve your problems with Marilyn and think about your children. They need their father and not on a part-time basis. Even when you're at home on weekends you are constantly finding excuses to get away and call me." John started to speak but Livvy let go of his hand and held her index finger to her lips, "I'm not finished John, I need to talk. I've never done this before and it goes against everything I believe in. It's simple really, you're married and even though I love you and I know you love me, we have to end this relationship. I'm not giving you an ultimatum and I don't want you to promise me anything, I just want us to walk away from each other and always think of each other as a lovely memory."

John paused, waiting to see if Livvy had finished and then seeing the tears beginning to form in her eyes, he slowly shook his head, "I can't let you go, Livvy, I love you too much. You said you don't want any promises from me but I've been thinking about this for months and I'm leaving Marilyn because I want to be with you."

Livvy protested because she still felt she had given John an ultimatum, "I can't let you do that; it wouldn't be fair to your kids."

"It isn't fair to them now. Whenever I'm at home, it's pretty tense. Marilyn and I hardly ever speak to each other and I know she isn't happy either. I'd like to wait until after Christmas though, it's only a few weeks away and if you could just wait that long, Livvy we can start planning the future together."

"I'm not sure it's the right thing to do. I feel like I'm putting pressure on you and maybe it would be better if we just stopped seeing each other. If you decide you still want to be with me some time in the future and actually leave home, I would feel so much better about it."

John looked stricken, "No, I can't take a chance on that, you might meet someone else. I promise I'll leave soon after New Year but I want to go on seeing you. I can't bear to think of coming to Toronto every week and not being with you."

As the evening wore on, John gradually wore Livvy's resolve down and she finally agreed she would continue to see him. In her heart she had hoped he would leave his family to be with her. She could no longer imagine her life without him. The next few months were extremely busy. Dan had acquired the printing plant he had always dreamed of owning and had added fifty people to their staff. He hired two more salesmen and moved them into offices at the corner of Spadina & King, only a few short blocks from the printing plant. Livvy was surprised to learn she would be taking a large corner office at the plant where she would be supervising an accounting staff of four, and be involved in job costing. This would mean she would be apart from the people she normally worked with, including Dan, and she felt rather isolated. At first, it was difficult for the existing plant employees to accept the new owner and the previous accounting supervisor, who had in fact been demoted, was particularly reluctant to co-operate. It took Livvy about a month before she was able to convince the staff of her credibility but, once she implemented some new procedures, which greatly improved the efficiency of the department, she began to notice a positive attitude change. This in itself gave Livvy a new found sense of importance but she still felt estranged from Dan and the sales staff and she wasn't happy.

Chapter Thirty-Eight

Christmas of 1975 came and went very quickly and Livvy was glad when it was over. With her father in the nursing home and John at home with his family, it was not a season for rejoicing. Together, with Rachel and Natalie, she spent Christmas Day at Matt's house and tried to make the best of it but her heart was elsewhere. Just before the holidays, she sat down with Natalie on one of the few nights they managed to eat supper together. Natalie had just left school, was working as an intern for the Ontario government, and spending most of her evenings with Robert. Livvy was also very busy putting extra time in to ensure the new printing plant was running smoothly and using her leisure time during the week to be with John. She had just thrown together a quick supper of tortellini pasta and salad, and was already seated at the table with Natalie, when she decided it was time to discuss her situation with John. She decided to take things slowly because she wasn't sure how Natalie would react to their plans, "I can't believe we finally found time to have supper together. We seem like ships passing in the night recently."

Natalie toyed with the food on her plate, "Yes, I know, Mom, but now I'm working and you are always at the office or out with John, I don't get to see you much anymore."

Livvy immediately felt guilty, "Are you saying you want me to spend more time with you? I thought you were out with Robert nearly every night and you were happy with that."

Natalie nodded and looked up, "I am happy, Mom, and as a matter of fact I wanted to talk to you about Robert."

Livvy reached across the table and touched Natalie's hand, "What is it, sweetie, you can talk to me about anything; you know that."

Natalie looked uncomfortable and squirmed a little in her seat, "Well, you know Robert and I have been seeing each other for nearly three years and we want to move in together. I know you've been planning your future with John and now I feel okay about leaving home because I know you won't be alone."

Livvy leaned back in her chair and breathed a sigh of relief, "Wow, here I was trying to figure out how I was going to tell you I wanted John to move in and you just made it all so easy for me. Are you sure this is what you really want though? I hope you don't think I'm pushing you away because that's the last thing I want."

Natalie finally relaxed and grinned, "This is what I really want, Mom, and I promise we aren't going to be far away. We've already started looking at apartments up at Yonge and Eglinton and want to move in just after New Year."

"Well you two have certainly been busy but you have my blessing. I have to be honest, Natalie, I'm not sure Robert is the right person for you but I know you love each other so I hope things work out for you both."

"Thanks, Mom, and I hope things work out for you and John too."

Two weeks into the New Year, while driving up to the Copper Lounge, John informed Livvy he had told Marilyn he was moving out but had been surprised by her reaction.

"Why, what happened?" Livvy asked.

"She broke down and cried. I didn't expect that and then she asked me if I could at least stay for my youngest son's birthday at the end of next month."

Livvy looked astonished, "That's it?? That's all she said? She must have said a lot more than that. She had to have asked you why you wanted to leave."

John shook his head, "No she didn't ask anything like that. She knows I haven't been happy and I haven't been around very much. I thought about telling her about you but I didn't." Livvy had begun to realize, although John always expressed how much he cared for her, he wasn't very forthcoming about the details of his life with his family and he was reluctant to confront any unpleasant situation, "So what's going to happen? Are you going to stay until the end of February?"

"Yes, I said I would. I'm sorry, Livvy, but it's only a few weeks away. Maybe I should start looking for a place to live on my own for a while before we move in together."

Livvy reacted quickly, "No, John, there's no need for that. I told you, Natalie is moving out and I have lots of room. I thought we'd already discussed this."

"We did, Livvy, but I don't want you to feel I'm pushing Natalie out."

Livvy shook her head, "She made the decision on her own and she wants to live with Robert. Please don't change our plans now, John. We've wanted to be together for so long and now we have the chance."

John had just parked the car and he reached over and hugged her tightly, "Okay, you win, right after Andy's birthday I'll be coming to Toronto."

Livvy couldn't wait for John to move in but things wouldn't turn out quite as she expected.

It was early March when John finally made a clean break from his family and arrived on Livvy's doorstep, with suitcase in hand. Livvy was overjoyed to see him and, after helping him find enough closet space for all of his belongings, they spent the evening getting slightly tipsy on wine and grand marnier and falling into bed to make love until the early hours of the morning.

In mid March, right after Livvy's birthday, she took John to visit her father for the first time. Harry greeted John with a feeble handshake but paid him little attention; it was Livvy he wanted to see. Whenever Livvy arrived at the nursing home she would see Harry sitting alone like most of the other patients, and her heart would break but, as she got closer and he finally noticed her, his face would light up like a little child. She was anxious to see how John reacted to her father but he was very quiet and added little to the conversation. She wondered if he was thinking about his own father, who died when he was in his early twenties, but she knew it was useless to try and encourage him to talk about the past. The next few weeks were a revelation for Livvy. She realized Natalie had given her the space she needed but John didn't allow her that luxury. He was not pleased when she worked late and wanted her to relax whenever she arrived home by sitting down and having a glass of wine with him. This was all very foreign to Livvy who often walked in the door and, without even taking her coat off, liked to start preparing supper. To please John, she did her best to do what he wanted but she would sit chomping at the bit, anxioux to get on with her chores so that she could relax in peace later. Often, after supper, Livvy would take a long hot bath and read a book just so that she could have some alone time. It was then she realized just how much she cherished those moments when she could be entirely by herself.

Livvy was soon beginning to notice her bouts of anxiety were becoming more frequent and were no longer confined to those times when she was traveling by car in unfamiliar territory. Sometimes, just going to the supermarket would bring on her symptoms and, for the first time in her life, she felt she was able to share her secret with someone other than a mental health professional. Because she thought she could trust John not to just brush off her problem as inconsequential, she decided to confide in him. She also knew, to be fair to him, it affected their life together and she owed it to him to be honest. It was difficult for her to approach the subject and John listened attentively but, based on his reaction, she wasn't sure how he really felt. She believed there was no way he could really understand her dilemma and he reacted accordingly. Making no comment, he neither judged nor placated her in any way, except for holding her close when she broke down in utter frustration.

Having now had the courage to tell John, Livvy decided Dan had to be told too. There were occasions when she had to make business trips out of Toronto by car and she wasn't sure how she could deal with it. She asked Dan if they could have lunch together and he readily agreed. Over fresh lasagna at a small Italian restaurant, with the requisite checkered tablecloths and racks of hanging Chianti bottles, Dan poured her a glass of wine and leaned back in his chair, "Well kiddo, this is really nice but what's going on? I hope you aren't thinking of leaving."

Livvy smiled, "Goodness no, I didn't realize you would think that, I'm sorry."

Dan let out a sigh, "That's a relief. I know you don't like it too much where you are but I think we'll soon have you moved over to the sales office."

"You're right I don't like it at the plant but that isn't what I wanted to talk to you about. I'm sure you're going to have trouble understanding what I'm going to tell you but things have gotten a bit difficult for me lately."

Dan looked concerned and grabbed her hand, "What is it, Livvy? Are you ill? Is it John? If I can do anything to help, I will."

"No, none of those things but you can help a great deal. I don't want to travel out of town anymore unless you are able to take me and I don't want anyone else driving with us."

Dan frowned, "What's going on? You're right I don't understand, explain it to me."

"I have anxiety problems. I've had them most of my life and I've managed to cope up until now, but lately things are getting worse and I need help. I've tried to get treatment but nothing has helped so far, however I haven't given up. I get so anxious when I'm driving anywhere unfamiliar especially by car and there are other circumstances too that affect me. I always felt pretty comfortable with you but, when I didn't, I was able to deal with it. I'm not sure I can anymore."

Dan pulled his chair closer to Livvy, "Wow, I had no idea; you're really good at hiding things. What happens now when you get anxious?" he asked.

"Well, that's the worst part," Livvy replied hanging her head, "some people feel faint or nauseous but in my case I always feel like I have to run to the bathroom. It's so embarrassing and I know it's illogical but it just happens spontaneously."

"Livvy, you don't need to feel embarrassed and you can count on me. I'll do everything to make it easier for you and if we have to travel anywhere I'll make sure I take you."

Livvy was so grateful, "I knew I could rely on you. It's too bad I don't know how to drive, then I'd be in control and I wouldn't have this problem."

"It's no big deal, Livvy, I told you; you can count on me."

"I know, and I just want to say one more thing. I really appreciate your help and the fact you never ever tried to change me in all the years we went out together, you always accepted me for myself. You don't know what that means to me."

Dan wasn't completely satisfied, "Am I reading between the lines here Livvy? Is something wrong at home?"

Livvy paused not wanting to admit that, in many ways, John had disappointed her. "John's a good person but he has trouble showing his emotions and he's not used to living with someone like me."

"What do you mean by someone like you?" Dan questioned.

"Someone who works every day and often stays late. He's not used to coming home to an empty place and he has trouble dealing with my independence. But I have to be fair, I'm not used to having someone around all the time and I need more space."

"Mmmm, I know what that feels like. I think you and I just need weekend partners and then we'd be happy."

Livvy laughed, "I think you're right, that would be ideal. Anyway, enough of my problems, let's talk about something else."

That's precisely what they did for the next hour, just relaxing and enjoying each other's company and Livvy felt more comfortable than she had felt for quite a while.

On May 16th, early in the morning, Livvy got a call from Rachel telling her Harry had been taken to the hospital and it was serious. Livvy immediately contacted Matt and then raced over to the hospital, only to find her father flailing about in his hospital bed and staring up at her with vacant eyes. Matt arrived at the hospital to comfort Rachel while Livvy attempted to find somebody who could tell her what was wrong with her father. It was only after Harry died, two days later, that Livvy found out he had developed liver cancer but she was thankful to learn he had only suffered for a very short time. On the day that Harry died, John was in Ottawa on business and when Livvy called him she was surprised when he asked if he should come right back to Toronto. Although distraught and needing a shoulder to cry on, Livvy asserted her independence and told him he could stay where he was but she would like him to be with her at the funeral.

Harry would have probably turned over in his coffin if he knew a small memorial service was being held for him, before the burial in Mount Pleasant cemetery. He had been an atheist all his life and even when he was dying, the word God never entered his vocabulary. Livvy's friends, Maggie and Susan, attended the service and stood by her side, on a brilliant sunny day, when Harry was buried beneath a huge maple tree. But while John stood silently by looking uncomfortable, it was Dan who comforted Livvy when she most needed it. As they walked away from the graveside, Dan approached her and she fell sobbing into his arms. Later back at Rachel's apartment, where everyone gathered, John seemed aloof and Dan was nowhere to be seen. It was almost an hour later when he came back to see Livvy and explain that he had needed to be alone for a while. Livvy never really knew what Dan had been thinking but if he had any regrets about ending their relationship, it was too late. He was now living with Diane in a new house he had bought in Cabbage Town and Livvy had committed herself to John.

Harry's death didn't really hit Livvy until two months later when she heard Smoke Gets in Your Eyes playing on the radio. This had been her father's theme song and it was only then that Livvy really broke down, hurling herself onto the bed and howling, until she was exhausted. John could only sit and pat her on the back when what she really wanted was for him to put his arms around her. It was then that Livvy admitted the truth to herself; John was incapable of showing any real emotion.

After that incident life fell into a routine. Livvy was introduced to John's friend Mark and his wife Gwen who lived in the suburbs with their two teenage children and Livvy came to understand the lifestyle that John had been living back in Sarnia. Gwen had never worked and was quite content to stay at home and look after the household and, while Livvy admired Gwen for her homemaking skills and her dedication to her family, she knew she would have been bored to tears.

In June they went on vacation to Florida and stayed in John's mother's mobile home in Pompano Beach. The thirty-four mile trip by taxi from Miami proved to be an ordeal for Livvy and her anxiety was at an all-time high. It was only when they arrived at the mobile home that she was able to relax and enjoy riding around on Mrs. Freeman's tricycle, to pick up groceries and find some time to be by herself. She persuaded John to rent a car for their return trip so that they could spend a couple of days in Miami and thankfully her anxiety failed to surface.

Later that year, they went to California and visited all the places where Livvy had gone with Natalie years before and they ended their trip by driving across the desert to visit the Grand Canyon, eventually stopping in Palm Springs. It seemed Livvy had become accustomed to driving with John and she trusted him enough to know he would stop the car at any time if she needed a break but, she also knew her anxiety was increasingly affecting other areas of her life. Back in Toronto, she decided to visit a hypnotist to see if he could get to the root of the problem but, even though she was a willing subject, the treatment didn't help her. In fact, it only reinforced the fact that deep down she equated John with her father. He even resembled the father she remembered as a child, tall, well built, handsome and with the movie star moustache popular in the days of Errol Flynn and Ronald Coleman. There was no doubt John was a very attractive man and he had a wonderful dress sense. Livvy was proud to be seen with him and, in the very early days of their relationship, she actually felt her heart turn over when he walked into a room.

Chapter Thirty-Nine

During the following year, Livvy was fairly content, although she was annoyed at John's irritation when she worked late and had no interest in what her job entailed particularly if it involved Dan. They continued socializing with Mark and Gwen but she soon realized that Mark was a womanizer and was constantly cheating on his wife. When she tried to pump John for details he was not forthcoming and his stock reply was always, "We don't talk about stuff like that!"

Every Friday evening, they would go out to supper and every Saturday morning, in hockey season, John would go off to play hockey with his buddies from work while Livvy cleaned house. John normally stayed out to have lunch and a few beers and then would come home, collapse on the sofa, and fall asleep. Livvy, who was invariably arriving home from shopping, would let herself into the apartment and pray that John was not in his usual prone position but he always was and often snoring. It was obvious that he drank a great deal but never seemed to get drunk. He always liked a beer when he got home from work and often had wine with dinner and on Sundays he added liqueurs to the mix. As his mother was an alcoholic, Livvy wondered if he had inherited her addiction but as long as he appeared to be sober, she felt she didn't have any reason to worry.

In the fall, Maggie married Byron, finally cementing their relationship. Both John and Livvy found Byron to be a wonderful, caring man and Livvy was overjoyed knowing that her friend had finally found the happiness she deserved. Meanwhile the tension between Maggie and Susan had not abated, even though Susan had been invited to the wedding, but Livvy continued to see Susan as often as she could and hoped she would eventually find someone to share her life with.

Business had begun to slow down and Livvy warned Dan he needed additional financing in order to keep the company afloat. After some serious negotiations with a well established label company located in London, Ontario he managed to acquire a partner willing to invest a substantial amount of money for a 49% share. With the change in ownership there was some restructuring in the plant and Livvy moved to the sales office at King and Spadina. She was so much happier in this environment despite the fact that, on many occasions, Diane would float into the office to use some of the equipment for personal reasons. Soon, though difficult to admit, she realized she liked Diane immensely and had no ill feelings towards her. In fact, when Dan and Diane invited her and John to attend a dinner party at there home, Livvy readily accepted but John was not so enthusiastic. On the night of the party, Livvy wore her favourite dress, a long halter style with a floral bodice and black skirt and she felt particularly elegant. Diane greeted her with a hug and then promptly asked if she could give her some tips in the kitchen because she wasn't sure what to do. Livvy was both touched and amused, as she had never been a great cook herself and, at that moment, Diane seemed especially vulnerable.

Early in 1978, John's friend, Mark, left his wife and moved into an apartment with Sherry Preston, an English girl who worked in his office. Livvy was upset about the breakup but when Gwen phoned her to pump her for information about Mark and his new girlfriend, Livvy had to tell her she was unable to help. She was well aware John's friendship with Mark would continue and she would have to accept Sherry as the new person in his life. As it turned out, Livvy had much more in common with Sherry than Gwen and, over time, they became good friends. Sherry was born in south London and just a few years younger than Livvy. She was tall, fairly attractive, always well groomed and an excellent cook but, most important, she worked and was familiar with the pressures of a full-time job. This was something Gwen had never really fully understood. In the coming months, the foursome formed a dinner club with two other couples and once a month they would rotate to each other's homes for a gourmet meal. Livvy was terrified the first time she was scheduled to make a meal for eight people and entertain them all evening but she made the one thing that she cooked well, tarragon chicken in a cream sauce, and the evening went off without a hitch.

It was during this time that Natalie came to visit Livvy with a surprise announcement. "I've got something to tell you," she said rather sheepishly.

Livvy had already suspected what Natalie was going to say, "Oh and what's that?" she asked.

"Robert and I want to get married and we'd like it to be in the fall. We don't have much money so we can't afford very much and we were thinking of getting married at City Hall."

Livvy was quick to respond, "Oh, Natalie, I want you to have a proper wedding and although I can't count on your dad helping out, I do have a little set aside so you don't have to worry about paying for anything."

Natalie was relieved and so grateful, "Thanks Mom, and I hope you're pleased about me marrying Robert."

Livvy hesitated because of her reservations, "If this is what you want then I want it too. I just want you to be happy, Natalie, and if Robert makes you happy then that's good enough for me."

The wedding took place on a glorious late September afternoon at Fantasy Farms, on Pottery Road in Toronto. Prior to the wedding, Livvy had been involved in a whirlwind of activity, arranging the menu, guest list, dresses etc. She had invited Russ and Ann, Dan and Diane, and naturally John would be there too. When many of the other guests became aware that Livvy's ex-husband, ex-boyfriend and current boyfriend, would all be at the same affair, there was quite a buzz and Livvy was enjoying all the gossip.

Natalie looked beautiful in a simple ivory dress, reminiscent of another era, and Robert made a handsome groom, in his brown tuxedo while Natalie's best friend Heather, who was the maid of honour, and her friends Gail and Colleen looked pretty in their yellow bridesmaid's gowns. Livvy had searched high and low for a suitable dress for a mother of the bride but this was the year when the blouson top was the latest fashion and, with Livvy's fairly ample bosom, the style didn't really suit her. Eventually, she found a raspberry silk dress but, despite many flattering comments, she would have preferred a more form fitting style.

Seventy-five guests attended the wedding, including Rachel, John's mother, Maggie and Byron, Susan, and even Baba. The one person who was not invited was Vivien and in that instance Livvy had put her foot down. While she was usually very ready to forgive anyone who caused her any grief and did not believe in holding grudges, Vivien gave her a reason to make an exception. She had learned that a few years prior, Vivien had informed Natalie that, when she was small, her mother used to leave her alone while she stayed out all night carousing and drank heavily. When Livvy heard this she was outraged but rather than confronting Vivien she decided to ignore her permanently.

Russ walked Natalie down the garden path at Fantasy Farms and Livvy was pleased to see that father and daughter had formed a bond that would endure throughout his lifetime. At the same time, it was strange seeing Russ back in Toronto and, although the reunion was cordial, they had little to say to each other, particularly with Ann looking on. John was used to addressing meetings and had taken it upon himself to write a speech. Livvy had seen him working on it for days before the wedding and he didn't disappoint her. He was both eloquent and amusing and looked particularly handsome in a light gray suit, white shirt, and dark gray silk tie. Livvy was very proud of him that day. After the wedding supper, when Natalie threw her bouquet, Rachel was the one who caught it. She almost pushed John's mother to the ground in her efforts and got an ovation from the crowd. At age sixty-six, her hair was still dark and she looked particularly lovely in a royal blue dress Livvy had loaned her but catching the bouquet was not a sign of things to come. Rachel had vowed she would never marry again and she had had enough of men.

Chapter Forty

In early 1979, Livvy applied to the Clarke Institute for treatment for her anxiety. The Clarke was one of the most renowned centres dealing with mental health in North America and Livvy did not expect to get accepted. She was elated, after only three weeks, to receive a telephone call setting up an appointment with a Doctor Adam Corelli and to learn that her condition had been taken seriously by such a distinguished organization. Dr. Corelli, as Livvy had expected, was of Italian origin but she had no idea he would be so young. He was extremely attractive with thick dark hair and the most amazing warm brown eyes and he was always dressed casually in a corduroy jacket, jeans and suede loafers. She liked him immediately and over a period of months she told him all about her life, her hopes and fears, and most of all her struggle with anxiety attacks but there was no magic breakthrough. It was a huge disappointment when, in September, Dr. Corelli informed her that he didn't feel he could do anymore for her. He admitted to having anxiety attacks himself, which always resulted in an upset stomach, and he had learned how to cope with it. He suggested Livvy would have to do the same and she left the programme profoundly disappointed.

One week later, John's mother was admitted to the hospital for an emergency operation. Without any warning she had fainted while walking home from a shopping expedition and it was obvious there was something seriously wrong with her heart. John and Livvy didn't even have time to get to the hospital before they received the news that Jane Freeman had died on the operating table. Her heart was so badly damaged, the surgeons were unable to save her and it was a miracle she had lived so long without having any serious symptoms. Livvy cried when the call came through but her thoughts were with John. She knew he had never been close to his mother and wondered how he was going to react. When she put her arms around him to comfort him he pushed her away and muttered something about calling his brother to make arrangements for the funeral and didn't even shed a tear. A little later, when he shut himself in the bathroom for a long time, Livvy listened at the door to see if he had broken down but there was silence. Once again, Livvy was puzzled at John's inability to show how he really felt inside. The funeral was held at the Rosar-Morrison Home, just two blocks from Livvy's apartment. Here, for the first time, she met John's wife Marilyn and his three sons and was introduced to his Uncle Raymond who was a priest and someone she would grow fond of over the next few years. She felt a little awkward being among John's relatives and family friends but she held her own and experienced minimal anxiety at the restaurant where several people congregated after the service.

All during the summer months, Dan had been negotiating to sell the printing plant to his London partners and in the fall, with the deal sealed, he purchased a house on Queen East near River Street with the intention of moving the business there. After some major renovations converting some areas of the house into offices Dan, Livvy, and the rest of the staff moved into their new premises and Livvy took the bright corner office on the south end of the building. Everyone was excited about the change and it felt like a new beginning, even though it had been nine years since Dan had started the company in his apartment on Wellesley Street.

Another exciting event occurred late that year, Natalie announced she was pregnant and Livvy was elated but found it hard to come to terms with becoming a grandmother at forty-four. The baby was due the following June and both Livvy and Natalie hoped for a girl, imagining her with the same fair hair and blue eyes as themselves. Natalie and Robert decided to move into a rented house in the North York area and they acquired a puppy, black with white paws, they named Snowshoe and, during the next months, Livvy watched her daughter's growing belly with increasing excitement. She hoped, with all her heart, her expanding family would stay intact and Natalie would remain in a happy marriage for the rest of her life.

In the spring of 1980, John and Livvy drove to the east coast for a vacation. Other than the time Livvy had arrived at St. John, New Brunswick, twenty-four years earlier, Livvy had never been east before. She was enchanted with the people and the hospitality they received wherever they went and gorged herself on lobster and other seafood delights fresh out of the ocean. After visiting St. John again and then taking the ferry to Digby, Nova Scotia, they travelled back by car to Maine and stopped in Bar Harbor. Livvy bought several small gifts in the charming shopping district and then they drove through Acadia Park with its wild and rocky shoreline. It was here that Livvy waded in the frigid waters of the Atlantic, roamed the beach searching the myriads of tiny pools for shells and enjoyed the solitude while John sat quietly on the pier staring out to sea.

On the third day of June, Livvy got a call from Robert to tell her that Natalie was in labour and they were on their way to Mount Sinai Hospital. Livvy immediately called John and told him what was going on. She was not surprised when he merely wished her luck and said he would see her later that night when he got back from playing baseball. She was too excited to worry about John's reaction and arrived at the hospital to find Robert pacing in the waiting room. So much had changed since Natalie had been born, when husbands were not permitted in the labour ward, and Livvy was thrilled when she was allowed to accompany Robert in to see Natalie, who had just been administered an epidural and was feeling quite comfortable. When the labour did not seem to be progressing too rapidly, the doctor suggested inducement might be the answer but, one of the nurses shooed him out the door and immediately sat Natalie up, piling pillows behind her, so that she was leaning forward. When the doctor returned just a short time later, he was surprised at how quickly things had changed and ordered Natalie into the delivery room. Meanwhile Robert and Livvy resumed their vigil in the waiting area but for Robert it was short lived when the doctor came bustling through the door and grabbed Robert's shoulder, "Come on Robert," he said, "it's time." and a reluctant father-to-be was whisked away.

Livvy tried to read a magazine but just couldn't concentrate and it wasn't long before Robert appeared in the doorway wearing green scrubs and grinning from ear to ear. Livvy rose and ran towards him, "Well, what happened? Tell me."

It was almost as though he was too overcome with emotion, he could hardly speak but then he embraced Livvy and, with tears in his eyes replied, "It's a girl and she's gorgeous."

Livvy was so happy she now had a granddaughter and could hardly wait to see her but her dream of a tiny infant with blonde hair was not to be. The baby was as dark as her father but her eyes were bright blue and in years to come people would comment on how striking they were. Natalie was holding the baby in her arms when Livvy entered the room and she turned to her mother with a look on her face Livvy would never forget as if to say "What do I do now Mom?"

When Livvy finally arrived home, the apartment was in darkness and she was disappointed John was not there. She had already phoned Rachel, Matt, Maggie and Susan and she was still bursting with pride and unable to settle down. It was just after midnight, when she heard John's key in the door but she decided to just lie there in the dark and wait for him to come into the bedroom. When he tiptoed in and started to put his pocket change quietly on the dresser, she couldn't contain herself any longer and sat up, "Hi," she said quietly, "how are you?"

"Oh, hi sweetheart, I'm fine," he replied.

Livvy could hardly believe her ears, "Aren't you going to ask me what happened?" she demanded with her voice steadily rising.

John continued to empty his pockets and without even turning to look at Livvy replied "Oh yes, what happened?"

Livvy was now more than a little frustrated, "I have a granddaughter! They decided to call her Jessie"

John sensed Livvy was getting impatient but he wasn't emotionally able to cope and merely replied, "Well, isn't that nice."

While Livvy was becoming used to John's lack of reaction to any change in her mood and constantly suggested she settle down whenever she became enthusiastic about anything, this incident reinforced her belief that she had made a terrible mistake. The problem was; what was she going to do about it?

Chapter Forty-One

Throughout the next couple of years, life continued along the same pattern and despite the added blessing of having a grandchild in the family, Livvy continued to question her relationship with John. She noticed that he never referred to her as his partner whenever they were introduced to anyone new and he never spoke about her in positive terms in the company of friends or family. It was almost as though she wasn't there except when they were alone together. Their sex life too, was now almost non-existent and Livvy realized John had a serious problem and urged him to see his doctor. When he claimed his doctor had suggested he was probably just under stress, she tried to persuade him to get a more professional opinion but he simply ignored her and she felt less desirable than ever. With her emotions beginning to have a profound effect on her, it was just a matter of time before Livvy snapped and, one bright summer afternoon, it was as though a black shade had been drawn across her mind. She was arriving home from work and pondering her problems when it happened and it frightened her but she let herself into the apartment and didn't mention it to John. He came into the kitchen where she was preparing supper and remarked, "You're really quiet this evening."

Livvy didn't look up from seasoning the salmon she had just removed from the refrigerator, "I'm just tired, that's all. It's been a busy day."

"Well, I'm sorry to hear that, sweetheart, but I've made arrangements for us to go away this weekend so that should make you feel better."

Livvy was surprised at this news, "Oh, that's nice John, where are we going? I could do with a weekend away."

"Well you know Mark has a time share in Huntsville, so we're going up there for a couple of days with him and Sherry. It's on a beautiful lake so we can go boating and fishing and they say the weather's going to be perfect."

Livvy looked horrified, "What do you mean? Are you saying you've made arrangements for us to actually drive up with them?"

John frowned, "Yes, why what's the problem?"

"You know what the problem is," Livvy said, her voice rising in frustration, "I can't go in a car with other people, I just get too anxious. Why on earth would you do something like this without asking me first? We can take separate cars and that's the only way I'll go."

"That's stupid!" said John sighing, "If you need to stop, we will."

"No, no!" Livvy cried and, at that moment, she felt such desperation that she looked over at the balcony door ,which was wide open, and for a moment was tempted to run through it and fling herself over the railing. Instead, just a moment later, she ran into the den and picked up the telephone.

John followed her into the room, "Who are you calling?" he demanded.

"I'm calling for help," Livvy said, now beginning to sob.

John attempted to stop her but she was not going to be sidetracked. She got the number of the Clarke Institute from information and started to dial while John looked on helplessly. When the receptionist answered, Livvy babbled that she needed to speak to someone, anyone who could help, because she was frightened at the thoughts going through her head. Seconds later, a doctor was on the line listening patiently while she rambled on pouring out her feelings to him. It was just a few minutes before she began to calm down and recognized the unknown person on the other end of the line understood what she was going through. She finally put the phone down feeling strong enough to deal with the situation in her own way. Slowly, turning to John, she said, "I'm not going anywhere this weekend."

Livvy knew John was having a difficult time coping with her at times, not only because of her anxiety but because she was impulsive and couldn't tolerate arguments. On two separate occasions, this had put her in a position where she had been left at a disadvantage but she still felt justified. Once at a company dance, held miles from their apartment, John got jealous because Livvy danced with a colleague of his more than once. They got into a spat and Livvy ended up prancing out of the hall and down a street completely unfamiliar to her. Because she was dressed in a sheer skirt, halter top and high heels and was crying, she became rather conspicuous and was stopped by two police officers passing by in their patrol car. They laughed when they heard what the problem was and offered to drive her to the Main subway station where she could catch a streetcar all the way home. It was a long ride and Livvy was aware of people staring at her but she was feeling rather superior and hoped John was worried sick about her. She was more than a little miffed to find he was asleep, or feigning sleep, when she arrived at the apartment. On another occasion, coming back from a trip to Florida, they checked into a motel just outside of Cincinnati and then went out to supper. There was a small dance floor in the restaurant and Livvy asked John to dance. When he refused, she got very upset reminding him they hadn't danced together for ages and how much they used to enjoy it when they were dating. No amount of cajoling worked and Livvy waltzed out of the restaurant into the night having no idea where she was or what motel they had checked in to. She soon realized she had made a terrible mistake and decided to go into a MacDonald's to check the phone book and see if any of the motels listed triggered something in her memory. It was while she was running her finger down the listing that she noticed their car pull into the parking lot and so she quickly ran outside, jumped in, and slammed the door. Ironically not another word was mentioned about the incident. Eventually, it was when Livvy found herself seriously attracted to someone else that she knew it was only a matter of time before her relationship with John would end. Business had begun to expand since the move to Queen Street but Jim, the Irishman, who had been such an asset to the company turned out to be a liability and had to be let go, after he made a private sale for his own personal gain and Livvy had discovered it. Dan then decided to hire his son, and Ben proved to be a driving force within the company. There were several occasions when Livvy was exposed to suppliers and she had several encounters with the trio of accountants retained to review their finances, as well as playing a part in the negotiations to sell the plant. The senior accountant, Trevor Bardwell, was a personable middle-aged man and the female of the trio, Linda Feldon, proved to be both friendly and efficient but it was the third member of the team who caught Livvy's attention. Dave Mackay was a tall, dark young man but it was difficult to determine his real age because of the beard he wore, which only served to enhance his masculinity. From the first moment she met him there was an instant chemistry, which was obvious to both of them, but there had been no opportunity to expand their relationship from one of a professional nature to anything more personal. A chance meeting in July of 1980 changed the dynamics to some degree when Dave finally had the chance to ask Livvy to have lunch with him and she agreed. He took her to Hy's, which was well known in the business district and a wonderful venue for relaxing and enjoying the superb menu, and they lingered there for hours. They were so comfortable with each other, time just flew by and Livvy was obliged to call the office and tell Ben she would not be coming back that day. This was so out of character for Livvy but she was enjoying every moment and didn't want to leave. It was supper time when she finally left Dave on Richmond Street, outside of the restaurant, and made her way home. She was on cloud nine but she had made it very clear to Dave, she could not see him again unless it was business related. When she bounced in the door of the apartment and John asked her what she was so happy about, she merely proclaimed it was a beautiful sunny day and why shouldn't she be happy but as usual he dampened her spirits when he told her to settle down. This attitude only reinforced her resolve that something had to change and, just over a month later, it almost did with what could have been a disastrous outcome.

Dan had decided that now they had been in their new premises for over a year and all the renovations had been completed, they should have an Open House. He planned on inviting a number of suppliers, neighbours, family and friends and one of the guests was Dave Mackay. In order to avoid any problem, Livvy asked John to come to the party and she was surprised when he agreed and very proud when he showed up looking exceptionally handsome and several of the females commented on his appearance. It was obvious after a while, however, that John was bored and when he suggested he would like to leave and go home Livvy was actually glad to see him go. This gave her the opportunity to focus her attention on Dave and just before the party ended in the early evening; they made a secret arrangement to meet at a popular bar just a few blocks away. Livvy was well aware she had broken her own rule but the temptation was too great and after two glasses of scotch, on top of the wine she had consumed at the party, she found herself holding Dave's hand and wishing for more. Two hours later, he was driving her home but stopped at the edge of a parkette where they were secluded from the streetlights and well away from the main road. It was a perfect summer evening and it didn't take long before they were caught up in the moment. Livvy was now painfully aware of the passion missing from her life but she had enough self-control to put an end to their lovemaking before they completed the ultimate act. Pulling away from Dave, she straightened her clothes and sighed, "I'm sorry Dave I just can't do this."

Dave looked disappointed but he had no intention of forcing her to do anything she wasn't comfortable with, "Its okay, Livvy, I understand. I shouldn't have parked here in the first place."

"No, it's my fault, I shouldn't have encouraged you. I have to admit though, I find you very attractive and you make me feel so special."

"But, you are special. Why on earth would you think otherwise?"

"Well, it's not easy living with someone like John. He isn't interested in anything I do at work and he never shows any real emotion. I've talked to him about it several times and he says he wishes he could be different but he just can't. Underneath it though, he's a decent person and I don't want my relationship with him to end because of someone else."

Dave shook his head, "Why is it men and women seem to have so many problems making each other happy? I've had my share and still keep coming back for more."

Livvy laughed, "Not all relationships are bad and you shouldn't just give up. You said you wanted to start traveling in a couple of years, now all you have to do is find some nice young woman who is as adventurous as you are."

"Too bad it isn't you Livvy."

"That's very flattering but I wouldn't be a very good traveling companion."

"Why not?"

"That's a long story and one I would rather not go into. One day, maybe I'll be able to see a lot of the places I've only ever seen in the movies or read about in books but for now I'm not going anywhere, except home to bed."

"Do you really have to go?"

"Yes, I do and until I can actually break away from John for good I just can't see you or anyone else for that matter. I've really enjoyed our time together and it's possible we could see each other in the future but not until I'm on my own. I have no idea when that will be. I just have to get up the courage to resolve this whole situation."

Dave took her hand, "You know I wish you well, Livvy, and I'll try to stay away. I'm actually getting transferred in a couple of weeks so I won't be working with Trevor and Linda anymore."

"Maybe that's just as well but I'm really going to miss you," Livvy whispered.

This latest encounter with Dave was a wakeup call for Livvy. She knew, for certain now, she would have to finish her relationship with John before she would consider going out with anyone else. At the age of forty-five, she also knew there was a possibility she might never find another partner and could spend the rest of her life alone but it was a risk she had to take. It took her almost another three years to get up the courage to make the break with John. There was no specific incident that spurred her on; it was just the slow erosion of their relationship.

One Tuesday, while at her office, Livvy phoned John to suggest they went out for dinner that evening. This was unusual, as they usually only ate out on Fridays, but John agreed without asking any questions. At six o'clock, Livvy entered the Quo Vadis Restaurant to find John was already seated at a table. When she walked through the door, being the gentleman he was, he got up and helped her into her seat, "Hi sweetheart," he said staring at her rather intently, "this was a nice idea but why did you want to eat out tonight?"

Livvy fiddled with her napkin, "Well, I wanted to talk to you but why don't we get something to drink first. Could you order me a glass of white wine?"

"I already did, in fact, here it comes now," and he nodded at the waiter as he placed the glass in front of Livvy and then waited for him to leave. "I had a feeling you had something on your mind. What seems to be the problem?"

"The problem is us, John. I think you know I've not been happy for a while and I believe you feel the same way but I also think you're content enough to put up with the way things are. It isn't enough for me and we need to do something about it."

John appeared to be perfectly calm, "What do you suggest we do?"

"I think we should separate. Obviously that means I'll have to ask you to leave and I know you'll need some time to find a place of your own but I want it to be soon John."

"I guess there's no sense in hashing this all out is there?"

"No, so let's have something to eat and talk about something else and we can discuss the details later. Meanwhile

I hope we can still be friends," and she reached across the table for his hand.

"Okay, if that's what you want, Livvy."

John's reaction was exactly as she had expected. He accepted the end of their relationship without a fight and three weeks later, after some gentle encouragement, and with Mark's help, he gathered his belongings and moved out. Livvy didn't take John's leaving lightly and was tearful when they said their goodbyes but they agreed to keep in touch.

John leased a furnished apartment on a month-to-month basis just a few miles north as he hadn't really decided where he wanted to live. Meanwhile, Livvy was contemplating becoming a first time homeowner and, after looking at a number of properties, she found what she thought would be the perfect place. Right opposite Maple Leaf Gardens, the home of Toronto's professional hockey team and accessible to all of the downtown area, she purchased a two-bedroom condo with a solarium, large kitchen, and two bathrooms, one with a huge oval tub. Rather than facing onto the main street she chose a suite on the south side of the building where she could see the CN Tower and be away from the noise of the traffic. When she decided she wanted some new furniture, she suggested to John that he take over the rental of her old apartment and she would leave him some of her old furniture so that he would only need to purchase a few things to make the place livable. She was ecstatic when he agreed and, in August, she moved into her new home and realized that John would only be about three blocks away. It was at this time that she got some other wonderful news, Natalie was pregnant with her second child and they were hoping for a boy.

In September, Dan asked her if she would like to go to a business forms convention in New Orleans and, although she was nervous about the actual journey, her desire to visit that part of the States took precedence over her anxiety. Any apprehension Livvy had about Dan's intentions were ill founded and although they spent most of the week together, not once did he ever make any advances towards her. It was a pleasant change to be able to enjoy the company of the opposite sex without having to worry about the dynamics of a relationship. Every evening they had dinner together at some of the finest restaurants in the French Quarter and some days they would be joined by people they had met at the convention. On one occasion, when they had a lot of spare time, they had a leisurely lunch in Jackson Square and then took a cruise on the Mississippi River. Livvy was glad she had made the decision to go and other than the ride to and from the airport, which seemed incredibly long, she was quite comfortable being with Dan.

When she got back from her trip, John called to invite her out to dinner. Livvy wasn't sure if it was a good idea but their breakup had been amicable and she wanted to keep John as a friend, so she agreed. It was only a matter of time before they were seeing each other on a regular basis and the initial attraction they had for each other resurfaced. When they talked about taking a vacation together over the Christmas season Livvy was happy about rekindling their romance but she felt guilty about leaving Rachel at that time of the year and was concerned because Natalie was so close to having her baby. When Natalie encouraged her to go and promised Rachel would be well taken care of, she began to make plans. The one place that really appealed to her was Hawaii and on December 20th, they flew out of Toronto for the nine-hour flight to Honolulu. Four hours into the flight, Livvy got restless and decided to go up to the jumbo jet's second level where she found six or seven people lounging about and chatting with each other. After ordering a pina colada from the flight attendant, she got into a conversation with a young Englishman who was on his way to Japan. He was originally from London so they had a lot to talk about and were enjoying their conversation until John appeared in the doorway and, frowning at Livvy, remarked, "Oh here you are, I was wondering where you had gotten to."

It was obvious to Livvy, that John was jealous and didn't approve of her talking to some man she had just met and she was annoyed at the intrusion. When she eventually returned to her seat, John was not in any mood to communicate and Livvy added fuel to the fire by pointing out that she was having a better time upstairs than sitting beside someone who was sulking. Unfortunately, this seemed to set the tone for the whole trip.They spent the first few days shopping in Honolulu, sunbathing on Waikiki Beach and touring Oahu and Livvy was overwhelmed with the lush green scenery. Then on Christmas day they spent hours in a bar while the rain came down in torrents and Livvy couldn't help wondering what her family was doing back in Toronto. After the first week, they flew to Maui and Livvy was nervous because she had not experienced flying such a short distance before. She managed to handle her anxiety without John being aware of how she was feeling and breathed a sigh of relief when the plane landed only twenty minutes after take-off. In Maui they rented a bungalow right on the beach and took their time exploring the island and enjoying the spectacular sunsets every evening. On one occasion they went out on a whale watching cruise and Livvy knew she would never forget the sight of the huge creatures as they swam near the boat and appeared to be performing acrobatics especially for the tourists. It was the highlight of the trip for Livvy but when John saw how excited she was, he reacted with his usual indifference and once again put a damper on the experience. Livvy expected that in such a romantic setting they might recover all of the feelings they had had for each other when they first met, but it was not to be and, after the vacation was over, she knew that any kind of relationship with John was not to be.

Chapter Forty-Two

On January 25th, 1985, when Natalie gave birth to a beautiful baby boy, Livvy felt a sense of contentment. Natalie now had the ideal family, a husband who doted on her and two wonderful children and Livvy took great pride in the fact that her daughter had grown up to be such a well-adjusted person and a responsible parent.

In April, Livvy flew to Florida to spend time with Maggie and Byron in their new condo close to St. Petersburgh. Byron was a businessman and had recognized the potential in renting out homes to people wanting to spend their winters in a warmer climate and he had purchased four other condos, just for that purpose. Maggie was now able to enjoy the finer things in life and she never stopped marveling over her good fortune. Livvy had been apprehensive about spending a week away from home and not being in control of how she would be spending her time but she found both Maggie and Byron gave her all the space she needed and she enjoyed her time with them.

One Friday evening just after returning from her trip, she was with Susan at Octobers, the newest place in Toronto to be able to dance as well as have a good meal, when she met Bill Carstairs. The lighting at Octobers was very low but that didn't stop her from noticing a man a few tables away staring intently at her, and she couldn't help staring back. He appeared to be quite young but that wasn't a deterrent for Livvy as it seemed, almost every man she had been out with had been a year or two younger. When he finally got up and started walking towards their table, she could see that he was of medium build, average height, average looking and clean shaven with a head of thick dark hair. As Susan was up dancing and her chair was empty, Bill took advantage of the situation and immediately sat down, "I hope you don't mind me sitting here for a minute," he said.

Livvy smiled at his audacity, "Well, I guess it will be okay until my friend gets back."

"That's great because I'd like to get to know you better. I couldn't help noticing you and I think you're very attractive."

"Thank you, but I think we should introduce ourselves before we go any further."

Bill grinned and held out his hand for Livvy to shake, "I'm Bill Carstairs."

Taking his hand, Livvy replied, "I'm Livvy Walker."

"That's an unusual name, is it short for something?"

"Yes, everybody asks me that, it's short for Olivia but everyone calls me Livvy."

"I see, and do you come to Octobers very often? I don't think I've seen you here before."

"We just started coming here the last few months. I think it's a great place. How about you?"

Their conversation progressed into more personal issues with Bill asking Livvy if she was married or had a boyfriend. It was only when Susan returned and introduced her dance partner, who turned out to be Bill's friend, Gavin, when the atmosphere lightened up. The foursome appeared to get along well and when Bill suggested they drive the girls home, Susan and Livvy felt comfortable enough to accept the ride. Livvy lived fairly close to the club while Susan lived a fair distance away so if Bill were able to get home himself, they would have to just drop Livvy off. When they stopped outside Livvy's condominium he asked Gavin to wait while he took Livvy to her door. After they entered the building and he saw the security guard, he commented, "Pretty ritzy, eh?"

For some reason, his remark made Livvy uncomfortable but outside her door, when he took her in his arms and kissed her so passionately that it took her breath away, when he said he would call her the next day to make a date, she was apprehensive but excited about the possibility of beginning a new relationship.

On their next encounter, she discovered that Bill was only forty years old, exactly nine years younger than she was, and she found the difference in age a little disturbing. Bill, however, was not in the least bit intimidated and, during their time together, he was constantly complimenting her on her appearance. This attention and the fact that he was an expert lover boosted Livvy's confidence to some degree but she was still coping with anxiety and had not felt comfortable enough to tell Bill about it. At the three-month mark in their relationship, Livvy began to get a little tired of the fact that he frequently complained about having to drive all the way from Brampton to see her and, when he wasn't with her, he would phone her and want to talk for hours. At these times, when she didn't feel like talking, she often just let the phone ring and when the ringing wouldn't stop she felt like screaming. The final straw came when he asked her to spend the weekend with him at a friend's house about sixty miles from Toronto and she knew she just couldn't do it. When she tried to make excuses, he wouldn't buy it and when she eventually broke down and told him the truth about her anxiety he just couldn't understand. In her heart, she knew she didn't need anyone in her life who was not ready to accept her, warts and all, but she was upset over the breakup and more anxious than ever.

A month later, she spent a week at Bally's in Atlantic City attending a software vendor's conference but getting there proved to be particularly difficult. She was to fly to LaGuardia airport in New York and catch a connecting flight to Atlantic City but, while waiting for her connection, she was surprised to hear an announcement over the public address system that the plane was ready for boarding. When she looked out of the huge plate glass windows onto the adjacent runway she could not see any plane but thought she should head for the boarding gate to find out what was going on. When she reached the gate, the attendant was very abrupt and hustled her through telling her to hurry up or she would miss the flight and she was horrified when she stepped outside and realized she would be traveling on a small six-seater aircraft which obviously had no bathroom. In a state of shock, she managed to climb the steps and seat herself at the back in a single seat near the window but she was shaking with anxiety and could not imagine how she was going to get through the journey. Whenever she travelled, she carried a novel with her and a book of anacrostic puzzles, and she immediately dug the puzzle book out of her purse and attempted to distract herself. Once they were in the air, she glanced out of the window and was amazed at the sight of New York below them. It was a glorious day and the view of the Statue of Liberty, the skyscrapers, and Central Park was magnificent and, for a brief moment, she was almost glad she had had this opportunity.

The trip took exactly one hour and most of the time Livvy was in a state of anxiety and she knew, without a doubt, there was no possible way she would get back on that plane for the return trip, let alone spend the whole week thinking about it. As soon as they landed, and even before she checked into the hotel, she went directly to the bus station and purchased a Greyhound bus ticket for her trip back to New York. After that, she finally breathed a sigh of relief and set out to enjoy her week in the city she had brought Natalie to so many years ago. The trip did not deter Livvy from traveling altogether because she was determined her anxiety would not take complete control of her life. Within the next few months she took another week long vacation and a weekend trip to Montreal with Rachel.

During this time Livvy had become disenchanted with her new home. She enjoyed the spaciousness and was proud of the way she had decorated every room in her favourite natural shades but she felt isolated without a balcony and found her neighbours to be particularly noisy. She finally came to the decision to sell and go back to renting for the time being. A new apartment block had been built just north of Allen Gardens and only three blocks from where she was currently living. After seeing the model suite, Livvy knew it was exactly what she needed. The apartment she rented on the fourth floor was pie shaped and there was a large balcony overlooking Jarvis Street, so she could now see the world going by. After settling, in she realized she had made the right move and she felt totally comfortable in her new surroundings.

Chapter Forty-Three

In March of 1986, Livvy turned fifty years old and was totally surprised when she discovered Natalie had arranged a party for her at Octobers, which was her favourite place to dine and dance. Natalie and Rachel had invited her out to dinner under the pretense that they were going to have a nice low-key celebration, particularly as Livvy was not exactly thrilled about reaching the half-century mark. She was bowled over when twenty-five people including relatives, friends, and business associates surprised her as she walked into the dining area but it completely changed her mood and she had one of the best evenings of her life.

Two months later Dave MacKay came back into Livvy's life and she was excited to hear from him. He had little to say on the telephone but wanted to see her so they arranged a date for the following evening. Livvy could hardly sleep that night and had trouble concentrating at work the next day, not only because she so desperately wanted to see Dave again but she had no idea where they were going to go and she was anxious about travelling anywhere unfamiliar by car. At six o'clock, she walked into a bar in the Bank of Commerce building and came face to face with Dave. He looked a little older, a little heavier, but still the same man she had been so attracted to years earlier and he was delighted to see her. After one drink and some small talk, he suggested they drive up to his house, not too far from where Rachel lived, so that Livvy could see his home, which he was obviously proud of. Livvy realized, with relief, she had no feelings of anxiety on the journey, and it was here she learned about the tragedy that had taken place in Dave's life. She took the glass of wine Dave handed her and sank back into the large comfy sofa in his country style living room, "So what have you been doing for the last few years?" she asked smiling up at him.

Dave sat down beside her and took her hand, "Honestly? Well, I actually met this woman and I thought we could make a real life together. She had a young daughter, only three years old, named Maddy and I really loved that child. When they both moved in with me I was the happiest guy on earth but it wasn't to be. I had no idea things would turn out the way they did."

Livvy squeezed Dave's hand, "I am so sorry", she said with sincerity, "what happened?"

Dave got up and started pacing the floor, "I didn't realize Lisa, that was her name, had mental issues. I think she was manic-depressive and her ex didn't help either, in fact he was a real bastard. I tried to hold things together particularly for Maddy's sake, she was so adorable, but I don't think anyone could really make Lisa happy and in the end she killed herself."

Livvy let out an audible gasp, "Oh no, how terrible."

"Yes, it was terrible and I was the one who found her. I came home from work and she wasn't anywhere in the house and Maddy was alone in her bedroom. I was frantic wondering what had happened to Lisa so I thought I'd check to see if her car was missing from the garage." He paused and then sat down again, "I knew, before I opened the door, what I would find. I could hear the car running. She was in the car and her face was blue. I dragged her out of the garage and called 911, then I tried to revive her but, when the paramedics arrived, they told me she was already dead."

Livvy could feel herself tearing up and she could see how deeply Dave had been affected by this tragedy. Very quietly she asked, "What happened after that?"

"The police investigated but it was pretty cut and dried. As for Maddy, her father came and just took her away. I tried to fight it because I loved that little girl but I didn't have a chance."

Livvy's heart went out to him and any problems she had experienced seemed to pale in comparison. Later, the mood lightened considerably as they enjoyed a wonderful supper at a seafood restaurant just a little further north of Dave's home but when he brought her back to the apartment and ended up staying the night, Livvy knew the spark had gone from their relationship. A few months later, after keeping in contact by telephone, she learned he had met someone new and they were going to South Africa to live for at least two years. She sincerely wished him well and hoped he had found the person he could spend the rest of his life with.

Now, being without male companionship, she decided to take another vacation alone and travelled to a spa in Palm Springs. There, she was surprised to run into Natalie's favourite soap star and she spent a delightful week getting to know her mother who was vacationing with her. Livvy found the spa to be an ideal place for her as she was able to immerse herself in activities throughout most of the day and there was always a movie or a seminar to attend in the evening. She didn't feel comfortable enough to go outside of the spa with any of the other women, but one day she ventured into town alone and, once again, realized the need to be in control of her surroundings had an enormous impact on her level of anxiety.

The following November, she took another vacation with Natalie and the two children in Montego Bay but it wasn't exactly an ideal place to be. The hotel they stayed in was rather seedy and the local people ambushed them wherever they went begging for money. It was dreadfully hot and Livvy had trouble with the traditional food served at most of the restaurants so they ended up eating at a Howard Johnson's most nights. They did spend one wonderful day at a nearby Holiday Inn resort where the beach area was spectacular but, other than being with her family, Livvy found the trip disappointing.

Chapter Forty-Four

In the spring of 1986 Livvy adopted two female kittens from the Humane Society, a five-month-old female calico, she named Tabitha, and a three-month-old female tortoiseshell, she named Peewee. Natalie was as pleased as punch that her mother had finally decided to have a pet but Rachel wasn't nearly as pleased. On the Sunday after the kittens had settled in, Livvy invited both Natalie and Rachel for supper and hid the kittens in the bedroom. After teasing Rachel for a while about a surprise, Livvy suddenly let the kittens out and they ran into the living room where Rachel shrank back into her chair. She just couldn't understand why anyone would want just one cat, let alone two, but in the years to come her attitude changed and she even cat-sat a few times when Livvy went away. Tabitha was the outgoing one but needy and liked attention while Peewee was extremely passive and held a special place in Livvy's heart. Livvy loved them both, to the point where she was unable to leave them overnight, and always came home right after work to feed them. She often wondered what would happen if she met someone new and the demands on her time would interfere with her commitment to her pets.

The following year, Matt's son, Colin, had a brush with death when a condition he had been born with suddenly surfaced. In an emergency operation doctor's implanted a shunt from his brain to drain off excess fluid. Matt spent every day at the hospital, never leaving Colin's side unless it was absolutely necessary, and later Kathy was to claim this episode was the beginning of the end of their marriage. Colin recovered to lead a normal life with the help of the shunt and medication but eventually, after Kathy had a series of affairs, Matt divorced her and she left the house he had built with his own hands to move in with someone else. This was one of the darkest times for Matt and, even though Livvy knew exactly what he was going through, he didn't reach out for help and struggled through this difficult period alone. It was only when he met his third wife, Irene that he felt truly happy again and finally found the only real love of his life. Irene was from Newfoundland and had a down to earth personality. She was a fabulous homemaker and loved to cook and, when they eventually married, Livvy attended the wedding and envied the wonderful relationship they had.

Life seemed to have settled into a real routine for Livvy and she was fairly content being alone but very aware that her life was still hampered by her anxiety. Six years after moving into her apartment, the building was converted to a condominium and she was ready to make the commitment and become an owner, with the idea that she would probably remain there for the rest of her life.

Over the following years she took many trips with Susan or Natalie, mostly to the Caribbean or Mexico, but it was always a struggle traveling away from home in unfamiliar places and she always felt relieved whenever they arrived back in Toronto. On one trip to Vancouver with Susan, they were called back after a day because Rachel had fallen and broken her hip while walking near Livvy's home where she had been cat-sitting. This incident was the beginning of a downward spiral as far as Rachel's health was concerned and, after a series of crises, Livvy had to move her into a resident care home in Willowdale. It was apparent, six months later, after another bout in the hospital, that she needed more than the resident care home could provide and Matt and Irene agreed to let her live with them.

Livvy was pleased her mother was now in such good hands but she had reservations about the commitment her brother had made and how long it would be before he realized he might have made a mistake. When Rachel had been in better health, Livvy had made it a habit to invite her for supper every two weeks but now, because of the distance to Matt's house which was only accessible after a long subway and bus ride, she was unable to see her at all. Matt had no idea about Livvy's anxiety and could not accept the fact she couldn't come to see Rachel. After a particularly bitter argument followed by letters being exchanged, they finally stopped talking to each other but, when Rachel intimated she wasn't happy because she felt so isolated, Livvy made arrangements to move her into a nursing home where she would get twenty-four hour care and be surrounded by people of her own age. Meanwhile, Livvy continued to work full-time until 2003, when she decided to cut her workweek to four days, and Dan fully supported her when she approached him with the idea. She was then able to spend one day shopping, lunching with Susan or Natalie, and doing all the things she had been restricted from doing on Saturdays because of her visits to Rachel in the nursing home.

In 2004 her beloved cat Peewee died at the age of eighteen and Livvy was devastated. She had already lost Tabitha ten years earlier, as the result of a blood disease, and so Peewee had been her sole companion for a long time. Peewee had been a passive and loving pet and Livvy missed her terribly so, a few months later, she adopted two more cats from the Humane Society. Both tortoiseshells, Lucy was already four-years-old and Kally, only two, but she had been with Lucy since birth and they could not be separated. It became immediately clear that their personalities were like night and day. Lucy, weighing close to seventeen pounds, had nerves of steel and followed Livvy everywhere while Kally, at only seven pounds, was like a nervous little kitten and ran away whenever approached. It took almost two years before Livvy could actually pick her up and hold her without her squirming to escape but sometimes, in bed at night, she would creep gingerly across the blanket looking for a pat on the head.

In October of that same year, Livvy again attempted to get help for her anxiety and stumbled across a website promoting a support group for social phobics. She didn't really feel it would be a suitable group for her but, after already trying every other type of treatment, she decided there was nothing to lose. She soon discovered this was one of the best decisions she had made in a long time and, when she attended her first meeting, she immediately felt comfortable and at home. Within a month, for the first time in her life, she confided her secret to family and friends and felt a tremendous relief. Even though they didn't really understand, they accepted it, and she no longer had to lie or make excuses when asked to do anything she was uncomfortable with. She got more and more involved with the group, setting up a monthly movie date, joining the newsletter committee, and hosting the annual Christmas party and, as time went by, she grew more confident and her anticipatory anxiety, before any event, became almost nonexistent. Travelling long distances by car or bus was still a problem and one she still hoped to overcome one day so that she could visit all the places she had only ever dreamed of seeing.

Rachel lived contentedly in the nursing home for five years until her death, at the age of ninety-four, in September, 2006. Whether it was the fact that her mother's death had been expected, and she had been prepared for the loss for some time, Livvy found it difficult to reconcile her reaction. Their communication had often been difficult and any time Livvy had attempted to draw her mother into a discussion on any issue of importance, she had always been brushed aside. Rachel just didn't have the capacity to understand Livvy's emotional needs and rarely ever complimented her on her appearance or her accomplishments. This disconnect seemed to continue after Rachel's death and although Livvy had always loved her mother and knew she was a good person and had always done the best she could, she was unable to grieve.

One event Livvy was grateful for was the fact that her mother had witnessed the reconciliation between herself and Matt, the year before her death. At Colin's wedding in

June, 2005, Livvy attended with the rest of the family and, on encountering her brother just before the ceremony, they exchanged their first words in over four years. This was the beginning of a new relationship that proved to be closer than at any other time in their lives and Livvy found it ironic that there were so many things that she and Matt had in common, despite their different personalities and lifestyles. They began to see each other more often and nearly every Saturday morning, Matt would interrupt Livvy's cleaning routine to chat, but she welcomed the phone calls. Then just a few years later, all that changed. In November, 2008, Matt began to experience some health problems. The following February, after being given a chest X-Ray, he was told he had chronic obstructive pulmonary disease. On Good Friday, Irene noticed he could hardly lift his cup to his mouth but he was advised to delay a trip to the hospital until the next morning because of the holiday. At seven o'clock, the next day, when he walked into the Southlake Regional Health Centre, he was immediately admitted. His oxygen level was alarming low and tests were ordered immediately to determine the cause.

Livvy was in her office when the call came through from Irene. Matt had terminal lung cancer. It was a moment she would never forget and she was unable to contain herself. She couldn't believe that, after almost four wonderful years, when they had finally connected again, it was all about to end. In the next few weeks, Matt went under several procedures to drain his lungs of fluid so that he could breathe. When he was sent home he was hooked up to an oxygen tank, told he had six months to live, and offered the option of having chemotherapy but he decided on quality of life rather than quantity. Livvy travelled up to his home in Bradford by train on two occasions so that she could stay overnight and, one beautiful warm evening, they sat in the garden and took several photos that she would always treasure. Matt looked so strong and healthy, it was almost impossible to believe he was so sick and she vowed to spend as much time with him as she could.

On June 10th, Matt was re-admitted to the hospital for a procedure in an attempt to alleviate the continual build-up of fluid in his lungs but three days later, on a Saturday evening, he took his last breath. That morning, the telephone rang as usual at Livvy's just as she was cleaning, but it wasn't Matt on the line. It was Natalie telling her to get ready because they were coming to take her to the hospital. Several members of the family and some friends kept vigil at Matt's bedside but it was Irene, Colin and Livvy who took turns holding his hand and talking to him, hoping he could hear all the loving things they were saying to him. When he finally slipped away, everyone left the room so that Irene could say her last goodbye.

Matt's death had a profound effect on Livvy and she often imagined the feeling of his hand in hers. Many Saturday mornings, the phone would still ring and there would never be anyone there. Livvy knew in her heart it couldn't be Matt but she fantasized that he was reaching out to her. Ironically, a year prior to the onset of Matt's illness, he had sent an e-mail to her and also to Colin. He was an atheist, just like their father, and wanted them to know his last wishes in case anything happened to him. He wanted to be cremated, with no religious ceremony of any kind, but hinted that he wouldn't mind a little party with a few friends. Livvy smiled about it later when a memorial get-together was arranged and well over a hundred and twenty people showed up, including several of Matt's former colleagues from the police force. Livvy was not used to public speaking but, on that day, she talked about Matt for ten minutes, after having practiced in front of a mirror several times. It was only near the end, when she glanced across at Irene, that she finally got teary eyed and couldn't continue. She had no idea then that her relationship with Irene was about to change. No longer just her brother's wife, in the years that followed, she would become a good friend.

In May, 2010, Livvy took Natalie on a trip to London. It had been over thirty years since she had been back to her home town. They visited with several of her cousins, including the only aunt she had left, who now ninety years old, and they visited all of the usual tourist spots. For Livvy it was nostalgic, while Natalie could hardly believe she was seeing all the places she had only ever seen in the movies. They even took the train through the chunnel to Paris and the short time there was even more memorable because Dan happened to be in Paris and took them out to dinner. The one place Livvy refused to go was the house she grew up in on Cavendish Road. The memories were too painful. She just wished that she had been able to tell Matt all about their trip but it was too late.

Maggie had remained Livvy's oldest and dearest friend and they kept in touch constantly, even going on a number of cruises together to the Caribbean and Alaska. Maggie, like Livvy, had ended up alone and was living in Victoria, BC after losing her beloved Byron to Alzheimers. Her spirit never changed, she was always optimistic and looking forward to the future and Livvy had treasured her friendship. That was why, in the fall of 2010, just eighteen months after losing Matt, she also lost Maggie to a heart condition she had been struggling with for almost a year.

Susan had also played an important part in Livvy's life and she surprised everyone when she moved into a senior residence and, at the age of sixty-seven, remarried after years of being alone. Marriage suited her and she was ecstatically happy and more than content having someone to look after. After this, the friendship continued but Susan's first priority was now her husband. Every month, she would go with Livvy to a movie or out to dinner and they would always get together on special occasions. So it was a shock when, just three years after losing Maggie, Susan was gone too. There had been no warning this time, she was just eighty years old and her heart suddenly stopped.

Earlier in the year, Livvy witnessed the marriage of her beloved granddaughter, Jessie, to a man she had been living with for five years, and someone the whole family had grown to love and respect. As Jessie had grown older, she and Livvy had developed a special relationship and even taken a trip to New York together. They loved to tease each other and cried easily. Any Hallmark moment or sad animal story would trigger teary eyes but seeing Jessie get married, only brought a smile to Livvy's face. It took place on a beach in Jamaica with over forty friends and family in attendance, including Natalie's father who Livvy hadn't seen for seven years. They spent some time together and it turned out to be a pleasant experience without even a hint of awkwardness. On the day of the wedding itself, it was typically hot for April with a strong ocean breeze and Jessie looked beautiful, but then she had always turned heads with her long dark hair and vivid blue eyes. Livvy's grandson, Ryan, was also there having flown back from a trek through South America with his girlfriend. For most of the guests, this was also a vacation and Livvy spent the week rooming with her sister-in-law, Irene, and although they both enjoyed each other's company, they were both happy to go home again. Neither one of them was used to being idle for too long.

Over the last few years Livvy had seen John on several occasions. He now lived in Burlington and would come to Toronto often, for medical reasons, and stay in town to take her to dinner. There was nothing romantic about their relationship and Livvy was constantly reminded of why they had failed to remain together but, for some reason as friends, they were able to communicate more freely and Livvy enjoyed seeing him.

As Livvy grows older and she mourns the loss of two of her closest friends, her family becomes even more important. Seeing Natalie and her grandchildren still brings the greatest joy to her life. She doesn't expect any monumental events in the future, except perhaps an addition to the family, which would be wonderful, but who knows? The last chapter is yet to be written.